JIM WALKER

BROADMAN
&HOLMAN
PUBLISHERS

Nashville, Tennessee

© 1999 by Jim Walker
All rights reserved
Printed in the United States of America

0-8054-1970-5

Published by Broadman & Holman Publishers, Nashville, Tennessee
Editorial Team: Vicki Crumpton, Janis Whipple, Kim Overcash
Typesetting: TF Designs, Mt. Juliet, TN

Map reprinted with the permission of Scribner, a division of Simon & Schuster from
Gettysburg: A Journey in Time by William A. Frassanito.
Copyright ©1975 by William A. Frassanito.

Dewey Decimal Classification: 813
Subject Heading: MYSTERIES—FICTION / CIVIL WAR—FICTION
Library of Congress Card Catalog Number: 99-17584

Published in association with the literary agency of Alive Communications, Inc.,
1465 Kelly Johnson Blvd., Suite 320, Colorado Springs, CO 80920

Library of Congress Cataloging-in-Publication Data
Walker, James, 1948–
Murder at Gettysburg / Jim Walker.
    p. cm. — (Mysteries in time series)
ISBN 0-8054-1970-5 (pbk.)
    1. Pennsylvania—History—Civil War, 1861–1865—Fiction. 2. Gettysburg (Pa.),
Battle of, 1863—Fiction. I. Title. II. Series: Walker, James, 1948– Mysteries
in time series.
    PS3573.A425334M86   1999
    813'.54—dc21
                                                            99-17584
                                                            CIP

1 2 3 4 5 03 02 01 00 99

To Ron and Lee,
two friends
who shine
in the darkness

MURDER AT

·GETTYSBURG·

The
MAIN
CHARACTERS

pril Wolff. April is a young schoolteacher who discovers that her father, Jonas, was murdered during Lee's march toward Gettysburg. Her family has always been opposed to slavery. They moved to Pennsylvania from Virginia to extract themselves from what they saw as the nation's great evil. Since coming to Pennsylvania, they have been involved with the Underground Railroad, helping with the smuggling north of runaway slaves.

Major Will Chevalier. Will is a major in the Confederate Army of Northern Virginia assigned to the provost marshall's office. He is a graduate of the Citadel and a native of Charleston, South Carolina. His father is a wealthy merchant who made his fortune in the slave trade. Will agrees to help April investigate her father's murder in exchange for a new assignment as a line officer.

Tillie. Tillie is a black house servant in the Wolff household. Formerly part of a group of escaped slaves, she decided to stay in Pennsylvania to help raise the Wolff children. She has been April's mentor and confidant since childhood. She may also be the only witness to the murder of April's father. There is, however, one problem: Tillie is blind.

Sergeant Jacob Perlman. Sergeant Perlman is a former police officer from the city of Atlanta, Georgia. He is assigned by the provost marshall to assist Major Chevalier in his investigation of the murder. Sergeant Perlman is Jewish.

Christine Wolff. Christine is the young second wife of April's father. Her father and April's father were friends in Virginia.

John Slocum. John is from Virginia and was the best friend of April's father. His farm is adjacent to the Wolff farm and they attend the same church.

Tommy Slocum. Tommy is John's youngest son. He is a simple-minded young man of twenty-two who has stayed out of the war to work on the farm.

General Alfred Iverson. Iverson is a man from Virginia, assigned to command a brigade from North Carolina. The tension between Iverson and his men has been a growing problem ever since he was given command. General Iverson is a historical character.

General Albert Jenkins. General Jenkins is a commander in the Confederate cavalry. His brigade represents one of the few cavalry units who made the march into Pennsylvania with the main force of Lee's army. General Jenkins is a historical character.

General Jubal Early. General Early is a divisional commander in General Ewell's Second Corps. His men saw action from the beginning of the campaign. General Early is a historical character.

Ulysses Sampson. Ulysses is an escaped slave who took refuge on the Wolff farm during the invasion. He has been sent north for his own protection and to insure that the Wolffs would not be compromised.

MAP OF GETTYSBURG

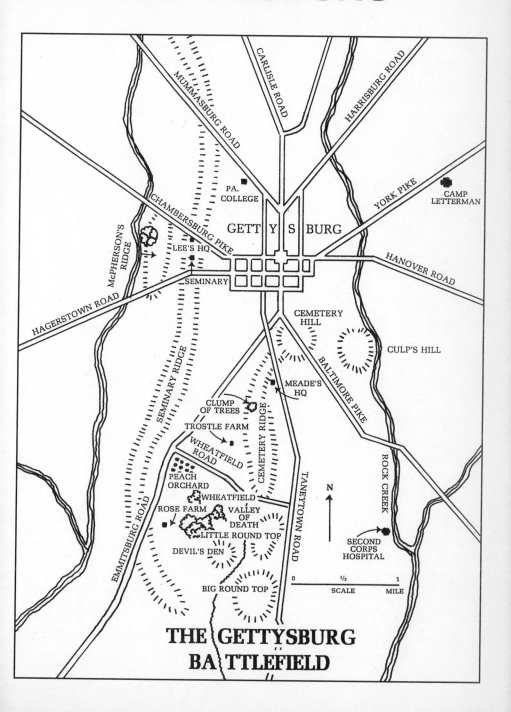

CARLISLE ROAD

MUMMASBURG ROAD

HARRISBURG ROAD

PA. COLLEGE

CHAMBERSBURG PIKE

YORK PIKE

CAMP LETTERMAN

McPHERSON'S RIDGE

GETT Y S BURG

LEE'S HQ

HANOVER ROAD

HAGERSTOWN ROAD

SEMINARY

CEMETERY HILL

CULP'S HILL

SEMINARY RIDGE

MEADE'S HQ

BALTIMORE PIKE

CLUMP OF TREES

TROSTLE FARM

CEMETERY RIDGE

ROCK CREEK

WHEATFIELD ROAD

PEACH ORCHARD

WHEATFIELD

TANEYTOWN ROAD

N

ROSE FARM

VALLEY OF DEATH

EMMITSBURG ROAD

LITTLE ROUND TOP

DEVIL'S DEN

SECOND CORPS HOSPITAL

BIG ROUND TOP

0   1/2   1
SCALE   MILE

THE GETTYSBURG BATTLEFIELD

PROLOGUE

I was never exactly friendless, but people saw me as someone who never quite fit in. Men snickered at me, and not behind my back either. Women were frightened of an educated woman who read books and chose to remain single at the age of twenty-six. I knew that men desired me; I just never wanted any of them.

My mother had been outwardly happy in marriage, but I knew that inwardly she was greatly disappointed. There was a cool look in her eyes when she took a walk and watched the sun set on the fields, a look of longing for a life that never would be hers. Books had been her window to the world. She loved them, but I could tell she wanted to be inside the story, making a difference, seeing the world and not just reading about it.

Perhaps that was why she had driven my father to move north to help escaped slaves find freedom. I admired her for that and pitied her at the same time. I couldn't help but think when we lowered her into the ground four years ago that she had found freedom too. She was with the Lord and free.

It was easy for me to think of her now while I labored to save Emma Slade, holding her while she screamed and wiping her sweaty forehead with what cool water I could find. Emma Slade was young and strong. She was younger than I was, but that didn't stop her from bleeding. When she finally pushed the baby free, I took it, but she could barely hear me tell her that it was a boy. She smiled slightly, a crease forming in her cracked lips. She lifted her arms.

I lowered the crying baby into her hands while maintaining my grip. There was no way Emma could hold the child and I knew it. Looking at the baby sent a sweeping sense of peace over her face, and she released her shaky grip the moment she could see the fresh, healthy face of her firstborn. She lay back on the blood-soaked feather bed and closed her eyes, hoping the end would come soon. Her blond hair was almost gray. It hung limp and wet on the pillow, her face a pasty white.

I wrapped the child and handed him over to Abigail, the little neighbor girl. "Here, take Harold his son."

Abigail nodded, reached out, and held the infant like a gossamer swan that was much too young to fly.

"And tell him if he wants to talk to Emma, he should come now."

I dipped a once-clean cloth into a pan of water swimming with the oily effects of perspiration. Wringing it out, I folded it gently and laid it on Emma's head. It was cool, and it was all that I could do. I had wanted to be there for the birth of her baby, but I had little desire to stay for Emma's death.

Harold came though the door, holding the infant. His trousers were rolled up above his ankles; his shoes had only a hint of leather still covering the soles. Tattered suspenders stretched over his bare chest to hold up his trousers, which glowed with a slick coat of sweaty dirt. "She doin' right?"

I shook my head. "I think she's lost much too much blood. You'd better give the baby back to Abigail and spend some time with Emma. I don't know how much time she has left."

He handed the baby to Abigail and swallowed. "We 'preciate you comin'."

"I'll stay on until she passes. You may need some help."

Harold raised himself to his full height and stuck out his chest. He took a deep breath. "Naw, you done enough, Miss Wolff, more than folks what ain't kin. You best be gettin' on home. Me and Abigail here can take care of what's left to be done."

"But Harold—"

He stopped me. "Ain't no point to you here no more. You ain't no doctor. You tell your daddy fer me dat I's mighty grateful for you comin' to help with Emma and her time."

I nodded reluctantly. Deep down, I was thankful to go. "I'm going home then." I looked back at Emma. "And so is Emma."

I stepped out onto what served as a front porch. The sweat rolled down my back, feeling like a horsefly crawling along my spine until it reached the belt that I had tied around my dress. The heat was unbearable. It seemed to rise out of the ground and dance along the cornfields in waves, like ghosts sent to torment the pure of heart.

The June sun hung directly over the green fields. I only wanted to get back to my buggy and whip my horse to get me home as soon as possible.

I stepped out onto the dirt where I'd tied my buggy the night before. Harold had been kind enough to feed and wash down my bay mare and, when the day was wearing on, he had hitched her back to the buggy. I untied her. She looked far more fresh and relaxed than I did, and I stroked her neck and patted down her withers. Untwisting my dress, the blue calico one that was now spattered with blood, I swung into the seat and slapped the reins on the mare's back. She stamped down the path and bolted toward the road.

The breeze was soothing against my forehead. My hat bounced on my back, suspended by the ribbon that was supposed to hold it in place. I was ever so glad it wasn't in place. The rushing air felt good through my hair, which fell in chestnut waves to the top of my shoulders and whipped across my face.

I was never cut out to be a nurse, and I knew it. I was a teacher. Taking people over the hump of learning was what I did, not easing them into eternity. Teaching was my gift, especially teaching women and slaves, people who the rest of the world said should never bother with learning.

I had mixed feelings about going back to my house. I taught school near Greencastle, and the town provided me with a comfortable cottage. But school was out now and I was at my homeplace, only it no longer felt like *my* home. Much of what I thought of as home had died with my mother.

Two years ago my father, Jonas, had remarried. It wasn't the idea of his marriage that bothered me, however. It was the fact that my new stepmother was four years younger than I was. I chalked it up to men's vanity and their desire to be young again and relive what was best confined to the past. There had been a brief period of time when my mother's memory hung over the house. I saw her everywhere and seemed to hear her soothing voice whispering in my ear. Now that was gone. The only place I could find comfort was with my Bible in the trees that surrounded my mother's grave.

I had no hard feelings toward Christine. By all rights we should have been good friends. It was just uncomfortable being in the same house with her and my father. I wasn't certain if it was a sense of jealously I felt at having been replaced as someone my father depended on, or if the jealousy was something I was feeling for my mother.

At times I wondered if, when I saw Christine, she reminded me of my own choice to remain single. I was attractive, but twenty-six was pretty much the end of the line. Perhaps I was trying to take my mother's place and was being overly protective of the one man either of us had ever depended on. No matter what the reason, I knew that my unhappiness was why people thought they could call on me for help. They knew I would prefer helping to staying at home. I was never very good at hiding my feelings, though Lord knows I tried.

It wasn't long before the mare rounded a curve in the road and came over the hill and into the valley that led to our farm. Sycamore trees gave some shade to that stretch of the road, and the Holsteins' farmhouse came into view. It was a large house with bright green paint and white trim. The porch was set on a layer of rocks with a swing and several rocking chairs.

The place was unusually busy. Riders leaned on their saddles as other men came from the smokehouse and chicken coup area, their hands full of fresh meat and squawking birds. It wasn't until I got closer that I saw the men were in uniform—Confederate gray.

Franny, the Holstein's oldest daughter, spotted me and ran in my direction. She lifted her skirts and raced across the yard to make sure she got to me before I came much closer. I watched her blond curls bounce.

"April," she screamed. "The rebels are here. Their whole army is coming up the road."

I pulled the reins on the bay and shuddered the buggy to a complete stop. "When did they get here?"

Franny was panting. "I don't know, maybe fifteen, twenty minutes ago." She looked back in the direction of the horsemen. "It seems like hours though. They're taking some of our hams and chickens."

"Thieves."

"Oh they're paying us for them, but with Confederate money and army scrip. It's worthless."

"Have they harmed you?"

Franny shook her head. "No."

One of the men spotted us talking. He barked out a few orders to the men around him and then swung into his saddle and rode in our direction. I sat up straight, bracing myself for what might come.

He rode up to where Franny was standing. The man wore a dusty uniform with a few polished buttons that were barely hanging on to the fabric. His face was ruddy in appearance with a swooping blond mustache and twinkling blue eyes. He tipped his hat. "Good afternoon, miss."

"It might very well have been, before you came," I replied.

He grinned slightly and brushed his mustache aside. "I can assure you that we mean you no harm. We're just purchasing some provisions for very hungry men."

"Stealing, you mean."

"No, ma'am, buying."

"With what you're using for currency, you might as well be stealing."

He glanced back at his men. "We're not taking everything, ma'am. The Lincoln cutthroats, on the other hand, ride into my state and take it all. Then when they're done with that, they burn the farms down around folks's ears."

"And you think what a few misguided men do can justify what you and your men are doing?"

His grin widened, and he made direct eye contact with me. "Those men have guidance, ma'am. They have orders too. We'll be gone before you know it, and when we do what we've come to do, that money will be worth pure gold."

"I doubt that very much, sir." It was plain to see the man did look drawn and hungry, and he was an officer. I might have been given to feeding the man out of Christian charity, even though I did hate the rebels and everything they stood for.

I raised my whip. "I'd better get to my farm and see just what your men have stolen there." I gave the mare a pop and once again she bolted down the road, this time leaving Franny and the rebel officer in the dust.

I drove the mare as hard as I dared, worry seeping into my head from around the cracks of what I knew my father's response would be to the invaders. We were Mennonites, and that meant a refusal to bear arms. It hadn't deterred my brother Gerald from joining the Union army though, and I wondered if it would really stop my father from using that shotgun of his if he felt that the farm was being threatened.

There was also the matter of the runaways. Our farm and the Wolff family in general had always provided a refuge for runaway slaves, and everyone knew it. We were a part of what had come to be known as the Underground Railroad.

The road sloped down a small hill and across the wooden bridge my father had built over the creek. Most of the time the running water kept the vegetables green and growing, and I loved the sound of it as it danced over the rocks. The mare's hooves hitting the bridge sent out a sound like distant gunfire.

When I neared the large red house, I could see the black iron stable boy. He had a red ribbon tied around his neck. Tillie sat on the porch in her customary rocker, smoking her infernal corncob pipe. Seeing her there sent a wave of comfort over me. The woman was an escaped slave, and even though she was blind and almost sixty, I doubted if she would be there if the rebels had come to the Wolff farm. Still, there was the red ribbon. I had to be cautious.

I pulled the buggy up to the hitching rail and jumped out. "Tillie, you have to hide. The rebels are coming."

She looked in my direction, her sunbonnet pulled down over her gray hair. The pipe stem quivered as she spoke, showing a perfect set of white teeth on the bottom and missing ones on the top. Her face was wrinkled, giving her the appearance of a prune. And despite eyes being empty of sight, I could almost feel her staring through my soul when she cast those black eyes in my direction. "I ain't got to hide no more, you's ought to know dat, chile. What dey want wif an old blind tar woman? I ain't fit fer nuffin no how, 'cept to wash clothes and care fer your daddy's new baby."

"Well, we'll see what he has to say about that."

Tillie rocked her chair harder. Her face tightened, and she clamped down on the pipe.

"Where is he?"

My question brought her chair to a complete stop. She pulled the pipe out of her mouth, knocked the dottle onto the porch, and dropped the pipe into her apron pocket. Slowly, she got to her feet and stepped in my direction. She opened her arms and waggled her hands for me to come closer.

I took a few steps. "What's wrong? Where's Father?"

Reaching out in her darkness and brushing her fingertips on my shoulders, she pulled me to her. She put her hands on the back of my head and slowly rocked me. "Dere jes ain't no good way to say dis lamb, but old Tillie's gonna try. He daid, honey. Dem men done kilt him late dis mornin'." She shook her head. "Tweren't no sense to it near as I can tell."

"No." I shook my head mindlessly.

She held me close and began to rock me just like she had done when I was a little girl and had skinned my knee.

"Why?" I started to sob. "Did they find the people? Did they find the hiding place?"

"Naw, dem folks is still put away. Dey is down in de hidey-hole. You don't have to worry none 'bout dem. But I tell you, chile, we's had folks comin' and goin' all day."

I tried to pull away from her, but she held me all the more tightly. "I just don't understand." I cried. "Why would they want to do this if they didn't find the runaways?"

"Lord only know dat, chile. You knows de meanness in folks. Man's liable to do jes 'bout anythin' iffen he gets his blood up. I was standin' right out on de porch when dat man come walkin' by after he done what he done. I heard him ride off."

"Where is he, Tillie?"

She kept her arm around me and stepped around, holding me to her side. "We got him laid out in de parlor, chile. Mr. Slocum heped us tote him in. Christine's in d'ere wif him, but she's all broke up. She ain't sayin' nuffin. I hears her jes sittin' dere all quiet like some lost dog."

"Where was he found?"

"In the barn."

I opened the screen door and stepped inside, then made my way to the parlor. My father lay on a table with a sheet pulled over his body, up to his neck. Even if the sheet had been pulled tight, it wouldn't have covered the man. He was tall. His feet stuck out from the bottom. His shoes were off, and his socks had been changed into the ones he wore on Sunday mornings. Someone had placed candles on the four corners of the table, and the candles were burning brightly even though it was broad daylight.

John Slocum, our neighbor, stood at the head of the table, his hat in his hand. He was a short squatty man, and his jet-black beard made him look harsh and withdrawn. Christine sat on the sofa, staring out the window. Her look was detached, almost as if she wasn't really there at all. The baby, playing at her feet, occasionally pulled on her dress for attention, attention that never came.

Slocum turned in my direction, his eyes never blinking. "It was a general who did this, not some common soldier."

I walked over to where my father lay and pulled back the sheet. Even with the clean shirt I was sure Tillie had put on him, I could see the open wound in my father's chest. "How do you know it was a general who did this?"

Slocum's eyes were hard, and he seemed to grind his teeth. "Those rebels were coming and going all morning. Tommy was on his horse up on the hill in the trees when he saw a general officer come out of the barn and ride off. Men were saluting him. Lots of bowing and scraping going on. Then Tommy came and got me. We rode down and found your father in the barn. We both figured your father wasn't about to take any of their scrip for what they took."

"Then we should find the man and make him pay for this—and not with Confederate scrip either."

Slocum crossed his arms. "How do you think you're going to do that?"

"No matter how bad they are, they still believe in justice. I'll talk to General Lee myself if I have to." I looked back at Tillie. "Besides, I have an eyewitness."

Slocum blew a half laugh out through his beard. "That's non-sense. You have an eyewitness who's a blind woman and an escaped slave to boot."

"But she hears well. She can tell the sound of a man just by the way he walks. And besides, they don't know she's blind. Sometimes I'm not so sure of it myself."

The
MARCH NORTH

CHAPTER 1

I
t took April Wolff less than a half-hour in the barn to hitch
the two mules to the wagon. The deliberate work seemed to
ease the bitterness bubbling inside her. If she could focus on
a task, even the simple discipline of putting two mules into
harness, then she could swallow without the sting of her
father's death burning her throat.

The mules twitched their ears and swished their tails to keep
the flies off. April wasn't about to take the mare anywhere near the
Southern troops, knowing how anxious they were to procure good
horseflesh. She also knew she and Tillie might very well need the
wagon to sleep in and carry supplies. It wouldn't be comfortable or
offer much protection in the rain, but rain might be a welcome
blessing from the sun beating down in the midafternoon.

The wagon was something her father pampered, not just used.
The sides were sturdy, and the edges still bore the marks of her

father's sanding. He had worked at buffing it down so that a stray piece of wood wouldn't tear one of the ladies' dresses. April reached over to a small keg hanging on the support post. She pulled out the stick with the cloth wound around the end. It was dripping with a thick bubble of grease. Moving around from wheel to wheel, she dabbed the grease into the hubs. It was just the kind of thing her father would have done.

Reaching over and dropping the stick back into place, she looked for the spot where her father had been killed. Slocum had said they found him in the barn, but where?

She stepped over to the hay and saw a few drops of blood. Her eyes followed the bloody trail across the straw, then widened in horror at the dark patch of color, matted straw, and dirt—a puddle of blood, her father's blood. She knew then that this was the place. She knelt down to get a better look at the place her father had fallen. She shifted some of the straw, which had been displaced when Slocum and his son carried her father's body into the house. She saw something odd. Her eyes widened and she leaned closer. Carefully she moved the straw and hay out of the way.

Written in the dirt, hastily scrawled, were the letters sn, and under them an X had been drawn. April sat back and stared at the drawing. She knew at once that her father must have written the scrawled letters in the dirt. He had been trying to say something. *What was he trying to say?* she wondered. *Are these the initials of the killer?*

She got to her feet and spotted two of her father's sawhorses. Walking over to where they sat, she picked them up and moved them over to the patch of straw and dirt that contained the writing. The sawhorses wouldn't guarantee the spot would remain undisturbed, but they would help.

Walking over to the door, she slid it open. She grabbed the lead mule's harness and marched the wagon out of the barn, pulling it alongside the house. Walking back, she carefully closed and secured the large door. April picked up her dress and raced around the corner of the house. Dust flew with every step she took. She then hurried up the stairs. "Tillie, you find yourself some clothes to wear for the next few days."

The old woman had retaken her seat on the porch, her pipe once again sending up a gentle trace of gray smoke. April's racing feet on the steps and sharp voice brought the old woman's chair to a halt. "You ain't 'bout to go 'round and do dis foolishness is you?"

The question stopped April in her tracks. She stood there with the door open. "It's not foolish. Somebody needs to do it."

"Why you, girl?"

"Have you ever known me to *not* do anything I set out to do?"

"No, girl, I ain't. Course, I ain't never knowed you to take on something so all-fired foolish afore. Dem rebs ain't 'bout to pay no attention to a Yankee girl. And you think dey is gonna stop dat battle what's a brewin' so's dey can have one of dere own big army bosses arrested on just your say-so? Tain't very likely, gal."

The corncob pipe bobbed in her mouth as she smiled; her eyes twinkled. There was no sight in them, but the woman could laugh with just her eyes and talk when there were no words to be heard. "You go in dere and manage to do dat, lammy pie, and you best not stop dere. You jes go head on and get General Lee to surrender. Put a end to dis here war altogether."

"There's no use in you trying to stop me. I'm going. If I don't do something, no one will. God is just. It's His justice I seek. Even the rebels can understand that. You can sit here as long as you want, but I'm going."

Tillie pounded her pipe into the palm of her hand. She slowly got to her feet. "Well, if you is gonna be a muley critter, I speck I'll go 'long." She smiled. "Sides, maybe dem boys in gray has gots better tobacco dat I can swap for some sugar or coffee."

April walked through the small sitting room to the large parlor where her father was laid out. Slocum was still standing at her father's head. It was as if he hadn't moved a muscle. Christine was sitting motionless by the window, her eyes focused on the fields outside. Her blond hair was tied behind her head and looked like a shock of ripe corn silk, ready for picking. Her blue eyes were light and airy in color, and her face a perfect milky-cream tone.

April dropped to her knees in front of Christine and picked up the baby. She smoothed the little boy's curls aside and spoke to Christine in a low voice as she petted the child. "I'm going to be gone a few days. I have to look for Father's killer. Did you see anything that might help me?"

Christine continued to look out the window, not even blinking. Her hands lay motionless on her lap. For all the world she looked like a wax figure, perfect in shape and full of life that was now only an illusion.

April put her hand on Christine's and squeezed it gently. "You just rest then. I'll find the man who did this."

She took the baby from her knee and got to her feet. Stepping over to the feet of her father, she tugged at his sock slightly, almost without thought, and looked at Slocum. "Will you take care of the arrangements?"

"Why don't you at least wait until we have your father buried?"

April shook her head. "I don't have time. I have to catch whoever did this before he gets away. You'll have to bury him yourself." She glanced back at Christine. "I don't think she's going to be much help."

"No." Slocum shook his head. "I don't expect she will."

April ran her hand over her father's body as she stepped around the table. He looked peaceful, more peaceful than she had seen him in a long time. It was almost as if he knew what she was trying to do. He had always had great confidence in her, even more than he felt for her brother, Gerald. She had never expected to be his favorite. That was a place reserved for a man's son, and Gerald had been his only son.

In many ways Gerald had been a disappointment. And when he had gone off to fight the war, all of her father's hopes for him had died. War was something the Mennonites shunned as man's great sin against man. Gerald was in disobedience, and as much as her father had tried to pretend that he no longer existed, she knew each bit of news about the war had shot pain through him.

Her father's hands were now placed across his chest, and April laid hers on top of his. They were cold to her touch. Everything inside of her wanted to talk to the man. He would be the only one who understood. "I love you, Father. I'll be back, and I will find the man who did this."

She looked up at Slocum's steely eyes. "When do you expect to bury him?"

He shook his head. "Probably tomorrow if we can. The Schneiders are making him a coffin, but it might take them awhile to get here. Because of the rebel army, people are hiding in their root cellars." He looked down at April's father. "And not without good reason."

April swallowed. "Maybe I'll be back before then."

"I doubt it, but you can try."

She turned to walk away but then stopped. "You didn't find my father's book of Psalms did you? You know the one, the leather-bound one. He carried it with him everywhere."

Slocum shook his head. "No, I didn't."

"Please find it if you can. I'd love to have it—to remember him by."

It didn't take long for both women to gather up enough clothes and supplies to last them for several days. April took extra food—some bread, ham, and coffee. She took a case of strawberry preserves, a jar of honey, and a jug of sorghum. From what she'd seen of the rebels, food was in short supply. The sweets might present an inviting bargaining chip for her, and she intended to use anything that might get her foot in the door.

The two women climbed up on the wagon, and April slapped the backs of the mules with the reins. They lurched forward. She watched as Slocum stepped out to the porch. It didn't take much to see the look of disapproval on the man's face. She'd seen the same look on her father's face many times, a condescending frown that said she should know better, while at the same time dismissing what she was doing as the emotional reaction of a woman.

Slocum's son, Tommy, had ridden in and tied his horse to the hitching rail out front. April thought of Tommy as no more than a boy. It was as if he'd been frozen in time for the last ten to fifteen years. He was simpleminded with a cruel streak in him at times, but April suspected it was because he saw himself as someone who wasn't like the rest. April had been with him when, as a child, he pulled the wings off butterflies. Many of the things he'd done to impress her only served to make her keep her distance from him. Not that it did any good. The boy was twenty, six years younger than she was, but he had a crush on her and often brought her flowers he picked in the field. At times it made her uncomfortable.

He nodded his head at her. His clothes were dirty and unkempt, a red-checked shirt crammed down into brown trousers. He had on a Union belt buckle that shone in the sun, but there was little about him that could be called army in appearance. What little facial hair he could muster was gathered in a smudge of beard on his chin. It almost looked like a piece of light horsehair glued in place on an otherwise slick and pasty face.

"Don't you worry yourself none 'bout what dem menfolk thinks." It was almost as if Tillie could see it all. "You gots to do what you think you gots to do. You always have, and dat ain't changed much since you was crawlin' 'bout the floor."

April had taken the time to change her dress, and she even felt somewhat clean. She had no desire to meet the enemy with blood on her hands or her dress. She was wearing a green skirt and white blouse that showed off her dark, chestnut-colored hair. The red ribbon she had used to tie her hair behind her head was set off with a red sash around her waist. People might easily mistake her as someone going to church, but that was the last place she had in mind.

She moved the wagon out onto the road to Greencastle. Before long she would find herself right in the middle of the rebel army. She hated them and everything they stood for, but it was a feeling she was going to have to work at concealing. The words of her father came racing back into her mind: "Girl, you never hide your feelings well. If you were a man you could never take up with cards. You'd be broke before sundown." This was one time she was going to work at proving her father wrong.

CHAPTER 2

The wagon moved along the road for hours with a slow and steady turning of the wheels. April could see the stalks of corn as they stood straight and tall. The wisps of corn silk were like brushes that painted the blue sky, and the sycamores cast a shadow over the road. The shade was cool as they rolled into it, but it was only a brief respite from the late afternoon sun.

Heavy wagons had worn deep gouges in the hard, parched dirt. The wheels of April's wagon tumbled over them with lurches and sudden drops. Each plunge in the road sent April and Tillie bouncing on the seat.

In the distance April could see the farm of Ebineezer Pender. The red house and barn were brightly painted, and she knew the Penders' well would give them cold water. They needed it, and so did the mules.

As they got closer April saw the four Pender girls sitting on the broken-down steps. They huddled together, carefully avoiding the splintered hole on the edge. It made April wonder. The man had two strong boys. Something like that cried out for repair. She also noticed how quiet the place was. The girls sat like statues. No dogs barked and no chickens scratched the ground.

Ebineezer and his wife, Julienne, stepped out of the door. The man crossed his arms as he watched the wagon pull up. He was wearing black trousers with a stark white shirt, and his flowing black beard plummeted down his chest to a point below his third button. The beard and flashing dark eyes made him an imposing figure. Julienne wore a simple blue calico dress. Her weak chin bobbed as if she'd been crying.

Aside from the broken stairs, the house looked prosperous even if the people didn't seem that way. Flowers were planted in boxes under the windows, and the impatiens were blooming a brilliant array of pink and white. April looked over the small vegetable garden next to the house. It was well cared for with neat rows of green beans, carrots, and turnips.

April smiled and pulled the team to a halt. "Do you mind if I water the mules?"

Ebineezer shook his head and motioned in the direction of the well. His cold look puzzled April. She knew these people, yet suddenly she felt like a total stranger. She climbed down from the wagon and, taking a bucket from the back of the wagon, walked over to the well. As she cranked the handle to raise the bucket in the well, she saw Julienne walk in her direction. The woman was wringing her hands.

"I'm sorry you weren't given a better welcome. Mr. Pender is just upset, is all. Our girls like you."

April continued to crank the handle on the well. "That's all right, Mrs. Pender. We're living in bad times."

Julienne wiped the palms of her hands on her dress. "You have no idea how bad. Troops came by this morning and mustered Evan and Earl into the militia. They have to protect Harrisburg, they said."

April lifted the well bucket onto the wooden bench in front of the well and began to pour water into her bucket. "It sounds like you don't believe them."

"I don't know what to believe anymore or who to believe."

April took the heavy bucket and swung it between her legs. She took careful steps in the direction of the team. Julienne followed along behind her. "We've been lied to so many times in this war a body can't trust what they hear or read. If we were winning it like they say, then the rebel army wouldn't be marching past our house all day, now would they?"

Holding the bucket in both arms, April held it for the lead mule to drink. "No, I suppose not."

Ebineezer stepped off the porch and walked in April's direction. He took the bucket from her. "I'm sorry about my manners. Let me water your mules while you and your darky woman get something for your own selves."

"That's all right. No need to apologize. Julienne told me about your sons being taken."

He stuck his lower lip out. "Only sixteen and seventeen; too young to fight in any war, especially this war. My chickens were taken too, all of them."

"The rebels took your chickens?"

"Weren't no rebels that took them. It was our own troops."

"The Union army took your chickens? They didn't pay you for them?"

"Pay! They didn't even offer us paper. They just took our sons and our poultry, killed our dogs, and almost cleaned out the smokehouse too. They would have if Evan hadn't pulled them off. They rode out of here with them boys of ours on the backs of two of our horses, horses we'll never see again. For that matter, it'll be the grace of God if we ever see the boys either. Those soldiers are all a bunch of brigands and thieves."

"Don't be too hard on them. I'm sure they're all lonely boys away from home."

"Boys my foot! Them was full-grown men. They may be away from home, and think that gives them an excuse to steal from folks they're never going to see again. *You* lose something to those people and you won't be so quick to defend them."

April swallowed hard and clenched her fists. "My father was murdered by the Confederates this morning."

Julienne slipped her arm around April. "I'm so sorry. We didn't know."

"I was told it was a Confederate general who did the killing. That's why I'm going this way. I'm hoping to find the man."

Ebineezer pulled the bucket away from the lead mule and held it under the second one. He shook his head. "That's a fool's chase, girl. They ain't gonna give you the time of day. What is your father's death to them? Pretty girl like you, no telling what them men are going to do."

"I brought my father's black-powder .44 with me. I can take care of myself."

He smiled for the first time. "The whole Union army's running from them, and you're going to take them on with a horse pistol. Them men that come by here today should have taken you 'stead of Evan and Earl. Looks like you got more reason to fight."

"I'm not going to fight. I'm just going to find out the truth."

"You're going to get yourself in a peck of trouble, that's all."

"Dat's what I done told her," Tillie spat out.

She had been sitting in the wagon patiently, but April knew that patience had never been a virtue with either of them. The problem was, Tillie could never decide if a conversation someone else was having was something she was welcome to participate in.

"I tells her and I tells her, but does she listen? Nooo."

"That's enough, Tillie. I've heard all I'm going to hear on the matter."

April had no desire to be ganged-up on.

Tillie sat back on the seat and crossed her arms. "Fine, den you jes get an old blind woman a drink o' water. Don't let me sit here and die o' thirst." She quieted down with a mutter. "Give dem mules a drink but can't see to old Tillie. Fine thing."

Julienne broke into a stammer. "I-I'll bring a bucket and a dipper for the both of you." With that, she scurried off to the well.

"Well, if you're bound and determined to pursue this foolishness, you won't have to go far. The whole danged Rebel army is up the road there. Been passing by all day it seems like. Those blue-coated thieves spotted them and took off like scalded dogs."

"Thank you. I'll find them."

It only took April and Tillie a few more minutes to quench their thirst and fill their canteens. They said their good-byes to the Penders, and April spent a short time with the scared and frozen girls on the steps. Climbing back on the wagon, she slapped the reins on the mules and lurched the thing back onto the road.

She looked over at the stone-silent Tillie. "You just never let anything be, do you?"

"Not when I's right, I don't. And I is right 'bout dis. You is wrong." She cracked a sly smile at April. "You and me is a lot alike in dat way. You tear into a matter like a hog goin' to de trough. You jes ain't 'bout to let up, no way, no how."

"Well, I'm right. That murderer deserves to be found and punished."

"Chile, dis here whole country's been killin' and murderin' one another fer plum near three years now. You get the first taste of what folks been goin' through, and you think it's high time fer justice. Dere ain't no such thing this side o' the great white throne. You of all folks ought to know dat, Christian woman dat you is."

"Father's death had nothing to do with war. It was murder plain and simple."

"And you best be leavin' it at de feet of Jesus, lamb. He's de only one what can put things right. He stay de steady course and keep His wheels grindin'. Dey may be slow, but dey is sure. I ain't never knowed Him to fail. Course, you hafta wait fer His time, and waitin' fer others to come round to doin' what's in yer head ain't never been nothin' you shine at."

It was little more than an hour later when April spotted the first Confederates. They were scattered along the road on both sides, sitting in a large cornfield and eating corn only partially ripe.

She slapped the mules with the traces and sent them moving a little quicker as they got closer. The men watched the wagon pass. Their eyes were silently riveted on April. It was a hollow look, mixed with fatigue and hunger. Many of the men had no shoes, and some had wrapped their feet with dirty cloths to keep them from getting cut by the rocks. Their dirty uniforms were a colorful mixture of grays, reds, and soft browns. A few even wore blue uniforms, or at least pieces of uniforms, that had once belonged to their enemy.

Two men stepped out into the middle of the road, and one of them grabbed the harness of one of the mules. "Whoa. Hold on there."

The man looked salty, with sweat beads pouring out from under his beaten cap. He had blue eyes, and a scar ran from his ear to the tip of his chin. It was a flame-like pinkish color. "Where you think you're bound to, little lady?"

"I'm here to see your general."

"Which one? We got ourselves a passel of generals, ain't we, Luke?"

The second soldier wound his way to the side of the wagon. April had covered the supplies she was carrying, and it was plain to see he was curious about what was under the tarp. He looked to be no more than a boy, his face unable to support any semblance of a beard. He started to lift the tarp.

"You keep your nose out of our things," April said, picking up a small whip. "Those are ours and things we are bringing to the general."

The boy jumped back.

"Like I said, which one? We got us General Iverson, General Ewell, General Jenkins, and General Early. Before long we're gonna get ourselves a few more."

"I just want the one in charge."

"Well, that there would be General Ewell. He's up the road a few miles. Might be pleased to see a handsome lady such as yerself, but the man's married and he's a Christian." He smiled. "Course we gots some up there that ain't given to revival particulars. You might happen on to one of them."

"I sincerely hope not. I'll just see General Ewell."

The man let go of the mule and stepped back, scratching his chin. He looked over at the younger man. "Well, Luke, you best escort the ladies here forward to see no harm comes to them. She appears to have business with the big dog, and it's best to get him afore he's nappin'."

The young man smiled and climbed up on the wagon. April didn't like it, but she scooted over. She could smell the odor of sweat mixed with tobacco juice. He took the reins from her hand and slapped at the mules. As they rolled past what appeared to be the Confederate army, April thought at any other time and place they would look like a shabby group of armed vagrants. Some were tending pots of boiling water with ears of corn bobbing in the swirling cauldrons. Others were stitching torn coats and shirts, and a few were stripped almost bare as they boiled their clothes in water. April turned her head.

She spotted the dirty tents beside the road in a clearing under some trees. Horses were tethered to a line that ran under the trees and men were cooking over several fires. Flags were snapping in the coolness of the evening breeze.

An officer stood up from a folding chair and walked in their direction as they rolled in to camp. He was the first man April had seen in a clean uniform, a young man who April measured to be in his early twenties. "Can I help you?"

Their young driver spoke. "Lieutenant, these here ladies is here to see General Ewell."

The officer wore a cap, and a sword that appeared to be too large for him to use dangled at his side. His face was smooth except for the trace of mustache he was obviously trying very hard to grow.

He blinked his brown eyes at April in an expression of disbelief. "And why would you ladies need to see General Ewell?"

"I am afraid that is for your general's ears, Lieutenant."

He reached out his hand to help April from the wagon. "I'm afraid right now the general is otherwise occupied."

April took his hand and climbed down. "Then you'll just have to tell him to get unoccupied, Lieutenant."

"Oh, ma'am, I couldn't do that. What you have to say, you'll just have to say to me. It may be that I could help you or direct you to someone who could."

April looked back at Tillie. The woman was chuckling. "I am afraid this matter is of grave importance. I can only tell it to your general."

The lieutenant shook his head. "Ma'am, if there's something you have to say, you'll have to say it to me. I am General Ewell's orderly. Nothing gets through to him without going through me."

April swallowed and clinched her fists. "What I have to say is about a matter of cold-blooded murder. My father was murdered on his farm this morning by one of your men, and I have an eyewitness with me."

CHAPTER 3

The young captain stood at the entrance of General Iverson's tent. He had kept Early waiting long enough, and even though it wasn't exactly his fault, he didn't like to face the frown of Jubal Early. If he hadn't been in Early's camp to deliver a message, he wouldn't have gotten this duty in the first place. He hesitated just a little. The general had his back to him, and he could see the man lift a bottle to his lips and drain its amber contents.

General Alfred Iverson was a hard drinker and everybody knew it, from the lowest private in the North Carolina brigade to the colonel whom Lee had passed over to appoint his fellow Virginian as brigade commander. It was resented too, not so much for the man's drinking as for the fact that he was from Virginia. Everybody knew Bobby Lee played favorites with the native sons from his home state, and Alfred Iverson had put a bold exclamation point to that murmured rumor.

The captain cleared his throat. "Uh . . . ahem. General Iverson, sir."

Iverson swung around on the small stool, the empty bottle still dangling from his right hand. His shirt was open, buttons hanging to the side. The man did have a shine on his boots, something those above him had made careful note of. No doubt they were the product of his orderly's labor, however. His trim brown beard glistened with the remains of his heavy drinking, and his warm brown eyes had a dull shine to them. "What do you want now, Captain?"

"General Early would like to see you, sir, to discuss the line of march tonight."

Iverson sputtered. "Tonight? That man's gonna keep driving us all through the night? We just found a good site to camp."

The captain shrugged as Iverson wobbled to his feet, slowly buttoned his shirt, then lifted and stretched his suspenders into place over his broad shoulders. "A man ought not to leave his camp every night to go marching in the dark."

"The men are almost done with their cooking, General." The captain smiled. "They are living off the land, and I think we have some ham if you'd like some, some ham and fresh biscuits. We have corn too." He forced a smile.

Iverson scowled at him. "I've been looking at that corn all day, Captain. I wouldn't exactly call it ripe for the picking."

"No, sir. I suppose not. But the men are ripe for the eating."

Iverson picked up his coat and pushed his arms into it. The sleeves on the gray coat had stitching that went from the cuffs to the man's elbows in fancy loops of embroidered gold. The cuffs were an off-white; the collar bore three stars on each side and gold oak leaves under them. He buttoned the two rows of bright brass buttons and tried to stand tall, throwing his head back. "That look presentable for Early?"

"Yes, sir. I would say so."

Iverson picked up his swooping hat and cocked it on his head. "Fine, then let's meander over there and see what form of torture he has in mind for us."

The captain stood aside and followed Iverson through the camp. Large fires were burning with crisp snaps of green wood, and the men were roasting some chickens and boiling corn in large pots suspended over the open fires. It was plain to see that there was no love lost for the general. Most of the men who saw him looked away. Few came to attention.

The Second Corps of the Army of Northern Virginia had seen more than its share of action. They had done a majority of the dirty work at Chancellorsville and taken most of the casualties. To top that off, they had lost their beloved leader, Stonewall Jackson. It was there that the former commander of the North Carolina brigade had also fallen. Rather than simply promote the second in command, the colonel from North Carolina who had been with them throughout the war, Lee had assigned Alfred Iverson to the post. He was a stranger to the men, and they treated him like one.

The captain noticed several of the men lying on the ground around the fires as they nudged one another. They pointed in Iverson's direction. They could see him teeter as he walked, and the sight brought chuckles to some and scowls from a few others. They were a disheveled looking group. But they had come to respect good officers, and it didn't take them long to recognize the bad ones. It was plain to see that the men from North Carolina thought Iverson was the latter.

Iverson stumbled slightly and then righted himself. That brought a few chuckles that could not only be seen, but heard as well. He looked back at the captain. "These men of yours have no discipline, Captain. I wouldn't call these roughnecks from your state soldiers. More like tramps with rifles."

"Yes, sir. But they do fight, General. They fire those rifles pretty well."

Iverson stuck his bottom lip out and lifted his head in a haughty manner. "I don't plan on letting them get behind me when we see the Yankees, Captain. They just might forget who they're shooting at." He turned and continued walking, his words trailing after him. "No, sir, not me. I plan on staying to the rear of this group."

The captain followed along behind him, watching the men as they devoured what they could pull out of the pot or tumble out of the fire. Food was one of the reasons they had made this invasion into Pennsylvania. Their normal daily ration was eighteen ounces of flour and four ounces of bacon, all of dubious quality. Active men easily lost weight on what they had to eat. There was little in the way of fresh vegetables, and many of the men had symptoms of scurvy. Each regiment was required to send out a detail every day to collect edible weeds such as sassafras buds, lamb's-quarters, and wild onions. Even some of the officers would rob their horses of an occasional handful of corn, which when parched in the fire, served to stave off hunger.

He smiled as he watched them eat. No matter who their general was, food was a cause for celebration. It would help them march during the night, and tomorrow might very well take care of itself.

The captain had picketed his horse next to the general's black stallion. He untied it and swung into the saddle. Watching Iverson try to mount was almost painful. The man lifted his foot and missed the stirrup, not once but several times before finally planting his boot firmly. He rocked back and forth as he held on to the horn of the saddle, building up a head of steam. Springing up, he landed in place with a thud.

Waving his hand, Iverson tried to give himself to business. "Lead on, Captain. Let's find this division commander of ours."

The captain spurred his horse into a trot, glancing back to make certain Iverson was still in the saddle. The captain then began to canter down the road. There was one thing about his long holdup that gave him some comfort. From the look of Iverson and the smell on his breath, it would be all too apparent just who had engineered the delay.

They rode for about five miles before the captain spotted the farmhouse that was serving as divisional headquarters. A Stars and Bars, the battle flag of the Confederacy, flew from one of the second-story gabled windows, and more than a dozen horses were tied up out front. Several soldiers milled about the front porch steps. The captain dismounted in front of the guards and handed over the reins to a private.

Iverson would have a more difficult time and he knew it. The general was bouncing up and down as he trotted into the small yard. He pulled both reins back and took several deep breaths, growing accustomed to the sudden stop. Bending over, he grabbed the saddle and lowered himself slowly to the ground. It wasn't pretty, but now he could at least walk.

The captain barked at the private, "Take the general's horse." The soldiers respectfully averted their glances from the man as he stumbled, but the captain was embarrassed for him nonetheless. He tugged slightly at the general's sleeve. "General Early will be waiting."

"Somebody's always waiting. Just once I'd like to be the one waiting." Picking up his feet, he waddled in the direction of the house and up the stairs. The captain hurried beside him and, opening the door, stepped aside.

The house was a comfortable place with red sofas and settees around the large living room. Heavy, emerald-green velvet curtains with tassels were pulled back from the large windows, and rugs were scattered over the spotless wooden floor. Just off the living room was a parlor, strewn with maps. Beyond that was a dining room, where Jubal Early sat at the end of a table covered with food. Around him were the officers gathered for his council of war.

Spotting Iverson, Early rose to his feet and beckoned him forward. "Come on in here, General. We saved a place for you." Early's coat was off, and his necktie hung loosely around his throat. His eyes blazed at Iverson, and he slowly pulled on his gray beard.

Iverson tried his best to hold his shoulders straight as he marched into the room.

"You took me unawares, General Early. I was about to have a meeting with my own staff."

"Your own staff?" One of the generals chuckled. The captain spotted him right away. It was Albert Jenkins, the cavalry commander. "John Barleycorn, most likely."

The remark brought a few stifled laughs from the men at the table, and once again the captain couldn't help but feel a sense of shame.

Jenkins was a young man with a deeply receding hairline. He carefully combed a small wave of what was left over his smooth head. Sharp ears stuck out from behind one of the largest beards the captain had ever seen. The full, black beard tumbled over his chest and down to a point touching the top of his belt. The captain was almost certain that a razor had never touched the man's face. Most likely, he'd been growing it since he was fifteen.

"Pay him no mind, Iverson, and take a seat." Early sat back down and picked up a plate. "We have some ham here. Had to rescue a few Yankee hogs."

Iverson carefully lowered himself into an empty chair on the far end from Early. That was best. He didn't have to walk far that way. He watched as the plates circled the table in his direction.

"We have orders to march on Chambersburg tonight and then on to Harrisburg. Ought to scare them scoundrels plenty to have one of their state capitols in our possession." He looked around the table. "What say, boys?"

There was a general murmur of laughter. The men nodded in agreement.

"My men are tired, General," Iverson said. "They're looking to rest up."

"I know this outfit's been pushed thoroughly, General. We've done more than is coming to us. Grates hard on me too." Early shrugged his shoulders. "But orders are orders, and we're about the only ones in a position to get our troops in to the field in front of Harrisburg." He smiled. "Of course, there are advantages to getting to these Yankee towns first. We get to visit the shops before Longstreet's boys get there. Your men might even find some shoes."

"And you might get ahold of a fresh supply of who-hit-John," Jenkins added. He snickered and looked down the table at the gathered council. He brushed aside his beard, allowing a smooth, toothy smile to form.

Iverson locked eyes with the cavalryman. Then a cool calm settled over his face. It was almost like a man slipping a dagger into an enemy. "Don't you have a sweetheart that married a farmer up this way, Jenkins?" he asked. "I hear she turned you over for a man your father's age. Could be she was looking for some maturity."

Jenkins's eyes flashed. He started to get to his feet.

"Sit down, Jenkins," Early barked. "We've got Yankees to fight. We can't be wasting our time or energy taking on each other."

Iverson deliberately loaded his plate with ham and sweet potatoes. It was evident he felt satisfied with dishing out pain, and now he intended to dish out dinner. He listened carefully as the next hour was spent talking over the plans for the coming march. Chambersburg would be the immediate target, and they would try to get in position to take the town while there was plenty of daylight left on the following day. Then it would be on to Harrisburg and the union troops that were gathering in the vicinity.

When the cigars came out, the plates were pushed away. The captain stepped back into the parlor as a number of the men started to leave. Early walked Iverson to the door, his arm around him. The captain tried to follow, but Early grabbed his arm and pulled him aside. "Not so quick, Captain. I want to talk to you."

"Yes, sir."

Early led him back into the living room. "I think your general can find his way back. He might even be able to get on his horse now that he has some food in his belly."

The captain nodded. "Yes, sir."

"Now, I want you to look after Iverson, Captain—what was your name, Captain?"

"Captain James Quinn, sir."

Early smiled. "Good Scotch-Irish name, Quinn. You ought to do well. Well, you watch out for Iverson. Do what you can to keep him off the bottle. Lord knows he has enough reason to drink. Do you know about the children he lost?"

"No, sir, I don't."

"He lost two little girls, poisoned by a runaway slave. From what I hear, the gal who did it wasn't much more than a girl herself. Figured with the general's girls laid up sick she could slip away in the confusion. Well, she got away all right, but she gave them too much of that oleander juice. It was supposed to make them sick, but it killed them dead."

Early looked out the door as Iverson rode off. "So, you see, the man's got some grief, plenty enough to drive him to drink. He's got revenge in his heart too. The trouble is, he doesn't quite know who to take it out on."

CHAPTER 4

pril and Tillie had been forced to make camp close to the headquarters of the Second Corps. It had been a long time since the lieutenant who had promised to help them had gone for a word with someone in command. All evening they watched as riders came and went, and April was growing more and more impatient. Tillie was stirring stew left over from the day before. She had brought it with them from home, pot and all. She hunched over the small fire, her drab brown dress spread out in front of the stool she sat on. She listened intently as April paced.

"You come over here, lamb, and get yerself some supper."

"I can't eat now. I'm not hungry."

"I don't care much if you is or if you isn't. It's what dat body of yours needs, hungry or not. You gonna be gettin' yerself all faintlike when you needs to be strong with them menfolk. You don't want dem thinkin' 'bout you is some weak sister now, does you?"

"No. I suppose you're right."

"You bet yer scrawny neck I is. Tillie is always right." She dipped her head and cocked it, smiling in April's direction. "Course, you only listen to me part of de time. You still ain't old nuff to reckon what's good fer you and what ain't."

She dipped a broad wooden spoon into the pot, piled some bubbling stew onto a tin plate, then held it out to April. "And when it come time fer you to finally choose yerself a man, you best be listenin' to old Tillie real good. You done turned more of dem away than a woman could fill a dozen hope chests with."

April took the plate and picked up a spoon from the gear Tillie had piled on a cloth. "I don't have much use for men. I'm a teacher."

"You is a woman first of all."

April blew on the first bite of stew. "We've been surrounded by men all day, and the more I see of them the less I like them."

Tillie cracked a broad smile, her bottom teeth shining. "Dat's jes 'cause you ain't seen de right one jes yet."

The old woman's vacant eyes twinkled. "When you do, you'll be singin' a different song. Maybe not wif yer mouth, but yer heart sure will."

April was almost finished with what Tillie had ladled out for her when she saw the lieutenant step out of the headquarters tent. He spotted her and started toward them. His feet clomped over a set of boards laid on the ground from the porch to where they had set up their camp.

"Dat be dat young man come back I reckon."

April looked down at Tillie. "How would you know who's coming?"

"Girl, I ain't got me no eyes, but I got ears sharp as a rat in the dark."

April set her plate down and stared at the man. "Well, can I see the general?"

The man quickly removed his hat. "I'm afraid not, ma'am. General Ewell is very busy. He does want me to take you over to the provost marshal's tent though. Maybe he can help you."

"And who is the provost marshal?"

"Colonel Eugene Sinclair of Virginia."

"And I suppose I am to be impressed because you are taking me to a Virginian. He has the kind of breeding to take care of wayward women?"

"No, ma'am," the lieutenant sputtered. "It's just his job, that's all."

April put down her plate. "I would have thought that murder was the job of your general. Your whole army seems to be dedicated to that proposition."

The lieutenant twisted the hat in his hands.

"Ma'am, it is the general's job to make war. The provost marshal's office is supposed to be the police. What you need is a policeman, not a general."

Tillie leaned back and laughed. "Go head on, girl. Half a hog is better than none at all."

April smoothed her dress and lifted her chin. "Lead on, Lieutenant. I'll see your colonel."

He stepped back. "This way, ma'am, if you please." With that he took her arm and led her over the stumps they had been using for firewood. She pulled her arm away and continued to follow him through the camp, drawing the attention of dozens of men gathered by their fires. When they got to a pair of tents on the far side of the camp, the lieutenant stepped inside and April followed.

"Colonel, General Ewell asked me to bring this lady to see you. It seems she has a matter that falls into your jurisdiction."

April studied the man. He was thin, with dark wavy hair and a mustache that was waxed and pointed at each end. The ends of the mustache hung down from his upper lip like the two legs of a mule-riding man about to give the animal a double kick. He stood up and smiled. His eyes were fixed on her with a softness to them.

Stepping around the table, he positioned a folding chair for her. "Please be seated, ma'am." He looked up at the lieutenant who was still standing at the door. "That will be all, Lieutenant. I can handle this from here."

"Yes, sir."

With that the lieutenant left and April took the seat offered to her. Colonel Sinclair stepped back and leaned against the table. He picked up a pipe, the likes of which April had never seen before. It was white and carved in the shape of a lion's head. The man picked up a pouch and began to stuff the lion with tobacco. "Now, why don't you tell me all about it? I take it our men confiscated goods from you they didn't pay you for."

"Most likely, but that is not why I am here."

Sinclair picked up a match and struck it, holding the flame over the lion and puffing the pipe to life. He shook the match out and dropped it into a cup on the table. "Then please go on with why you are here."

"One of your men murdered my father in cold blood. My father wasn't even armed."

April could see shock registering on the colonel's face. His thin eyebrows bent inward. "This is serious."

"Yes, very serious."

He wiped his forehead with the fingertips of his right hand, then motioned for her to continue. "Please go on."

"The man who committed the murder was a general officer in your army."

Her words almost made the pipe drop from his mouth. He gripped it. "You saw this?"

"I have an eyewitness."

Sinclair got up from the table and walked to the door of the tent.

He motioned for a corporal standing outside. "Go find Major Chevalier and Colonel Drummond. Bring them here at once."

In only a matter of minutes, the flap on the tent was pushed aside and in stepped two officers. One was older with white muttonchops and darting blue eyes. His tunic was buttoned to the top of his neck and, with his bulging neck and portly girth, he looked to be uncomfortable in any position. "What seems to be the trouble, Colonel Sinclair?" he asked.

Sinclair stepped back to allow them a better view of April. He cleared his throat. "Gentlemen, allow me to introduce—" His words were cut short by a look of embarrassment, followed by a slight smile. "I am sorry, madam. In my haste I did not get your name."

"April Wolff."

The second officer was young. He stepped forward with a broad smile. He was wearing a white shirt open at the collar and tucked into his gray trousers. One look at him almost made April blush. He was strikingly handsome, uncomfortably so. His face was clean shaven and had a strong, dimpled chin. He filled his shirt tightly and stood ramrod straight. "Miss April Wolff?" he asked with a smile.

"Yes." Now April was blushing. She could feel the blood surge into her face, warming it.

"Miss Wolff, these are two of my best officers, Colonel Drummond and Major Chevalier."

The young major clicked his polished boots and bowed slightly, and the older man took a seat on a stool. It creaked slightly under his weight.

"I take it you gentlemen are familiar with General Lee's order number 72."

Both men nodded. General Lee had issued the order at the beginning of their invasion of the North. It severely limited what might be taken from enemy civilians and the form of payment to be given.

"Miss Wolff's complaint does not fall under that decree, but it severely violates the spirit of that order." Sinclair looked back at April, almost hesitant to speak the words. "It would seem the lady's father has been murdered. There is no better way to say it. And from reports and an eyewitness account, one of our own general officers is suspected."

"Who?" Drummond blurted out the question.

"I'll let Miss Wolff give you her account."

For the next several minutes April slowly repeated what she had seen and heard about her father's murder. The men were riveted to her story, although Drummond seemed restless. "Is that all you have?" he asked.

"I am afraid so. I do have an eyewitness, and if we can interview those officers who passed this way today, I'm certain we can find the man responsible."

Drummond looked over at Sinclair. "Surely you can't be serious? You expect us to go around to the general officers and interrupt their councils of war with this cock-and-bull story from a Yankee woman?"

"All I know is that General Ewell asked us to tend to this matter. I am open to your suggestions."

Drummond slowly raked his hand through his whiskers and over his face, as if by doing so he could make the problem go away. He then put his hands on his legs, rubbing them back and forth to bring life into them.

April watched as Chevalier studied the man. He seemed almost amused at the sight of the older man's discomfort.

"I think the entire notion is ludicrous. It might even be a Yankee plot to stop our advance while we chase our tails," Drummond said.

"We will have to give a report to General Ewell," Sinclair said. He shook his head. "I wouldn't want to be the man to tell him that we've done nothing here."

Drummond looked over to where Chevalier was standing. "Then let the major handle it. He's a college man. He thinks himself so bright. Perhaps he can determine the killer without being allowed into his presence."

"How about it, Major? Would you like this case?"

April watched as Chevalier locked eyes with Sinclair. He brushed his hand through his thick black hair. "Colonel, a man would have to be the buffoon of all time to take this. Even if I find the man, I'm going to make a lot of enemies."

"You already have a lot of enemies," Drummond added. "What are a few more where you are concerned, Chevalier? You have no career where this army is concerned and you know it."

Chevalier ignored the man and continued to stare at Sinclair. "If I do it, I'll have my price."

"I know you will, Major."

"And I'll have to have your solemn promise to fulfill it during this campaign."

"This campaign?"

Chevalier jabbed his finger toward the ground as if to nail down the point. "This campaign."

"All right. You have it, Major. I'll find something for you."

Drummond glanced at April, then back at Chevalier. "I shouldn't think you will find your duty here that unpleasant, Major, given your reputation with the fairer sex. From what I understand, there isn't a father in all of Charleston who will so much as let his daughter go for a ride with you."

"I'll ignore that remark, Colonel. You have your job; I'll have mine." He looked at Sinclair. "And Colonel Sinclair will have his."

"Yes, Major. I'll do my best for you."

"Then I have your word as an officer, a gentleman," he smiled, "and of course, a Christian."

Sinclair shook his head. "Yes, Major. You have my word."

Drummond got up from his stool and pushed his bottom lip out in Chevalier's direction. "This sounds like a match made in heaven, Major." He looked back at Sinclair. "Now, if I can be excused."

Sinclair nodded, and the older man waddled out of the tent. He turned to April. "I am sorry you had to hear that, Miss Wolff, but you are in the best of hands with Major Chevalier. He is exactly the man I would have chosen for this."

April got to her feet and looked first at Chevalier, then Sinclair. "We'll have to see about that, Colonel, won't we?"

Chevalier stopped at the entrance of the tent. "One thing more, Colonel."

"What is that?"

"I will need Sergeant Perlman."

Sinclair slouched his shoulders forward and shook his head. "How will I survive here without my best people?"

"That is your problem, Colonel." He motioned in April's direction. "I have mine; it's only right for you to have yours. Think of it this way, when it comes time to file your report with General Ewell, you can tell him you put your best men on the job and actually mean it."

Sinclair waved him off. "All right. See to it. Just come back with something for me to say."

April followed Chevalier out of the tent. He turned to her. "Miss Wolff, I'll get my things and my horse, and Sergeant Perlman and I will join you in a few minutes."

"Why?"

"We'll first need to go back to your farm before we can do anything else."

"We are wasting time with that."

"Miss Wolff, let's get this straight from the start. I am the policeman here. I decide what needs to be done, and nobody else. If you want my help, you'll have to receive it on my terms. From this point on the risk is all mine, so I get to make the decisions. Am I making myself understood?"

"Perfectly, Major." April clenched her fists by her side. "You are an arrogant man who won't take advice from a woman."

Chevalier smiled. "Yes, then you do understand."

CHAPTER 5

appy swung down from his horse and held the reins. He had spent most of his day in the saddle, and he swung his arms from side to side to work out the pangs shooting through his back. His trousers were worn at the cuffs, and his tobacco-colored shirt was ripped and hung in tatters below his waist. The cuffs hung around his wrists for the lack of buttons. His hat, which looked like it had been trampled by a stampede of horses and subjected to a driving rainstorm, hung down around his ears and served only to cover his head. His beard was beginning to obscure the outline of the crisp mustache and goatee that he usually sported in more polite society.

To anyone passing by, he would appear to be a vagabond, someone trying to escape the war itself by finding odd jobs. He only hoped any federal pickets he might come across wouldn't give him too hard of a look. His horse was a beautiful blood bay that stood fifteen hands high, far too nice for a man with visible means of support. But good horseflesh was something he needed, although he wasn't much of a rider. His boots were new and hand tooled, purchased just three weeks ago in Washington city; and his side arm was a Colt dragoon.

He could only hope that it would be his smell that kept people away. He hadn't had a bath for three weeks or even scrubbed his face in four days. It would have been enough to make him retch, had he not become so accustomed to the odor that rose from his clothes, tickling the edge of his mustache.

He watched the road below him where the soldiers stood around their fires. He'd been doing his best to keep his distance from the bluecoats all day. His sharp, black eyes darted over the dark horizon as he counted the fires. It seemed that the entire Union army was on the march now. He could make out the men directly across the road below him and even hear the music of a mouth organ one of them was playing. Most of them were spooning hot food into their mouths. The taste of hot food was something he wanted very badly. He walked the horse to the tree and looped the reins over a low-hanging branch.

Reaching into his saddlebag, he took out a tin plate, a fork, and a spoon. Even life on the road didn't preclude a man being a gentleman. He stuffed the utensils into his back pocket. Crouching behind the tree, he began to dig in the soft ground. He scooped out clods of dirt with the edge of the plate, forming a windbreak. Reaching around the base of the hole, he picked up a number of rocks and began to form what he hoped would be a shield that would cover his small fire.

It took him a short time to find dry branches, and he piled them with care over the ads of the paper he'd bought in Washington two weeks before. He made a tepee of the dried sticks and lit a match to it. It burst into flames. The fire in the small hole wouldn't give off light to the men in the valley below. That was just what he wanted. He needed some hot coffee without attracting any attention.

He took a small coffeepot from his bag and poured water from his canteen into it. He settled it over a small grate he had with him, and it took only a matter of minutes before the growing fire was licking at its bottom. He tossed some coffee grounds into the water and settled back to watch it foam.

A short time later he heard the sound of two horses as they picked their way across the ridge. He stood up and, lifting his shirt, drew out the Colt dragoon. Stepping over to the tree, he carefully laid the revolver on a low limb and sighted down the heavy barrel. He squinted at the oncoming figures in the growing darkness. They were riding slow and steady, their heads outlined against the deep indigo sky.

With his thumb he pulled back gently on the hammer, which gave off a series of clicks that sounded like a string of miniature firecrackers before finally coming to rest.

The sound of the Colt was enough to stop the two riders in their tracks. They drew rein and strained their necks to search the darkness.

"What do you want?" Nappy asked.

"Nothing," a shrill voice answered. "We just smelled yer coffee, is all."

"You soldiers?"

"Not anymore we ain't."

"Then climb down from those horses of yours and keep your hands where I can see them."

They threw their legs over their saddles and slid down to the ground. They didn't appear to be much more than boys. "Now you just step forward and keep your hands up in the air so I can see them. A man can get nervous traveling alone."

The two riders walked forward with their hands extended over their heads. Nappy stepped around the tree trunk. He shook the revolver at them. "If you aren't soldiers, why are you creeping around out here in the dark?"

He could see them now. The two riders appeared to be teen-
agers with sandy hair and checked shirts tucked down into their
trousers.

"We're just trying to make our way back home, is all. We figured to come this way to miss all them army troops on the roads.
Please don't take us wrong, mister. We been traveling all day and
trying to stay close to the trees and such."

"Come on up to the fire so I can get a better look at you."

Nappy stepped up to the smoldering pit and watched the two
boys walk toward him. One was tall and lanky and wearing a straw
hat. His cheeks were smudged with soot, and his eyes shone in the
flickering fire. He had made himself the spokesman for the two of
them and, from the way the other boy looked, it was plain to see
why. The shorter of the two had a baby face, and his bottom lip was
trembling with fear.

Nappy wagged the revolver at them. "What's yer names?"

The oldest boy answered. "I'm Evan Pender. This here's my
brother, Earl."

Nappy smiled. It was hard not to with the unconscious looks of
complete innocence on the boys' faces. He took off his beaten hat
and swept it across his body and toward the ground, as if he were
presenting himself at a grand ball. "You are welcome to my humble
fire, gentlemen, and to what I have to offer as a cavalier of the open
road. My provisions may be humble indeed, but I can assure you my
generous spirit more than makes amends for what I lack in condition. You had better picket your horses with mine on the tree over
there. I'll give you some coffee and a little to eat if you're hungry."

The two boys looked at each other, blinking. "We are, mister.
Thanks."

Nappy rummaged in his bag for some cheese and ham along
with a crust of bread he had left. The bread and cheese wouldn't be
nearly enough to feed them all, but the smoked ham would go a
long way, he figured. The two hams were the size of small canta-
loupes. He pulled out a sharp knife and cut several slices.

The boys walked back to the fire and squatted down. Nappy handed them a piece of ham. "The soldiers down in the valley would have more to feed you. Why didn't you ride down there?"

Evan tore the slice of ham in two and handed his younger brother a piece. "We just come from the army. We don't much want to go back."

"You deserters? You hardly look old enough. But upon my soul if you are, then I should take you captive and claim my reward from our gallant men in blue."

Evan bit into a piece of ham, snapping it back into his mouth with a pull. "We ain't deserters 'cause we never did join up. They just took us."

"Took you?"

"That's right. They rode into our farm and took the meat in the smokehouse, the chickens, and us. Said we had to do our duty to protect this here state."

"And you don't seek to protect the glorious state of Pennsylvania, I take it?"

Evan gnawed on the meat. "We don't much mind that, but we ain't about to save Mr. Lincoln or that Joe Hooker's hide."

"And you believe that is what you would be doing?"

The boy nodded. "Yes, sir. We figured that aplenty."

Nappy reached back and picked up the tin cup he carried. He filled it with coffee and handed it over to the boy. "Treat that sparingly, my good man. I haven't got all that much."

Evan gingerly held the cup, passing it from hand to hand as he sipped the top off the black coffee. "We had to come this way." He took another sip. "The rebs is all over to the west of us, and our men is everywhere else."

"Where were you?"

"North of Chambersburg."

"How many Union troops up there?"

"Looked to be aplenty to us." He glanced at Earl. "Course we ain't seen much in the way of the army, so we couldn't say for sure."

"Any infantry, or were you just with the cavalry?"

"We didn't see any foot soldiers, but we heard there was some around."

"Did you see any cannons, any artillery?"

Both boys shook their heads. "Not much to speak of. Everybody looked plenty scared too. That didn't do much for our brass either."

Nappy smiled. "I just bet it didn't." He leaned toward them. "Would you boys like some cheese?"

"We sure would if you got some."

"I may have a little."

Nappy got up and walked back to his sack. He pulled out a small portion of a wheel of cheese and the folded map he was carrying. Walking back to where the boys were seated, he spread the map out in front of them. "Now, boys, I want you to do me a favor. Show me where you were today on the map and what you saw."

"What you want to know that for?"

Nappy smiled. "I'm just a knight of the open road trying to stay out of this war, just like you boys. You show me what you saw and where you were, and then I'll know just what I need to avoid."

For the next few minutes Nappy watched the boys pick out spots on the map where they had seen troop movements. He cut small pieces of cheese off the hunk in his hand and handed it over to the two boys as they gave him the lay of the land and descriptions of just what they had seen. The cheese was like a treat given to a dog that was being trained. The more he cut, the more they remembered.

"Fine, boys, that's very good. You're both going to spare me a peck of trouble, and I do appreciate it." He folded the map and stuck it into the front of his pants. "Would you like some more coffee?"

"Yes, sir. We would at that."

Nappy got to his feet and poured them a fresh cup. He watched as they passed it between them. "How far are you boys from home?"

"Not far," Evan gulped. "We ought to be there in the morning." He looked up. "Where you from?"

"I've been all over." Nappy chuckled. "A man such as myself seeks his own comfort and finds beauty in every place the sole of his foot touches. I have no obligations and no allegiances, just my heart to give me directions."

"We just been right here. Ain't never been nowhere and hope we never go nowhere neither."

Nappy packed up his supplies and then took the cup from the boys. He drank a cup of his own and stuck it back in the bag. "I suppose I'll be on my way now, lads. I should be making good time while it's still dark."

He tied the bag to his saddle and swung himself onto the big bay. "You boys should be getting home now. Your folks will be worried about you."

The boys got to their feet. "You didn't give us your name, mister."

"Napoleon Batist, but folks just call me Nappy."

"We're sure glad we come upon you, Mr. Nappy."

Nappy grinned. "Just make sure you don't ride up on me again. If I catch you following me, I'll kill you."

CHAPTER 6

W hen Chevalier and Perlman walked up to April's wagon, she and Tillie were loading their supplies. Chevalier was leading a large gray horse, and the sergeant was jerking on the reins of a swayback mule. It struck April as comical.

The sergeant was even more amusing than what he intended to ride. He was stoop shouldered and as bowlegged as a broken-down rooster. His uniform was tattered and his gray jacket, with bold yellow chevrons on each arm, was open. He wore a straw hat that was frayed at the edges, giving him the look of a farmer. A small, round, red nose peeked out from his wild and unruly gray whiskers. The man's face looked like a wilted salad with a bright red radish in the middle. His eyes were a lightning blue, crisp and clean, and full of fire. Under his arm he carried a large orange-and-white cat.

"Miss Wolff, allow me to present Sergeant Perlman."

April smoothed her hands on her dress. She would never be so rude as to laugh in the man's face, but she wasn't about to shake his hand.

"You can call me Jacob if you like, ma'am." He held out the cat for her to get a better look. "This is Elmer. He goes his own way most of the time, but he's been with me for two years now. I like him, even though he's a Virginia cat."

April turned and busied herself with loading the grate she had used to cover the fire. Even though she was usually given to making conversation with people, she refused to give either of them the satisfaction of knowing that she would give in to being pleasant. April had been taught to hate slavery and everyone who supported the institution. To her, slavery was the embodiment of evil. Men who fought for it were evil themselves.

Chevalier dropped his reins and picked up a stool the women had been using. He put it in the wagon. "Sergeant Perlman is one of our best. He was a policeman in Atlanta before the war."

April shot Perlman a glance. "Then you're accustomed to investigating murder, I take it?"

Perlman nodded his head and put the cat on the ground. It scampered off under the wagon. "Yes, ma'am, I seen me a few in my time."

"And have you ever seen one committed by a man who can't be arrested?"

"No, ma'am. I can't say that I have."

"Then perhaps this will be a first for you, Sergeant."

Perlman chuckled. "Been a long time since I seen me a first."

"Miss Wolff, if we find the identity of your father's murderer, I can assure you there will be an arrest."

"Major, your assurances are of little comfort to me. I came here for the consideration of what I thought were civilized people, and all I've gotten so far is a man who is looked upon as being at the end of his career by his own army and," she glanced at Perlman, "a broken-down former policeman."

"You do have a sharp tongue, missy," Perlman said. He raked his finger under his nose, pushing his whiskers back. He grinned at her. "Let's hope you have a mind half as sharp."

April set down the bag she was loading. She wrung her hands. "I'm sorry I was short with you. My attitude was not Christian. You're just doing your job, I suppose. This day has been a trying one for me, and I've lost what little patience I have."

Perlman nodded. "That's all right, ma'am. The major here told me about your father, and I'm real sorry to hear about it."

"The sergeant is right," Chevalier said. "Times are hard enough without something like this happening. We'll do all we can."

"Thank you, Major. I know this assignment won't make you the most popular man in the army."

Chevalier smiled. "I've given up on that. I'd just like to be the most effective." With that, Chevalier walked off and started to help with the loading of the wagon.

April looked at Perlman. "I'm afraid I just don't understand. Your Colonel Sinclair seems to think he's competent."

"Being from the North, I don't think you could possibly understand, Miss Wolff. The major is from South Carolina. Worse than that, he's a Charlestonian and a graduate of the Citadel. This is an army run by Virginians and West Pointers. He could walk on water and sing the 'Hallelujah' chorus at the same time, and everyone in the upper echelon of command would just try to find him singing off-key. Being popular is the least of the major's worries."

"I see. It's a matter of class."

"More like envy, I'd say. The major is a blue blood if ever there was one. Blue bloods and other blue bloods just tend to get into spitting contests."

"Sounds awful."

"Might be a good thing for you. If Chevalier there can pin your father's murder on one of them 'gentlemen' from Virginia, it would be a feather in his cap. He would have gone and spit a lot farther than the rest of them boys. So don't you go to doubting the man.

He might not be doing this for you, but he's gonna give you the best that's in him."

Chevalier came back with two sacks of pots the women had brought to cook on. He loaded them in the wagon. "You two getting to know one another?"

April looked at him, her eyes piercing his. The man was handsome. She doubted if that made him very popular with the other officers either. "I think we are," she said.

"Good. I'm glad to see it."

On the other side of the wagon, Tillie poured water on what remained of the fire. She hobbled around to the back where the three of them were standing. "Don't you gentlemens let dis here gal get you all riled up." She laughed. It was a cackle that sounded like a handful of rocks tumbling down a tin roof. She swung the empty coffeepot into the back of the wagon. "She ain't much used to folks tellin' her no, is all. Never has been, no ways."

"I can believe that," Chevalier said.

"This is Tillie. She helps out at the farm. She was there when my father was killed." April watched the two men carefully, wondering how they might treat a black woman.

"Pleased to meet you, ma'am," Chevalier said. He grinned. It was a large smile that showed off his sparkling white teeth. "Maybe you can help us."

He caught April's eye. "It's plain to see you've raised yourself a spirited young woman here. She can't take no for an answer."

Tillie nodded and let out another cackle. "I have at dat. Lord knows I been workin' at dat fer more than a few years. She don't set much store by menfolks though and gets plumb excited when dere's one abouts dat she sets her fancy to."

April saw Chevalier's quick glance and sparkle in his eyes. She was quick to change the subject. "I just don't see the point of going back to the farm tonight. My father's dead. What more do you need to see?"

Perlman walked over to his mule and swung himself into the saddle. "For one, I'd like to know what killed him."

"He was stabbed."

"By a knife or a sword?"

"What difference does that make?"

"It makes a great deal of difference, young lady. If your father was stabbed with a sword and one of our men was responsible, I'd say the murderer was a cavalry man or an officer. If he was stabbed with a bayonet, then an enlisted man in the infantry is to blame." He chuckled. "If by a letter opener, then it was a clerk."

"Well, I wouldn't know."

Chevalier smiled at her. "It would seem that we have found something that you don't know. Maybe we are making progress after all."

He turned, but April put her hand on his shoulder and tugged him back into facing her. "Listen to me, Major. I don't know police procedure, but I'm a fast learner. No doubt that will be quite different for you. You may have had a lot of experience with women, but you haven't with me. I'm not your type. I have a brain."

"I'd say you have. And you conceal it well too, with one of the prettiest packages I've seen in a long time."

The gleam in his eyes sent a flush into April's face.

With that he stepped into his stirrup and swung his leg over the big gray. "I suggest we get going. We've wasted enough time here pretending to be—how did you put it, Miss Wolff?—civilized."

April helped Tillie into the wagon and then took her seat. April slapped the traces to the backs of the mules with a snap and the wagon bolted toward the road, its wheels grinding into the soft ground. They drove the wagon for some time behind the two men and watched them as they worked at clearing men off the road. It was not an easy task. Many men were lying on the soft ground in the darkness, and April could hear the murmurs and complaints as they crawled and hobbled to one side.

"Why you want to give dem men such a bucket of burs, gal? Dey is jes tryin' to help."

"I don't like the way they are helping."

Tillie smiled. "What dat man look like, girl?"

"He has a gray beard and walks like a duck."

"You knows de one I mean, de young one."

April was silent. Tillie never missed a thing, and April knew it. The louder her protest, the more Tillie would hear her mind. "I never paid much attention."

"Don't lie to me, gal."

"He's all right, I suppose, for an enemy, a man I hate."

"Hate. Now dat's a mighty strong word fer a man you don't even know."

"I know enough about him. I can see the uniform he's wearing."

"You and yer people don't care much fer anybody's uniform to hear you tell it. Why is you so all fired steamed up 'bout his?"

"The man's a slaver, Tillie. That's enough for me."

The stars were bright overhead when the wagon topped the hill leading down to their farm. April could see the lights were still lit in the parlor. John and Tommy Slocum's horses were gone, and that gave her some measure of relief. At least there wouldn't be a confrontation.

The two men walked their animals to the hitching rail in front of the house. She drove the wagon around the house to where the barn door stood open and climbed down. She stood there looking at the door.

"Is you gonna help me?" Tillie asked.

April caught herself. "I'm sorry." She went around to the other side of the wagon and helped the woman to the ground.

"Somethin' botherin' you, gal?"

April continued to stare at the door. "The barn."

"What about it?"

"I was sure I closed the door before I left, and there's a lantern burning inside."

Tillie scooted her dress into place. "Maybe somebody had call to go in dere."

April looked at Tillie and, even though the woman couldn't see her, she seemed to know what April was thinking.

Tillie shook her head. "No, I reckon not. From de way Christine was all somber like, I'd be surprised if she's moved from outta dat spot she was in. Poor baby's probably fell asleep on de floor."

They heard the sound of the two men walking around the house, the dirt and rocks crunching under their feet. The place was silent now, and anyone moving could be heard without too much trouble. "You need us to unhitch that team?" Chevalier asked.

"No, I can take care of that later while you're looking over father." She pointed at the barn. "It's just that the barn door was closed when I left here, and now it's open. And there's a lantern lit."

Chevalier lifted the cover of his holster and drew out his revolver. He signaled for Perlman to circle around the barn. "We'll see to it. You ladies just stay right here."

April watched as the men moved quickly to their assigned spots. Chevalier waited until Perlman had gotten to the other side, then he stepped through the door.

"You don't think whoever did this came back?" April asked.

"Ain't no tellin'. Is you worried 'bout dem men?"

The thought sent a sudden shock through April. She *was* worried. "No, why should I be?"

Tillie smiled. "No reason. I's jes askin', is all."

A few minutes later Chevalier reappeared in the door. "Everything seems to be all right in here." He holstered his gun. "You can take a look and make sure nothing is missing."

April headed for the barn door, followed by Tillie. When she stepped inside, she made her way over to the stalls. The horse was still there, along with several sheep. She checked over the tack and the few tools her father hung in the barn. "Everything seems to be here."

Then her eyes fell on the area where she had placed her father's sawhorses, the place where her father had been murdered. She walked over and stooped down to the ground. The area had been carefully raked. All of her father's writing had been rubbed out.

"Is everything all right?" Chevalier asked.

April got to her feet. "No, it isn't." She pointed to the ground. "This is where my father was murdered. He left a note scratched on the ground, and now it's gone. Someone has been here, someone who knew what he was looking for."

It was then that Perlman came through the back door. He was dragging a young black woman by the arm. The woman wore a tattered calico dress and was barefoot. "Look at what I found me back there. There was another one, but she run off into the house."

CHAPTER 7

Two bucks a jigger! Two bucks a jigger!" The barefoot man in overalls walked through the camp with four canteens hung over his shoulders. Tin thimbles were tied to the wooden spouts. With each step the man took, the thimbles danced on the ends of the strings that held them in place. The sound was almost musical.

The man had a long, hawklike nose with a full browned-from-the-sun face, and small dark eyes, like blackberries floating in a bowl of oatmeal. His shirt was the color of burned squash, and half of it hung out over the opening in his overalls, giving him the appearance of a man who had been in a hurry when he got dressed. If the truth were known, he really didn't care how he looked or who he saw. At first glance you might have even called him a businessman but, in point of fact, he had revenge on his mind.

Rifles were stacked like the poles of tepees. The fires glowing behind them caused their stark, skeletal shadows to fall across the path that cut through the camp. The dried wood snapping in the flames made a popping sound. A gauzy veil of smoke rose over the camp. The man stiffened a little when he saw stacks of fence rail beside the fires. No doubt there wasn't a fence left standing in this part of the state. The rails made convenient firewood that didn't have to be cut. The men in gray simply pulled them down and carried them over their shoulders to where they were going to make camp.

He walked past men on the ground, their bare feet stretched out, broken and callused. Some of the soldiers sat cross-legged, inspecting the damage of the day's march as they held their feet closer to their faces. A few had shoes, broken brogans with toes or heels missing. If it could be said that an army traveled on its feet and its stomach, then the Army of Northern Virginia didn't have far to go.

"Got some good Pennsylvania corn here, boys. Only thing is, this here's in liquid form. It'll be good fer what ails you. Make your step lighter and put a smile on your lips."

A number of the reclining troops struggled to their feet and formed a circle around the man who had become a traveling distillery. No matter how poor they were, they dug into their pockets and haversacks to come up with what it took for a thimbleful of the promised pain reliever. They fumbled for coins, paper money, or any form of payment that could be found. One soldier took out a watch on a chain and swung it in the face of the salesman, asking for and receiving three thimblesful.

A poker game was taking place on a nearby blanket, and the men dropped their cards and rolled to their knees. They were soon taking places in the mob around the man, gladly moving on from one form of disapproved vice to another. General Lee had spoken about the evils of gambling and drinking. He had even gone so far as to doubt the blessings of God if men in the army gave themselves over to the debasing habits of cards and liquor.

"Here now. What goes on here? You men break this up."

The sudden booming voice behind the group caused several heads to turn, followed by moans and murmurs. The young captain continued to shout at the men as he stepped out of his tent. His arms were flapping like a rooster at the break of day. He strode forward and began to peel the grays at the back of the crowd away from one another. "Get back to your gear, men. We're pulling out of here right away. We've got ourselves a night march. There's no time for this."

The man with the canteens grinned as the captain came into view between the separating men. "Everybody deserves something to smile about, Captain. Let the men live a little before they die."

The captain quickly grabbed several of the men and turned them around to sheepishly face the man with the canteens. "You men see what you got here? A Yankee who's trying to take your last dollar. He doesn't care if you live or die. The man would just as soon spit on your grave if he thought there was a dollar in it." He glared at the man. "What is your name?"

"Lee Twombly. I farm near here, and I figured to just show a little profit with the bounty of my land. Your men took a lot of my corn today. What's wrong with selling them a little of the squeezings?"

The captain waved him off. "You haul your lousy carcass out of my camp Twombly, and don't ever let me see you here again. I want you away from these men of mine. These men have enough trouble with lice without the human kind."

Twombly shrugged his shoulders. "All right. I'll move on. There's a cavalry group up ahead." He smiled. "They got more money than your boys anyway, and they're eating better too, from what I hear."

He ambled through the path of soldiers who were packing their haversacks and picking up their rifles. Some looked back at him with empty, hollow eyes; others with passion, with a deep-down pride that went beyond clean uniforms and shoes. Many were little more than scarecrows, their ribs bouncing around in what still passed for shirts. Twombly shook his head as he walked past them. These were the men who had fought the Union army to a standstill for two years.

They were marching through the North as the victorious army that could seemingly do no wrong. Even though he couldn't see much meat on their bones, it was plain to see the fire in their eyes.

He stepped out onto the road and continued down to where he had seen the Confederate horsemen camped. The soft ground squashed between his toes, and he could smell the strong aroma of wood smoke everywhere. He kicked at the ground, maligning his luck with an overzealous and obviously righteous officer. It was something he was going to stay away from in the future if he could help it.

The stars hung in the sky like lanterns sent to lead the way to what he hoped would be the destruction of this army. Ahead he could see the soft glow of campfires that painted the blackness with a pale pink light. That would be the cavalry. Their fires were burning brightly, and even from where he was, he could hear the sound of singing, which picked up his spirits. Men who were having a good time were men who might just be tempted to have a better time.

As he rounded the bend in the road, he saw the rebel battle flag standing in front of a very large tent. The tent was smoky in appearance with streaks of brown and black covering what otherwise would have been a tan canvas. The sight of officers coming and going from the tent gave him caution. Whisky drummers were very appreciated by the men, but as he had already seen, not well thought of by the officers.

He picked up his pace and made it into a stand of trees. He would lay low for a while and wait to circle the group of officers.

The ground was soft, and the leaves on the sycamores made a slight rustle as the evening breeze blew though them. He could smell the grass and the scent of fresh hay that was being used to feed the horses. He took a slight step and felt a twig under his foot. He backed off, ever so slightly. He was grateful he had no boots on. One misstep would make a noise, something he couldn't afford to do.

He watched as two men appeared at the door of the tent. A lantern hanging inside set aglow their shadows against the tent. One man was tall and straight. His hands were clasped behind his back, and he appeared to be listening to the second man at his side. The other man was shorter. He hung his head as he spoke, and Twombly could barely make out the sound of his voice. They walked over in his direction. He began to hear the words more clearly.

"Your horse looked a little lathered up from your ride tonight, General. You must have gone a long ways."

"I did."

"You find the Yankee cavalry, General? We do need to locate them if possible. I know General Lee is quite anxious about Stuart's whereabouts. Most of the men on his staff that I've spoken to say he's been quite exercised about our plumed knight."

The general was wiry and balding, with a beard that flowed from his face to a point near his belly. He appeared to be young.

"I had to try to see a friend."

The man stepped off to a point near the trees where Twombly was doing his best to hide. The general seemed to be staring into the darkness, lost in thought. The other man followed, keeping to the general's side. Twombly wanted to move away from where the two men were talking. To be discovered might mean to be thought of as a spy. The thought terrified him and excited him at the same time. He might very well pick up some casual word spoken that he could turn over to the Federal troops. The idea froze him in place despite his uncomfortable crouching position.

"The woman you spoke of?"

"Yes." The general began to stare at the ground.

The other man shook his head. "Nothing good ever comes from trying to find a lost love, General. Many a man has done just that. More often than not he finds that she's changed. Even if she hasn't, he's changed. A man does best to just ride on and let the yesterdays stay a pleasant memory."

"She hasn't changed." He lifted his head and stared at the man. "I saw her. I touched her cheek." He turned and walked a few paces. "But she's married now."

The general turned to look at the man without responding. It was a cold look, one that would stop most men from following up such a line of questioning. In this case it didn't help.

"Women of a man's past are like ghosts in the night. You hear them, you even see them on occasion. You always see signs of their passing: a hint of perfume, a note of music, a favorite flower. I suppose there are things a man can never shake about a woman; most of them, though, are about the way she made him feel about himself. It's a feeling a man can't escape, I suppose." He shook his head. "It's like carrying around a lock inside when the key is missing. You know it's out there someplace, and you know it fits. Until you find it, the lock stays shut."

The general nodded slowly. "I think that about sums it up, Colonel. I've carried feelings about this woman for five years now, and her being married to someone else hasn't changed them one little bit."

"But that door is closed, General."

"I never have liked closed doors, Colonel. A door hasn't been made that wouldn't open. You just have to want what's inside bad enough. That's all. When a man spends his life turning away from the closed doors in life, he soon forgets how to open them. I love her and somehow, someway, I know that she loves me."

"Well, General, there are closed doors and then there are impossibilities. A man would be well advised to discover the difference between the two."

"Colonel, this army has been fighting an impossible war for years now. We don't have the men to fight it, and the Yankees seem to have an endless supply. Already we have two hundred thousand Yankees stiff in Southern dust, and still they keep turning them out to fight. We have no supplies to speak of, although plenty are growing in the ground. We just can't ever seem to figure out how to get the food to the troops."

He looked up to the far dark horizon. "Our enemy has an endless supply of trains filled to overflowing with pork that rots because he cannot eat it all, butter, flour, vegetables that are fresh, and every kind of pleasant victual that an army could ever want. We crawl along on bad flour and rancid bacon. So don't speak to me about the impossible. If I believed anything was impossible, I'd be in Virginia right now with my hand to a plow, not here listening to my men's stomachs rumble."

"I suppose you're right, General. We are being asked to do the impossible."

"And we all believe it can be done. If we didn't, we wouldn't be here."

"I just think, General, that there's nothing to be served at this point by your taking off after a lost love. We need you too much right here, all of you, including your mind. The more you torture yourself about this matter, the less energy you'll have to think about what's best for the men. General Lee may be lamenting the absence of Stuart, but he still has cavalry here with him. We are it, General. We are exactly what Lee keeps pining away for. He may not have Jeb Stuart, but he has Albert Jenkins."

Jenkins smiled. "I guess somebody needs to tell him that."

"You can tell him, General. You can tell him by some stroke of boldness. You can tell him by bringing him what he wants most to hear—the whereabouts of the Union army."

The general nodded. "I suppose you're right, Colonel Updike. I have been behaving badly here. I've been lost in my own world. It's so very hard being close to her and yet far away. One minute I think I can reach out and touch her, and the next moment she disappears into the night."

"I understand, General. Believe me, I do."

"Good. Then let's just keep this other matter to ourselves. I wouldn't want anybody to think I was acting like a schoolboy smitten on the playground."

"Then no more long rides at night by yourself?"

The general dropped his gaze to the soft grass. "No, Colonel. No more long rides at night." He looked up at the man. "But I do have a funeral to go to tomorrow."

CHAPTER 8

hevalier motioned for the group to go into the house, and they made their way around the building and up the steps that led to the large, oversized porch. The farm looked prosperous. Wicker furniture and a rocker dotted the porch. A swing was suspended from the overhanging roof by a chain. Most people didn't have such nice furniture inside their houses, to say nothing of leaving it exposed to the elements on the outside. They walked up the steps and through the main door, Perlman still holding the black girl by the arm. Behind him, the orange tabby climbed the stairs.

"You can let her go," April said. "She isn't going anywhere."

"You're darn right, she isn't," Perlman shot back. "Not until we find out just what's going on here."

They stood in the hallway and could see the body of Jonas Wolff still laid out on a table in the parlor. It almost surprised April not to see Christine still sitting there by the window. Evidently one of their guests had helped her upstairs and put her and the baby to bed. Candles flickered at the four corners of the table, giving the room a shadowy, reverent feel.

Chevalier motioned across the hall toward the living room. "We'd better go in there. It might be more conducive to talking."

The five of them took their places around the living room on the red sofas and chairs. Yellow tassels hung from the edges of the furniture, and ornate smoked-glass lamps were burning, sending thin wisps of quivering smoke into the air. Crystal drops of beveled glass hung from lamps, and the light on the floor was mixed with a collection of the rainbows they produced. Small slices of brilliant colored light danced over the polished wood.

The shimmering colors on the waxed and shiny maple floor had always been a favorite of her father. He said it made him look forward to the end of the day and the darkness so the lamps could be lit.

Just sitting in the chair and watching them made April smile. She was determined to go through life remembering the good things about life with her father, not just thinking about the day he died.

"Do you know this young woman?" Chevalier asked, motioning to the black girl.

"Yes. Mandy is a servant—and a friend."

"For someone so opposed to slavery, you seem to have more than your share of servants."

"We do our best to give gainful employment."

"Then why did she take off running when she saw me?" Perlman asked.

"I couldn't say. You'll have to ask her." April caught herself. She didn't like being questioned, and the last thing she wanted was for Chevalier and Perlman to be the ones asking Mandy questions. "Because you are in the uniform of the Confederacy, perhaps she just assumed you were here to steal from us—again."

Perlman listened to her, but it was plain to see that he wasn't totally convinced. He wiggled his index finger on the side of his mouth, nervously scratching his beard. His blue eyes were almost cold, looking right through her. Without responding, he got to his feet and left the room. The big cat, like a lap dog used to being with the man, followed him.

"Who is in the house here with you?" Chevalier asked.

"Just my father's wife, Christine, and their baby, along with Tillie."

"Baby?"

April could see the look of surprise register on Chevalier's face. "Christine is my father's second wife. My mother died several years ago."

"We will have to talk with her."

April glanced nervously at the stairs. "You may not get many answers. When I saw her earlier today, she wasn't saying much of anything to anybody. I think the shock of my father's death was too much for her."

"Perhaps she saw more than you think she did."

April shook her head. "She was frozen with grief."

"So it's just you, Tillie, and your father's wife and child."

"Yes."

Chevalier glanced at Mandy, who was anxiously sitting on the edge of a chair. "And, of course, Mandy here."

April shot the nervous girl a glance. "Yes, Mandy."

Chevalier got to his feet. "Then why don't we start by taking a look at Mandy's room?"

"I don't think that's necessary. Why would we do that?"

"You do have a room for Mandy, don't you? She doesn't sleep in front of the fire?"

"She get by," Tillie said. "She make do jes fine." Tillie grasped the arms of her chair and, wobbling, got to her feet. "I'm gonna make you boys some supper." She started across the room, then paused and looked back in Chevalier's direction. "You don't mind some ham and eggs, does you?"

Chevalier cleared his throat. "We don't want to put you ladies to any trouble."

Tillie waved her hand at him. "Ain't gonna be no trouble, no trouble at all." She broke her grin wider, showing off her bottom teeth. "Course we ain't got no grits jes yet. I knows you boys takes grits wif yer eggs."

"Whatever you have will be fine with us."

"Fine, fine. I likes dat in a man. Ain't too particular and is appreciative of whatever womenfolk does." She shook her finger at him. "Dat's gonna serve you well, boy. You jes hangs on to dat. I gots to go out to dat henhouse. Maybe dem soldier boys left us wif some eggs to eat. Lawsy, I sure hopes so." With that she shuffled her way across the floor and out into the dining room and the kitchen beyond.

April had to smile. The woman couldn't see her hand in front of her face, but no one would know it to look at her. The years spent in the Wolff house had taught her the place by feel and now by sheer memory. She knew every step. Even the way she had looked at the major showed that she was making eye contact.

Perlman stepped back into the room, the big cat at his feet. He glared at April first, then at Mandy. "I didn't find her."

"Who?" April asked.

"The woman who ran away when I was in the back of the barn. I know she came into the house, but she's not downstairs."

He looked back into the hallway at the stairs that led to the upper level of the house. "Maybe we should go upstairs and look through the rooms."

April got to her feet. "You can't do that. Christine is sleeping up there, and so is the baby. She's not up there."

Chevalier took a step in her direction, his dark eyes fastened onto her. "Then perhaps you can explain her and show us just where she is."

April put her hands on her hips and looked back at Mandy. "I told you not to leave the house, didn't I?"

Mandy nervously nodded and kept nodding, her head bobbing up and down. "Yes'm, you sure nuff did. I's sorry. I's plenty sorry. But you weren't here, and Tillie was gone too." She wrung her hands in her lap. "We had to get out. We jes didn't know what to do. We can't stay penned up whilst dem soldier mans is around."

April looked back at Chevalier. "You might as well know this. You seem to be determined to find it out anyway. We keep runaway slaves and send them north when it's safe for them to travel. You want to know who these people are"—she paused—"Well, that's who they are."

Chevalier looked at Perlman and then back at Mandy. "Where are you from, miss?"

"I's from Gaw'gia. Come up here all the way from Albany, I did."

"And did you see the man who killed Miss Wolff's father?"

Mandy shook her head. "Nah, sir, I surely did not."

"You aren't going to take these people and send them back, are you?" April asked.

"Miss Wolff, I do think you are misguided. You are encouraging people to leave the only home they have ever known and move off to someplace cold, someplace where someone will pay them starvation wages and think themselves holy for doing that. You may think us cruel for having black slaves, but we house them, feed them, put shoes on their feet, and most slave owners treat them like their own children. You have slaves in the North too. You keep them in squalor and pay them meager wages they have to use in company stores and for company houses. Then publicly you shun them." He leaned toward her slightly as if to make his point. "You call them the Irish."

"I am afraid, Major, that you simply do not understand the passion people have for freedom. You've had these people as chattel for so long that in your mind they cease to be human beings with the longing to set the course for their own lives."

"That is where you're wrong, Miss Wolff. That happens to be the thing we're fighting for. This nation of ours was founded on the idea of self-determination, and now when the shoe's on the other foot, you and your kind don't think that a portion of the states have the right to determine their own destiny. You enslave us with a tyranny of the majority that is far worse than the chains you think we keep these people in. To make matters worse, you think that a nation that has to be kept by the point of a bayonet is worth keeping."

April stepped over to where Mandy was shivering. She put her hand on the girl's shoulder and looked back at Chevalier. "You can't send this child back to where she came from. That would be cruel."

"I have no intention of doing any such thing. I think you forget. We have a war to fight and a murder to solve. I'm no slave chaser. The sooner you put politics out of your mind, the sooner we can find your father's killer. These people, as you call them, just may know something that we should hear. If you try to keep them from us, you try to cover up what you and your father were doing, and you aren't helping us one bit. We might as well go back to camp, and you can let me write the report to General Ewell explaining why we couldn't help you. Do you want that? Because if you do, that's just what I'll do."

"I just thought—"

"Thought what? That since I'm a Southerner I'm not interested in the truth or in justice? That I wouldn't care if one of our officers is guilty of murder? That all I am interested in is your politics and the meager endeavor you have in flaunting the law if it serves your purposes? Or is it that you just don't trust me? If that's so, let me tell you, Miss Wolff, I am the only man you can trust, the only one you have left."

"Are you finished?"

Chevalier clasped his hands behind his back.

April looked over at Perlman. "Does he always go on like this?"

"Not usually, ma'am. Only when he gets a head of steam up."

She looked at Chevalier. "Or I suppose when he's lecturing some poor woman. Major, you must have had a great deal of experience with flighty women who blush at you and wag their fans to cover their smiles. Either that or you're practicing your stump speech for Congress. In any event, you're wasting your words with me. I'm sorry I didn't tell you sooner. Frankly, I didn't think what we did was any of your business."

"Miss Wolff, when you came rolling into camp complaining about a murder, it became my business. Now are you going to trust me or not?"

"Call me April, Major. I find it hard to trust any man who cannot use my first name." She extended her hand for him to shake it.

He smiled and took her hand. "I suppose the absence of decorum won't be an issue for the two of us then, April. You can call me Will." He glanced at Perlman. "But, Sergeant, to you I'm still Major Chevalier."

The older man bowed slightly and smiled. "I wouldn't have it any other way, Major."

"Now why don't we see just where Miss Mandy's bedroom is?"

April led the way into the hall and down to a point about halfway to the back door. A large wall was to their left, which made up the support for the stairway. A blazing candle sat in the middle of a side table that was positioned under a picture of sheep in a pasture. April pushed on the wall, and a small section gave way and fell off into the darkness under the stairs. April picked up the candle and pushed it into the opening, leaning through the hole. "It's all right. You can come out now. Everything is safe."

CHAPTER 9

I t took over a half-hour to interrogate the slaves who had been living in the wall. One by one they related their stories, which all boiled down to one thing: They had seen nothing. Will wondered if the color of the uniforms he and Perlman wore had anything to do with the sudden onset of forgetfulness.

He and April took their places at the table where Tillie had set out three plates. The table was large, stretching out across the country-style kitchen. It was oak with ornate claws carved into the legs. Tillie had spread a red-and-white-checkered cloth over it. In some ways it reminded Will of home, although his own home looked out on the bay at Charleston.

Tillie carried a pan from the stove. It was popping with grease, and she set it down on a pad on the table. "I gots yer eggs and some for the sergeant man too, when he comes."

Will looked up at her. "That's nice of you, Tillie, but you didn't have to fix us anything." He looked down at the silver. Tillie had evidently set out their best. Floral patterns were carved into the handles, and each piece shone with a luster that spoke of polish and careful buffing. It was the kind of silver that people hid in times like these.

Tillie reached out and touched the edge of Will's plate with her left hand. "Lawsy sakes. When I gonna get to fix anything fer men round here? Woman's got to be 'preciated some ways, ya know. Menfolk do dat best, I found." Her right hand had an egg suspended on a spatula. She laid it gently on the plate. "You be wanting two, I reckon."

"Yes, ma'am, if you've got them." Will watched Tillie's eyes.

Tillie grinned in April's direction. "Ain't he so polite-like to a poor old black woman? I jes bet he's got his self some mighty fine words locked away in dat head of his."

She reached back and scooped another egg out of the pan then brought it forward. Her hand was still on the edge of Will's plate, and she laid the egg down. Repeating the same procedure, she ladled out a slab of sugar-cured ham. The shell of the brown sugar was like a rind around the pink meat.

Will cut into the ham. "Maybe I should ask you a few questions, Tillie."

"Shore." She waddled back over to the stove with the pan in her hands. "Hope your sergeant man gets here shortly. Don't want these eggs of his to get too greasy or form a crust 'round them, ya know."

"I'm sure anything will be fine. We aren't too particular when it comes to our food these days, and to be honest with you, this is the best either of us have had in over a year."

"I's glad fer dat. Lady wants to be remembered, ya know."

"Now, when was it that Mr. Wolff was killed? That could be important."

Tillie turned around and tugged on her chin. "Musta been near to midmornin'. I knows dat, cause I was on the front porch rockin' and smokin' my pipe. Dat sun was on my face, but tweren't too hot jes yet. Dat's how come I reckon it was midmornin'.'"

"You couldn't narrow that down more?"

She scratched her head with her index finger. "Don't believe so. Ya see, I ain't got me no watch."

"I understand. Did you see the man ride in who did this?"

She shook her head. "Nah, sir, I sure nuff didn't. I heared him though. Heard the rattle of a sword and heard some things in the man's pocket. I'd recognize him jes by listening I'd be willin' to bet. Dat horse of his favored one foot."

"You have a keen ear, Tillie." He continued to study her.

"Dat I does, Mr. Will. Dat I does." She picked up the coffeepot and made her way to the table. "Hand me up yer cup."

Will reached for his cup. It was ornate and dainty fine china, pure white with a gold rim around the top. It matched the rest of the dishes and could have set any table in Charleston. He held it up, and Tillie found his hand. She poured the coffee to a spot that was half-full. "Men folks like dere coffee hot. I don't give 'em a full cup. Bottom gets cold too soon."

"I appreciate that." Will held the cup to his lips and looked at her while he sipped it.

"Tweren't too much after dat when Mr. Slocum come ridin' in. He went to the barn, and dat's when he come back and told me Mr. Wolff was dead."

"Who is Slocum?"

"He's a neighbor," April said. "He goes to our church."

"He rode right to the barn?"

"Yes, sir, he did."

"That unusual? Didn't he stop and ask where April's father was?"

"Nope. Guess he figured Mr. Wolff to be in the barn, and he was. He surely was."

"What happened after that?"

"His son, Tommy, come on the place. Him and Mr. Slocum carried Mr. Wolff's body into da house and laid him out. I cleaned him up, mind you, but dey done carried him in."

Will put his fork to the eggs and began to eat. "Good, Tillie. The eggs are mighty good. I haven't had a fresh egg in over a month."

"Perhaps your men can give you more then," April said. "They took most of the chickens."

Just then Perlman came into the room. He took his seat.

Will put a forkful of egg into his mouth. "You are going to love this, Sergeant; fresh eggs, ham, and coffee—real coffee, not that chicory."

Tillie took the pan off the stove and repeated the process of serving the ham and eggs to Perlman. She then poured him a half-cup of coffee. She held up the pot. "You be needing some more, Mr. Will?"

"I surely do."

April quickly took Will's cup out of his hand and held it up for Tillie to pour. She then gave it back to Will.

Will lifted the cup to his lips. His eyes were fixed on April. "You said there was something your father wrote on the ground? Something that had been rubbed out?"

"Yes," April said. She stood and picked up a piece of paper and a pencil from the counter. Leaning over the table, she drew on it and slid the paper across to where Will sat.

He looked it over. "The letters S and n with an X on the bottom?"

"That's right."

"Do you know anyone with those initials?"

Will passed the paper over to Perlman.

The sergeant chewed his ham vigorously and then looked at the paper.

"What do you make of that, Sergeant?"

The more he studied what April had written down, the harder Perlman chewed. He turned the paper upside down and chewed harder. Tearing off a strip of the meat, he lowered it to the floor for the big cat. He pushed the paper back in Will's direction. "Try this."

Will looked it over. "I see what you mean." He passed it over to April.

"I don't understand."

"Well, you don't exactly know how your father fell do you?"

"No, I don't."

"You didn't see the body?"

"No, I didn't."

"Well, just maybe this is the way it was supposed to read."

"**US** with an **X**?"

"Yes."

"That would mean . . ."

"That would mean you are looking at the wrong army. Perhaps your murderer is a federal trooper."

"It was your army that was marching past our farm all day."

"Stragglers and deserters have been known to do bad things, April."

"But Mr. Slocum said the man who rode in was a Confederate general."

"And where might we find this Slocum? If he saw the man, then we ought to question him."

"He will be here for father's funeral in the morning."

"Will Mrs. Wolff be up and around for that? I think we would like to question her."

April shook her head. "I can only hope so. She wasn't saying a word this afternoon. She was in a state of shock."

"Let's hope a good night's sleep will help her."

"There's something else you ought to know," Perlman added.

"What is that?" April asked.

"I examined your father's wound. It wasn't made by a sword, a bayonet, or even a letter opener, for that matter."

Perlman sipped his coffee.

"Well, go ahead, Sergeant," Will said. "Don't keep us in suspense."

Perlman put down his cup. "First of all, there were three wounds, not just one."

"I could'a told you dat," Tillie said. "I washed him."

Perlman hunched over the table, sliding his elbows forward. "Two of them almost side by side, and another grazing wound at his side. It was like whoever did it took aim to make sure they were equidistant. I've never seen anything like them. They look like bayonet wounds but are much cleaner. I've seen more bayonet wounds than I care to remember, and these wounds weren't like any I've ever encountered."

"Why would you say that?" April asked.

"The wound was deep, right to the liver, but it was narrow. Clean, not like a bayonet. It took him awhile to die. I suppose that's why he had the time to write you his note. He might even have crawled a little ways."

April took out a handkerchief and dabbed her eyes. Her eyes welled up with tears, and she did her best to keep them from flowing.

"Sergeant, you have less subtlety than that mule you ride. I'm going to stop taking you into polite society if you have to bring up delicate matters in front of ladies." Will looked down at his plate. "And over a good meal too."

Will picked up his cup and glanced at April as he sipped. "We just need to get a better description of the man who rode in here yesterday. Perlman and I need to talk to your witness."

April sniffed slightly and wiped her eyes. "Mr. Slocum said the man who rode onto our farm was a Confederate general," April repeated herself. It was almost as if by finding the man responsible, she might be able to bring back at least a piece of her father. She went on. "He said he saw him ride in and ride out."

"Then I suppose that's a matter we need to take up with your neighbor." He shot a look at Tillie, a sly smile crossing his face. "Of course, we do have another witness here."

"Yes, we do," April added.

Both Will and Perlman prepared to bed down for the night in the barn. They were pulling fresh hay out of the loft and clearing a spot for two beds when April came though the large open door. She was carrying two quilts and a pair of large feather pillows.

"I brought these for you two gentleman. I still think you should sleep in the house."

Perlman took the quilts and pillows. "Ma'am, I am sorry for my conversation at your table tonight. I suppose I've spent too much time with men lately."

"We'll be fine here, April," Will said, changing the subject. "I'd kind of like to be here. Whoever it was that erased that message from your father might just come back. Besides, if your stepmother wakes up and goes to wandering around the house, I wouldn't want her running in to us. The shock might be too much for her."

"You're right. I didn't think of that."

"We'll be real cozy here, ma'am," Perlman said. "Can't tell you how long it's been since we had any kind of a roof over our heads."

April turned to leave the barn, and Will spoke to Perlman. "I need to walk Miss Wolff to the house. I'll be back in a moment."

Will stepped out of the barn behind April and walked with her to the front of the house. "I know tomorrow will be hard for you, and Perlman and I being here won't make it any easier. We'll do our best to keep our distance. I don't think there's anything we can do about changing the color of our uniforms, but we won't intrude."

"Thank you. You have been most kind, and I treated you badly."

Will reached out and took her hand. "This war and its politics have taken many people who might otherwise be friends and made them enemies. I only hope that you and I can look past all that and become friends."

"I doubt that will ever happen, Major." She took her hand away from his and started up the stairs.

"One thing more, April."

April stopped and turned around.

"We do trust each other, correct?"

April nodded. "Yes, Major, of course we do."

"Then you're not going to lie to me or try to hide anything."

"Of course not. Why should I?"

April turned and hurried up the steps, leaving Will standing at the bottom of the stairs. She jerked open the door and disappeared into the dark house. Will continued to stand in place. She had disappeared, but he could tell that she was still there, watching him from behind the glass in the door. He pulled off his hat and bowed low, sweeping the hat across his body. He smiled. "Good night, my fair young maiden. Sweet dreams."

It was several hours later when Will's eyes bolted open. Outside the door he heard movement, a rustling. He threw back the quilt he had covered himself with and got to his feet. Perlman was still fast asleep, snoring. Will moved to the door and watched as it slowly opened. A figure dressed in white stepped into the barn. It was a woman with long flowing blond hair that caught the moonlight. The major reached out and grabbed her from behind. "Not so fast. Who are you?"

The woman struggled, then screamed. She arched her back and shook her arms, trying to free them from his grasp.

Perlman was now on his feet. He lit the lantern and held it up, stepping closer. The woman struggled in Chevalier's hands, bolting and kicking like a colt refusing to be broken. "You want to tell us just who you are?" he said.

"I am Christine Wolff. This is my farm. Who are you?"

CHAPTER 10

M orning came early, with the one remaining rooster crowing to his heart's content on the fence behind the barn. It was almost as if he knew he was the only one left; and while the count of hens was now quite low, they were all his. Perlman reached over to the mound of orange fur nestled next to him and gave the tabby a scratch. The big cat turned over on his back, playfully pawing at the man scratching his belly. Perlman then rolled out of the mound of hay he had lain down the night before. He stood up straight and began to stretch, listening to Chevalier mumble under his quilt. "That old bird out there is a mighty lonely feller, I reckon." He took both hands and scratched his beard vigorously.

Will kicked off his quilt and sat up. "You're probably listening to the last chicken in western Pennsylvania."

"Maybe not. We did have eggs last night, and they didn't come from that rooster." He picked up the quilt, shook it out, and then began to fold it neatly.

Perlman stepped closer to him, and they each started picking the strands of straw matting out of the other's hair and off their backsides.

"Mighty strange thing with that Wolff woman last night," Perlman said. "Christine."

Will nodded and took his tunic from the peg he had hung it on.

"Did you believe her?" asked Perlman.

Will stuck his arms in the jacket and straightened it. "Just wanting to visit the spot her husband was killed? It does sound like something one of these women would do."

Perlman blew a breath through his mustache, rippling the long gray hair. "If you ask me, she was looking for something, something she might have dropped."

"You do have a ripe imagination, Sergeant."

"Maybe so, but it's what I'm trained to do. You have a good talk with the other woman when you walked her back to the house?"

"You might say I did."

"You talk with her about the black woman?"

"About what?"

"You know what. You must know."

Will chuckled slightly. "No. I just couldn't bring myself to let on that I knew." He buttoned his tunic. "When did you know?"

"Almost from the first. I didn't say anything about it because I wanted to see how long it would take you to figure it out." He laughed. "You were so busy training your eyes on Miss Wolff, I figured it might take you some time to notice."

"You have a point there. The old woman is smart though, and she's good. She served my ham and eggs and never missed a beat. Of course, she had to touch my plate to know where it was, and my cup too. She can look right at you like she can see through you. It's almost spooky. But up close you can tell she's looking at you and not at your eyes."

"What are we going to do about her? She's our 'eyewitness'."

"The woman has a keen sense of hearing. She just might tell us something. If we keep her at a distance, we need not let anyone know our eyewitness is blind. Nobody needs to know."

Perlman laughed. "You going to bluff a confession out of one of our general officers?"

"Why not?"

"We're going up against a full house with a pair of deuces, you know."

"It's been done before."

"And if they catch you doing it now, they're going to think you a bigger fool than they already do."

"Sergeant, I don't have much farther to fall in this army. I'm a line closer, remember?"

"Are you going to tell the Wolff woman we know about Tillie?"

Will raked his hands through his hair. "I don't think so, not just yet. It's almost comical to see her try so hard to hide things from us and frankly, I'd like to see her reach the point where she trusts us. If I let her be the one to tell me about Tillie, then maybe I'll know just when that point arrives."

Perlman stuffed his shirt into his trousers and lifted his suspenders over his shoulders. In the far stall a cow was beginning to bellow. "I see old bossy there wants to give us some fresh milk. It won't be long before one of those women comes out here to take care of her, I shouldn't think."

He walked over to where a pail was sitting on a stool. "I might just get a jump on them. No sense leaving this cow uncomfortable."

"I'll go up to the house and see if they have some of that good coffee on. If they do, I'll bring you back a cup." Will ran his hand over his face. "I think I might need to find me a basin and mirror too."

Perlman laughed. "Yes sireee. Man like you with all them pretty women around has got to keep lookin' his best."

As Will left, Perlman squatted down on the stool beside the cow and set the bucket underneath her. He blew on his hands. "All right, bossy old girl. I done you a favor. Now you do one for me. I ain't got no cold hands, and you got to give me milk." He then looked over at the big cat. "Elmer, you hit the jackpot this morning, son. I got something here to help you wash down that mouse you took last night."

He grabbed hold of the cow's teats and began a slow squeeze, sending spurts of chalky white milk into the tin bucket. The first of the milk hit the empty bucket with a hollow sound, rolling down the side. He then turned one teat sideways and shot out a few spurts of milk in Elmer's direction, hitting the cat squarely in the face. The cat backed up, brushing his face with his paws. Then catching the taste of the milk, he moved forward as Perlman created a small puddle on the floor of the barn. Using both hands, Perlman took up a rhythm of pulling and rattling the sides of the bucket with fresh milk. It wasn't long before he heard the door to the barn open. "You got my coffee?"

"Lawsy, no."

Perlman looked under the cow and could see the feet and long dress of Tillie. She took a few steps forward.

"I jes come in here to milk dat cow is all."

He released his grip on the cow and got to his feet. "All right then. I'll let you take over. I just couldn't stand to see her needing to be milked." He looked down at the big tabby who was waiting for more. "Besides, my friend here was hungry."

He backed up and watched as Tillie put her hands on the cow's rump. She stepped around it and bumped into the stool. Then she took a seat and found the bucket underneath. He smiled but said nothing.

"I can't have you men takin' over old Tillie's chores now, can I? What would people say? Dey's liable to think I's no good at all 'round here."

"Oh, I'm sure you'd have no problem in proving them wrong on that score."

Tillie began to milk the cow. "What be your given name, Sergeant?"

"Jacob, Jacob Perlman."

"What kind of a name is dat, pray tell?"

"It's Jewish. I'm Jewish."

Tillie stopped her milking and leaned back, glancing in his direction. "Jewish. Dat's mighty strange for a Johnny Reb, ain't it?"

"I suppose it is, but I'm a Georgia cracker all the same."

Tillie laughed. "*Cracker.* I used to wonder just where dat come from. I heard tell it was from men what cracked de whips. Then I reckoned it was jes de color of y'alls skin, white as a soda cracker."

"I'm not sure I could tell you that. I just know I am one, that's all."

"And you was a policeman?"

"That I was. Now I'm just a line closer." He reached down and began to scratch the big cat's ear.

Tillie cocked her head. "What's a line closer?"

Perlman stepped closer to her. He wanted to see how well she could focus on him and what her eyes looked like. "I serve with the provost marshal's office. It's a kind of military police, but the men call us line closers because we close up the lines going into battle."

"How you do dat?"

"We march along behind the men and shoot anyone who turns to run. The other side has them too."

Tillie leaned back under the cow and began to milk. "Dat sounds like a mighty dirty job, Jacob. Probably not many men want anythin' to do with dat, I reckon."

"You got that right. Not many want anything to do with us either."

"I's sorry fer you."

"I am too sometimes." He continued to scratch the cat's ear. "I guess we're just loners. Maybe that's why I like this old cat. He goes it alone most of the time, just like me."

"Well, now you boys got yerselves some real police work to do. Dat ought to make you happy."

"Well, I ain't fighting this assignment, if that's what you mean. I've finally got the chance to do what I've been trained to do. A man spends his life chasing down lawbreakers, and you want to do what you know to do, even if you do wear a uniform. Of course, the major has plenty of reasons to do a good job here."

"What might dey be?"

"He made our colonel promise to give him a line command in the upcoming battle."

"Ain't dat gonna be dangerous?"

"I suppose it will be, but it's the reason a man goes to war in the first place. Nobody wants to go into battle afraid he's going to kill more of his own men than the enemy."

"I reckon not."

"So tell me, Tillie, you an escaped slave?"

She looked back at him and cracked a half-smile. "Why you want ta know dat fer? Is you gonna arrest me?"

"No, we've got bigger fish to fry."

"Well then, the answer's yes. I come up from Mississippi twenty year ago on the Underground Railroad. I got dis far and didn't want to go no farther. April was jes a little girl then, and I took care of her and did my chores 'round here. I miss the warm air, but I don't miss Mississippi none."

"You must have seen a lot of slaves come through here."

"A passel of dem. Dey is passin' on though. I never got to know dem much."

"Any of them ever want to stay?"

"More than a few. Dis here is a good place to be, and Mr. Wolff was a nice man."

"But April's father wouldn't let them stay?"

"Nah, he wouldn't. He said it was better dey moved on."

"Any of them ever get upset or angry because of that?"

"A few, I reckon."

"Any malcontents lately?"

Tillie stopped her milking and leaned back on the stool. "We had one a short while back." She shook her head. "Didn't think de roads was gonna be safe wif you men marching north. He thought fer sure he's gonna be catched and sent back to North Carolina."

CHAPTER 11

The captain rode hard down the road, smoke and dust trailing behind him. He took off his hat and began to wave it back and forth. "That's far enough. Break ranks and get to the side."

Like a snake that was being split in two by a knife, the men in the column parted down the middle of the road, some collapsing in a heap and others leaning on their rifles. Noncommissioned officers mixed with the troops, shouting, "Stack arms, men. We're going to rest awhile."

A number of the men looked toward the east where the sun was peeking over the hills. Its glaring light promised another hot day. Most of the men knew if they were going to get any sleep it would have to be in the next few hours. By the time the sun had crawled to the top of the late June sky, it would be too late to sleep. The heat would be oppressive, and the flies would be buzzing.

Two of the soldiers fell into the stubble of a wheat field. One kicked off the remains of what had once been shoes, and the other one simply crossed his legs and wiggled his toes. They watched the officer as he rode to the rear of the column and continued to shout his orders. The man with the shoes began to rub his toes that stuck through the wool socks on his feet. "I guess this is why we was called the 'foot cavalry.' Only thing is, we ain't got no horses."

The barefoot man pulled his hat down over his eyes to shield himself from the rising sun. "You better enjoy this here spell of sittin'. When Iverson finds out we is stopped and there ain't no bar hereabouts, he's gonna have us back on our feet until we find one."

"I ain't gonna grouse 'bout that none. I could use me a cold beer right about now."

"Yer dreamin'. You don't really think he's gonna give us none, do you? We give him ten minutes in that place ahead of us, and there ain't gonna be nothing left. Man's gonna drink it all, and all we're gonna get is the belch."

Captain James Quinn got to the rear of the column and pulled his horse up near the shade of some large trees. It took him some time to pick his way back through the men slouched along the road. A creek ran near the road, and the trees gave shade to a patch of cool water. The water ran fast in that spot, skipping over polished stones and fanning out as it widened. It ran south of them along the road and then meandered back to the east. The grass was high and green with dots of yellow and purple flowers waving on top. They were winks of color in a sea of lush green.

He could see several men near the water, among them General Alfred Iverson. A cook in an apron had coffee boiling over a fire. He had made biscuits, which were situated around the fire on plates of iron.

Quinn got down from his horse and landed on the ground with a thud. He walked his horse over to the trees and picketed the animal on a low hanging branch. Standing there, he could see that the general had a bottle in his hand. Iverson tipped his head back and drained the last of its contents and then flung the empty bottle into the creek. It bobbed in the fast moving water, rounded the bend in the stream, then made its way south along the side of the road.

Pushing his shoulders back, Quinn stepped up to the general and the two officers close by the man. He caught the general's eye, then came to attention and saluted. "Sir, General Early's compliments, sir."

Iverson placed his hands on his hips. His gray coat was open, and the hands on his hips spread it out like a turkey showing itself off to the other birds. He lifted his chin. "And what does our commander require now?"

"Nothing, sir. General Early's in Chambersburg. He suggests that our men rest alongside the road and wait for his further orders."

"How far are we from Chambersburg?"

"About two miles, sir. I just came from there."

Iverson bowed his head and shook it. "Two miles!" He cursed. "We march all night, and we don't get to take the town? By the time we get there the best places will all be gone. We'll be left with nothing but the dregs." He stepped back from the stream and walked away. "It isn't fair."

He turned to look at Quinn, who was following him. "You hear me, Captain? This isn't fair."

"Yes, sir."

"Why do you suppose the man treats us so badly?" He looked Quinn in the eye, hoping to find some sympathy for his note of suspicion.

"I wouldn't know, sir. I suppose the general thought the men could rest better out here in the open."

"Balderdash! Men need something to sink their teeth into, not grass to lay out in the sun. What kind of nonsense is that?"

Iverson pointed to a group of horses picketed under the trees. "Have my orderly bring my horse. Captain, you and I are going to pay Early a visit. I'll have a word with him."

"Yes, sir."

Minutes later the two men were riding toward Chambersburg. They rode past men who were stacking their arms. Other small groups were finding places along the road to lie down, stretching out on the ground like an army of collapsed scarecrows. Some were building small fires and preparing what little they had to eat. All of them looked tired. The night's march had left them spent, and their faces were drawn and lean.

"Who gave the order to do this?" Iverson asked.

"I'm afraid I did, sir. I was carrying out the general's orders."

"Captain, you only have one general that you need to care a whit about his orders, and that is me. Am I making myself understood?"

"Yes, sir. Perfectly, sir."

A short time later, the two men trotted into town. It was quiet except for the troops that were making their way from building to building shaking doorknobs and trying to pry the locks from the doors of shops and bars. Iverson grunted his disapproval at the men who were making their rounds. Quinn knew, however, that it wasn't that the general objected to their actions; it was the general's jealousy that it wasn't his men carrying out the looting.

The sight of Colonel Updike, General Jenkins's second in command, walking the streets did nothing but cause Iverson to bristle. Updike turned and smiled as the two rode by. Iverson rose in the saddle and fixed his gaze forward, down the main street, his eyes riveted on the sight of the town square. Quinn heard him mutter under his breath. It was a deep mumble of disapproval.

The courthouse was a white building with white columns that held up a red roof. The green shutters were closed tight. Iverson and Quinn drew rein at the hitching rail and climbed down off their horses. A rebel battle flag hung over the front door, and a guard stood on either side. They snapped to attention as Iverson climbed the stairs.

Quinn followed along behind the man. He knew Iverson was somewhat sober, but that might mean even more of a problem. Drunk, he was easy to handle. Partially drunk, he just might let his mouth get in the way of his brain. Quinn knew the man was in a dangerous state of mind. He could only rely on the slight sympathy Early had shown for Iverson the night before.

Iverson threw open both outside doors and stomped into the hallway between the offices. He spotted a corporal standing guard. "Where can I find General Early?"

The corporal nodded toward the open door. "He's in there, General. Should I tell him you're here?"

"Never mind that." Iverson brushed him aside and stepped into the office.

Jubal Early sat behind an oversized polished, almost black mahogany desk. He wore a starched white shirt and a narrow clipped tie with the ends stuffed into his shirt between the second and third buttons. His gray-and-brown beard was combed and looked recently washed. He wore a pair of reading glasses, small and round with gold wire rims. Two colonels were looking over his shoulder and pointing to positions on a map that was spread across the desk.

Iverson marched up to the desk; the sound of his boots and spurs rattled in the large office. He grabbed hold of the edge of the desk and leaned over. "What do you mean by having my men camp outside of town?"

Early looked up. He smiled. "Alfred, you're here."

Early's smile and friendly greeting didn't stop Iverson. "Yes, I'm here, but my men are not." He stood up straight and pointed to the window. "They are out there in the hot sun, and we've marched all night to get here. Now we hear we have orders not to come into town, to sleep through the hot day in the road like dogs."

Early looked up at the two officers. "That will be all for now, gentlemen. If you will excuse us, it seems that General Iverson and I have matters to discuss."

The two officers snapped to attention and saluted, then marched out the door past Quinn.

"Sit down, Alfred. You look tired."

"My men are tired, General, too tired to lie on the road when there are beds here in town."

Early folded his hands and pulled them to his belly. "I had no idea you had such sympathy for your men, General. From what I've heard, you don't think much of our North Carolina troops."

Iverson waved his hand, as if to dismiss what was said. "That has nothing to do with it, General. It has to do with what's right. My men deserve this town, not what is left that Jenkins and his men don't want."

"General Iverson, our goal is Harrisburg. To reach that we're going to need infantry. If I turn you and your men loose in this town, it may take us a day to muster them again. We simply don't have a day to spare."

"But they're tired, General. They need a rest."

"The entire Second Corps needs a rest, General. If you boys do what I need you to do, you can have your town, but it will be Harrisburg, not Chambersburg."

Iverson balled up his fist and laid it knuckles down on the desk. "My men won't do it, General. They don't have what it takes to keep going on and on without rest or decent food. They deserve this town."

Slowly, Early peeled off his glasses. He folded them and dropped them into his coat pocket. "Your men will do what I say they will do, General. If you cannot successfully command them and see that they carry out their orders, then perhaps I should find someone who can."

Early picked up a large cut glass decanter that was filled with amber whiskey. Taking off the top, he poured a glass and pushed it toward Iverson. "Try some of this, Alfred. It's really quite good." He once again pointed to the chair beside the desk. "And sit down, for God's sake. You'll feel better with a little rest."

Iverson's gaze came to rest on the glass of whiskey. He slowly took his seat as directed and picked up the glass. "My men need

some time in town now, General, not tomorrow or the day after."
He shook his head. "I fear they will not be ready to fight if I do not
give them rest and something to eat."

"They will be ready to fight when we say it's time to fight,
General. I have the utmost confidence in you and your men."

Early watched as Iverson held the glass to his lips and began to
drink. "Now isn't that better? That's some mighty fine stuff there;
I'd say it's sipping whiskey from Kentucky. The mayor here was well
stocked. I'll give you a couple of bottles when you leave."

Quinn watched Iverson's shoulders drop. Evidently the promise of
Kentucky liquor was more than enough to make him forget his men.

Early reached over and picked up a small leather-bound book.
He opened the pages and began to turn. Finding his place, he set
the book down. "Do you know what I have here, General?"

"No, sir."

"It's the book of Psalms. You know the Twenty-third Psalm, I'm
sure." He picked up the book and began to read. "The Lord is my
shepherd; I shall not want." He set the book down and looked into
Iverson's eyes. "Perhaps that is exactly what He wants us to be to
our men, General—shepherds. I admire your concern for your
troops, General. Keep doing that. But you just let me decide what
is best and where we go from here."

CHAPTER 12

W ill took a walk with the cup of coffee in his hand. He sipped it and watched a meadowlark dart over the wheat field. The high wheat almost seemed sad that no one was there to harvest it. A slight breeze rippled over the field, and behind the field he could see the men digging Jonas Wolff's grave.

There was something about the death of a man who still had work to do that made it an especially sad occasion. Will had seen the baby at the breakfast table. Now looking at the wheat that was ready for harvest drove the point home. No man was ever ready to die, and the death of any man seemed to lessen what was left for the rest. Stonewall Jackson's death had been a time for mourning for the entire nation. Ewell was a good man, but he could never begin to be a Jackson. No one could. In some way, every man's death Will had seen these past years was the same, only on a much smaller scale. All over the nation women were crying and children were growing up with only photographs of fathers they would never know.

It made him almost hate politics and the gaudy phrases of glory and honor that served to rally men to their graves. No issue, however glorious, no cause, however noble, could dry the eyes of one child's tears.

Sipping the last of his coffee, Will watched as the men dug the grave. They had brought a handmade coffin by the house during breakfast and then had begun to dig the man's grave by the clearing near the creek. He would be buried next to his first wife, and there would be space to spare for the other members of the family. Christine had been quiet while the site was selected—silent, almost brooding.

He heard the door open and shut, then looked up and saw April standing on the porch. She was wearing a black dress with a green sash tied around her waist. She came down the stairs and walked toward him. The woman was beautiful; there was no getting around it. Her figure was well proportioned, and she moved with grace even when walking through the grass. Her hips swayed gently, and her fingertips brushed at the tops of the flowers as she came closer.

"I didn't know where I would find you," she said.

Will shook the cup dry. "I just thought I would come out here and collect my thoughts."

"I see."

"You're surprised?"

She bowed her head. "Yes, I suppose I am."

He began to walk, and she kept pace. "I do like to be alone with my contemplations from time to time. It helps to clear the head."

"Most men find it very difficult to only think and not do. I tend to think of men associated with action, not thought."

"Doing a little thinking before you act can save a lot of grief."

"And has it saved you?"

Will stopped and looked at her, deep into her eyes. "I've had more than my share of hard times. I've tried hard to be my own man. I didn't take to the sea as my father wanted me to, and I've paid for that."

"Your father is a seaman?"

"You might say that. He owns a shipping company out of Charleston. A successful one."

"The slave trade?"

"Every kind of trade known to mortal man. Now it's mostly blockade running. While most of the South lies in poverty, he's doing quite well for himself. The table is never empty."

"Is that why you're looked down on by the commanders of your army?"

"It's only part of the reason. Charlestonians for the most part see themselves as a cut above everyone else. Ours is an old and dignified town, unflinching in the face of the rest of the world. Everyone knows his place and everyone stays there, where God intended him to be."

"It sounds harsh."

"Far from it. It has glamour and glitter at times. The balls are ablaze with lights and polished carriages. Women wear the finest dresses from Paris, France. Champagne flows like water from a stream. You'd like it for a day, or maybe even a week."

April shook her head. "I don't think I'd like it at all."

"But it would like you, to look at you at least. As long as you never told them your last name, you'd do fine."

"My last name?"

"Everyone knows everyone in Charleston. You'd have no place there."

"You do think deeply, Will Chevalier."

"A product of my education, no doubt."

"My mother would have liked you. She read a lot and always talked of going to the places she read about in books. She wanted me to be a teacher just so I could be close to books, I think."

"And far away from people."

"No, books draw you close to people you never knew. They introduce you to the world and its struggles. They make you feel what others feel and hurt where others hurt."

"April, there is no place known to mortal man that brings you closer to people than the battlefield. You see them close up, smell their sweat, hear their cries of terror, and see their blood. God is one breath away, and many would say the battlefield is a sanctuary."

"That sounds monstrous."

"It is."

"I do hope your thoughts spare you from some of the pain of that place."

"Maybe they will. A man can never tell just how much grief he has around the corner. It does pay to avoid it if he can."

They began to walk again, and then Will stopped her. "There are some things I'd like to know about your stepmother. Do you know she came to the barn last night?"

"Why?"

"She said she wanted to see the place where her husband died."

April raised her head, as if in thought. It was always interesting for Will to watch April think. The woman's eyes seemed to stare off into space, even if she was looking right at you.

"Can you tell me where she is from?"

"That does seem to be important to you people, doesn't it?"

"A sense of place is something we carry around with us."

"She is from Virginia. Culpepper."

"And how did your father come to know her?"

"My father was from Virginia. He and our neighbor, John Slocum, grew up there. They moved up here together to start their two farms."

"So your people have ties to the South?"

"None that we like to brag about. Less and less all the time. But some things are hard to shake. Mr. Slocum even has a best friend who is one of your generals."

The notion peaked Will's interest. He sharpened his look into April's eyes. "Who might that be?"

"Your General Jubal Early and my neighbor were boyhood friends. They grew up together. He even has photographs of the two of them as young men."

"And why did your family and the Slocums leave Virginia?"

"Slavery, Major. They saw it as an abominable evil. My father came north with my mother to establish this farm, but it was also to be a place of refuge for runaway slaves. He was determined to do whatever his conscience would allow to end the dreaded trade in human lives."

"And his connection with your stepmother?"

"She is the daughter of one of his other boyhood friends in Virginia. The two of them wrote when my mother died, and then she decided to leave the South and marry my father. It was quite a traumatic experience for her. She had to leave her home and the people she had known all her life. She even left a fiancé to marry my father."

"Why would she do that? Your father was obviously a much older man."

April crossed her arms and looked at the house. "I was never quite certain of that. Perhaps it had something to do with the impending war. I think she knew the South would be devastated and, as you see, my father has a prosperous farm."

"For the money then. I thought most women wanted love."

April dropped her hands and balled her fists. "I can't say that." She waved him off. "Forget what I said. It's just a jealous daughter talking. Christine is a sweet woman. Frankly, I think it had more to do with slavery than anything else."

"And what about her fiancé? Did he just forget her?"

"I don't think so. He wrote her letters during the first year of my father's marriage to her. The man was obsessive."

"Do you remember his name?"

April thought for a moment. "Albert, I believe. She used to talk about him. I don't remember his last name."

They walked up to the house. They could see inside where the body of April's father had been transferred to the coffin, which sat

on the table in the parlor. April stepped into the room, followed by Will. She walked up to the coffin and placed her hand on it. Will walked over to the bookshelf and began to pull down some of the family's volumes.

A few minutes later April sauntered over to where he was reading their titles. "I see you're looking at *Uncle Tom's Cabin*."

"Yes, some would say it's the book that caused this war."

"It might very well be. It's a wonderful book."

"It's sheer nonsense, complete fiction from a Yankee woman who never saw a slave."

April took the book from his hands and put it back on the shelf. She ran her fingers over the shelf, as if searching for something. "I don't know what happened to my father's book of Psalms. He was never without it."

"Maybe that is what your stepmother came into the barn looking for last night."

April thought it over. "It could be, but why wouldn't she say so? That seems harmless."

The sound of people coming through the front door stopped their conversation. April darted into the hall and led the way into the dining room. Women were bringing in plates of food. Hams and stacks of ribs piled high on platters and bowls of potatoes and corn.

For the next hour Will and Perlman watched the people come by horseback and carriage. They first watched them from the dining room, and then they moved out to the barn. Will was sensitive to April and her need to explain the presence of the Confederate army. The woman had enough on her mind, and he knew it.

Perlman took out a precious cigar from his pocket and bit off the end. He held it up and stared at it. It was long and crooked, the wrapper broken in places. "I've been saving this, and now I don't remember for what."

"For the end of the war, no doubt."

Perlman curled his lip. "Yeah, and then somebody gets to find it on my body." He reached into his pocket and pulled out a match. Raking it over the box he was sitting on, he held the flame to the end of the twisted cigar. He blew out a cloud of gray smoke. "Ah, tastes like Atlanta." He winked at Will. "At least the memory of Atlanta."

The door rolled open, and April, followed by a tall thin man, stepped into the barn. The man was dressed in a black suit, white shirt buttoned up to his neck, and no tie. His full black beard would have covered it anyway.

"I'd like to introduce you gentlemen to John Slocum. He's our neighbor and the man who found my father's body."

Will got to his feet. He nodded. "Pleased to meet you, Mr. Slocum."

Slocum grunted and then remained silent.

"Has April explained our presence here?"

"Yes, she has." He shot April a quick glance. "I just never thought . . ."

"Never thought the Confederate army would take her seriously?"

"No, I didn't."

They spent the next half-hour questioning Slocum. Both Will and Perlman knew that if the man was to believed, he might very well have seen the murderer. He might be their only real eyewitness.

"Did you see anyone on the road that day?" Perlman asked.

"I saw a Confederate general. He was riding with his staff."

"And who might that have been?" Will asked.

"Don't know. I never asked."

"Can you describe the man?" Perlman asked.

Slocum shook his head. "I'm afraid not. I really didn't look him in the eye, just saw his uniform. You know how it is; you look a man in the eye, and you're afraid he might want more. I didn't want those people ransacking my farm."

As he turned to leave, Will asked, "One thing more, Mr. Slocum. I understand you and General Early are good friends."

"Yes, we are. Why do you ask?"

"Did General Early pay you a call on the march north?"

"Yes, he did. It was just a short visit. He only had time for a glass of lemonade."

"So that makes two generals you saw that morning?" Perlman asked.

"Yes, I suppose it does." Slocum started to leave, then turned back to April. He took his hat off and held it in his hands. "I've made your stepmother a fair offer for the farm, April. She hasn't given me her answer yet, but I wanted you to know. A place like this needs a man to look after it."

April nodded.

When the man left the barn, April stayed behind.

Will looked at her and, crossing his arms, stroked his chin. "Do you believe him?"

"Why wouldn't I? The man's our neighbor. He goes to our church. He and my father have been friends all their lives. What reason would he have to lie?"

Will looked at Perlman. "What about you?"

Perlman flicked the end off his cigar. "Some parts maybe, others no. I find it hard to believe that Jubal Early would stop for a social call. I also can't believe this Slocum feller would meet a general on the road and get close enough to know his rank and then not look him in the eye so he could recognize the man."

"He didn't exactly look us in the eye."

Perlman stuck the cigar back into his mouth and puffed on it. "No, he didn't."

"It could have happened the way he said it."

"I don't understand," April said. "What reason would John Slocum have to lie?"

"That seems to be exactly what we need to find out, April." Will shook his head. "Finding a murderer means crawling into another man's thinking."

The funeral wasn't a long one. Will and Perlman stayed near the rear of the group, almost out of sight. Will was sure that even having them close by would be a matter of some discomfort to those who were gathered. But it couldn't be helped. He leaned over to Perlman and spoke in a soft voice. "You really think a killer attends his victim's funeral?"

"I've seen more than one do just that." He shook his head. "I don't know why, maybe a sense of completing the circle for him. I had me a child killer in Atlanta. By the time the same feller showed up for four different funerals, we knew we had our man."

"We may have some explaining to do to April as to why we were here in the first place," Will said. "I'll expect you to explain."

Perlman nodded toward the Slocums. "I see Slocum and his son are here."

"Yes." Will looked toward the rear of the group to where a man in a gray uniform had ridden up. The man dismounted his horse and stepped into the rear of the crowd. Will nudged Perlman. "We seem to have a distinguished visitor, Sergeant."

Perlman turned his head and looked. His eyes widened. He studied the man with the long beard. "Is that who I think it is?"

Will nodded. "Yes, that's General Albert Jenkins, the commander of our cavalry."

Will had related the conversation he'd had with April to Perlman, and the name caused the sergeant's eyes to widen, then fix on the sight of Jenkins. "Do you think?"

"The name fits. He is from Virginia, like our grieving widow over there. And I dare say he's more her age."

They watched as Jenkins and Christine glanced at each other. It was only for a moment, and then Christine turned her head.

CHAPTER 13

I t was midafternoon before they were ready to leave the Wolff
farm. April and Tillie had loaded the wagon, and Perlman
had saddled Will's horse. He walked over to where the big
cat was standing and picked the animal up, giving him a few
strokes to show that he was safe. Walking over to the wagon,
he handed the tabby to Tillie. "We'll let him ride with you. I think
he gets a little tired of the bag on my saddle."

Tillie took the cat and set it on her lap. "He'll be fine here wif
us." She patted it. "I don't get to pay much attention to cats normally. Ain't never had one dat was a people cat."

"He goes his own way, same as me."

They sat waiting as Will came out the front door and down the
steps. He mounted his gray horse, and they trotted down the road
ahead of the wagon.

"Were you paying your respects to the widow?" Perlman asked.

"Yes, I was."

"And what did you find out?"

"Not what I wanted to."

"Is that right?"

"I wanted to know the name of her fiancé in Virginia that she broke up with in order to marry April's father. The woman clammed up tighter than a drum. All I got was a *good-bye* through clenched teeth."

"Sounds like you hit a nerve."

"I'll say I did. I wouldn't want that woman on the outs with me. I can tell you that."

The sun was hot overhead, but the mules that pulled the team were fresh and moved at a steady pace. The road showed signs of wear. Deep ruts promised that any wagon found in them might not get out again until it had arrived where the ruts ended. Artillery on a dirt road had a way of doing that, and they were fortunate that where they were going was most likely the same place the artillery had gone.

The road closest to the Wolff farm veered from the main road and led through their valley. Even though it was not the shortest way to Chambersburg, a number of the Confederate units had taken it to free themselves from the traffic.

The valley had hills on both sides with a clear running creek down the middle, unlike the main road and flat plain that led into Chambersburg. The unspoiled terrain was lush with green vegetation and trees along the creek. They even spotted signs of deer.

They trotted beneath a number of shady trees, and each sudden cool dip away from the sun's rays was all too short-lived. The glare of an almost cloudless sky made the heat nearly unbearable. The sun bored down on them, like a hot poker driving through their clothes and down deep into their skin.

Will jerked on his reins and swung his horse around to face the wagon. "Are you ladies bearing up under this sun?"

April had done the smart thing and changed out of her black mourning clothes into a light and airy white dress. The sleeves were loose around her arms, and her hair fell back and down her shoulders. Tillie had taken the precaution of bringing a bright yellow parasol, which was keeping the two women in the shade.

"We are holding up just fine, Major," April said. "Could you be so kind as to tell us just where we're going now?"

"We're going as far as these ruts will take us, Miss Wolff. I should imagine all the way to Chambersburg."

"And just what will we do there?"

Will let out a broad smile. "Well, ma'am, we're going to do just what you've wanted us to do all along. We're going to question general officers about your father, men who were close enough to have been there on the day he was killed."

"It's about time. All this intrigue of yours is useless, in my opinion. I'm quite certain the only reason for my father's death was pure thievery."

"And was anything stolen that you know of?"

"I don't know. I can't say for sure."

"I'm afraid, ma'am, that I can't quite place one of our generals riding into your farm and killing your father, only to ride off with a couple of chickens."

Tillie laughed. "Man's got his self a right good point dere, girl. Dem was mighty scrawny chickens too."

They heard the shot, a loud distant boom that echoed through the valley, before they saw its effect. Wood exploded on the side of the wagon, almost directly in front of where Will sat on his horse.

The big gray bolted and threw Will to the ground. He rolled behind a wheel, where he could see Perlman kicking his mule and galloping in the direction of the shot.

He looked up the road and spotted his horse. The animal was in full flight down the road, a cloud of dust flying off his hooves. It was apparent that he wasn't about to stop anytime soon.

Will reached up and grabbed Tillie, hauling her out of the wagon and pulling her down behind the wheel with a rush of brute strength. The big cat flew out of her arms and scurried under a tree. Tillie moaned and let out a sigh of pain as she hit the ground.

Will put his hand on her shoulder and shook her slightly. "Are you all right?"

Tillie swallowed hard, then shook herself. "You jes leave me be, Mr. Will. I's fine. Go on an see to April."

Looking back up, he spotted April. The woman was on the bottom of the driver's box, flat against the floor. She raised her head. Her eyes blazed. "Leave me alone."

"Not with that rifle up there. You get down now."

"I will not. I am fine, I tell you. He's shooting at you, not me."

"Have it your way, April." Will scooted up to the edge of the driver's seat and, swinging his hand over, caught April by the back of her dress. He yanked hard on her, dragging her forward. Then he lifted her up and over the side of the wagon. She screamed, kicking as she tumbled to the ground.

"You take your hands off me." She twisted in the dirt. "I can take care of myself."

Another rifle shot rang out. A portion of the driver's seat was torn off by the impact of the bullet. Chips of wood flew.

April sat beside the wheel panting. She looked at Will. "You just have to be right, don't you?"

He grinned. "It's my habit to be right. Just lie still and keep out of sight."

Will drew his revolver out of its holster. He ducked under the wagon and crawled forward. He edged his way to the far wheel.

The mules were nervously stamping their feet when another shot rang out. It kicked at the dirt beside the mules. They suddenly lurched forward. The wagon rolled as April screamed. Will saw the wheels moving and spun himself quickly, rolling over with his shoulders digging into the dirt. He barely cleared the wagon, tumbling out the other side. Scrambling to his feet, he ran for a tree near the road. He craned his neck around it and could see Perlman as he galloped his mule up the hill and into a stand of trees on top.

He heard another shot from the rifle and then took off running through the field. Even though he was exposed to the man shooting at him, it would take the man some time to reload. With every step, Will's heart beat faster. Being a single target silhouetted against a field of fire had never been his idea of a good time. His boots dug in the soft ground. His run in the soft earth was slow and deliberate, making him feel like he was in a dream.

The weeds were thick and the trees loomed ahead along the banks of the creek. He hit the high grass and kept running. Within minutes he was stamping in the trees and then wading his way across the creek. When he got to the other side, he settled down behind a tree and waited. Then he heard the sound of Perlman's carbine.

Will hit the rise out of the creek bed, running. He cleared the top and continued with full abandon in the direction of the crest of the hills. The hills were brown with the summer heat and dotted with rocks and trees. Brambles and berry bushes formed a barrier near the bottom, and Will ran right through them, tearing and jerking the material in his pant legs.

He heard another blast from the rifle and saw a puff of smoke from the outcropping above him. He felt the sting of the bullet as it creased his left arm. The burning sensation stopped him, but only momentarily. He watched the flow of blood start, then he began to run.

He ran up the hill and was almost halfway to the top when he spotted Perlman's mule. The animal was picketed to some low-hanging limbs of a tree. His ears were back, and his tail swished back and forth like the pendulum on a very fast clock.

Will pressed on toward the top of the hill. Fifty yards farther he spotted the sergeant. The man was lying in a prone position and taking aim. Will moved up to lay beside him.

"What do you see?"

Perlman pointed to a group of rocks up the hill. "He's up there, behind those rocks."

"Yankee sniper?"

Perlman shook his head. "I couldn't tell. It could be anybody." He looked at the blood on Will's arm. "You've been hit."

"It's just a scratch. I'll circle around to the left and come up on him. You fire a couple of rounds to keep his head down."

Will backed down the hill and moved to Perlman's left. He waited until Perlman had fired his first shot, and then he took off at a dead run. He had to make it to the trees on the crest of the hill. The rocks were in the open, but the trees would give him some cover. He danced over small stones and ran straight through the brush and brambles. There was no time to lose, and he knew it.

In what seemed like minutes but was most likely only a few seconds, Will collapsed near the base of an oak tree. He lay flat and panted, working to catch his breath. Down the hill he heard Perlman continue to shoot. There was no return fire. Will could only hope that whoever had taken the shot at them was still there, still hunkered down behind the rocky ledge.

He held his revolver out and then rolled over the grass, winding up in a prone position with his gun trained on the boulders. Slowly he got to his feet. He crouched, then made a run for the outer edge of the rocks.

He eased his way around the boulders. Edging the hammer back on his revolver, he pointed it in the direction of what he hoped would be their sniper. He stepped around the outcropping cautiously, taking care not to break a twig or anything that might give away his position.

With one final burst, he jumped clear and stood on the backside of the formation. It was empty, only a makeshift breastwork. Slowly he moved to where the sniper had lain. The grass was pressed down into the earth in the outline of a man. He knelt down and picked up a brass cartridge.

Getting to his feet, he waved for Perlman to come forward. He looked off to his left. Whoever had been there hadn't gone around to where he was coming up the hill. The man must have gone south, back in the direction of the Wolff farm. The terrain there was broken by trees and rocky formations. Anybody might be waiting under cover, waiting for them to show their faces.

It took Perlman a few minutes to ride the mule up the hill. He got off and ran to where Will was standing. "You didn't see him?"

"No, I didn't." Will bounced the shell casing in his hand. "He wasn't using a carbine, I can tell you that. This shell belongs to a Sharps rifle. He may not have been a sniper, but he sure was using a sniper rifle."

The two of them moved to the edge and looked down the slope to the numerous ravines that lay south of them. "You reckon we ought to go after him?" Perlman asked.

"Whoever it is, no doubt he has a good position by now. We won't see him until it's too late."

"So should we go get the ladies and find your horse?"

Will nodded. "Yes, I think so. The sooner we get out of this valley and onto the road to Chambersburg, the better." Will looked down the hill. "We should get back to the women. I don't want that sniper circling around to get them."

Perlman walked back to his mule. "I'll ride down there fast. You take your time. You need to catch your breath. We'll wait for you."

A short time later Will climbed out of the trees and back onto the road. His pants were soaked from the creek and were torn in several places.

"Are you all right?" April asked.

Will nodded. "I am now."

"We was worried 'bout you, boy," Tillie added.

"So was I," Will said.

April spotted the flow of blood. "You've been wounded."

Will looked down at the blood trickling down his sleeve. "It'll heal."

April lifted her skirt, took hold of her petticoat, and began to tear off a strip from the bottom. Jerking it free, she took Will's arm and began to wind a bandage around it. "I won't have you bleeding on account of me."

His mouth curved, a smile breaking into the corners of his lips. "I can't think of a man who wouldn't trade a bucket of blood for a look at your petticoat, ma'am."

She tightened the bandage and he winced. "Hush your manly nonsense. I'm trying to help you, and that's all."

"Who you reckon dat man was after?" Tillie asked.

"There's only one of us we can be sure he wasn't gunning for." Will pointed to Perlman. "The sergeant and his mule."

"Maybe there's something to being an object of pity," Perlman said.

CHAPTER 14

N appy swung his horse around the rocks and began a slow trot along the crest of the hill. He had heard the sound of gun-fire up ahead, and it made him cautious. No doubt some skirmish was taking place, and he had no desire to be a part of it.

He stopped and, reaching into his bag, pulled out a brass tube. He pulled the telescope open and held it to his eye. He would try to avoid the troop movement in the valley below. He watched as a brigade of Union cavalry moved below him. The men were dismounted, leading their horses to give them a rest. Several of them rode back along the marching line, shouting orders and giving a report of what lay ahead. They would be edgy now at the sound of gunfire, much too edgy to suit him.

Nappy moved the scope along the valley below and then looked at what might be ahead of him. He moved his line of sight along the trees and rocks and then stopped. He thought he saw some movement.

He collapsed the telescope and dropped it back into his bag, then got down from his horse. If someone was up ahead, he had no intention of presenting a good target. He tugged the horse's reins to run uphill, to a stand of trees that might offer some cover and still provide a place to see.

When he reached the trees, he hunted for a low branch to tether the horse. He soon found one and slung the reins over it, giving them a turn. He sat down for a moment, waiting. Whoever or whatever it was that he had seen would come along shortly. He just wanted to be sure that he saw him first.

Then the thought occurred to him: If it was cavalry, he had to see them long before they saw him. He looked along the side of the hill and saw a rocky outcropping that might make a good vantage point. It was still close enough to allow him to slip away. He got to his feet and moved stealthily away from the trees.

Keeping low, he skirted the crest of the hill. He was moving quickly, thankful for his new boots. The grass and brush were dry, and they made good cover for what he was wearing. His dirty tan shirt and trousers blended in well with the undergrowth, and he made certain he stayed low.

It took him only a few minutes to cover the ground between the trees and the rocks, and when he made it, he cautiously peered around them. They were hot to the touch, baked by the sun. The sensation made him feel alive and sharpened his senses. He began to climb the rocks, one step at a time, his feet feeling where he might jam his boot into a secure place and haul himself up. One cautious step at a time, hand over hand, he climbed. He got to the top and hugged the rock.

The sun was high, and he took off his hat and held it up to shield his eyes. He squinted. It was hot and getting hotter. He watched a hawk making lazy circles in the distance. All at once he spotted a bevy of birds take to the sky. A dozen of them took off from the ground for no apparent reason. Certainly with that hawk overhead, it would not be in their best interest.

It was no doubt what he had seen in the telescope. He only hoped it wasn't something he hadn't seen, like scouts from the soldiers in the valley. The possibility, however remote, caused the hair on the back of his neck to bristle. Right then the sight of Union cavalry was the last thing he wanted to see. He would have to stay out of sight and close by the big bay horse. If it was a blue-coated trooper, he wanted to make himself scarce and be quick about it.

He lowered himself onto the rocks, hugging them and watching. Suddenly he saw movement. It was something low to the ground, however, not a horse. He squinted into the sun-drenched hillside and then he saw him. It was a man, alone. He had a rifle and was running like a weasel, darting between the rocks and brush, his nose to the ground.

Nappy could tell the man was going to pass close to where he was hiding. There was no telling where he might go, however, and the last thing Nappy wanted was for the man to discover where he had tied the bay.

He scooted carefully back down the rocks, pointing his toes and feeling for a secure place to bear his weight. When he got close to the ground, he looked down. The last step might be the most noisy with the brush he had seen. He edged his way down until he touched solid ground.

He pulled the big dragoon out from his holster and waited. The man he had seen wouldn't take long to get there, and from the way he was moving, he wouldn't see anything or anyone that wasn't directly in front of him. Nappy had been a hunter and a stalker all his life. He knew that for a man to find what he was looking for, he had to keep distance in mind. He always had to keep his eyes open to what was a long ways off, not just something that was squarely in front of his eyes. By the time a person saw anything in front of him, it was much too late.

The lone man rounded the rocks, and Nappy stepped forward and trained the revolver on him. The man stopped in his tracks and lowered his rifle.

"What are you doing here?" Nappy asked.

He was no more than a half-man, half-boy. He stood under six feet, and his brown hair hung down from a slouched black hat. He was thin and had a scrawny neck. His Adam's apple twitched as he tried to speak. "I w-w-was huntin', that's all."

Nappy noticed the boy's eyes. They were filled with a mixture of fear and hatred. He could see the fear from the way he was shaking, but there was something more, something he couldn't quite put his finger on. "Hunting? Up here in the heat of the day? What for, pray tell, rabbits?"

The boy nodded. "Yes, rabbits."

"You sure you're not running away from something?"

"No, sir."

"You see army troops back where you came from?"

The boy glanced back behind him. "No, sir. I didn't see anybody. Honest I didn't."

The boy looked nervous. He was still shaking. "You look like you're running from the devil himself."

The boy shook his head. "No, sir. I'm just huntin'. That's all."

"Let me give you some advice, son. You'd better pick a time to hunt when this valley isn't filled with army troops. Any animal with half a brain is long gone by now, and the ones that are still here can be found only in the early morning. Besides, you sneak around like this in the middle of a war and somebody's going to shoot your behind off."

The boy swallowed hard. "Oh. All right."

Nappy shook his head. "Some people just need weeks on end of stomping the ground to figure that out. I expect you're one of them. You live close by?"

The boy pointed over the hill. "Just over there a ways. I don't go too far from home."

Nappy laughed, then tried to stifle his need to laugh harder. He lowered his revolver. "I've been watching you, boy. I don't think you could bag a snail." He looked at the boy's rifle. "That is a mighty fine gun there, son. It's one of those Sharps rifles, isn't it?"

"Yes, it is."

"Your father let you use it?"

"It's mine."

"Can you hit anything with it?"

"I don't do too bad. I hit lots of things."

Nappy snickered. "I just bet you do, when they let you get close enough. If I do find some rabbit attempting suicide, I'll be sure to send it your way. That gun looks much too big for rabbits too, boy. You won't have anything left but a clump of fur, if that."

Nappy caught sight of a long knife behind the boy's belt. He reached over and pulled it out. "That's some spear you're carrying there, son. You expect to go running after them rabbits and stabbing them in their holes?"

"No, sir. I plan on skinning them."

Nappy turned the blade over and felt its sharp edge. "Then there's another thing you've got to learn, boy. This blade's no good for skinning. It's much too long. You need a small one for that." He handed the knife back to the boy. "I'd say you've got quite a bit to learn. You'll be running and fall down and kill yourself with that."

The boy swallowed. "I'm not under arrest, am I? You ain't the law, are you?"

"Not hardly. I'm just a fellow fool trying to stay out of the war." He grinned. "The only thing is, I think I can provide better for myself than you'd be able to. I hope you're a farmer boy, because you aren't worth warm spit when it comes to hunting."

"I do farm."

"Well, that's good. Then you'll eat."

The boy looked over his shoulder, then back at Nappy. "Can I go now? My pa will be expecting me home."

"No doubt you've been lost before, boy. I don't doubt that your father has the dogs out looking for you even as we speak. What is it with you boys from Pennsylvania? You're either lost, hungry, or escaping the army."

"I ain't lost."

Nappy waggled his revolver to motion the boy on his way. "Then you'd better get to where you belong, son. Do your meat hunting in the smokehouse from now on because I don't think you're going to do much good out here."

The boy nodded. "Yes, sir."

Nappy watched the boy begin to walk and then run. He obviously hadn't listened to a thing Nappy had said. He just knew the boy was going to fall down and kill himself. He also didn't believe a thing the boy had told him. Some men were passable liars, but in Nappy's opinion the boy couldn't do even that well.

CHAPTER 15

J enkins rode east down the road from Chambersburg. He had searched for Jubal Early and his men in town, and everyone had pointed him in this direction. Two regiments of his own cavalry were with the man, and unless Jenkins showed up to explain his whereabouts, it wouldn't look good.

It was close to an hour later when he spotted the general. He was on a rise with some of his staff officers. A pair of civilians appeared to be standing beneath his horse. From the looks on their faces, Jenkins could bet they were doing more than their share of pleading about something.

He rode up to where the general was listening to the men. "Afternoon, General."

Early looked at him. "Well, well, the prodigal has returned."

Jenkins looked down to where Early's men were starting fires. Evidently Early had something else in mind besides pitching camp, and from the look of the buildings that were in the small valley below them, it was plain to see just what that was. "What do we have here, General?" he asked.

Jubal Early rose in the stirrups and pointed to the buildings. "It would seem that we have quite the find, General Jenkins. This is the Caledonia Furnace Ironworks and its outbuildings." He smiled and brushed his mustache and beard aside. "To make this even more sweet is the fact that the owner of this illustrious ironworks mill is none other than Thaddeus Stevens."

"*The* Thaddeus Stevens?"

"That's right, General, the leader of the radical Republicans in the Yankee house of Congress himself. Ain't that a pip?" He pointed to the buildings. "My men slept here last night. This morning they took out about four thousand pounds of bacon, molasses, and other items from the store down there."

"Those supplies will be good for the men."

"Yes they will, but it's this part that's the sweetest for me. We're going to have a fire, a big fire."

"What sort of buildings are down there, General?"

"I am told the ironworks has a large charcoal-burning furnace, a forge, a coal house, shops, stables, a sawmill, and a storehouse—" he grinned— "where we requisitioned our supplies this morning."

He pointed to a group of cottages. "That is where the men who work here are housed. Yankee slaves, I'd say. Of course, Stevens isn't here."

Early pointed to the man standing at the foot of his horse. "This is Stevens's manager. A Mr. John Sweeney."

Jenkins eyed the man. He was large and rotund. He wore suspenders to hold up his pants and a bright yellow shirt that was only slightly dirty. His round cheeks were rosy, and a brown goatee bobbed beneath his chin as his fleshy lips quivered.

"He thinks I'm going to take him prisoner. Quite prosperous looking, don't you think?"

"Yes, sir. I do."

"Well, Mr. Sweeney here was just explaining to me why I should spare Thaddeus Stevens's ironworks." He winked his eye. "It ought to be good." He motioned to the man. "Go ahead, Mr. Sweeney. I'm sure General Jenkins would love to hear your explanation."

Sweeney began to stammer. "G-g-g-general, these ironworks aren't p-p-p-profitable at all. Mr. Stevens loses money on them every year. He just keeps them open to feed and house the p-p-poor in the area."

Early smiled. "You see, General, we'd do more damage to Stevens, to hear Sweeney here tell it, by leaving his mill open and running. Why, you'd think that we'd drive the entire Yankee nation into the poorhouse by allowing them to keep their white slaves making iron for the Union army."

"What about General Lee's order number 72, General?"

Early shook his head. "Lee's order has nothing to do with this. The federal troops burn everything in sight when they come into Virginia. And the speeches Stevens makes on the floor of Congress are nothing more than torches being lit for the South on a daily basis. The man has a vindictive spirit for the people of the South. I figure I just ought to give him something to justify his mean-spirited nature."

Sweeney bowed his head, shaking it.

"As to Mr. Sweeney's claim that Stevens just keeps this place open to house and feed the poor, have you ever known a Yankee to do business that way? Those people will skinflint their way into every corner of your pockets and would take your last dime. I figure we're doing those workers down there a favor by freeing them from slavery, just the same as they say they are freeing our slaves by burning down our plantations."

Early gave out a sigh. He turned to one of his staff officers. "Colonel French, you may apply the torch."

Jenkins watched as French saluted and rode down the hill to where the men had built their fires. The men gathered around the bonfires and, pushing their torches into the flames, drew out burning brands. They ran down the hill and circulated among the buildings, setting the dry wood into a blazing inferno. Within minutes the structures were burning, sending up a column of smoke into the blue, late-afternoon sky.

"Didn't you graduate from a college up here in Pennsylvania, Jenkins?"

"Yes, sir. Jefferson College, sir. I also graduated from Harvard Law School."

"Quite impressive. Served a term in Congress too, as I understand it."

"Yes, sir. But I can't say that I'm proud of that."

Early turned to Jenkins. "Now, General, why don't we discuss your galavantings around the Yankee countryside?"

Jenkins swallowed hard. "Yes, sir. There is something I would very much like to discuss with you. I am afraid I am going to need your protection."

Early stared hard at him, his flat unspeaking eyes prolonging the moment. "Suppose we ride over the hill for a bit, General. Then you can tell me whatever it is that you have on your mind."

Jenkins tugged on his reins, and the two of them rode over the rise of the hill. Jenkins waited until Early stopped before he drew rein. He couldn't help but notice the gloss on Early's boots. They were freshly waxed and buffed, giving off a luster that looked like coffee in a cup—black, wet, and shiny. He had polished his own boots that morning before he rode off to the Wolff funeral. Now, however, they were caked with the dust of the road, and he noticed that one of them, his right boot, was beginning to lose its sole.

Early got off his horse and dropped his reins on the ground. Jenkins followed his lead, and both men walked over to a group of stumps left by the men who had been cutting wood for the now burning ironworks. Early took out a handkerchief and swiped at a stump, knocking off dust and what remained of cut pieces of wood. He took his seat. "Now, General. I am all yours."

"Sir, I don't quite know where to begin."

"Just spit it out, son. Spit it out."

"Sir, I believe I am going to be the subject of an investigation by the provost marshal's office."

"And why would that be? Have you been freeing Yankee pigs?"

"No, sir. Murder."

"Murder? And just who are you supposed to have killed?"

"A Yankee farmer named Wolff."

Early's eyes were flat, hard, passionless. "And just how would that involve our provost?"

"I don't know, sir. All I know is that I was at the man's funeral this morning, and two members of the provost marshal's office were there. They were looking at me very carefully."

"And why would they suspect you of such a thing?"

Jenkins rubbed his beard, running his hand down its massive length. He then worked his way through his beard and began to twist his brass buttons. "Because I was there." He looked at the ground. "In fact, I must have been there before the man was killed."

Looking back up at Early, Jenkins made direct eye contact. "But I didn't kill him, General. I just rode into his farm and went to his barn."

"And just why were you there in the first place, General?"

Once again Jenkins dropped his gaze to the ground. He shuffled his feet slightly and held his hands in the front on his beard, as if to give himself some comfort. "This is very hard for me to say, General. I feel like a fool."

"Go on, Alfred. We're all fools from time to time."

"I went there to meet the man's wife."

"His wife?"

Jenkins jerked his head and put up his hands. "It's not what you're thinking—at least not exactly what you're thinking."

"And how would you know what I'm thinking?"

Jenkins shook his head. "I just know what I'd be thinking, and I wouldn't blame you one bit."

"Please explain then."

"Do you remember that note I gave you and asked you to deliver? You said you knew someone who lived in the area, someone you were going to see."

Early nodded. "I remember, and I did what you asked."

"Well, that note was for Christine, Wolff's wife. We were once engaged to be married." He shook his head slowly. "It seems like such a long time ago. She broke off our engagement to come here and marry Jonas Wolff. The man and her father were good friends. He has—or had—a prosperous farm, and Christine was afraid of what the war would do to me and my holdings." Jenkins shook his head. "And I think my politics were wrong in her thinking."

"The slavery issue?"

"Yes, sir."

"Many a good home has been broken up over that one."

"Yes, I know. But I just couldn't get her out of my head. I sent her a note saying that I was going to ride down to meet her in the barn that day. When I got there, I found her along with her husband."

"I see."

"And then"—Jenkins became animated and started to wave his hands—"we had words. I just got out of there, and right quick too. I know I should have informed someone, but I panicked. I did talk to Christine later. I rode back that night."

"She was waiting for you?"

"Yes, on the road. I didn't see her at first, but she was there, just standing beside the road." He bowed his head. "I didn't say anything about what happened in the barn. I don't know why. Perhaps I was ashamed. We talked, but I know I must have seemed quite agitated to her."

"You were wise to say nothing. Women can become hysterical."

Jenkins began to beat on his chest with slow soft blows from his knuckles. "I just knew that I would be suspected. I had every reason to want the man dead." He continued the beating of his chest. "I loved her. I couldn't stand the thought of losing her."

"Did anyone see you ride in?"

"I think there was a woman on the porch when I rode up, a black woman. She didn't look up at me though. I also met one of his neighbors on the road, a Slocum." He shook his head. "I don't know if he remembered me or not."

"John Slocum?"

Jenkins looked him in the eye. "That might have been it. Do you know him?"

Early waved his hand at him. "That's immaterial." He leaned forward. "Who do you think killed him?"

Jenkins nervously wrung his hands. There was an almost pleading quality to his movements. "I don't really want to get into that, General." He paused. "Let me just say that it wasn't me." His voice trailed off. "I don't want someone trying to pin the blame and trying to hide . . ."

"To hide a murder? To blame it on the Confederacy? Perhaps on you?"

Jenkins bowed his head and shook it. "I have been such a fool. I'd never have thought it possible to be used like that by a woman. I feel that I'm being trapped by this thing." He looked up at Early. "What am I to think?"

"And who is in charge of this investigation?"

"I've seen him before. He was at Wolff's funeral. A Major Will Chevalier, I think. Do you know him?"

Early smiled. "Yes, I know of him. He's a Citadel graduate, from Charleston. A very bright man, but not well thought of. He is a line closer. I shouldn't think you will have any trouble from Chevalier. No one will give him the time of day."

"I hope you're right, General."

"When have you ever known me not to be right, Alfred?" Early smiled. "You say you were seen only by a black servant woman and Wolff's neighbor, Slocum?"

"That's all, General. Of course my second in command, Colonel Updike, knows I've been out riding alone. I also told him about Christine. But I'm sure he won't say anything. He's loyal."

Early got to his feet. He walked toward Jenkins and put his hand on his shoulder. "You were right to come to me with this, Alfred." He patted his shoulder. "I need to have you thinking about killing the Yankee army, not some Yankee farmer. I'll keep your secret." He smiled. "Of course, you'll owe me."

"I owe you so much already, General. You've stuck by me."

"Then don't worry. I'll have something up my sleeve for Chevalier. You just go on about your business and rejoin your unit. Your brigade and Iverson's have been assigned to Rhodes's division. There is a railroad bridge near Scotland that you're supposed to destroy. Are you feeling up to blowing up something the Yankees have built for a change?"

Jenkins came to attention and snapped a salute. "Yes, sir. Very much so, sir."

CHAPTER 16

W ill led the group out of Chambersburg that next morning after they had been told that Early had gone east. With every stretch of road, the four of them encountered returning townspeople and Confederate stragglers. Many of them had fresh news of where Early had gone, but most agreed that he would wind up in York before long. Will trotted along beside the wagon while Perlman rode ahead.

April slapped the reins on the mules' backs. "I must say, Will, you sure know how to show a girl a good time. If we had gone on and questioned those men before they lit out like bats after a shotgun blast, then we'd have this solved by now."

"And we wouldn't exactly know what questions to ask, April. You don't expect me to just say, 'General, did you kill this lady's father?' now do you?"

"But at this rate we'll never find them. Every time we get to where this Early was, he's already gone."

"It's a war. You've got to expect that. At least we have some names."

"You chillin fight like dogs wif tin cans tied to dere tails," Tillie said. "You get so busy tryin' to gnaw off what's on your own tail, you forget why you's dere in de first place."

Will laughed. "Tillie's right. We're both on the same side."

April looked at Tillie and then back at Will. "For now, at least. After we find my father's killer, we'll be on opposite sides."

"Without a doubt, April." Amusement flickered in his eyes. "I just bet, though, it would be hard to find someone you weren't on opposite sides with."

Tillie let out a cackle. It rumbled from her throat like a rake being dragged across rocks. Then she slapped her knee. "Dat man sho' nuff got you pegged, girl. He surely do. You can be ornery, and you got a surly mouth to beat anybody I ever did see."

"Perhaps you should consider a run for Congress, April."

April shot him a look that would have stiffened a cow in a stampede. "That's nonsense."

"Now why is that? With the edge on you always showing, no one would ever be able to pull the wool over your eyes."

"Women can't even vote. How could I win?"

"I'd sure vote for you."

April slapped the backs of the mules with the traces once again. She muttered as she looked straight ahead. "Fine thing, I get one vote and I can't even vote for myself." She looked at him. "Do you realize how unfair that is, Major, that women can't vote?"

"Some would say it's only right. The men do the fighting and dying: they should do the voting too."

April looked straight ahead at the road. "That would suit you, I'm sure. You just want to continue to treat us like brainless china dolls to be displayed on your shelves. If we followed your line of reasoning, then women should be the ones to make all of the decisions about children, since we are the only ones who give birth."

Will laughed. He had an infectious laugh, a deep baritone that practically sang. "I can see we have another cause for you to fight after the war. Some people never tire of fighting wars they cannot win."

"And you think you can win this one, Major. If you ask me, yours is just as much a hopeless cause as mine. The North has too much for you to overcome. It's only a matter of time, and I know you're too smart of a man not to see it."

Will took the idea in silence for a while. Then he spoke. "Miss Wolff, some men fight for what is right, their freedom to choose what government rules over them. If a man can't die for that, then nothing is worth dying for. I know you think this war is all about slavery, but in reality that is only a ploy to recruit Northern troops. It's about power. One section of the country is growing in political power and seems determined to force its will on the other. Individual rights and freedoms are of little consequence to the almighty federal government in Washington. You may not see it now, but even if you do win this war, you will have lost in the long run. We will never again be a nation of free people."

"Once again, Major, it is you who are running for Congress. But you do see, even if you fight a losing cause, the fight alone is worth it. It makes you human to know right from wrong. It makes you a creature of God."

Will smiled. "April Wolff, you are a most unusual woman. You're a politician, a policeman, a teacher, and a rabble-rouser. I'm not sure how any man could ever stand up to you."

Tillie leaned across April and grinned at Will. "It would take a mighty smart one, Mr. Will, and one wif sand."

They camped for the night and spent the next day traveling toward York. It wasn't until the early afternoon that they pulled in to the town. The town had fallen to Confederate forces, and from the murmur around the streets, Old Jube, or Jubal Early, was soon to be there.

People were coming back from church in their Sunday best. Bells were ringing, and a carnival-like atmosphere was rippling through the crowded streets. Will halted the wagon, and the four of them sat and watched the parade.

Leading the line of troops was General Billy Smith. His brigade was evidently the first to enter York, and they were more objects of curiosity than animosity. The old gentleman rode in front of his troops with a blue cotton parasol over his head. Men, accompanied by barking dogs, walked beside the troops. Many were asking questions of the southerners. Others pointed and shouted.

Billy Smith, ever the consummate politician, started doffing his hat and being the gracious gentleman to any lady who presented herself on the street. Will could tell the man was invigorated by the display because his chest was swelling with every smile.

Smith turned to the band and had them strike up "Dixie," followed by "Yankee Doodle." Brass instruments and drums echoed in the street. Some children clapped their hands, and others simply beamed with the pride of being entertained.

Smith wheeled his horse around. "Brigade, halt."

The men trickled to a stop right in the middle of the street.

"Stack arms, men, and stand at ease."

The order brought the curiosity seekers to the tips of their toes to see over those in front of them. Men in their butternut uniforms stacked their arms in tepees and formed lines. Many pulled at their uniforms to knock off the dust.

Smith removed his hat and stood in his stirrups to address the growing crowd. His voice boomed as it rose. "Ladies and gentlemen of Pennsylvania. You will pardon our intrusion, but the sun was too hot in Virginia, and we've just come up here to enjoy your fine weather. You might say that we have come up here to join the Union, after a fashion."

A ripple of laughter carried through the crowd.

Smith swept his hat back over the standing troops in the street. "As you can see, our army is composed of decorous Christian gentlemen, not monsters."

The laughter increased.

"You are welcome to remain here and make yourselves entirely at home. You are to be most welcomed as long as you behave yourselves pleasantly and agreeably as you are now doing." He smiled in the direction of his troops. "Are we not a fine set of fellows? You must admit that we are."

The people in the square broke into applause. Will watched April. Her expression went from one of shock to anger. She bit her lip.

Hay's brigade was following Smith's and they ground to a halt in front of the crowd. Will could see Jubal Early riding up. The man wasn't the least bit amused at Smith's show of goodwill. He became even more irritated when the crowd almost knocked him off his horse.

He kicked and spurred his way to the front. Reaching out, he took hold of Smith by the shoulder, spinning him around. "What the devil are you about? Stopping this column in the midst of this cursed town. You conduct your men north of town and camp there by the railroad."

Early rose in his stirrups and shouted. "Send me your mayor." He pointed to a white hotel, the Metropolitan. "Send him to me in there."

Will turned to April. "It would seem that we have found our general. I'm not too certain of his mood, but it's most likely the best we're going to get. We had better make our way over to the hotel and see if we can find out where we can find Jenkins."

This wasn't going to be a long stop and they had no desire to stay the night in York, although it would have been much more comfortable than the road. They pulled the wagon into the alley behind the hotel. The big orange tabby bounded out of the wagon and scurried down the alley, then between the buildings.

April pointed. "That cat of yours, Elmer, is running away."

Perlman laughed. "That cat's probably the only one of us with sense. And he ain't mine. Cats don't belong to anybody but themselves. It's even sort of ridiculous to name them. A body should just call them *cat* since they don't come when you do call them."

"Then why are you so attached to him?"

"'Cause I know he's going to run off on me. There are no sur-
prises with a cat. People run off and befuddle you. They disappoint
you, and you get your heart broken. With a cat you presume it.
When you expect so little, you always get more than you count
on."

They tied the traces of the mules and the wagon in the back
alley and started around the corner to the front door of the hotel.

Guards were already posted, but Chevalier led the way up the
stairs and through the glass-paneled doors. The hallway was abuzz
with activity as officers were busy establishing what would be Jubal
Early's divisional headquarters. Officers carrying rolls of maps and
satchels filled with papers hurried toward the parlor off the lobby.
Several officers escorting a man in a black suit into the parlor
pushed aside Chevalier and the group.

One of the men bounced Tillie aside as he hurried past her.
"Dis is a busy place," she remarked.

Will steadied her. "You just stay behind me."

They walked through the two open doors, and Will found a
chair for Tillie. They stood and watched Early, who was now seated
behind a writing desk. Behind him, men were tacking a rebel flag
to the wall. A young lieutenant stood at Early's side.

Early looked at the man in the starched white collar and black
suit. The man was tall and lanky, with gray hair that came down to
his shoulders. His cheeks were bony and chiseled, and his nose
sloped down from his forehead to a point that seemed never to end.
"You are the mayor of York, I take it."

The tall man nodded his head. "Yes, sir, I am. We were certainly glad to hear about your intentions here, General."

Early's face was hard, and his eyes narrowed. They looked like
black olives set in wrinkled parchment.

"Well, you can forget that poppycock dribble from the old man
out there. I'm in charge here, and you will do as I say."

The mayor shifted his weight nervously.

Early picked up a piece of paper from his desk. "I have here a list of our demands, Mayor. We will require 2,000 pairs of shoes or boots; 1,000 felt hats; 1,000 pairs of socks; 165 barrels of flour; 3,500 pounds of sugar; 1,600 pounds of coffee; 32,000 pounds of fresh beef; and 21,000 pounds of bacon. And one other thing, and this is most important: we will require $100,000 in cash money. These demands will be met, and you will deliver everything on this list to the market by 4:00 P.M. today or your town will be burned to the ground." He handed the piece of paper to the mayor. "Have I made myself understood?"

The man nodded slowly. "Yes, sir. I don't know if we will be able to come up with that kind of cash, however."

Early smiled. He looked at the ceiling of the parlor and lifted his hand to point out the ornately designed pressed plaster. It was white with angels dancing over clouds. "You have a lovely town, Mayor. Either you meet my demands or this place will be no more than a memory by this time tomorrow. Now go and do your job. I have mine to do right here."

Will put his hand on April's and squeezed it. He could see the anger rising in her face. "You stay here with Tillie and Perlman."

As the mayor walked out of the room, Will stepped up to the desk, snapped to attention, and saluted. "Major Will Chevalier. My compliments, sir." Reaching into his pocket, he pulled out his set of orders and laid them on Early's desk. "Those are my orders, sir. I am here to investigate a murder. What I need to know from you is the whereabouts of General Alfred Jenkins."

Early looked at the lieutenant. "Lieutenant Reynolds, this is one of our graduates from the Citadel. He's Charlestonian." Early said the word dripping with sarcasm. "We must be careful how we treat him, or his father will buy and sell us as if we belong on that slave block of his."

Will noticed the smile on the lieutenant's face. The man had blond hair combed straight back. His skin was perfect, and his sky-blue eyes seemed to dance over Will's grave as he looked at him.

Early picked up the orders and read them. He stroked his beard. "Major, I've heard all about this matter. You don't have a murder that involves this army. It's purely a civilian matter, something for the local authorities."

Will glanced back in Tillie's direction. "But we have an eyewitness, sir, that places one of our general officers at the scene of the crime."

Early looked at Tillie, a long careful look. "You talking about that black servant woman over there?"

"Yes, sir, and a farmer."

"Major, you are wasting your time and mine too. I've already solved this crime of yours. Jenkins came to me with his story. I know about the murder of this man who was married to Jenkins's former sweetheart."

Early reached down to his feet and picked up a battered leather case. He set it on the desk, unbuckled the flaps, and pulled out a leather-bound book.

"That is my father's book of Psalms," April shouted. She walked forward, pointing at the book. "He always carried it with him. He had it with him when he was killed. I'm certain of that."

Will reached out and took her hand. "This is the murder victim's daughter, a Miss April Wolff."

Early looked at her and then opened the book. He took out a piece of paper with handwriting on it. "Then perhaps she should see this."

April took the piece of paper and read it. Her eyes moistened with tears, and she began to shake her head.

Early sat back in his chair and smiled at Will. "What Miss Wolff has is a letter from Jenkins to the man's wife arranging a meeting between the two of them, a meeting in the victim's barn at the time and place the murder occurred. This note was in the man's Bible. Evidently he found out about the meeting. Jenkins showed up, but the wife wasn't there, only the body. Isn't it obvious, Major? The woman murdered her own husband and hoped to pin the blame on our brave but foolish General Jenkins."

Will took the letter and read it. He looked at April. "It would explain why your stepmother came to the barn that night we were there." He held out the letter. "She was looking for this."

"I simply can't believe it," April said.

Early folded his hands and smiled. "So you see, Major, this wild-goose chase of yours is over." He waved a hand. "Have the woman arrested if you like and hold her for civil authorities. Meanwhile, you need to get back in the war."

"First I will need to see General Jenkins," Will said. "I must have him confirm your story."

"Isn't my word good on this matter?"

Will nodded. "In order to do my job, however, I need to follow all the leads. We have our eyewitness, and we'll need to place the whereabouts of Mrs. Wolff. It would seem to me right now that General Jenkins still had the best motive."

"Well, Major, you'll get no more cooperation from me. So far as I'm concerned, you're just a horse fly in the middle of a cavalry charge."

Early held up Will's orders from Ewell and tore them in half. He then folded them and tore the paper once again. "Your orders have been rescinded, Major. You'll have to rejoin your line closers and pester someone else for a change." He jabbed his finger in Will's direction. "You stay away from my men and my officers. Now you are dismissed."

"Not so quickly, General." April stepped forward. "You have something that belongs to me." She reached out and snatched the leather book. "This was my father's. You can take all the food and money from this town you like, but you can't have my father's Bible."

Will started to walk away, then turned back to face Early. "One thing more, General. I'm interested. You know Wolff's neighbor, Slocum?"

"Yes, I do. So what?"

"From what I've been given to understand by Slocum, you went to see him on the day Jonas Wolff was murdered?"

"What if I did?"

"That does place you near the crime scene, General."

"What of it?" Early got to his feet and placed his hands on the desk. "What are you suggesting?"

"I'm not suggesting anything, General. I'm just curious. How did you happen to come into the possession of the man's book of Psalms?"

"That's enough!" Early shouted. "I've heard quite enough from you. The next time I see you, I want it to be in front of a firing squad. Not one you're in command of either, but one that is executing you. And I will if you keep bothering me. I'll have you up on charges of insubordination."

CHAPTER 17

ill turned the brass knob embossed with the wreath of oak leaves and pushed open the glass-paneled door. He was the last to leave the hotel. He walked down the steps with his shoulders square and fixed his hat to a jaunty tilt. Jubal Early hadn't taken one bit of starch out of him, and he was determined to show it. In spite of everything Early had said, Will had stayed in the lobby and continued to ask questions. A few of the officers inside had told him that Jenkins was no longer under Early's command but was under the strict supervision of Rhodes. Evidently Lee had found the conduct of his troops to be less than desirable. Will had also found out that Jenkins was now making his headquarters back in Chambersburg, so he could be as close to Lee as possible.

Perlman was waiting for Will on the sidewalk at the bottom of the stairs. April and Tillie were talking to a runaway slave who had been captured. The man's hands were tied behind him with a lead rope dangling on the sidewalk. A guard was smoking a pipe close by, watching him.

"What did you find out?" Perlman asked.

"I'll tell you later."

Pushing up his cap, Perlman scratched the back of his head. "What are you going to do about those orders that man tore up?"

"Get new ones."

"Who from? Once Old Jube there passes the word, I don't think anybody's going to give you permission to do anything."

A number of soldiers passed by them, one hobbling on a crutch. The man was barefoot. His trousers were torn from the knee down, giving him the appearance of a street bum. His gray hair and stubbly beard would have made him a grandfather in anyone's book. Here, though, he was just another private in the Confederate army. Will didn't respond to Perlman's question while the man limped by. He simply smiled at the wounded soldier and nodded.

"Whose permission are you going to get? I don't know a general who would be foolish enough to stand up for you now."

Will smiled. "There might be one, just one maybe."

Perlman rocked back and forth on the balls of his feet, his hands clasped behind him. Will noticed the man's boots, scuffed and deeply gouged. They had long ago seen the look of polish, and the blood brown they had once been was now faded to a pale tan, the color of clay. "You should see about getting yourself a pair of those boots the mayor is digging up."

Perlman stopped his rocking. He lifted one foot and looked at his torn sole. Repeating the action, he looked at the other one. It was in worse shape than the first. "They'll do for now." He glared at Will. "Stop changing the subject. Who're you gonna find that's a soft enough touch to buy that swill of yours? It would have to be someone they'd listen to, and I can't think of many that would fit that bill."

"I know of one." Will's lips trembled with the need to smile. He was relaxed. There was something about the guessing games he always played with the experienced sergeant that amused him. Jacob Perlman was a man of grit, and one that few people ever put one over on.

"All right, college boy. You got me. Who is it?"

Will leaned closer to him. "The one man who doesn't much trust Jenkins—or Early either, for that matter—General Lee."

Perlman slapped his hand on his face and pulled it down slowly, raking it through his beard and forming a frown. "How do you think you're even going to get close enough to Marse Robert to let him hear your case?"

Will looked over to where April and Tillie were still talking to the runaway slave. He broke into a slow smile. It spread across his face. "A pie."

"A pie?" Perlman put his hands on his hips. "Are you crazy, boy?"

Will shook his head. "Not in the least. I hear that General Lee loves blackberry pie. We passed some blackberry bushes on our way into town. I figure if we can get Tillie or April over there to bake the man a pie, we just might have a fighting chance of getting to him." He looked back in April's direction, his drawl becoming more pronounced. "Especially if it was being delivered by a beautiful young lady with Virginia roots."

Perlman laughed. "Son, if I didn't know you any better, I'd say you was either crocked or still suffering from the frets over Early. You really think you're going to get that woman to be even a little bit domestic? I think she'd rather run through them bushes barefoot than bake a pie. And if you tell her who it's for—the commander of the Confederate army—that's going to be the corker for the girl."

"Five dollars says you're wrong."

Perlman's eyes widened. "Five dollars? Confederate or American?"

"American, of course."

"You're on, college boy. You may know your facts, figures, and ciphering, but when it comes to womenfolk, you don't know beans from road apples."

A half-smile crossed Will's face. "You're forgetting, Sergeant. Women are what I know best."

Both men nonchalantly stepped over to where the two women were talking to the slave.

April grabbed Will's sleeve. "You have to do something." A sense of desperation was in her face.

Will looked at her. Her brown eyes shone like glassy volcanic rock, liquid but hot with emotion behind them. "Do what?"

April reached over to the slave. "This is Ulysses." He was tall, bare chested, and wearing tattered trousers with no shoes. His toes were like mushrooms, pink and peeling underneath, black and crusted with dirt on top. "He was on our farm." The man's lips were full and pouting and his eyes looked as if they might bore right through you. There was a sadness to them, a sadness of having seen much too much suffering and misery. "He's from North Carolina."

"An escaped slave, I take it."

"Yes, he is." April looked at Ulysses, pity written all over her face. "He came from a horrible situation. We sheltered him for almost a week, and father sent him on his way several days ago. General Iverson's men captured him after he left us, he says. They are from North Carolina too. Now they're turning him and all the other recaptured slaves over to some men who are going to take them back to the South. They are even taking people who were born here in Pennsylvania."

"So Ulysses here was part of your Underground Railroad?"

"Yes, he was. I'm only sorry we couldn't keep him. As it turns out, we could use him now."

Tillie reached over and patted Ulysses on the back. "He a good man too, Mr. Will, big and strong. He'd do a right smart of work on de place iffen we could get him back dere."

Will looked him over. "I'm sure he could."

"Looks strong as a mule," Perlman said.

"Not a mule," April shot back. "A man."

Tillie shook her head. "Folks be always confusin' black folk with animals. You go to treat 'em dat way and you buy and sell 'em like cattle, and pret' soon you forget dat things wif souls is people."

"I stand corrected," Perlman said.

"See that you do," April agreed.

Will stepped closer to the man. "Did you see Iverson?"

Ulysses nodded. "Yes, suh. I did."

"He question you?"

Ulysses continued to nod. "Yes, sir. Dat man question me a whole lot."

"About what?" Perlman asked.

Ulysses turned his attention to the sergeant. "He axed me where I come from and how I come up to be here."

"Did you tell him about the Wolff farm?"

"Yes, suh. I surely did now. I didn't want to, but dat man's looks is so terrible. He was gettin' madder and madder. He shout and scream ever which a way. I thought he's gonna bust a blood vessel in his head." He circled his head with a slow motion. "Or worse, bust one in mine."

April took Will's hand. Her warm eyes would have melted the snow in the dead of winter. "Can we bring him with us? Is there any way we can free him from being returned to North Carolina?"

Will looked at Perlman, and Perlman shrugged his shoulders. "You're the boss man, Major. Personally, I'd say it was a fool thing to do. It might compromise our investigation and bring Early's wrath down on you even more than it already is."

Will studied April's face. "You know you're going to owe me, Miss Wolff, owe me in a way that might be unpleasant to pay back."

April nodded. "I'll do anything, anything it takes to get Ulysses back."

"I might just take you up on that tonight, Miss Wolff."

Will saw April's face register a look of surprise. Her eyebrows arched, and the corners of her mouth drooped slightly. He could tell that she was thinking of a romantic favor, perhaps even a kiss. It amused him and made him smile.

"I don't know just what you have in mind, but I'm willing to do anything reasonable." The emphasis in her voice on the word *reasonable* was unmistakable.

Will stepped over to the private who had been assigned to watch over Ulysses until they could find a place where he could be kept. "Private, I'm going to do you a big favor."

The soldier snapped to attention.

"I am taking this man with me."

"I don't know, sir. I have orders."

"Well, I am giving you new orders. You can go back and rejoin your unit."

The man hesitated, then saluted and started down the street. Will and Perlman watched him walk away. Then Will spotted something else. The lieutenant who had been in the room with Early was watching them from the top step of the hotel. The man turned and walked back through the front doors.

"We'd better get going," Will said, "and right now."

They walked around the corner to the alley where the wagon and horses were tied. They watched as the big orange cat ran out of the space between two houses and jumped into the wagon. "He's back," April said.

"Like a crippled foot," Will sneered. He cut the ropes off of Ulysses, handed the knife over to him, and then helped Tillie and April into the wagon. As he took April's hand, he asked her, "Do you bake blackberry pies?"

Tillie chuckled. "She sure do now. Bakes some a de best blackberry pie dat's ever gone into a gentleman's mouth."

Will looked over at Perlman, who had mounted his mule, and grinned. He held out his hand.

"All right. All right." Perlman dug into his pocket. "I can tell when I've been whipped."

CHAPTER 18

I t took the group the rest of the day to find a place to stop for the night on the road to Chambersburg. Will's horse and the mules were bathed and set out in a field that seemed to be covered with clover. The small white blossoms dotted the lush green, and the animals fed noisily, the sound of their grinding teeth carrying into the camp.

The next morning they set out for Chambersburg, passing a number of cavalry units who were foraging for food and paying in Confederate scrip that they swore was as good as gold.

April slapped the traces to the mules' backs. She had been thinking what a lovely day it was when suddenly she noticed storm clouds as the wagon neared the top of a hill.

Will rode back. "Tillie, you and Ulysses get in the bottom of the wagon." Tillie seemed to hesitate. "Do it now."

"Why?" April asked.

"Don't ask questions. Just do what I say." He turned his horse and spurred back to where Perlman was seated on his mule.

In a few short minutes the wagon was at the top of the hill. Then April could see why Will had been so cautious. A group of cavalry was slowly riding through a wheat field. Their swords were out, and they were using them to slice through the waist-high wheat. Occasionally, a black man or woman who had been in hiding would jump up and begin to run. They were chased down by men on horseback, tied, and led back to a group that was being assembled.

Will rode back to the wagon. He drew rein and leaned toward April. He took a quick look at the back of the wagon and could see that both Tillie and Ulysses were out of sight, covered up by a lightweight cotton tarpaulin. "It's some of Jenkins's cavalry. They have orders to arrest and detain anyone who looks like a runaway. I suppose they're shipping them south."

"That is horrible. How could you people do such a thing?" April said.

Will bit his lip and looked back at the butternut-clad horsemen. "I don't know who gives an order like that, but there's no excuse for it. We're not here to make war on civilians."

"Unless they are black in color."

"What can I say? It wouldn't be my idea of how an army should conduct itself. But I wouldn't be so high and mighty if I were you. I've seen what your federal troopers do to civilian property in the South, Miss Wolff. There seems to be neither rhyme nor reason to it, only hatred. They looted the homes in Fredericksburg without any intention of carrying anything away. They only wanted large bonfires to show our troops on Marye's Heights what the sight of our burning property looked like. I saw clocks, china, and family portraits torched in the Yankee bonfires, to say nothing of the homes. Frustration will cause a man to do almost anything."

"Including murder?"

Will sadly nodded his head. "Yes, ma'am, I would say that too. It pains me to say it, but it is possible."

Perlman trotted his mule back to the wagon. "It looks bad. I'm not sure we should leave the Wolff woman alone with the two darkies, but I wouldn't want to drag them all over looking for Jenkins."

"Can we find a safe spot to hide them?"

"We might be able to find a place in Chambersburg. The woman's from Pennsylvania and her two Negroes just might get by, providing we can find a sympathetic family to put them with."

"You're not going anywhere without me," April said. "Tillie maybe, but not me."

Perlman tapped Will on the shoulder and motioned him to ride off a few yards from the wagon. He slowly turned the mule around and trotted off, followed by Will. April watched the two men talk. Both of them looked back at her repeatedly, and she wished she could have been a part of the conversation. Will would shake his head, but Perlman seemed to drive home his point by jabbing his index finger in Will's direction. Then Will nodded, and they both rode back to the wagon.

Will looked at her, thinking the situation over. He cleared his throat nervously. "April, we may just have to violate your conscience."

"And just how do you propose to do that?"

"We could say that you're my fiancée from Virginia and that Tillie and Ulysses are your slaves. If they were found, our soldiers wouldn't take your property away from you. They would be safe, providing you are believed."

"But I am a Christian. I do not lie about anything to anyone."

"Your roots are in Virginia."

"Yes, but as to the rest of your passel of lies, I don't know what seems the most repugnant to me, owning slaves or being betrothed to you."

Will smiled and shrugged his shoulders. "It's your conscience we're talking about here, ma'am. You make up your own mind. You either lie, have us do something to allow you to tell the story, or risk having those two being sent back to the South. We could work on making the story sound true."

April glanced back in the wagon where Tillie and Ulysses were huddled together under the tarpaulin. "What would we have to do to make the story true?"

"One way or another, we're going to have to trod on some of your precious toes."

"Just tell me. Don't beat around the bush."

"Do you have a dollar?"

"Yes, I think so. Why?"

"Give it to me."

"Why?"

"Don't argue with me, just do it."

April fished in her pocket and came up with a federal greenback. She handed it over to Will.

He stuffed it in his pocket. "Those two seem to be contraband. As an officer of the army, they are within my rights to dispose of as I see fit. I have just sold them to you, Miss Wolff. So now you are an official slave owner."

April swallowed hard.

Will leaned in her direction. "A little tough for your conscience to take, isn't it?"

"Yes it is. You have no idea."

"Well, you'd better tell them who owns them now so they can get their stories straight."

April leaned back over the seat. "Did you two hear that? I own both of you now."

"We heard it!" Tillie screeched. Her voice was muffled under the tarpaulin. She laughed. "You better takes good care of us, girl."

April turned back to face Will. Her face was flushed with anger.

"Now to the other matter," he said.

"What other matter?"

"You don't want to lie, do you?"

"Of course not. I won't do that."

"Then you have to become my fiancée."

"I won't. I can't do such a thing."

"Suit yourself." Will grinned. His wide smile showed off his teeth. "We could find a preacher and you could become my wife."

"You're an idiot, Major Chevalier. You're an idiot and I'd be one too if I agreed to such a preposterous thing."

"We're playing this by your rules, April. You'd have no reason to be here unless you had some attachment to me. If you and I can't make these people—and the others you're going to find who want to take slaves—believe us, then Tillie and Ulysses will be part of a wagon train heading south. It's all up to you. Either you lie or you do what I tell you to do."

Tillie's voice sounded out from under the tarpaulin. "Go ahead on, you foolish chile. Do what dat man say to do."

"Thank you, Tillie," Will replied. "The voice of reason."

April looked at him, flustered and angry. "All right. All right, blast you. Get it over with."

Perlman laughed. It was more of a roar than a laugh. "Now that's got to be the most eager woman you've ever come across, college boy."

Will leaned over on his horse, closer to April. He swallowed, then forced a smile. April could see Perlman grinning. The man was obviously enjoying this. "April, would you do me the high honor of becoming my wife?"

Tillie threw off the tarpaulin. She sat up in the wagon and put her hands on her hips. "Dat ain't right, boy. I thought you knew womenfolk better dan dat." She shook her finger at him. "You gots to tell the woman some sweet things. Tell her you love her and such like dat."

Perlman laughed even louder, if that was possible. "The woman's got a point there, Major. You thought you were going to have some fun with Miss Wolff's conscience, and now it's your turn to pay the fiddler."

"This is nonsense," April said. "Just get on with it."

"No, it's not nonsense." Will shook his head. His smile had become more subdued, but he still couldn't resist seeing the fun in what he was having to do. "We're just making this easier on your conscience. If you're asked questions, you're going to have to look some people in the eye and tell them your story. When that happens, I don't want you to flinch, not even a little."

"All right. Just get it over with."

Will got off his horse and stepped around the wagon to where April was seated. "April, I love you."

"Oh, stop it."

"Hush up girl," Tillie said. "Let de man say his piece."

Will cleared his throat. "I love you, April, and I want to marry you. Would you do me the high honor of becoming Mrs. Will Chevalier? Would you marry me?"

Tillie beamed, a smile crossing her lips from one end of her face to the other. "Dat was nice, Mr. Will, real nice." She reached out and pushed on April's shoulder. "Now go 'head on, girl. Say yes to de man."

April gave a hard nod. "Yes, yes. Of course I will. Now is that good enough?"

Will grinned in Tillie's direction, then at April. "What about it, Tillie? Did that sound sincere and honest to you?"

"Not by a long shot it didn't. Come on, girl. Make it count. Tell de man you loves him."

"This is ridiculous."

"It's your conscience, April. If it's ridiculous, then you have only yourself to blame."

"Oh, all right." April looked up at him sarcastically. "I love you, Will Chevalier. I would be happy to marry you and become your wife."

"Dere." Tillie cackled and pushed on April's shoulder once more. "Now dat weren't so hard, was it? I been waiting to hear dat for such a long time, gal. You makes me proud."

April settled back into her seat. She forced a smug smile. "I'm sure the major knows how I really feel about him. I can take some comfort in that."

"And now you can also take some comfort in the fact that we've done the things it takes to soothe your conscience. Now we can tell your story and you won't have to confess sin about the matter. Your heart can remain pure as the driven snow."

April grunted at the man. It was a long, low grunt that rumbled deep in her throat.

"Kiss de man," Tillie screeched from the back of the wagon. "Dat'll make it legal like."

Will smiled. "Yes, don't I get a kiss?"

April spit over the side of the wagon. "Not now, not ever."

Will leaned back and looked at the grinning sergeant. "You hear that Perlman? Not ever."

CHAPTER 19

L ights were on in the shops, and the streets of Chambersburg were busy with soldiers coming and going, bundles in hand. The soldiers were spending Confederate scrip, and those who had been in town more than a day were being well fed. Bosworth's smoke shop had opened its doors to sell pipes, cigars, and pipe tobacco, mostly acquired from Cuba. The lights behind the glass were glowing, and written in red paint on the windows were the words TOBACCO—PIPES—CIGARS.

Will was riding next to the wagon on the eastern edge of town. They had already had more than one opportunity to explain the story of Tillie and Ulysses. April had told it very convincingly. With each telling she looked at Will, narrowing her eyes and turning up her nose. She had paid quite a price for having a clear conscience, a price extracted at the cost of her dignity. Her eyes registered the contempt at having to repeat the fact of their engagement, and Will thought it was perhaps an even greater problem for her than claiming to be a slave owner.

Perlman had ridden ahead in the hope of finding a place they might stay, and to listen for news of Lee's and Jenkins's whereabouts. It was some time later when he trotted his mule back down the road east of town. Will recognized him at once. It was hard to mistake Perlman on the back of his mule, even in the evening twilight. The man's legs dangled over the side, and the sergeant's kicks at the animal's sides seemed to unleash a raucous series of brays and bellows.

He pulled up alongside Will and heaved a sigh. "I guess we passed by where Lee is camped, in Messersmith's Woods. Jenkins has gone on to Carlisle with Ewell and Rhodes to join up with Lee there. Appears to me they're getting ready to attack Harrisburg. We could stay here tonight and go on to Carlisle tomorrow. Ewell has already authorized Sinclair's orders for you. He might sign a set of them himself."

"Or he might not. Early may have poisoned the waters."

Perlman nodded. "Yep, he might. And if Ewell refuses you, I don't think it would be a good idea to go over the man's head to Lee."

"Then, sounds to me like we'll be camping in Messersmith's Woods tonight."

"That's the way I figure it too."

"Lee's our best chance."

"Might be our only chance, Major."

Will turned his horse and circled, easing it up next to the wagon. "I hope you ladies don't mind camping again tonight."

"There's no place for us here?" April asked.

"Lee's camped in some woods east of us. If I'm going to get a new set of orders that will allow us to question his general officer staff, then we should try to see the man tonight. The cooperation we get with orders signed by General Lee will make a world of difference. You saw Early's reaction."

"General Lee is a fine Christian man," Tillie said. "He'd be wantin' to help us iffen he could."

"We just have to figure out a way of getting in to see him." Will looked at April. "That is where you come in."

"Me? How do I fit in with seeing Lee?"

Will shot a glance back at Perlman. "The sergeant and I have been talking it over."

"Me?" Perlman burst out with the question. "Don't go dragging me into that woman's wrath, Major. It was your idea, not mine."

"But you agreed it might work."

Perlman put up a hand. "It might, but it was your thinking."

"All right." Will looked back at April. "I didn't think you would mind, especially if it got us in to see the general."

"Mind what?"

"That bucket of blackberries we picked. From what I've heard, General Lee is quite fond of blackberry pie." Will leaned over toward her in his saddle. "I thought if we could prevail upon you to bake the general a pie, it just might get us in to see him."

Tillie pushed April in the back. "You can do dat, girl. Dat man like his pie, you can give him one dat would make his mouth sing."

"You'll have to find me an oven here in town that I can use. I won't bake a pie in the field."

Moments later Will found himself tapping on the back door to Bosworth's smoke shop. The door was opened, and an attractive blond woman in her early forties stood in the doorway. "You will have to go around to the front of the shop," she said. "It's open."

Will took off his hat. He had the bucket of ripe berries in his left hand. "I'm sorry to bother you, ma'am. We're not shoppers."

"Speak for yerself, sonny boy," Tillie screeched.

Will looked back at her. The woman was pounding her corncob pipe in the palm of her hand, a grin on her face. He looked back at the woman in the door. "At least that's not why we're here. Do you have an oven, an oven we might borrow for a short while?"

"I don't understand."

April stepped forward. "We're sorry, but I need to bake a pie."

The woman's eyebrows arched. "It's a long story, ma'am," Will said, "but if we could just borrow your oven, then we'll be gone in no time."

She stepped back into the kitchen. "Come in then. My oven is hot. I was baking brownies." The woman had a thin face, and when she smiled, her mouth opened wide with both sets of teeth forming a tunnel. It was a jack-o'-lantern smile.

The five travelers stomped into the kitchen, Will and Perlman wiping their boots on the back of an iron dog placed by the door for just such a purpose.

Perlman held up the cat. "You think you could spare a dish of milk for the old cat here?"

"I'll see what I can do."

They then wiped their feet on a grass mat. Ulysses wiped his bare feet on the mat. The woman brought a small dish of milk over to the door and set it down. She stepped back to watch Elmer begin to lick it up. She then took April to the cabinets and set her up to wash and prepare the berries. The woman looked back to where the four others stood. "You can go through that door to the shop and look around if you like."

Perlman led the way, with Tillie and Will following. Ulysses stayed behind in the kitchen. The hall wound past a workshop area where a teenage boy was scraping away at a large piece of root with a file. The hall emptied into the store. A number of men in butternut uniforms were mixing and perusing the displays of pipes on a series of racks mounted on the wall. The men bent low, inspecting the pipes, and bobbed up and down like the stream whistles on a circus calliope. Others were lifting the lids from clay jars and smelling the sticks of tobacco and cigars.

A broad-shouldered man with curly black hair, wearing an apron, spotted them. He stepped over to where they were standing. "I'm Bruce Bosworth. Can I help you?"

Will smiled. "Your wife was kind enough to let us use your kitchen."

"You can hep me," Tillie interrupted, holding out her corncob pipe. Her gnarled fingers clutched the thing like a flower freshly picked in the field. "Think you can do better by me dan dis here thang?"

Bosworth took the beaten and burned pipe from Tillie's hand. He turned it over, smiling. "I think we can do better than this almost anywhere in the store. Let me show you something." He handed the old pipe back to Tillie, then stepped over to a display and picked up a small stubby pipe. It was polished and had carvings depicting a man's face around the bowl. He handed it to Tillie.

She held it in her hands, almost as one would hold a rare jewel. Will watched her empty eyes fill with thoughts.

"I ain't never had me a pretty one before." She closed her hand around it and tested the weight. Then she ran her fingers over the man's face in the bowl. "I bet it feels real nice to chomp down on."

"I make my own pipes with the help of my son and daughter. Each pipe is a piece of art to me. I like to take care with each one of them. A pipe is not like a cigar. You don't just use one and throw it away. You care for it and hold it close. In that way, it is like a friend, a warm friend that gives you comfort and doesn't talk back to you."

Tillie smiled and touched the man's face on the bowl. "Dis here would be jes about de first man what didn't do dat to Old Tillie." She cocked her head. "How much you reckon to sell dis here one fer?"

Bosworth smiled. "For you, five dollars, and only because I'd like to see it with someone who would love it. Cash money, though, American."

Tillie handed the pipe back to him. Her smile quickly disappeared. She clutched her corncob pipe tightly.

"I just be to puttin' dat foolish thought outta my head den. Fer old Tillie, five dollars might as well be de moon and de stars."

She turned around abruptly and headed back toward the hall. Will and Perlman watched her as she bumped into a display, felt her way around it, then, with hands feeling the empty space, found the hall.

It was sometime later when the two of them made their way back to the kitchen. April had made three blackberry pies. They sat on a cutting board, cooling off.

"Goodness sake's alive," Perlman said. "They look beautiful."

The Bosworth woman agreed. "They taste good too, I'd bet." Once again she flashed her open-mouth-smile.

April wrapped one of the pies in a checkered cloth, its frayed edges folded over the sides and tickling the crisp, brown, sweetened crust. A light coating of sugar caught the light and sparkled like crushed diamonds. She slid the pie in the woman's direction. "This one's for you, Mrs. Bosworth, for your kindness and hospitality."

"Oh, you don't have to do that. You'll need them."

"These two will be fine." April motioned to Perlman. "You take that one, and Ulysses can carry this one."

Perlman grinned. "With pleasure." He wrinkled his nose, twitching his mustache. "Just the smell alone is worth the trouble."

The woman smiled. "You never did tell me who you were baking these for."

Will held the door open, and April stopped and smiled at the woman. "This pie is for General Robert E. Lee of Virginia."

Will watched the woman's mouth fall open, then he closed the door as the cat and the group stepped out of the kitchen.

After Tillie and Ulysses had settled down in the back of the wagon, Will helped April up. "You give dem pies back here to Ulysses and me," Tillie said. "We'll keep 'em from bumping and jostling around. Don't want dem crusts broke now, does we? And where'd dat cat go to? I done got myself kinda used to cuddling wif him. You know how it is wif a single woman." She turned her head in April's direction. "All dey need is to get used to a little cuddling."

Perlman reached to the ground and scooped up the cat. Then he handed it to Tillie.

Will started to his horse, then turned around. He leaned over the side of the wagon in Tillie's direction, leaning his arms over the side of the wagon in a relaxed manner. "I have something for you."

Reaching down, he fished in his coat pocket and came up with the pipe Tillie had been shown. "It's a new friend."

Tillie's eyes widened to half-dollar size as he pressed the pipe into her hands. "Mr. Will, you didn't."

"I sure did." His smile was soft, looking into her eyes and past them. "I thought you could use it, and then when I saw you holding it, I knew you had to have it." He reached back into his pocket and pulled out a large bag. "And this is a pound of tobacco for you, whiskey soaked for flavor."

"Go on now. Don't you be funnin' me none."

"Smell it for yourself."

Tillie opened the bag and held it to her face. She breathed a deep sigh, her upper lip trembling. She wrinkled her nose as she inhaled deeply. "Dat sure is mighty fine stuff." She lifted her head, arching her thick black eyebrows. "Where'd you get five dollars in Yankee money to spend on the likes of me?"

Will took a glimpse at Perlman. "I happened to come on to five dollars just recently, and I can't think of a prettier lady I'd rather spend it on."

Tillie pushed at him playfully. "You is full o' de nonsense, boy." She turned her head in April's direction. "Dis man is sure gonna spoil some girl."

Will patted her hand. "Right now, I'd just like to spoil you, Tillie."

CHAPTER 20

T he woods east of town were filled with the smell of smoke. Fires lit up the rolling hills, and the shadows of men around them seemed to blend into the trees. Banjo music rattled various tunes, blending with the soft noises of idle men ready at any moment for war. But that evening, war was no more than an idea among the neighing of horses and the snapping of rifles being cleaned and stacked.

April looked up at Will as he rode beside the wagon. The man had taken the time at the pipe shop to shave and brush off his uniform. His buttons, shiny moons that glistened in the growing darkness, were polished. His hat came down to a point that set off his dark eyes. He looked every inch the perfect soldier, with eyes that glared into the darkness and saber that rattled as he rode.

April noticed the small scar on his chin. It was like a nick on an otherwise perfect statue of a Greek god. It curved slightly over the corner of his chin, ending in the middle of his dimple. Something about the small flaw made him seem vulnerable. "The noise of camp," April said. "You must be used to this. You were prepared for this in that school of yours, I imagine."

Will rubbed his hand over his freshly shaved chin, lightly fingering the scar. "I was trained as a child in the fine art of obedience. My school was dedicated to the prospect of training Southerners. Men of the South, you see, possess a simple, magnificent, glowing obsession with all things military. We are taught to love command and authority. As boys we march to church and school, salute flags, train with rifles, and brandish swords, even if they are crude sticks. We snap to attention when a woman drops her handkerchief. It has been my impression that Yankees are trained with ledgers and pens, pouring over long columns of ciphers in search of a profit. But the soul of the South is the long gray line of crisp discipline. The Citadel, in the end, seemed to be a place where the blade of my soul was polished and the rough spots smoothed out. But the sword had been forged long before that, beaten into a sharp saber. Because I am a Southerner, a military school seemed to be the natural place to strangle the last of my innocence. It made me a final gentleman."

"Your father did this to you? He trained you to obey?"

"My father and my mother."

"Your mother?"

"Does that surprise you? It shouldn't."

"I suppose I look on a woman's role as that of a comforter, someone who will be tender and kind. It's hard for me to think of a mother as a disciplinarian, someone who drives a child with a rod."

"My mother is perhaps the most beautiful woman I have ever laid my eyes on. She is well-bred and cultured, like a magnolia blossom one would put in a vase of imported cut glass with vanilla to scent the water. She's a lady, a typical Southern woman of breeding, the type that keeps her talons carefully hidden until it's time to kill. She hides them behind shining eyes and speaks with self-effacing drawls that conceal the steel she uses to rule the family. You remind me of her a great deal, only you have more of your fire on the surface."

"But you love her?"

"With all my heart." He smiled. "I don't hold it against her that she is a Southern woman. All that steel inside helps them survive the tyranny of Southern men who feel more comfortable living with an illusion than a flesh-and-blood woman."

April was intrigued that Will might open up his heart to her. There was a tantalizing sense of mystery to the man. He was like no one she had ever known, and up to this point he had been so proper. There was also a note of fear that rang in her mind. It was very much like the feeling she had as a child on Christmas morning when she untied the string on her gift. She didn't really know what she would find. She knew what she wanted, or she thought she did. She also knew that if what was in the wrapper was something that didn't suit her, she would still have to feign a smile and pretend that it was just what she had wanted all along. She couldn't just walk away and leave it under the tree. That wouldn't do.

Just then she knew that no matter what she discovered about this man who was helping her, it would have to mean her being respectful of his convictions. She wouldn't be able simply to walk away and leave him feeling exposed. What he had said was too emotional for that. He had left himself open and in the raw, and it made her feel slightly uncomfortable.

The other, and perhaps even greater, fear was that he might tell her something that would endear him to her—a mark, a scar of vulnerability like the one on his chin. She knew that if this newfound measure of tenderness managed to tug at her heartstrings, she couldn't just walk away. She would have to run. She hated Will Chevalier's politics and everything he stood for as a man. How could she find a man so attractive and appealing and still hate what was in his heart? He captivated her, but he was dangerous. And he frightened her with his high-minded eloquence at the same time. She was used to talking down to men, not to being challenged by them.

"Your mother must love you very much."

"She loved me as one would love her own soul. You see, I was the chosen champion for that part of her that was too polite to fight. It would never be proper for her to pick up a gun. That was not the way my mother did battle. And so she sent me on to war with her name on my lips. But she won my undying love by going into battle with my father whenever he abused me. It was then that she showed her claws, then that I discovered what war was truly like. War is never found in the sound of shots being fired. It is found in the hot hatred of adversaries who square off at one another knowing that only one will survive. It is a contest of death played out by two people who live with each other and hate every moment of their mutual existence."

April shifted in her seat uncomfortably. There was a note of calm, collected hatred in Will's words that she was not accustomed to hearing in connection with a family. The thought was totally foreign to her. A cold chill in Will's voice ran down her spine. Her hands suddenly became sweaty holding the reins. "Your parents were like that?"

"Yes. Perhaps it's why I understand this war so well. You see, I've lived in a war like this all my life. I've seen and felt the icy silence of days and weeks on end, punctuated by explosions that were well thought out, words that were like daggers. In a way, when I fight for the South, I fight for my mother. This war has become a final explosion of bitterness from the woman who is the South, a bitterness that has been smoldering under the abuse of a tyrant for many years. I hear the patriotic soundings of politicians from your side who want to preserve this union at the cost of blood, and I only see my parents and their marriage."

"But God intends for people to stay together whom He has joined, and He intends this nation to survive intact."

"You presuppose that it was God who joined them. Perhaps it was a woman's desire for comfort or merely survival. It may have been a marriage arranged for them by their parents, or even an adolescent fling based on carnal desire or infatuation. To attribute such things to some edict from above is like calling those lanterns we see over there stars."

"But once it is done, it is done."

"And then it will go on, one who is stronger with greater assets subduing one who will outwardly bow the knee but inwardly hate the oppressor. They will live silently together exchanging icy glances, only to be buried in a churchyard side by side while their children, who know the truth, place flowers on their grave."

"I'm not sure just what you're talking about Will Chevalier, marriage or this war?"

"Perhaps both."

"But divorce is unthinkable for Christians."

"I know, and my parents are very Christian, at least for the public to see at church and parties. And so they will go on, hating the thought of each breath the other one takes and waiting for the final victory when one will stand over the other's grave. The survivor will feel some measure of grief and may even shed a tear. But the joy he or she will feel inside for the final victory will be too much ever to admit to anyone. That is what we're doing in this war. We are attending a funeral of very private joy."

April wiped her hands on her blouse, exchanging one hand on the reins for the other and shifting nervously in her seat. "If you're talking about marriage, Will Chevalier, then I'm glad I never took other people's advice. Since I was fifteen, people have been trying to get me to settle down with a nice man who could make me happy. I've never trusted my happiness to someone else. I've always figured that if I couldn't be happy on my own, I would never be happy with a man."

A broad smile spread across Will's face. "Then you're wise. I don't find too much wisdom in teachers—a lot of knowledge, perhaps, but little wisdom. They talk about places they've never been and things they've never seen."

"I have seen my parents' marriage, and it was a happy one."

April hated the look Will gave her. It was as if he were searching for her soul and had found just exactly where it was hiding.

"Then why aren't you married, April Wolff? Why aren't you breeding cannon fodder for the Yankee army like your neighbors?"

"Because . . ."

"Don't tell me it's because you haven't met the right man. You just told me you didn't need a man to make you happy."

April's brow wrinkled, as if she were trying to force the thought out of her mind. "Women are told they need a man to make their lives complete. My mother was happy, but I never got the idea from her that she felt complete. She always wanted to do something, something more in life. I don't know what that is for me, but I want to find it and do it before I find a man. I don't ever want to be like your mother."

"Then once again, you are wise. My mother is trapped by the expectations of her church and Charleston society. I suppose the pit of hatred and loneliness she lives in is better for her than the unknown feeling of freedom."

April shook her head. "I can't imagine divorce for a woman—the shame."

"And my mother can't force her mind to grasp the freedom. She seems to see misery and unhappiness as part of her Christian duty. My father is her cross, and the more she labors under her marriage to him, the more holy and godly she sees herself."

He slowly shook his head. "I just can't see that God takes any pleasure in our sorrow."

"But He does take pleasure in our duty."

Will held out his ring from the academy. "This is the ring that speaks to me about duty, not a wedding ring."

"I think you're wrong, Will Chevalier. Life is a duty."

"I'm sure my mother would agree. And so she will continue to live in pain and be nurtured by whatever pity I can show her. Marriage is quite a risk in our world. It should only be attempted by people who can't live without each other. It should only be agreed upon by two lovers who are best friends. You must never marry a man you can't respect, no matter what he promises you in the way of comfort. You are a very attractive woman, April. I'm sure many men are willing to endure your tongue just to lie next to you in the wee hours of the morning. But you are wise to remain a single teacher. As for me, I will stay a single soldier."

April straightened her spine and stuck her chin out. "Then we both know what's best for us, being a wise teacher and a wise soldier."

Will laughed, his rolling baritone voice carrying through the trees. "Then does that mean our engagement is off?"

April nodded abruptly. "Just as soon as this mess is over with." April looked at him, studying the man. "You do wear the ring though. You must have some loyalty."

Will held his left hand out to her. "My graduation ring binds me to my polishing. It reminds me not to trust the softness of my heart. I went to the Citadel as a boy, a child, really, and wanted to quit a thousand times. In a way I hate the school and love it at the same time. I hate it for what it did to my soul, and I love it for what it did to my spine. It taught me duty first and last."

"And so you don't care what people even in your own army think, as long as you do your duty."

"No, ma'am, I do not. Most of that comes from being Charlestonian; the rest comes from this ring I wear."

CHAPTER 21

I t didn't take them long to find Messersmith's Woods where Lee had set up camp. Fires blazed, and guards marched in staggered rows of six to eight men. Lights winked in the woods, and the aroma of tobacco mixed with wood smoke and the smell of burning meat. The scent of sizzle filled the air, as fresh beef and ham turned on spits over open fires. Lee hadn't billeted himself in the comfort of a hotel in Chambersburg; he had chosen to sleep with his men on the ground.

Riding on a little farther, the group was confronted by a soldier standing picket duty. The man was large at the shoulders and wore a tattered shirt that sported bright corporal's stripes. His brown beard looked like dirt in the darkness. It was tangled and flew in all directions as if he had taken both hands and scratched it furiously in a vain search for fleas. April guessed that it was no doubt just exactly what the man had been doing. The picket pointed his bayonet at them. "Who goes there?"

"Major Will Chevalier of the provost's office. I have business with General Lee."

The man walked around the wagon, carefully looking over Tillie and Ulysses. He then glanced at Perlman, nodding with a knowing smile. "All right, you follow me, but on foot from here."

They walked in file behind the soldier, through the trees and into the bright circle of a clearing in the woods. A creek flowed through the meadow, musically tripping over rocks and flattening, then meandering through a vast expanse of open grass where horses were feeding. April spotted General Lee's horse. Traveler was as well-known and admired as the general who owned him. The tall gray's ears twitched forward, alert and aware. His big brown eyes followed the group. *Almost like he knows we're here to see Lee,* thought April, smiling. The regal horse reminded her of Will's. Traveler was the one animal in the army that she was sure everyone could recognize, and even though the horse looked remarkably like Will's, he had a regal stature that spoke of royalty.

A number of tents were pitched in single file, and others bent around the pasture like a huge canvas snake. Hanging lanterns painted dirty shadows on the inside of the khaki canvas. Rows of men lay at the feet of arms stacked around the creek bed. Some were trying to sleep while others were playing cards or smoking.

A large tented awning stood in the middle of the camp with fires blazing on either side. Four lanterns were hung at the corners of the large canopy. The dull glow of the flickering light highlighted a number of men standing around one man who was seated at a table. April recognized General Robert E. Lee, who had a reputation for being a thoughtful listener. Everything about the man was rare for a general officer.

"We got us some of the men we need to talk to right here," Perlman said.

Will nodded. He looked at April. "Iverson and Jenkins are there, standing over Lee's shoulder. Jenkins is the man pointing at the map. If I can get Lee's permission to continue this investigation while these officers are in Messersmith's Woods, my job will be easier. There will be a lot less riding for us to do too. That ought to please you."

"Yes, let's hope you can."

Perlman grabbed Will's arm and pointed to a young blond lieutenant standing next to Lee. The man was bending down and pointing to a piece of paper on the makeshift desk. "Hey, don't we know that man?"

Will nodded. "Reynolds. He was at Early's headquarters."

"That Early don't let no grass grow under his feet, does he?"

"It would seem that General Early has more than a passing fascination with this case of ours."

Perlman stroked his beard. "It would appear so. And with this war to fight, you'd think the man had better things to do than obstruct justice."

"The bond among officers of the general rank is strong. You almost get the feeling that they consider the men who wear the stars some sort of blood relative that they're sworn to protect at all costs."

Perlman grinned. "There are a few notable exceptions to that rule, Major, as I'm sure you are well aware."

"I take it you're talking about Jackson and A. P. Hill," Will said.

Perlman could only be alluding to the running feud between Generals Stonewall Jackson and A. P. Hill. Jackson had brought the man up on charges, and it was only Stonewall's death that brought the feud to a halt. Even then, some men had their doubts. Most thought A. P. Hill was vindictive enough to carry the dispute to Jackson's grave.

Perlman nodded. "That I am."

Will grunted. "Hill can only take orders from the mirror. His own image is the only thing he respects."

April noticed that Jenkins had spotted their group. He riveted dark eyes on Will, then once again bent over Lee's map to point.

Will stepped over to the picket. "Corporal, could you tell the general's aide that the provost's office would like a word with General Lee." He glanced back at April. "Also tell him we have a young lady here who has baked him a blackberry pie." Reaching over, he took the pie from April, carefully laying it in the corporal's outstretched hands.

The man grinned, baring yellow teeth that seemed to turn gold in the moonlight. He hefted the pie up and down, testing its weight. "Yes, sir, I surely will now."

Will faced the group. "You might as well make yourselves comfortable. There's no telling how long we'll be here." He smiled at April. "I'm sort of counting on that pie of yours to move this along."

They pulled up a number of barrels and boxes that had been piled near the edge of the fire. Perlman eased Tillie onto a large box marked cheese. "That ought to do you."

She looked up in his direction. "Is you sayin' dis here tar woman is too fat?"

"Why no, ma'am. My mother raised me better than that."

"You better hope she did, Mr. Sergeant Man." Tillie pushed her hand into the pocket of her dirty apron and pulled out the pipe Will had bought her. Opening the bag, which she had refused to even put down, she scooped the tobacco mixture into the pipe. "I ain't got no patience wif men what ought to know better. I don't spect no politeness from Yankee men, but y'all boys what was raised in the South ought to know better."

"We do our best to be gentlemen, dear lady."

Tillie stuck the pipe in her mouth and grinned up at him. "Den you jes go and get old Tillie here a match so's I can rake it on dis here box and light my fine new pipe."

Perlman probed his pocket and produced a match. He handed it over to her, making certain she could feel it. April and Will watched her as she struck the match to life and raked it over the aromatic brown mixture.

She sucked on the pipe, sending up a cloud of intoxicating smoke. "Ehhh . . . dat sure does taste mighty fine."

Will noticed a man who looked like a tramp leaning against a rail fence. His hat was pushed down to his eyes, and he smiled broadly. His arms were crossed, giving him the appearance of terminal smugness. It was an attitude, being from Charleston, that Will had seen many times before. Will stepped over to the man, and April casually followed. "You seem to be enjoying yourself."

The man snickered. "I suppose you might say that. I don't often see majors leading such an unlikely group of people: slaves, mammies, and women. I'd place you as a group headed for a church bazaar."

"We have business with General Lee. What about you? I don't see many tramps at army headquarters."

The man got to his feet. "Well, pardon me." He took his hat off and, in a mocking gesture, swept it to his side in an attempt at formality. "I am Napoleon Batist of Louisiana, late of the stage, but now in the employ of the army of the Confederacy."

Will motioned with his hand to the man's clothing. "I take it this is your uniform?"

Batist grinned and held up the tattered remains of his shirt. "You like it? I've seen more than a few of your men in no more than this." He held up his chin proudly. "Frankly, I consider myself as doing quite well to have what I have. I'm a scout, you know." He leaned in April's direction, widening his grin. "A spy, you might say."

Will frowned. "Some people will do anything to stay out of the shooting war, even act." He started to walk away but turned back to face the man. "By the way, as a spy you could do better."

Batist's mouth dropped open slightly and he lifted his eyebrows. "How is that, sir?"

Will's face beamed, and a sly smile crossed his lips. "Your boots. They're much too nice and new for a man of the open road. They might keep you comfortable, but you won't feel them at all on the end of a rope."

Will and April made their way back to the group. She tugged on his arm. She knew his mind was preoccupied with seeing General Lee and that he might even be a little nervous at the prospect, but there was something she needed to say to him first. "I need to have a few words with you, Major, before you see General Lee."

April watched the men milling around Lee and once again caught sight of Jenkins's glance in their direction. She stepped off into the gloom, away from the fires, and Will followed.

"You're assuming the general will see us. He is a mite preoccupied with the war, you know."

April smiled. "It would seem that I have more confidence in my pie than you have in your office, Major."

"I'm glad of that, because right now my notion of just how important I am is at an all-time low. We may be doing the right thing here, but the war is unfolding and we're no more than a sideshow."

April turned on her heels abruptly and clasped her hands. It was a move of nervousness. She was trying her best to appear to make a bold stand. She held her head erect. "There is something I need to tell you, Major, and I am afraid it cannot wait." She rubbed her hands together.

Will crossed his arms. "What have I done now?"

April felt more than a little embarrassment. Being wrong was not new to her, and admitting when she was wrong was something she saw as a virtue. But Will Chevalier was someone she never wanted to be wrong with. The man was haughty. He saw himself as almost perfect, and to the casual observer, he might even have been right. Where women were concerned, April knew deep down in her heart that the man was far from perfect. It was easy to see how women would cast themselves at his feet, and it was even easier to speculate how he had taken advantage of them. Being one of the groveling herd of females who adored Will Chevalier was the last thing she wanted to be at the moment. "It's not what you've done; it's what I've done."

Will's teeth showed in a broad smile. "I should have known. If I'd done something wrong, you wouldn't have any hesitation in telling me so in front of the world." He uncrossed his arms and gestured her on in a circular motion.

"I just thought that before you talked to General Lee, there's something you should know. I don't want you to make a fool of yourself."

"Well, that's quite a change for you, Miss Wolff. I would think you'd take great pleasure in that."

April bit her lip. This was something she wanted to get over with, and he wasn't making it any easier. "I might under any other circumstance, and I will tomorrow. But not tonight." April shot a quick look back to where Tillie was sitting. "It's about Tillie."

"About her being blind?"

April's eyes widened. "How did you know?" She swallowed. "Did she tell you?"

Will's grin broadened. "No, the sergeant and I spotted it the first night we were together."

"Why didn't you say anything?"

"And spoil this touching little scene of you displaying your humility? I wouldn't do that for the world. Besides, I sort of like it when you think you have something to apologize for. It gets you off that righteous high horse of yours where we can look each other in the eye."

April burned on the inside. "You are barbarous. You may think I'm a silly child or a plaything in a skirt that you can trifle with, but I can assure you that I'm not. I won't be toyed with."

She started to walk away, but Will took her arm and spun her around. "Listen here, Miss Wolff. No matter what you think of me, everything I do is in the best interest of doing this job. I didn't say anything to you for two very important reasons. One, I wanted people to think Tillie was an eyewitness just as badly as you did. I figured it just might make someone say something if they knew they could be confronted with the truth."

He leaned toward her. "Two, I wanted to see just how long it would take for you to trust me, to know I was on your side. I figured if you were holding something back from me, that maybe, just maybe, there might be more in that head of yours that you were keeping to yourself." He pulled her closer. "Now is there? Is there anything else that I need to know?"

"Well, you know we kept runaway slaves." Will was holding her arm tightly, a determination to his grip.

"Yes, another thing you didn't tell me on your own."

"My brother is in the Union army, a cavalry officer."

"What else? Any jealous lovers or suitors your father turned away?"

Her eyes flashed. "Why of course, wagon loads of them. Whole squadrons."

The look of momentary astonishment on his face was delightful, but the audacity of the man still infuriated her.

She pulled away and put her tiny nose in the air. "I don't see where my love life is of any concern to you, Major Chevalier. I handle my own affairs. Who and when I marry will be my own decision. I won't be sold or given away like some heifer."

"And everyone who has ever talked to your father knew that, I take it?"

"If they had their wits they did."

"All of them knew it?"

She knew what Will was getting at. Traditionally, a suitor asked the father for his daughter's hand, not the young woman. Fortunately, April knew that was an arrangement her own father would never have consented to. He never babied her or censored her, and he knew she had her own mind. But now he was dead. No man had ever understood her as her father had. Grief sliced through her like a knife. Her throat tightened with the effort to control tears that this Southern soldier could never understand. The Wolff home was far from customary. The only exception might be if someone was so preposterous a match that April would be offended or even amused at the notion. If such a would-be beau had been someone close to the family, her father might have concealed the matter. There would be no need to poison April's mind to a man whom she saw frequently. "I'm sure they did," she lied.

Will was watching her closely, waiting patiently. He tried to look into her eyes, but she intently looked away from him. "Well, Miss Wolff, if there should come a time when you're not so sure all of them did, will you be so kind as to tell me?"

April walked back and Will followed. If she had known what was going to happen, the guilt she already felt would have been too much for her to bear. She had concealed the facts, and covering up the truth might prove deadly.

CHAPTER 22

T he crickets in the field began to sing, followed by the hoarse croaking of frogs from the edge of the creek. There was a melody to the night, with men playing banjos and harmonicas, some humming and singing. Fires hissed and crackled as the flames bit into the green wood.

The card games being played were all at a safe distance, away from Lee's notice. Everyone knew the general was opposed to cards or anything that might cause the Almighty to look unkindly on his army. Lee was the type of man who saw God's blessing as something more valuable than cannons. Others might call the strike of lightning luck. Not Lee, however. Providence went to the pious, not to the well-equipped. Where the Union army had the vast supply of arms, equipment, and manpower on their side, Lee wanted to make certain that the blessing of God was in ample supply in the Army of Northern Virginia.

Will watched as the men vying for Lee's attention took their turns. The braid and polished brass buttons on their uniforms shimmered in the lamplight. Their tunics were brushed, and the hair on their heads shone with oil. For some of them it might be their only chance to impress the man the troops called Marse Robert.

The corporal slid up to a tall officer who Will imagined was Lee's aide, tugged on the man's sleeve, passed on Will's message, and then handed him the pie. The colonel turned and glanced back in their direction, carefully studying them. He was assigned to keep Lee from being pestered, and no doubt he took his job very seriously. Sharp dark eyes and a close-cropped beard set off the colonel's angular face. The pie was a godsend, however. The colonel looked awkward holding it, as if he weren't quite sure what to do with it. He turned and waited until Lieutenant Reynolds had finished talking, then stepped over to where Lee was seated and put the pie down in front of the general. Leaning over the table, he said a few words. Everything depended on the general's response, and Will knew it.

Reynolds marched back from the gathered staff in Will's direction. His actions were efficient; he was evidently on his way to making captain as rapidly as possible. He twitched his blond mustache, faking a smile, then brushed the swooping curve of hair that had fallen over his forehead. "Nice to see you again, Major Chevalier."

"You sure of that?"

The young lieutenant fingered his polished buttons nervously, as if to reassure himself that he was still in the army. His blue eyes reflected the firelight in their depths. "I didn't know I'd see you here." He eyed Tillie and April. "And this is your witness, I take it?"

Will looked down at Tillie. "You'll find that out at the court-martial, Lieutenant."

"Is that so? And what makes you think there will be a court-martial?"

"Justice, my passion for justice."

Reynolds chuckled. "I'm afraid not everyone in this army shares that desire with you, Major."

"They should, Lieutenant. It's why we're fighting this war. There may be a few brass diapers like you who hope to gain glory and the hand of some proper woman at home, but most of us just want to survive this war with dignity and a little justice. You be sure to tell her of your gallantry as Jubal Early's errand boy. That ought to impress her. How you led the charge against a woman whose father had been murdered. It will no doubt make her very proud."

Will's words brought a flush of anger into the man's face. He tightened his chin, his mustache drooping straight down the sides of his mouth. "If you will excuse me, Major. I need to return to my command."

Will spoke to Reynolds's back as he turned to walk away. "Tell General Early that I will be around to see him with new orders, ones that he dare not tear up. Tell him I will want to question him as well." He watched as the man took several paces. "See you at the court-martial Lieutenant."

April stepped up to Will. "Talk about my sharp tongue, Major. You seem to delight in it as a sport."

He grinned sheepishly. "I suppose we'd make quite the pair after all."

"No, in a man a sharp rebuke is admired. Women, however, are supposed to quietly paw the ground with a toe and bat their eyes. We're supposed to be more wily in our confrontations. It's sad, really. I find male honesty so much more efficient. Why do you suppose men can't tolerate that in women?"

Will laughed. "Maybe it's just the farm boys you've known. Personally, I like a woman who has a mind and speaks it. Why would I want to spend more than an hour with a woman who can't think? Or worse, one who played silly games in order to make her point? No, ma'am, give me a woman who speaks her piece." His dark eyes danced. "There are times when knowing where I stand is of utmost importance."

April laughed, enjoying his witty comebacks. "Then I take it you've spent some time with women on an hourly basis."

Will chuckled, a smile spreading across his face. "The indiscretion of youthful stupidity, I'm afraid. Frankly, any time with such a woman is almost a waste."

"Almost?"

"Yes, almost. Of course, in spite of how you may think, I do enjoy my time with you, Miss Wolff. You and your moral high horse."

April noticed that Reynolds had stopped by one of the fires to sip a cup of coffee. He was staring at them. "He doesn't like you, does he?" April asked.

"He fears me, and I like that. I'd just like to know why."

It was only a matter of minutes before Lee's aide made his way through the group of officers and stepped over to where Will was seated. Will and Perlman got to their feet and stood at attention. "I am Colonel Charles Marshall, General Lee's military secretary. I understand you want a few words with the general?"

"Yes, sir."

The man looked at April and smiled. "And you must be the lady who baked the pie for the general."

"Yes, I am."

The man nodded. "Any hint of home is much appreciated by General Lee." He glanced back in the direction of the officers. The meeting was slowly breaking up. General Iverson stepped off into the darkness, and Jenkins paused for a last word and then mixed with a group walking toward one of the cooking fires. "I think he can spare you a few minutes now."

Will and April followed the man through the group of officers under the awning. Lee had gotten to his feet and was talking to several officers who remained behind. His hands were clasped behind his back, and he was pacing back and forth behind the makeshift table that was serving as his desk. Will couldn't help but overhear the man.

"We must have General Stuart. An army cannot afford to go into battle blind. I simply do not know where the enemy is to be found and in what strength. How can I be expected to know that without Stuart?"

"We have Jenkins and his cavalry, sir," one of the officers said.

Lee cleared his throat and rocked back and forth. "The man has his limits."

Will stood to attention in front of Lee's desk and saluted. He was beginning to feel like an intruder, overhearing things that he shouldn't.

Lee waved away the salute. "Be at ease, Major." He looked at April and began to button the brass buttons on his coat, trying his best to look presentable. "And you must be the dear lady who baked me this pie." He smiled. "It is my favorite, you know."

"I'm glad, General."

"This is Miss April Wolff, General," Will offered.

"I am pleased to make your acquaintance, my dear." He looked down at the pie. "And more than pleased to make the acquaintance of your berry pie." Lee turned to one of the officers standing next to him. "Get me three plates and some utensils and chairs for these people." He smiled. "The Bible says that it's right for the ox who grinds the grain to share in it."

It took only moments for the men to gather up the necessary forks and plates and to provide chairs for Will and April. Will pulled April's chair back and seated her, then took his own chair. Lee waited until April had taken her seat before placing himself in the chair across from the two of them.

"Now why don't you cut our pie, Major, and explain the nature of your business."

Will picked up the knife and began to cut. "I was assigned by General Ewell to try to find the murderer of Miss Wolff's father. Unfortunately, my orders were torn up. It would seem that only a set of orders signed by you will allow me to interrogate the officers that I need to question."

"I am very sorry to hear about your father, Miss Wolff. It must be a great loss to you."

"Thank you, General. He was a wonderful man."

"I'm quite sure he was, to have raised such a thoughtful daughter." He looked at Will, his calm eyes carefully studying him. "And you have reason to believe that this matter is one that belongs to the Army of Northern Virginia?"

"We have a witness, General, and I am afraid our suspects are general officers in our army." Will dished out pieces of the pie onto the three plates and passed one to April.

"I have just received a report on this matter, not ten minutes ago."

"By General Early, I'm sure."

"Yes, as a matter of fact."

"I am not quite certain how to tell you this, General, but we have reason to believe that General Early is protecting someone. There is further evidence that he may even be involved in the incident himself."

Will took his first bite as he watched Lee think the matter over and take a bite of his own. "General Early is the one who tore up my orders from General Ewell."

Lee balanced his second bite on his fork and looked at April. "This is wonderful, Miss Wolff. I had forgotten just how much I missed it. There have been times when I thought I should never be reminded of what it was like to be home. It is something like this that reminds a general not to grow too fond of war."

"You do remind me of my father in some ways, General. He hated war and everything it stood for. He saw it as unchristian for men to vent their meanness and hatred with a gun."

Lee studied her eyes deeply. His look, an expression of kindness marked by intelligence, was one that could melt into her very heart. "War is the cruelest of man's invented sins. I do hate it, Miss Wolff. I hate it with all my heart." He looked at Will. "I have heard reports on you, Major. You seem to be quite zealous."

"Overly zealous is what you have heard, I'm sure, General."

"Is that possible, Major?"

Will leaned forward. "General, I was raised to do my duty. That is all. That is all a man can and should do."

Lee smiled. "And this matter of great embarrassment has become your duty."

"Yes, sir. One that I did not seek."

Lee nodded. "I can understand that, Major. I am performing a duty that I hate, one that I have done everything possible to shy away from. It was given to me by God, and to resist my duty is to resist Him. That I will not do. That is why I want this war over with as soon as possible. I am quite certain you can understand that, Major. You seem to have inherited an unpleasant task along with me."

"Yes, sir. Very unpleasant."

Reaching over, Lee slid a piece of paper in front of him and picked up a pen. He dipped it into a well of black ink. "Major, I am going to issue your orders personally. I want you to help this dear woman and find justice for her. There is so little of it available in this nation of ours these days. We must do what we can to provide it."

He began to scribble his orders on the paper, writing rapidly with a great flair. Signing his name at the bottom, he shook it and blew on the ink. He then folded it and passed it across the table to Will. "Here, Major. I wish you Godspeed."

Will and April got to their feet. "Thank you, General."

"Don't thank me. I have just made you some powerful enemies, and a large group of your fellow officers will resent your intrusion into their lives and their command." He pointed to the paper. "You will see, however, along with anyone you show those orders to, that I expect a full report from you, complete with the names of those who refuse to cooperate. We are not here as conquerors to abuse the law. We are here to gain our freedom, not to take what does not rightfully belong to us."

April reached over and put her hand on Lee's. "I am very sorry we are fighting you, General. If I could change that, I would."

"So would I, my dear, so would I."

When Will and April rejoined Perlman, the orange-and-white tomcat was curling himself around the man's legs, weaving in and out. The cat stopped and looked up at her, almost expecting her to speak. April peered out across the camp. "Where is Tillie?"

Perlman shrugged his shoulders. "Ulysses and her took a little walk. I don't know where they went off to."

April grabbed Will's arm. A pained expression was on her face. "We have to find them. If your people stick them in a wagon heading south, I'll never forgive myself—and I'll never forgive you."

Will pointed to Perlman. "You'd better take her and look through the camp. I'll go off in the direction of the wagon. They might have gone back that way."

CHAPTER 23

P erlman watched Will fall in behind a squad of four men and then disappear into the gloom. He stood with his hands on his hips, feeling somewhat disgusted. He didn't much like being stuck with April. This was Will's job. Chevalier was the ladies' man. He had the smooth talk. As far as Perlman could tell, he even liked the woman. April Wolff was mouthy, and he wasn't certain just what he could say in response. Women were far from being his specialty. The fact was, most men doubted he'd even had a mother.

He resolved to just be what he was, a policeman who got stuck in the army. He'd say whatever was on his mind and let the devil take the hindmost. "I wouldn't worry if I was you, Miss Wolff. They probably just wandered off to get something to eat. We'll find them. Just leave it to me. You better let me do the talking, though. You're a Yank, and a woman at that. You stay close to me."

"What does that have to do with it?"

Perlman fixed his eyes on her. "I gotta tell you, ma'am, war is about the most immoral place there is. Men get real edgy about women when they're about to go into battle. Lots of men just want their mothers. You'd be pretty safe with them. But some want to touch something soft, and they don't much care who or what it is. We don't have many camp followers in this army. Marse Robert don't allow it. But ever once in a while one will sneak in, hoping to ply her trade." He looked out on the camp full of men. "I just don't want you getting separated from me and having somebody trying to force their way with you. Not that it would happen, mind you, but you just might get asked. So you stay close to me."

April took hold of his sleeve. "You don't much like me, do you, Sergeant?"

Perlman nervously brushed the beard on his chin with the back of his hand. "I wouldn't say that, ma'am."

"Then what would you say?"

"You make me uncomfortable."

He shuffled his feet, disturbing the big cat who'd draped himself across the toes of his boots. The animal meowed in protest and glared up at April as if she were responsible.

"Why would I make you feel uncomfortable?"

"Ma'am, I ain't like the major. I've never had much dealings with women. I don't much like feeling responsible for one. That's all."

"Well, you needn't worry about me, Sergeant. You just take care of Elmer, and I'll take care of myself."

Perlman cocked his cap to the side. "Then stay with me. Don't go to wandering off."

April nodded, touched somehow by the plaintive look on his homely face. "I will."

Jacob had a sense of relief with her agreement. Women had always worried him, which was why he was a confirmed bachelor. A man like him needed as little to worry about as possible. With his job, he needed all of his mental capacity to think about what needed to be done next. He didn't need to worry about a wife who would complain about a policeman's late hours or a pack of kids running around to make him feel guilty about not having enough time for them. He liked his life simple. No wife. No children. No dogs. Just one big tabby cat who could take care of himself and provide an occasional snuggle when it suited the animal. In some ways Jacob Perlman saw himself as similar to the cat: shrewd, cunning, a creature of the night, and fiercely independent. He reached down and picked up the big cat, cuddling him under his arm. "We'll just go through the camp and see if anybody's seen them. Maybe we can get some cream for Elmer along the way."

They began to walk down the line of reclining men. Men in gray were sprawled over the ground. A few were darning socks. Some were finishing what little dinner they had left, wiping their hands and jumping to their feet when April got close. The sight of April was more than enough to cause men to sit up. Many jumped to their feet. Some bowed. All smiled. Perlman looked over each group they passed, repeating the same question. "Did you see a pair of darkies come this way?" Each time the question brought a shaking of the men's heads.

Perlman set the cat down on the ground. The tabby was all too happy for the attention he got. He wound in and out of the men's legs, stopping for occasional back rubs and sidling himself up to anyone who had a morsel of meat left to give. For many men the sight of some living thing that didn't have a uniform on was an occasion. They fondled the cat, picking him up and passing him around. After a while, all the attention got to be too much even for the old tom to take. He slithered away from one pair of hands and pranced off through the ranks of outstretched feet.

Perlman chuckled. "Sometimes a little loving can go a long ways—for anyone. Folks get used to being alone; they want to stay that way forever."

"Do you want to stay alone?" April asked.

Perlman thought the question over. It was something he'd pondered from time to time. "I just am alone, that's all. I think for most single people, they make decisions to be by themselves early on, and after that the decision makes them. They just are alone and that's it."

Perlman looked April over. This was a woman who shouldn't remain by herself for long. She was pretty, very pretty, and smart too. But he got the feeling there was loneliness underneath all that bravado. Maybe it was grief. After all, she'd just lost her father in a horrible way. But his policeman's instincts told him something else. He sensed something oddly familiar. A solitary soul himself, he'd long ago learned to live with reduced expectations. After all, he was homely. Had been even as a boy. What few women had wanted him, he hadn't wanted back. He could live with that. It suited him. But April, he felt, wasn't comfortable with the solitary life. Jewels need the right setting, he remembered someone saying once. Until then, they're just rocks.

April spotted a wagon at the edge of the camp and started toward it. Perlman lunged forward to catch up with her. "Where you going?"

"I think that's our neighbor over there." She shook her head. "I don't know why he'd be here."

He followed April over to the wagon where a young man was selling things out of boxes. He stood under six feet and his brown hair hung down from a slouched black hat. He was thin with a scrawny neck, and he wore brown pants, a red checked shirt, and hobnailed boots that had no black on them at all.

"Tommy," April shouted. "Tommy Slocum."

The young man looked over the heads of the men who were standing in front of him and saw her. He frowned and looked away. Bending down, he continued selling. Several soldiers were buying ears of corn and slices of ham. Two of the men were passing around a jug of what appeared to be corn liquor.

April squeezed her way in between the men. "What are you doing here, Tommy Slocum?"

He jumped down from the back of the wagon, forcing a smile. He seemed nervous. "I'm making money, that's all. I'm doing what Daddy done told me to do."

He reached out and snatched the jug of liquor from the hands of a man who was taking more than he had paid for.

"You're not taking their money, are you? It's worthless, you know."

Tommy waved his hands at the men standing around. "That's all for now. Come back in a little bit, and I can sell you more. Just find some hard type money I can use."

As the men mumbled and walked away, Tommy bent his head and smirked. "I ain't taking their paper stuff. Daddy won't let me. Sides, I ain't stupid, you know." He reached back into the wagon and pulled out a box. "I'm taking gold and silver, just hard money."

He shook the box. Perlman could see that it contained coins along with an assortment of silver spoons, knives, and forks and some larger serving spoons. All the flatware was worth something. Perlman also spotted the brass buckle and leather belt that held up the boy's pants. It was a union buckle that had been turned upside down. Many of the troops used captured buckles just like it. It was meant to read US but when turned upside down, it read SՈ. The Confederate troops said it stood for Southern Nation, not United States.

"You hungry?" Slocum asked.

April glanced back at Perlman. "Yes, we are a bit hungry."

The boy pulled a long knife from behind his belt and turned around to cut the ham. He cut four or five clean slices and turned back with them balanced on his obviously dirty hand. He held the meat out. "Take this, then. It's good stuff, smoked in our smoke-house." His smile widened. "You don't even have to pay me for it."

April picked up the ham and handed several of the slices over to Perlman. She bit off a piece. "I just didn't imagine your father making a profit from the war."

"He says it's here and we're here. He figures to make up this-a-way for things taken what don't belong to people, I reckon."

"And so you come into camp masquerading as a Southern sympathizer," Perlman said. "But all you're doing is peddling your goods."

"Don't blame me, mister. I'm just doing what Daddy tells me to do. He sets the prices. I just sell things."

Perlman chewed the ham. No matter how dirty Tommy Slocum's hands were, the meat tasted wonderful. He spotted the cat circling a group of soldiers, and he crouched down, tearing off a piece of the meat. He held it out and the tabby trotted over to him and began to nibble.

"I am sure glad to see you, April. Wait till I tell Daddy." Slocum took off his hat, his hair falling down into his face. He brushed it aside. "I got me something I needs to tell you. I ain't none too proud of it either. I didn't know you was going to be here. I did see—"

"I just can't get over you visiting Confederate troops with food to sell," April interrupted. "It sounds almost immoral."

Slocum shook his head. "Daddy says ain't nothing wrong with it. He says the men need food and we got some. He says it's biblical to be thrifty with what we got and make a profit. You remember the Bible story about the talents, don't you?"

"Of course I do."

"Daddy says it's just like that. God gives us stuff, and He expects us to make a good return on it. That's all. Daddy says it's in the Bible."

"I'll have to have a talk with your father when I see him."

The boy rocked back and forth on the balls of his feet. "You do that. I think he wants to talk to you too."

"About what?"

Slocum smiled. "You know."

"No, I don't know."

"I best let him tell you then. It's about you and me and what's going to happen to you now."

"I don't see that's any of your father's concern."

Slocum grinned. "He thinks it might be. I'll have to let him tell you, though. It's a secret." He held a finger up to his lips and hushed as if quieting a child. "It's a big secret I ain't supposed to talk about to you. He'd whip me if I did." His grin turned to a sudden frown. "But I needs to tell you 'bout something else, somethin' I should have told you before."

April shook her head. "I'm not really interested. I'm certainly not going to make you do something that would give you a whipping."

The boy's Adam's apple bobbed as he took a hard swallow. "I sure am glad to hear that. You know how bad I is at keeping a secret."

"Yes, I recall."

"We had better keep up our search," Perlman said.

April started to turn away, then looked back at Slocum. "Have you seen Tillie and Ulysses? They seem to be missing."

The boy's eyes widened, and he shook his head vigorously. "They ain't bought nothing from me tonight." He called out after April as she turned to walk away. "I didn't sell them anything. I really didn't."

Perlman picked up the cat and walked off after April. He glanced back at the boy. "He didn't exactly answer your question."

April looked back at where Slocum was standing, still watching them. "I'm surprised he could make sense out of anything. That's one of the reasons I'm so shocked his father would send him here to sell anything. I'd expect him to sell his entire wagon for a few brass buttons. The boy thinks with great difficulty. He's really about my age. We played together as children. The only problem is, his body grew up but his mind didn't."

Perlman stopped. "Maybe he didn't send him."

"What do you mean by that?"

"Just a thought. Either the boy took off on his own or maybe the old man is here with him."

CHAPTER 24

Will softly made his way through the woods. The moon was like a dinner plate in the dark sky. There was a sparkle to it, like elegant bone china when first pulled from a sink of soapy water, squeaky clean with warm soapsuds sliding over the surface. The soft light filtered through the trees, fingering its way through the branches overhead and curling around the limbs. The moonlight covered the leaves and twigs on the ground with a cool, pale glimmer.

He had left the marching men just moments before stepping into the woods. Like most men in camp, they were full of talk, and right then Will just wanted to listen to the quietness of the trees.

He had sent Perlman and April through the camp looking for Tillie and Ulysses, but he really didn't think they would have gone that way. Escaped slaves would find greater comfort in the darkness than they would in a noisy camp full of rebel soldiers. Walking through the camp by themselves would be much too risky. There was still the feel of master and slave between the races, a haunting sensation of the whip and chain. Will knew that such thinking was ridiculous, but Tillie and Ulysses would feel it nonetheless. The sight of Jenkins's cavalry rounding up blacks had been enough to open the wounds of slavery for both of them. No doubt they had felt uncomfortable in camp, even with Perlman standing right next to them. The darkness might be the only place they could go to ease their minds.

He walked toward the meadow and stood watching the horses crop grass. He could see them standing, their heads bobbing up and down as they fed, their flat teeth making a dull, grinding noise. Some horses walked from place to place, sampling what was near the water. Others moved to the creek to drink long, slow gulps. Will could see three riders circling the horses, weaving in and out of the trees. The men lazily sagged in their saddles, almost falling asleep.

Will knew at once that the scene was much too peaceful for Tillie and Ulysses to be wandering about. The woman was far too noisy, and that would cause the horses to pick up their heads, to say nothing about the pipe. The aroma would carry. They had to be deeper into the woods, unless they had gone back to the wagon.

He turned and walked toward the road, to the spot where they had entered the camp and left the wagon and their mounts. The sentries would still be in place and other men walking picket duty. Perhaps the officer in charge would know something about them. Security around Lee's camp was just too good to allow people to roam about unchallenged.

A few minutes later, he hit the road and stood for a moment. The light of the moon made the orange dirt underfoot glow with borrowed warmth. As he walked up the road, he spotted two of the pickets. They stepped forward from where they had been leaning against a tree and snapped to attention.

"Good evening, gentlemen."

"Evening, sir."

The men clutched their rifles in front of them, the straight shafts of the barrels running up the edge of their buttons and parting their faces in half. One of the men had dainty fingers, almost like a child's. He squeezed the rifle to get a better grip. "At ease, men."

Both men eased their rifles to their sides. Their bodies relaxed. They were no more than boys, probably not more than sixteen. It was why they had stood at panicked attention upon the approach of an officer. "I'm looking for two slaves. One is an older woman and the other is a young man. Have you seen them?"

Both men shook their heads. "We ain't seen nothing pass in front of us. Can't say fer sure what's gone on behind us."

The boy had a harelip that quivered as he spoke, and his words had a slight whistle to them. His blond hair fell down his face and the sides of his head, like a haystack mashed down under a gray tarpaulin. His sharp nose and beady eyes made him look like a hairless squirrel.

"If you see them, hold them for me. Don't send them back to camp. Just keep them here with you."

"Yes, sir."

Will walked off down the road, leaving the two young privates looking at each other in a state of semiattention.

Moments later Will rounded a curve in the road and saw the wagon. Perlman's mule and his horse were still standing where they had tied them. He walked up to the wagon and looked over the side. It was empty. The tarpaulin Ulysses and Tillie had been hiding under was missing.

As he stepped around the wagon, he heard a deep, hoarse growling noise, like wet rocks grinding together. He cocked his head in the direction of the sound. The corner of the missing tarpaulin was peeking out from between the wheels. He stooped over, and there beneath the wagon was a mound that could only be Tillie and Ulysses, huddled under the khaki canvas. "All right, come on out. It's me." He waited a moment. "You hear me, Tillie. I said, come on out."

A small flap of the tarpaulin was pushed back, and one shiny dark eye peered at him. "Iz dat you, Mr. Major Man?" It was Ulysses. He pushed his head out like a turtle sleepily awakening from a long snooze. The man's flat nose was covered in dirt, and his big eyes sparkled. "It's jes me. Tillie ain't here."

"Well, come on out from there and show me where she is. Why are you sleeping under there?"

"I's scared people be coming by, so I hid myself under dis here wagon. Must'a gone to sleep." The big man kicked at the tarpaulin, bouncing it from underneath the wagon with his bare feet. He clubbed his elbows on the ground swinging his hips from side to side. Planting his hands under his chest, he drew himself up from the belly of the wagon like a snake shedding his skin.

"Why did you two leave camp?"

Ulysses shook his head and began to beat some of the dirt off his pants. "I wasn't none too happy back dere. I told Tillie I gots to get out and make my way back to dis here wagon. She said she wanted to come wif me."

"Well, where is she?"

"I left her down by de creek. She was smoking on dat pipe you gots fer her. Said I was to come back and gets her after you done gots back to the wagon."

"Then why don't you take me to her. April and the sergeant are looking for her. We can't leave until we find her."

"Yes, suh. I'll take you to her."

Ulysses walked across the road and into the trees and then broke into a slow, gliding run. He had a loping trot and picked his feet up when they hit the bare branches on the ground, allowing them to remain only a split second. Will jogged along behind him, his boots snapping twigs and crushing leaves. They headed down the slope of the hill and toward the creek and the meadow beyond.

When they reached the edge of the creek, Ulysses stopped. He swung his head from side to side, surveying the trees. Looking back at Will, his eyes widened. "She was here when I done left her." He walked around in a circle, waving his arms. "About here."

"You sure you have the right place?"

"Yes, suh. I is sure." He pointed to a tree, mangled and blackened by lightning. "I remembers dis here tree."

"Why did you leave the road?"

Ulysses began to nervously slap his arms back and forth, fending off mosquitoes. "We done started back on de road, we shore nuff did. Dere was some o' dem white soldier men what was following us, some men dat come outta dat time under de big tent. So we cut off through de woods down here. We figured to circle round and come up on the wagon dis-a-way."

"She couldn't have gone far. The woman's blind." Will stepped over in Ulysses's direction. "Let's just make a wider circle. She's got to be here someplace." He lifted his hands to his mouth and called out. "Tillie! Tillie! Where are you, Tillie?"

Both men turned around, straining to hear the woman's voice. There was nothing, only silence.

"Maybe we should go down to the creek. She might have gone there for water."

"Yes, suh. She might have done just dat."

The two of them walked down to the creek. It was bubbling over the rocks and flattening out as it surged through the meadow. The light from the moon created a glare over the dark water, kissing it with bright footsteps. One of the riders Will had seen earlier rode up. "Who goes there?"

Will stepped up to the edge of the creek. "Major Will Chevalier of the provost's office. Have you seen an old black woman? We're looking for her."

"No, sir. I ain't seen nothing tonight."

"The woman's blind. She would be hard to miss."

The man shook his head. "Ain't seen her, but I'll keep an eye open."

"Thank you. We'll just keep searching."

Will and Ulysses moved upstream, in the direction of the camp. "You move uphill a ways, Ulysses. I'll stay down here by the creek."

"Yes, suh. I shore will."

Will tracked through the grassy mud, watching the creek up ahead. He danced through the soft ground and onto a flat rock beside the creek. Up on the slope, he could hear Ulysses calling out for Tillie in a soft voice. It was troubling. The woman's blindness wouldn't prompt her to wander too far, especially in unfamiliar territory. He had heard how the blind could remember the obstacles found in their own homes and even make it appear as if they had sight. Tillie had certainly given a good impression in her own kitchen. This was different, however. There were no walls to give her a sense of orientation. She could roam in any direction, but why would she? Will hadn't been concerned about her while she was with Ulysses, but now he was growing more worried by the minute.

They both made their way to a point below the camp. As far as Will was concerned, this would be the last place the woman would go. Troops came down to the creek there for water, and after all, the reason she and Ulysses had left the camp in the first place was to get as far away from the rebel troops as possible.

Suddenly he heard the sound of April's and Perlman's voices. They were calling out for Tillie and heading his way. He could see them in the moonlight. Perlman had a flaming torch in his hand, and April was below him, walking along the edge of the creek. He bent low and could see the outline of April's dress. He saw something else up ahead as well. It was a small huddled mass in the moonlight. It turned in his direction and its eyes flashed. It was Perlman's cat.

Will stepped softly through the grass in the direction of the cat. It looked at him and hissed.

"Take it easy, cat. It's me, the man who helps to feed you. What're you doing so close to the water anyway?"

He stepped forward and what he saw made his blood run cold. The cat was standing on a body lying facedown in the water, and even from where he stood, Will could tell that it was Tillie. Her feet and legs were on the bank of the creek, and the upper part of her body was in the shallows.

Taking several steps to where the woman lay, Will shooed the cat from her body. He crouched down and took hold of her hips, dragging her up to the bank. He turned her over. The woman's eyes were open, staring deeply into space. Her body was still warm. She was dead, but hadn't been for long. He might have just missed being here when it counted the most.

Lifting his head, Will shouted to Ulysses. "I found her. She's down here." He looked off to where April and Perlman were still making their way down the stream. "Over here!" he shouted. "I found her. She's over here."

It took Ulysses only moments to run down to the bank. He stood and watched as April and Perlman ran up to where Will had cradled Tillie in his arms. April stepped forward. "Is she . . ."

"Yes," Will said, "She's dead. Don't come any closer. Not just yet."

April began to cry.

"Here, hand me that torch. But don't step in the mud."

Perlman reached over and passed Will the torch.

He laid Tillie down gently, getting to his feet. Stooping down, he passed the torch over her.

"Any signs of wounds?" Perlman asked.

"Not that I can see."

"Then how?" April's voice cracked as she tried to ask the question all of them were thinking. She broke into a sob.

"It would appear that she drowned." He held the torch high. "Back up, all of you. I want to get a look at the ground here."

They all backed up as Will stepped back, waving the torch over the ground. Scuffle marks cut deep into the mud near where Tillie lay. He could see deep boot prints and the marks of Tillie's shoes in the mud. Bending down, he lifted her feet, first one, then the other. They were caked with fresh red mud. It came over the tops of her shoes and up to her ankles.

He heard the sound of Perlman as the man walked out into the middle of the creek.

"Major."

Will looked up.

Perlman was standing in the middle of the creek. The dark water was flowing around his boot tops. "I'd say if that woman drowned in this creek, she had to have some help. A child couldn't drown in here."

Will nodded. "She had some help, all right. The man, or men, wrestled with her on the bank. They probably had their hand over her mouth and then dragged her down to the water. I'd say they held her head under."

April collapsed to her knees in the mud. "It's all my fault. I made her the eyewitness, and now she's dead. All because of me."

Ulysses stepped closer, shaking his head. "Den it had to be somebody what didn't know Tillie was blind."

Perlman tracked out of the water. "Not necessarily," he said. "It might just be someone who knew what a good witness she was, someone who knew her very well."

The
FIGHT

CHAPTER 25

They buried Tillie in the Cashtown cemetery. Cashtown was a small place, not unlike many of the towns in central Pennsylvania. There was a general store, a post office, and a boarding house that served as a hotel. The store had a bar that was nothing more than planks of wood stretched over two barrels. There were plenty of trees, however, and a small church surrounded by an old cemetery dotted with listing and weathered markers. There was also a section of ground dedicated to casualties of the war. The earth was soft there, and the graves fresh. Tillie would have liked the place. Her plot was out back of the main area reserved for families. It was a spot set aside for former slaves and those with no home or family.

A local farmer with a short blond beard dug and maintained the graves. He was broad at the shoulder and even broader around the middle. His dirty red-and-white striped shirt was pulled out of his trousers, giving him the appearance of a walking circus tent. A faded slouched hat was pulled down to the tops of his brown eyes. He leaned against his shovel.

It was early. Dawn was breaking over the hills east of town. Dogs barked in the distance, and smoke rose from several chimneys in light airy puffs that meant breakfast coffee was being prepared. Cashtown was taking its first morning yawn. Normally it was not the time of day for a funeral, but this was not an ordinary funeral.

The church was a white, boxlike structure with a steeple trimmed in red. The cross on top was worn, but sparkled with fresh white paint that someone had risked life and limb to apply. The windows were long and narrow with red shutters. There was a lonely silence to the place, but the echo of hymns could still be heard, if one listened with the heart. Right then that was just what April was doing as she stood at the foot of the open grave. She found it comforting to think of hymns when her heart was heavy.

April was wearing her black dress and bonnet. She opened her father's book of Psalms. The feeling of guilt was something she found hard to shake. Her anger at the murder of her father had driven her to pursue the killer. Her blind anger didn't care whom she stepped on or whom she involved. Now the bitter gall of anger had turned into deep depression. The blue sky overhead was a mockery. Brushing back a tear from her eye, she began to read.

> He that dwelleth in the secret place of the most High shall abide under the shadow of the Almighty.
>
> I will say of the LORD, He is my refuge and my fortress; my God; in him will I trust.
>
> Surely he shall deliver thee from the snare of the fowler, and from the noisome pestilence.
>
> He shall cover thee with his feathers, and under his wings shalt thou trust; his truth shall be thy shield and buckler.
>
> Thou shalt not be afraid for the terror by night; nor for the arrow that flieth by day;

Nor for the pestilence that walketh in darkness; nor for the destruction that wasteth at noonday.

She closed the book and they stood there for a moment, looking down at the rough-hewn coffin. "She can see now. She can see me."

Will looked at her and put his hat on. "I think she's always seen you. Seen right through you too."

April nodded. The woman had had an uncanny ability to know people. Maybe her blindness was her gift. Tillie had always seen with her heart.

"What are you thinking about?" Will asked.

She shook her head slowly. Just then she didn't want to let anyone else in on her thoughts. They were private thoughts about Tillie, about April's life as a small girl with the woman. She stooped down and picked up a handful of the fresh soil. Holding it over the grave, she dropped the soil on top of the coffin. It bounced like buckshot on a shingled roof. "I think I'm looking for ways to ease my guilt in the matter."

"You did the right thing by coming to us."

"Did I?" She didn't really believe him. She knew he was trying to be comforting, but the last thing she wanted was to be comforted. What she wanted was pain. Only pain could ease the guilt she felt.

"Of course you did."

April looked down at the simple coffin. "She didn't want me to come. She thought the whole idea was nonsense, that I was an angry woman who ought to know better."

Will smiled. "The people who love us always have our best interests at heart. They don't think about the situation. They think about us."

"But I took her with me. She was like a piece of bait I was feeding to the fish to get them to come to the surface. Don't you see? I used her."

"Don't confuse *use* with *need*. You needed her. Just as you need me, too, to find your father's killer. And I need you. If I do a good job, I get my own line command." He swallowed hard. "And Tillie needed you. She needed you to fill up a mother's heart when her own family went north and left her here. It's no sin to need, or to be needed, for that matter."

He reached for the saber at his side and drew it out. "You see this sword of mine?" He shook it. "I love it. I keep it sharp and polished because I intend to use it. I need it. We all use the things we love." Putting the point of the saber back into the scabbard, he slammed it back into place. "When we don't use them, they rust and are worthless. You might as well throw them away."

"I see your point, Major."

"I'm glad you do. Now we need to turn that thought-filled head of yours to more worthwhile pursuits, like finding your father's killer and Tillie's."

They turned and walked back toward the road, their heads down, refusing to look up at the sky, listening to the farmer's shovel bite into the pile of dirt beside Tillie's grave. Clods of earth hit the coffin with a hollow thud.

April stopped. "I can't stop thinking about who could have done this."

Will nodded. "Most of the men we need to see were there that night."

"Or people they sent," Perlman added.

"You mean Reynolds?"

Perlman nodded. "He was giving us more than a casual glance."

April shook her head. "And we saw Tommy Slocum that night. But I just can't believe such a thing is possible from him. He's too simple to be devious. But he and his family do know Tillie."

"Then they know she's blind," Will added.

"It might make her even more dangerous," April said. "She can tell one man from another by the way they walk, the way they breathe. She didn't have to see them. She could just feel them."

They walked on a little farther. "That was a beautiful psalm," Perlman said. "Number ninety-one, as I recall." He stopped and looked up at the sky. "Let's see. How does it go? I seem to remember. 'A thousand shall fall at thy side, ten thousand at thy right hand; but it will not come nigh thee. Only with thine eyes shalt thou behold and see the reward of the wicked. Because thou hast made the LORD, which is my refuge, even the most High, thy habitation; There shall no evil befall thee, neither shall any plague come nigh thy dwelling. For he shall give his angels charge over thee, to keep thee in all thy ways. They shall bear thee up in their hands, lest thou dash thy foot against a stone.' Isn't that how it goes?"

April looked up at him, and Perlman laughed. "Don't think it strange that I know that, Miss Wolff. I'm Jewish. We had that in our Bible long before you did."

April smiled. It was a slight smile, but a smile nonetheless.

"I'd say that's a perfect psalm for a soldier," he went on. "Before this thing is through, we'll have thousands falling beside us. We're going to need those wings the psalmist talks about."

A man's yell along with the galloping hooves of a horse brought all of their heads up. Down the road, a Confederate horseman was bearing down on the small hamlet of Cashtown. He was waving his hat and shouting with a series of bone-chilling rebel yells. "Yeee-haaa." The noise echoed over the road.

Will ran toward the road, waving his arms for the man to stop. Perlman, April, and Ulysses ran after him. The sweating rider skidded to a stop, jerking hard on the reins and causing the horse to rear back and circle wildly. The animal panted heavily, and clouds of dust burst around his hooves and settled along the road.

The man had a black feather in his hat, and the stripes of a corporal stood out in blazing gold on his gray coat. His boots were polished but caked in dust.

"What's happening?" Will yelled.

"We're after some morning fun, Major. General Archer's on the Chambersburg Pike with men from 'Bama and Tennessee. Heath's whole corps is behind them, with Marse Robert himself riding with them. We're going on to Gettysburg and get us some shoes. Lee's ordered the army there, kind of a meeting-up place."

"What about Union troops? What about the Army of the Potomac?"

The man shook his head, a broad smile showing a perfect set of teeth. "Ain't nothing there but militia, from what we hear. Meade, the old snapping turtle, is in charge of the Union army now. He'll be moving slow." He laughed. "He's probably still camped out in Maryland."

"What about Stuart? Has he reported in?"

"We ain't seen hide nor hair of the glory boy, but that ain't gonna stop us none." With that the man slapped his spurs to the side of his horse and went clattering down the road, a trail of dust following him.

Perlman took off his hat, wiping the inside leather band. "I guess that means we're going to Gettysburg."

"That's exactly what it means," Will said. "If that's Lee's gathering place, then we'll have everyone there that we need to talk to. We won't have to go galloping all over Pennsylvania."

CHAPTER 26

I t was still early in the morning when they came upon the Chambersburg Pike. April's eyes widened at the sight: a steady, rolling current of men was surging over the road. On the hilltops, mounted cavalry rode in a sweeping maneuver designed to protect the marching column's flanks. The horsemen would suddenly appear riding up the ridge and just as quickly vanish out of sight as they rode down the hill.

The men on the road were marching four abreast. The day was going to prove hot, and many had already unbuttoned their shirts and tunics. Some marched stiffly at attention, rifles at the ready in front of them, while other men sauntered leisurely, rifles slung over their shoulders. Relaxed and laughing, the latter soldiers were celebrating victory. The sky was blue, and no bluecoats were in sight.

The soldiers smiled at April as they passed by. Some were so young, no more than boys. It saddened her that they would be introduced to death and dying before they had finished with play. *These boys should be out climbing trees,* she thought, *not preparing to kill or be killed.*

Perlman found a spot on the road for the wagon, and they fell into place. They found themselves in a gray mob being marched down the road in lines of four. But the sight of the wagon with April driving it was more than a little distracting. The men began to gather around the mules and drift back to where they could walk alongside the wagon, gawking and smiling at April.

"What's a pretty lady like you doing out here?" one soldier asked with a pronounced grin.

"You come here to cheer us on?" another asked.

One of the sergeants marching along with the men gave them a shove back into position. "Keep up with the rest," he ordered.

It was obvious that each man was going to try to get a word from April. Perlman drifted back with his mule until he was riding beside her. "Where you boys from?" he asked the soldiers.

"Mississip'," one of the men shouted. "Archer's up ahead yonder. This here brigade's commanded by Joe Davis. He's Jeff Davis's nephew, don't you know."

"Yes, I know. You boys ready for a fight today?"

"We is always ready fer a fight. We got plenty of scrap in us. There ain't much up the road yonder, though, from what we hear. They got them shopkeepers and farmers they handed a gun to today." The man laughed. "They get themselves a taste of Mississippi shootin' and they'll be rushing outta there like a coon with his tail set on fire."

Perlman spoke up so Will could hear him. "Will Archer know what to do up there?"

Will nodded. "He should. The man's bright, a Princeton grad. He's a veteran of the Mexican war too, so he's seen his share of gunfire."

It was then that they heard the first of the shots, not just one or two, but a volley of gunfire. The sound of the shooting caused the men around them to walk a little taller and pick up the pace.

Suddenly they could hear shouts from up the line. They watched the men begin to trot. The intensified run began with the group of men rounding the hill ahead of them and then rippled through the entire line. The pulsating line of gray-clad men was like the head of a snake racing for dinner while the end of the animal was just now getting the idea. In a matter of minutes the men from Mississippi also broke out into a run.

Perlman pulled Elmer out of the bag he'd been carrying. He dropped the cat in the wagon and then shouted at Will. "What about it, Major?"

"We're in no hurry. We'll just stay like we are and keep moving." He looked back at April. "I don't want her coming into any gunfire. The most deadly shots in this war are the ones not even aimed at you."

April saw Will's face suddenly turn white as a pail of milk. He grabbed the traces on the mule and jerked them. "Get this thing off the road. Now!"

April picked up her whip and cracked it over the backs of the mules. She sent the team bolting over the shoulder of the road and into the soft grass. It was not a moment too soon. Down the road, a team of horses were galloping with a caisson and cannon behind them. They took the turn on two wheels, racing for the sound of the gunfire up ahead. Several more batteries of guns quickly followed. Men were whipping the horses, and the animals seemed to be barely held in check by their harnesses. Clouds of dust and debris settled down onto the road.

April's heart raced. There would have been no way the carriages carrying those guns could have stopped in time. Men on foot might be able to jump clear, but not a slow-moving wagon.

Ulysses was panting. "Missy, we just made it over here. I thought we was dead sure 'nuff."

It took them some time to clear the crest of the hill. All during that time, the rest of Henry Heth's division had marched or run past them in quick time. Will had ridden up ahead. He held his hand up for them to stop.

April and Ulysses climbed down from the wagon and ran to where Will was seated on his horse. They could see the men spreading out over the field to their right. They were forming a battle line, and that took some time. Officers were barking orders, and men with guidons were waving them back and forth to form the troops into position.

All at once, the guns that had passed them boomed out from a ridge nearby. Clouds of smoke rose from the distressingly loud weapons. Explosive plumes of death crashed into the lines of the men in blue.

Will held up a pair of field glasses and stared at the Union lines. "Cavalry," he said. "Dismounted cavalry."

"We ought to send them running in no time," Perlman offered.

Will took the glasses from his face. "Don't be so sure, Sergeant. Those men may be cavalry, but they have position." He looked at Perlman. "They also have those breech-loading carbines. With enough ammunition to shoot all day."

The gray line, which stretched for more than a mile with flags flying and officers waving their swords in the air, began to move on the blue troopers. April watched as they advanced, studying first one man and then another as they seemed to trip and fall. She turned and held on to Will, and he put his arm around her. "Those men are dying out there," she said.

"It's not a pretty picture, is it?"

"No. I just didn't ever think it could be like this, young boys that I just spoke to, marching off to be slaughtered like sheep."

"The next time you hear one of those politicians talk about the glories of the war, you just remember this. In reality, there is never much to cheer about."

They watched as the battle unfolded. The long gray line buckled and wavered as shot after shot was poured into it. They stopped and held their own. Their returning volleys were accompanied by the batteries of cannons fired from the ridge near them. Smoke blanketed the field. The sudden screaming of men stabbed at

April's heart. The dreams and hopes of men were dying in an instant of time, only to be replaced by pain and agony.

Will took April by the hand and led her back to the wagon. She sank to the ground and put her head in her hands. "This has got to stop. Nothing is worth this pain. It's the stubbornness of it all. Both sides are taking the moral high ground, and each is refusing to budge."

Will put his hands on his hips and looked back up the ridge. "I think what gets to me are the innocents in this thing."

"The innocents?"

"Yes, women like you who wait for men who will never come home, men who will wind up buried in some shallow grave up here with no one to tend it or even grieve for them. One can almost hear the mourning at night, the deep sigh and bitter crying of the whole nation. The languishing never stops in my head, and I was born in a town accustomed to bitter political debate. I can no longer hear the speeches, just the wailing of widows and their children."

"My father was right. He said that all war is evil, and now I know why."

"Then one could only wish it was your father sitting in the White House. Not one life is worth this glorious Union."

April could only look up at him and bite her lip. For a soldier, Will Chevalier hated war. She admired that. "How long will this go on? Will the hatred go on forever?"

Will nodded. "Yes. Long after the war is over, the spite and anger will be there. People will forget what it was all about, but they won't forget the bitterness. This marriage will end when one mate stands over the other in triumph. The hatred is too strong. The love is too shallow. They have each chosen what it is about the other that they can no longer abide, and they will never be satisfied until the beating heart of their mate stops and beats no longer."

"How ugly."

"Yes, amazing, isn't it? Three days from now there will be great celebration of the marriage of this country while each mate plots the murder of the other."

"It always comes back to the same illustration for you, doesn't it, Will Chevalier?"

"It's a part of my life. I've grown accustomed to the feeling of it. I suppose that will never change."

"What about two mortal enemies who fall in love? Can the war end for them?"

It was apparent that the thought had taken Will by surprise. He blinked his eyes and then stared into hers. There was a warmth to his look. April hadn't been talking about the two of them, but Will was thinking about it. That was clear. "I've never seen that."

"But it could happen?"

He paused. "Yes, it could."

April's heart raced. She knew the man wasn't saying that he loved her, but in her mind he was saying that it was possible. What she didn't know were her own feelings. Up until this time she had never dreamed it would be possible for her to care about any man. Will Chevalier was the most unlikely man she could ever imagine. He was an aristocratic, blue-blooded Southerner. He was a slave owner, and she wasn't even certain the man was a Christian in the way she was accustomed to thinking of one. He might have respect for what it meant to be a believer, but that didn't make him one.

Perlman came running back to where they were, with Ulysses right behind him. "We've got us a battle on our hands here, Major. For a while it looked like our boys were going to collapse their line, but then some Yankee infantry showed up, those black hats from Michigan. If I didn't know any better, I'd say the whole Union army is out there." He pointed to the north. "We do have a right smart number of troops coming in from the north, though. If it don't get any worse, it ought to be just a matter of time."

"Maybe we should head north then," Will said.

"That would be the way I would go." Perlman looked over at April and then back at Will, staring him straight in the eye. "What about this here investigation? It would seem that we have more pressing matters here."

Will patted his pocket. "I have my orders, Sergeant, and I intend to carry them out." He glanced down at April. "We may have wholesale murder going on here, but there's nothing we can do to stop it. Right now there's only one murder I care about. It's the only one I can do anything about, and I intend to do just that."

CHAPTER 27

I t took the wagon the better part of four hours to climb the hills to the north and circle around the sound of the ongoing battle. The noise didn't stop. Cannons, along with a vicious sea of musket fire, crashed in the hills below them. They could see the smoke rising, a gentle fog of acrid stink that curled around the tops of the trees and blanketed the hills. One could almost hear the played-out gunpowder softly hitting the grass.

When they reached the top of the ridge, they could see fresh divisions of Southern troops coming in from the north. The gray-clad soldiers were marching down the road. Others had fanned out over the top of a hill that was just to the east of where they had stopped the wagon. Will sat on his horse next to April and the wagon, and Perlman rode his mule farther. He looked the scene over carefully, then turned around and rode back to the wagon.

Draping the reins of the mule over the saddle, he leaned forward. "That'll be Ewell's men," he said.

"Yes, I expect so."

Perlman turned his head and stared down at the soldiers, then looked off to the area of the farm where the battle had begun taking shape. The fresh troops were in a perfect position to crash into the flank of the dug-in Yankees and sweep the Union troops from the field. They couldn't have had it any better if it had been carefully planned. "You suppose Iverson's down there with him?" Perlman asked.

"He's got to be."

April watched Perlman flex his jaw. No matter how important it was for these men to complete their investigation, she knew that nothing was of greater importance to them than winning this war. It was why they had joined the army. While the army was on the march, other matters might be dealt with, but the men were soldiers first and foremost. She could see that the sound of the guns had changed Perlman's sense of priorities. He seemed to tighten up all over. He leaned over the saddle and stuck his chin out in Will's direction. "And you want to go down there and question him?" Perlman leaned back and shook his head slowly.

April recognized the look. It was like the one Tillie had repeatedly given her when she knew April was wrong. It was a hard expression that seemed to say, *You idiot, if you can't figure out what to do, I'm sure not going to tell you.* She knew Perlman would never say such a thing to Will, but it didn't stop him from thinking it.

"You have a problem with that, Sergeant?"

Perlman fixed his eyes on Will. A slow burn was in his blue eyes. "Am I free to speak, sir?"

"Of course you are. I couldn't stop you anyway, from the look on your face."

"No, sir. I suppose you couldn't at that."

"Then tell me what's on your mind—all of it."

"All this hunting around after some hearsay evidence is well and good when that army of ours is chasing their tails and sleeping fat and sassy in the grass of this here state, but when the shooting starts we need to be down there with them. I'm not saying we're on a wild-goose chase. I don't think we are." He pointed his finger down the hill to where the fighting was raging. "All I'm saying is that there is where we need to be, not up here out of harm's way."

April could see Will bristling. He rose up in his stirrups. She reached over and gently put her hand on his arm.

"Are you finished? Have you said all you're going to say?"

"Yes, sir. Pretty much."

"Then let me enlighten you as to our job, Sergeant Perlman. You think we're out here simply to solve a murder. You see it as something that's important, but not vital to what this army does. You might even think that since it's a Yankee and some slave woman who've been killed, it ought to wait until this thing's over with. Am I right?"

"That about sums it up, Major."

Will breathed a deep sigh. "Look, Sergeant, I can understand your problem with being here. The battle's down there, and we should both be in it, even if we are only closing the line. We joined this army to fight. Both of us have a sense of duty, and even though we feel it for this job of ours, there's a higher duty we both recognize."

Perlman looked at April, and April had no doubt that the man thought Will's growing affection for her had clouded his thinking. "What about Miss Wolff here? I wouldn't exactly call this place the safest in the world for her."

Will gave her a careful look, as one would give a prize piece of china. "Now hold on," April said. "If you think you're going to turn me loose on that road with all those men, you've got another think coming. If your men don't take me prisoner and send Ulysses south to slavery, then I just might run into Union troops. They could take me for a spy for all I know."

Perlman grunted.

"Then perhaps we'll have to find a safe place for you and Ulysses, some place for you to wait until all this is over."

"And where might that be?" Perlman asked.

"We'll know it when we find it."

"And what about our jobs. Just what is our job right now, the one we ought to be doing?"

"That's a good question, Sergeant. It bears some pondering. We do have this set of orders from General Lee. No one could fault us for doing what he's asked us to do."

"And nobody would complain if we dropped the whole matter." He glanced at April. "At least for now."

"Then let me prod your head in another direction. Do you really want some cold-blooded killer leading our troops into battle? Do you think that if a man can kill a couple of innocent civilians that he's going to stop with that act of rage?" Will shook his head. "I don't think so. If we have someone in command who thinks so little of human life that he can dispatch it on a whim, then that same man will think nothing of ordering our troops into a blood-bath just to save his own sorry hide. He might even need to perform some heroic act no matter how many men he kills in the process. No, we're not just trying to solve a murder here, we're trying to stop a murderer."

April could see the thought was having its effect on Perlman. It was a new idea and one that was compelling. The man leaned back in his saddle, stroking his beard.

"You remember those murders in Atlanta you solved, the ones with the children who were being killed?"

Perlman nodded. "Yes."

"Think how many children are alive today because of what you did back there. You can multiply that by the thousands here. We have enough problems on our hands in this war without having a homicidal maniac in command. We don't have enough supplies, weapons, or manpower. Men are the one precious resource we can't afford to squander. We'd be doing our whole army a favor to find out if a general officer is responsible for what we've seen. It might be the most important thing we do during the entire war."

"All right, Major." Perlman nodded his head and forced a small crease of a smile. "You've almost got me persuaded. But remember, if you have a hard time convincing me, you're going to have a dickens of a time down there. Bullets are flying. You might say they're kinda busy."

"The trouble with you, Sergeant, is that you know me too well, or at least you think you do." He shot a glance at April. "You think because there's a woman involved that I'm going to find a way to do what I wouldn't otherwise do."

"You said that, Major. I didn't."

"You didn't have to. Push those notions out of your head. I do my duty first. I do the important things second." Will pulled Lee's orders from his pocket and drummed them on the back of his hand. "As far as those people down there are concerned, I don't have to convince anyone, Sergeant. I have to get them to obey orders."

Because of the wagon, it took them an hour to get down the ridge to the place where the Confederate reinforcements were arriving. Perlman grabbed one of the men. "What outfit is this?"

The man stopped in his tracks, weaving with excitement. "It's the Twenty-third North Carolina."

Perlman looked back to where Will had gotten off his horse. "It's Iverson's unit."

They watched as Iverson and his staff rode over the hill. The general got down clumsily from his horse as several of his staff set up chairs and a table. He took his seat and began to bark out orders to the men around him. The unit was being dressed into a battle line company by company. Officers and noncommissioned officers were shouting out orders. One staff officer held out a pair of binoculars for Iverson to survey the field. He propped his elbows on the table and held them up to his face.

"It would seem our modern day Caesar has arrived," Will said.

Perlman nodded. "I believe he has, Major."

They watched Iverson take out a bottle from a bag and hold it to his lips. He tilted his head back, drained its contents, and then threw it to the ground. Several riders rode up to where Iverson was holding court. They dismounted and stepped up to the general. After a brief discussion, they got back on their horses and rode off.

Perlman smiled. "I think he brought his courage with him."

They watched the officers and senior enlisted men march up and down the rapidly forming line. The men appeared to be in fighting shape, even after what could only be supposed as a long march. They fanned out over the hill, doing their best to make fresh lines out of what had been a traveling formation. It would take some time to do that, and Will and Perlman both knew it.

"Perhaps we should have a word with the man," Will said.

"I think we should." Perlman fell into place beside Will as they marched in the direction of the general and his staff.

When they got closer, one of the officers standing close to Iverson stepped over to them. The man was a captain. His brass buttons were in place and his eyes were steady as they looked at Will. "Can I help you, sir?"

"I'm Major Will Chevalier of the provost's office. This is Sergeant Jacob Perlman. We're here to ask General Iverson a few questions."

The man looked back over his shoulder to where Iverson was conferring with his officers. He had taken out a fresh flask of whiskey and was beginning what Will was sure would be a fast trip to the bottom of the bottle. "I'm Captain James Quinn. There must be some way I can handle any questions you might have."

"Look, Captain Quinn, we're investigating a murder."

"You can't be serious." Quinn's thick brown eyebrows curved downward, and a frown spread over his face. "We've got a battle here. The general can't be disturbed with your questions."

Will smiled. "I think he can." He reached into his pocket and pulled out Lee's signed order. "I'd suggest you look this over before you act too hastily."

Quinn took the paper and began to read. His mouth dropped open as his eyes followed the words down the page to the signature. "This is amazing. You are serious." He handed the paper back over to Will.

"Deadly serious," Will said.

"What is this about?"

"It's about a man who was murdered, a farmer. We have reason to believe that your unit was in the area when the killing took place. A witness said the murderer was a confederate general."

"My Lord." Quinn shook his head. "I can't believe this."

"Has Iverson gone out on any night rides alone?"

Quinn shook his head. "No, he hasn't. I can tell you that much. The man finds it hard to ride in the daytime."

Will looked over the captain's shoulder to where Iverson was taking another drink. "I can see that. Do you know if he's talked about a grudge he might have against anyone in this state? Just come out with it and tell us. We're going to find out anyway."

"He lives with a grudge, but it's more of a general nature."

"Such as?"

"The man's daughters were poisoned by a runaway slave. They died in his arms. He's been drinking ever since."

Both Will and Perlman exchanged glances. "Has he tried to do anything about it?" Will asked.

"Besides pickle himself? No, I don't think there's much he can do."

"Unless he found someone who sheltered runaway slaves," Perlman added. "He might bring himself to do something then."

"I don't see how. The man's never sober enough to see what's right in front of him. I'm not sure he could shoot anyone who walked up to him and slapped him in the face."

They heard the sound of the officers in the line bark out the order to forward march. The order rippled in quick succession up and down the line. Suddenly the line of men moved forward. They lurched as one down the hill and toward the wheat field that stood below them.

"Aren't you going to send out skirmishers?" Will asked.

Quinn turned and watched as the men walked down the hill. The flags were flying at various positions in the long gray lines, and the men were working hard at keeping their lines straight. "It would appear that we are not."

"Fool thing to do," Perlman added.

"Perhaps we can ask the general a few questions now," Will said.

"Follow me," Quinn replied. "I'll take you to him."

The captain turned and led them to where Iverson was taking another drink. They stepped up to the table, and the three of them saluted. "General, these men are from the provost marshal's office. They have orders signed by General Lee and would like to ask you a few questions."

Iverson wiped the back of his hand across his face and broke into a sickening smile. "Orders from Lee himself? Must be a heavy burden for you two men." He held out the bottle. "Would you care for a drink?"

Will shook his head. "I don't think we'll be drinking for quite some time, General." He glanced back at the troops, who were continuing their march. "Is there some reason you're not leading your troops, General?"

Iverson waved his hand at the troops. "They're from Carolina, and they're slow. I'll catch up with them directly."

"Shouldn't you have scouts in front of the formation, General?"

"Are you a West Point man, Major? That sounds like the kind of question a Point man would ask."

"No, sir. I graduated from the Citadel."

"Oh yes, I see your ring." Iverson grinned. "An Institute man then. You got your military education from a chalkboard." He waved his hand in the direction of the troops. "Just leave them to me, Major. I'm in command here." He leaned forward, his elbows on the table. "Now what questions would you like to ask me?"

"Do you know a man named Wolff?" Will asked.

"Never heard of him. Is he an officer?"

"No, sir, a farmer."

"A farmer? What business would I have with a farmer?"

"We wondered if you knew the man or had ever had an occasion to speak with him."

Iverson held the bottle to his lips and drank a few swallows. He put it down and wiped his beard. "I am afraid I can't be of much help to you gentlemen. I don't know the man." He blinked his eyes. They were watery and bleary. "Now what is this all about? Why should I know the man?"

"What if we told you the man helped runaway slaves and was murdered?" Perlman said.

Iverson held the bottle to his lips until the words registered in his mind. He slammed it back on the table. "I'd say he was burning in hell and good riddance."

"He was murdered," Will said, "and his farm was not far from where you marched your men when you came into Pennsylvania."

"And you think I had something to do with it?" He raised both of his shoulders, then dropped them with a sigh. "I only wish I had. It might make it a little easier for me." Shaking his head, he went on. "If I had done what you suggest, Major, I'd be the first to tell you. I'd be proud of it, and no court in this man's army would convict me of anything other than littering."

There was an explosion of gunfire below them. The men from North Carolina were in a wheat field, and to their left was a stone wall. From behind the wall a line of Union infantry had suddenly appeared. The federals were laying down a withering fusillade of fire into the flanks of Iverson's troops. The men in gray were falling in line, stretched out in the midafternoon sun. Sheets of flame poured out from the wall, stabbing at the edges of the field. Will and Perlman watched the men from North Carolina twist in midair and then fall in waves. Flags fell in rapid succession.

Iverson was on his feet, pointing and shouting at the officers around him. "Why are they down? Get them back up on their feet. Those lazy, good-for-nothing sloths from Carolina. They should get up and meet the enemy."

Will looked over at him. "They can't, General. They're dead."

CHAPTER 28

The streets of Gettysburg were filled with troops, gunfire, and the echoing sound of canister shot being unleashed on the advancing rebels. Will had placed April in the bed of the wagon with Ulysses driving. She bounced on the hard boards as the wagon rattled through the holocaust on Chambersburg Pike. "Where are we going?" she yelled.

"Keep your head down," Will hollered. He was on horseback directly behind them. "We're going to find you a place where you won't be shot."

April poked her head up slightly. She couldn't imagine that such a place existed, not in Gettysburg. April had never imagined such confusion and commotion. Thick, sulfurous clouds of gray smoke wafted through the air. Men surged around their wagon from every direction. Will's horse danced and bucked in near panic, and it was only Will's tight rein that kept him in check. Perlman's mule, on the other hand, seemed content to plod directly into whatever got in his path. April could see more than one soldier leap aside when he came nose to nose with the determined animal.

"I said keep your head down. Stray shots are everywhere."

Pushing through the men alongside the wagon, Will rode up next to Ulysses, who was clucking and whistling to the plodding team of mules. "Ulysses!" Will had to shout to make himself heard in a sudden thunderous roar of cannon fire. "There, that house! Follow the fence! You see it?"

Huge muscles worked in the black man's massive arms as he expertly worked the reins. "Yes, suh."

April peeked her head up and spotted a long line of fence posts. The white rail fence led up to a rather imposing house. The two-story house was embellished with gingerbread latticework. The structure was brick, however, and that seemed to be what Will had in mind.

Ulysses drew rein in the yard. Will came off his horse like a madman. "Perlman, you and Ulysses take the horses and mules and get them put away in the barn," he yelled. "I'll take April in the house and see she gets settled."

With that he reached over the edge of the wagon and lifted April to the ground. Taking her hand, he ran in a crouch for the front porch. He drew his revolver and threw open the door. Confederate soldiers were stationed around the windows, all of which were broken. The glass was strewn around the carpets, and furniture was arranged in piles under the tall windows to provide makeshift breastworks. April could also see dead men heaped in bloody piles, arranged helter-skelter in the dining room and the hallway. The corpses wore a mixture of blue and gray uniforms. "Who's in charge here?" he asked.

A young lieutenant got to his feet. "I am, sir. Lieutenant Jeff Victor of the Third South Carolina."

"How many men have you got here?"

The young lieutenant began to count. Over a dozen wounded men in gray uniforms lay writhing on blankets spread on the hardwood floor alongside several more bloodied Union soldiers. "I've got fourteen wounded and twelve men besides them."

"I only see six," Will said.

Victor nodded. "Yes, sir, but I've got six more upstairs. They're sharpshooters."

"Well, get them down here. You have a hospital here, man. I don't want any Union cannon battery to fire on this place, so take those sharpshooters of yours out. Also, I want you to get a red flag to hang out the door."

"But I still have men who can fight, sir."

"Then take them out into the street where they can do some good. Do whatever you want. I don't really care. I just don't want this place fired upon. Am I understood?"

Will pointed to the dead on the floor. "Get those men out in the yard too. They will be buried later."

April could see the wheels turning in the lieutenant's head. The man was young, an inexperienced soldier thrust suddenly into the maelstrom of war and the responsibilities of leadership. He wavered, uncertain. The men he had left still had plenty of fight in them. "What's happening out there, sir?"

"The Union Eleventh Corps is in total retreat. They're being chased out of town. There is still plenty of fighting on the other side of town near the cemetery, but I think you're safe here for a while. I just don't want some stray Union cannon to think they can take a parting shot at this house. As far as I can tell, those men of yours upstairs are not much more than a nuisance now."

Perlman and Ulysses burst through the front door. "We got the animals put away," Perlman said. "They're safe unless they get stolen." He sized up the young lieutenant with a skeptical squint. "What do we have here?"

"Lieutenant Victor and men from the Third South Carolina." Will looked at the lieutenant. "Where is the rest of your unit, Lieutenant?"

The man shook his head. "Darned if I know, Major. They're to hell and gone by now." He glanced at April. "I'm sorry, ma'am. Pardon my language."

"This is Miss Wolff," Will said. "I want you to see to her. She can do some nursing work for you."

He quickly turned to April. "You can do that, can't you?"

April nodded. She'd mended plenty of broken bones and cauterized gushing wounds around the farm. Blood and gore didn't scare her. In fact, she was energized at the thought of being needed, not just dead weight for Will to have to fuss over. "Of course I can," she said, rolling up her sleeves.

He looked back at the lieutenant. "There you are, a nurse. You just take care of her and see that no harm comes to her and that she stays put here with your wounded."

"Yes, sir. I can do that."

"See that you do." He looked at April. "I noticed this place has a root cellar. I'd suggest you and Ulysses spend as much time down there as possible. Perlman and I will get on about what we have to do here and come back for you as soon as we can. The quicker we get our job done, the quicker we can get you out of here. Maybe by then this whole business will have died down. If that army of yours does as it always does, it won't be here for long. It'll be headed back to the gates of Washington faster than a skinned cat." He reached over to where Perlman had the orange tabby in his arms and scratched the cat's ear. "My apologies."

"I'll just leave ol' Elmer here with April," Perlman said. He stooped over and dropped the cat to the floor.

April followed Will to the door. "When will you be back?" she asked.

Will opened the door. "Just as soon as I can. I don't feel right about leaving you here, but I'd feel even worse if I had to accompany you home while all this is going on. I feel derelict enough in my duties without having the sound of gunfire at my back."

"I understand." April did understand. She was beginning to know Will Chevalier. The man was dedicated to his work no matter what else he was. There was also a growing feeling inside of her that this investigation was far beyond what she had envisioned. In the meantime, she was beginning to see and understand war through Will's eyes. It still sickened her, but she felt a growing respect for the men who felt duty bound to fight for their principles.

She put her hand on his arm. "More than anything else, I want you back. If you find out anything or nothing, it will make little difference to me if anything happens to you."

Will smiled. "I appreciate that, coming from a woman so driven by justice."

A low moan from one of the wounded men caused their heads to turn. April looked back at Will. "None of that seems very important to me right now. I'm only interested in the living, not the dead."

Will patted her hand. "I know you are." With that he followed Perlman out the door.

April turned to the young lieutenant. "I think, sir, that we should get busy here." She rolled up her sleeves and went to work inspecting the wounds of the men on the floor. She looked at Lieutenant Victor. "Could you have someone boil water? I'll need lots of hot water."

"Yes, ma'am."

It took her some time to make her rounds, and then she began to explore the house, searching for bandages or anything that could be torn to make them. She found a number of bedsheets and pillowcases in a set of bureau drawers. They were white and seemed to be clean and pressed. Loading them into her arms, she carried them back into the living room. Spotting one of the men coming down the stairs, she thrust a stack of sheets into his arms. "Could you tear these into strips? I'm going to need a supply of bandages."

The sharpshooter looked surprised and glanced at Lieutenant Victor. "Do as she says," the officer nodded curtly.

April looked at Lieutenant Victor. "I still haven't found any medical supplies. I'll look down in the cellar. Whoever owns this place may have stored some emergency supplies there. Perhaps your men can explore the house upstairs. Bring me anything you find."

"I'll do that, ma'am."

She reached over and picked up a candle in a pewter candleholder. A small red-white-and-blue box of matches was there, marked THE UNION FOREVER. She opened it, and taking out a match, raked it over the top of the table. She touched it to the wick. Bending down, she picked up Perlman's cat. "You're going with me, Elmer. I may need the company."

She moved down the small hall that led to the back door. A small alcove contained the door that led to the cellar. She opened the door. A rich damp smell of earth rushed up at her. Wooden stairs anchored to a mossy brick wall disappeared into the blackness. The steps were worn and shaky, and she stepped lightly on them, balancing the cat in one arm and the candle in her hand. Holding the light in front of her, her foot pressed on a step. It sent out a loud squeak.

When she reached the hard-packed dirt floor, it seemed cool and relatively quiet. The thick walls stifled even the sound of gunfire. Massive wooden pillars supported the house, rising up from blocks of stone and disappearing between the rough-hewn beams in the low ceiling. Bags hung on nails in the beams, filled with potatoes and onions, April imagined. In the flickering candlelight she spotted a workbench to one side and a wall of shelves and cabinets on the opposite side of the cellar. Lifting her black skirt high, she made her way between stacks of boxes and crates to the open shelves lined with canned goods. Placing the candle on a nearby barrel and Elmer on a box, she set about opening the storage doors one by one.

For a moment she was lost in her search, but then Elmer stiffened and spat; with a screeching hiss, the cat bounded down and hit the floor, arching its back and hissing.

April jumped back. There in the darkness stood a man. She could see him faintly in the light of the narrow window that was level with the yard. "Who are you? They need your help upstairs."

The man stepped forward. He was wearing a sword and carrying a pistol in his hand. She could see him more clearly now. His head was bare with black hair and shiny black eyes that drilled into her. Muttonchop whiskers drifted down the side of his full face. He was wearing a Union uniform with stars on his collar. He braced himself, sticking out his chest. "I am General Schimmelfennig."

CHAPTER 29

Will and Perlman led their mounts out of the barn. The gray horse seemed skittish with the gunfire and it was plain to see Perlman's mule was irritated. Its ears were pinned back and it had a wild look in its eyes. "I hope he lets you keep your seat," Will said. "He doesn't seem too happy."

Perlman watched as a group of soldiers ran by, shouting. "I know just how he feels. Me and him have a kind of understanding. I don't take him into trouble, and he don't leave me there if we find it."

Will smiled. "Sounds like a good arrangement, but it looks like trouble has found us."

Perlman climbed on the mule and straightened himself in the saddle. He checked both revolvers. Men in the provost marshal's office were accustomed to carrying two side arms. "Where we off to now? You gonna hunt down somebody else to question?"

Will swung himself into the saddle. "We're going to find General Lee."

Perlman looked puzzled. He brushed his mustache aside.

Will patted the pocket where he was carrying Lee's orders. "I know I wanted these orders. I even asked for them. Right now, though, with all this going on, they seem like the weight of the world."

Starting through the streets of Gettysburg, they could see the Union troops fleeing to the south of them, abandoning the town in the face of the fresh Confederate troops and their own collapsing lines. From where the two rode it seemed like another Union disaster. Will had seen it often enough, and the feel of a possible rout was in the air. Soldiers clad in gray were shouting, and spirits seemed high.

Whenever Will spotted someone he thought might be in command, he stopped to inquire about the whereabouts of the Confederate high command, specifically Lee and Jenkins. All of them pointed to the hills west of town, near the place they had left Iverson.

When they came to some unfinished railroad tracks, they followed them west out of town. All along the tracks, groups of soldiers sat rummaging through their haversacks for ammunition and food to sustain their strength. Bodies clothed in blue and gray were strewn like matchsticks scattered from a card table. Some lay with their faces down and their feet up on the abutment of the tracks, their heads pointing to the rough ties. Others were stretched out as if they had fallen asleep and were relaxing. They looked at peace. Piles of bodies were crumpled like rag dolls on the bottom of a child's toy box. It was as if some great unseen hand had grown tired of the order of the lines of men in battle and had simply swept them from the table with one mighty stroke.

As they rode on, it was increasingly difficult for Will to concentrate. The battle was underway and it promised to be a victory, perhaps the great victory they had been hoping for. They seemed to be on a fool's errand. Will kept reminding himself what he had told Perlman that morning. They needed to catch a murderer before he could do something rash, something that might involve thousands of victims, not just one or two. He fought hard to force the thought of joining the battle out of his head. And when he glanced at Perlman, he could tell the man was thinking the same thing. It was like a bond of icy silence between them. They wouldn't say the words, but neither of them could help but think the thoughts.

Will drew rein beside a colonel who was barking orders to a group of officers along the tracks. "Can you tell me where to find General Lee?"

The man raised his head and stared at Will with large black eyes. His neck was scrawny and sweaty. He had unbuttoned his collar for comfort. He lifted a bony finger and pointed in the direction of a ridge. "Last I heard he was up there on Seminary Ridge. You see him, you tell him my men need more ammunition. We've got too many Yankees down here to kill with what we got, and I don't know where the supply train is. You tell him that for me, ya hear?"

Will gave a halfhearted salute. "Yes, sir, I will."

Will rode off in the direction the man had indicated. It was hard for him to shake the look of the man, the hollowness of his eyes. He knew the man had no doubt turned back to his task at hand, but it was hard not to think of him just watching them ride away, wondering what they were doing and why they weren't in the fight. It sent a cold chill down his back.

They soon spotted the group of officers on the ridge, among them Lee on Traveler. The men were taking turns staring at the battle through binoculars. A sense of hope flooded through Will as he rode. Lee had given him his orders to investigate; perhaps now, with the battle being fought, Lee might find it necessary to rescind the orders. Will hoped the man would do just that. It would free his conscience.

Will and Perlman rode up the ridge and into the trees. They heard the strange sound of dreadful howls. They brought their mounts to a halt. On the ground were large numbers of wounded men from both sides. Several seemed to be mad, foaming at the mouth and screaming, their eyes blankly staring at the sky, mindless and in great pain.

Will and Perlman circled them and wound their way through the trees. Moments later they rode up to General Lee and the officers who were in conference with him. Looking off to their left, they could see the fighting below them. Union forces were being driven out of Gettysburg and others were digging into a hill that lay just south of town. They watched as fresh Union troops slowly joined those who were feverishly working to prepare breastworks on the tops of the hills.

Will edged his horse up next to the group of officers. He recognized General A. P. Hill at once. The man looked frail and delicate, almost as white as biscuit dough.

Lee turned to him. "General Hill, those people down there are digging in. They will be more difficult to take with every hour that passes by. I suggest you take your Third Corps and drive them from that place."

Hill cleared his throat. "I agree, General. That position must be taken if we are to carry the day, but my men are exhausted. Anderson's division is still miles from here. Heth's men are shattered, and he is unconscious. General Pender's furious charge has left his men exhausted and out of ammunition. I simply no longer have men on the field to command, General, none that can fight."

Lee nodded. He looked off to the north, to the town of Gettysburg. "Then that leaves us with General Ewell. We have four hours of daylight left, and he simply must push those men off of that hill."

Lee looked at Hill. "He will want support from you, however."

"I have none to give him, General."

"Then he must act and act quickly."

Will watched as General Longstreet rode up the ridge. The man had a long, well-kept beard and sat on his horse like a cavalryman. His high boots were polished, and they gleamed in the sun. There was a light in his eyes that marked his intelligence, almost as if he knew what was to come next and was ready with a response before being asked. Old Pete, as he was called, though one never knew why since his given name was James, took out his binoculars and surveyed the enemy lines.

Will watched Longstreet scan the terrain. A broad low ridge extended from the hill, which had a cemetery on top of it, to a pair of conical hills. The Union positions resembled that of a fishhook. Neither of the round hills appeared to be occupied by Union troops, though it was obvious they commanded the entire position.

Longstreet put down the binoculars and smiled like a man whose prayers had been answered. "General, I don't think we could find a better position. All we have to do is swing our army around the enemy left and come between those people and Washington. Those people will have to attack us on ground of our own choosing."

"No," Lee said. He pointed toward Cemetery Hill. "The enemy is there, and I am going to strike him."

"If he is there, it is because he is anxious for us to bear the burden of the attack. That is precisely why we should not do so, in my judgment."

Lee shook his head. "They have been running. They will not stand and fight if we strike them now. We can roll up their entire line. It must be here. It must be now. I am going to whip them or they are going to whip me."

Longstreet clamped his mouth shut, but Will could see his mind racing. Will had silently listened to the men, not wanting to interrupt. He already felt more than useless and didn't want to draw attention to that fact by speaking out of turn. He could see that if Lee was right, they would have to attack immediately. More Union forces were arriving every minute, and the key to victory was to drive the enemy from the high ground.

Lee spotted Will, a cool smile forming across his face. "It's you, Major. Have you done what I asked you to do?"

The question shocked Will. He would have thought the battle might have driven out any thought from the man's head except that which was necessary at the moment. He didn't want to report failure, but it was something he had to do. He could only hope Lee would think better of the order now and tell him to report to duty. "I've been working at it, General, but have found nothing so far. I was thinking in view of the fight here that you might want me to rejoin my unit."

"Then who would do what you are doing, Major?"

Will bowed his head. "No one, sir, I suppose. However, it would seem to me that I might be more useful in the line with the troops, sir."

Lee shook his head. "And how would the blessing of God remain on our army, Major, if this great sin were allowed to remain unpunished?"

"I don't know, sir."

Lee put his hand to his face and stroked his beard. "I know that you as a young man are anxious to join the battle. That is understandable. We need you and you need to do your duty. However, I want you to complete this other matter first. Others can perform your task in the field, but no one can do what you are doing. Am I making myself clear?"

"Yes, sir, unfortunately. Perfectly clear."

"Fine, then perhaps I can put you to further use at this time."

"Anything, General."

"We need to get General Ewell moving down there and take that hill. You will go with my adjutant general, Colonel Taylor, and find General Ewell." Lee pointed down at the Union forces digging into the cemetery. "Tell him to press those people and, if practical, take that position before nightfall." Lee smiled. "This may not get you into the fighting directly, Major, but it is important. And when Ewell does launch his attack, you may go with him."

Will snapped a crisp salute. There was a smile on his face. "Yes, sir. Thank you, sir. You won't be disappointed."

CHAPTER 30

A pril stood frozen in the semidarkness. The blast from the cannons outside shook the small narrow windows in the basement, rattling them in their frames. She watched as the man stepped forward. At the sound of the artillery, his expression changed from a fearless look of haughtiness to one of a small boy who had been caught up in an apple tree by his mother. And if April had been that mother, she would have sworn he had eaten too many green apples. There was a sick quivering to the man's lower lip.

He self-consciously looked down at the revolver in his hand. It was a look of disbelief, almost amazement, at how he could be holding a gun on a woman. He lowered the pistol and stuck it back in his holster. "I'm Schimmelfennig," he repeated. He nervously glanced toward the stairs. "They may be searching for me."

"Who?"

"The rebels. I'd be quite a prize for them."

April swallowed her fears of the man. He was more frightened than she was. The idea of any kind of search for this man, however, was almost amusing. "Those men up there are just looking to stay alive. But your army is retreating out of town. When the action subsides, that may change. How did you get here?"

The man clasped his hands behind his back and nervously paced the floor. He stopped at one of the small windows and looked outside. "My horse was shot out from under me. I ran to the first place I could find." Once again he glanced at the stairs. "But they'll find me. I really don't know what has detained them until now."

"Look, General, whoever you are . . . "

"Schimmelfennig. I am Prussian."

"I don't care what you are. Right now you're wearing a blue uniform. Those men haven't come down because they were looking for high places to shoot from. This basement doesn't afford a very good view."

"I suppose not."

"But you can't stay here."

"Can you help me?" There was a pleading to the man's voice. It cracked slightly.

"I can try. It won't do you any good to know this, but I'm not sure when the men who brought me here are coming back. We may not have much time."

"I need to get back to my men."

In the distance the cannons were backing off into a low growl. They sounded like vicious dogs, snarling and ready to pounce at any given moment.

"I'll do what I can." April glanced at the low basement window. "Do you think you can get through that window?"

Schimmelfennig put his hand on his belly and stared at the narrow opening. "I don't know." He shook his head. "I could try."

"I could give you one of my mules in the barn, but I think you'll have to wait until dark."

The man swallowed. "I was waiting for the army to return."

April shook her head. "I don't know about that, General. Your army may never come back. For all I know, tomorrow it may not exist."

"Then do what you can to get me out of here."

"I'll try. If I can distract them tonight, you might be able to slip out the front door."

"Please." He nodded his head. "Do what you can."

April stepped over to the cabinets. "See if you can help me find some medical supplies. I need to get back upstairs."

They spent several minutes rummaging through the cabinets. "I found bandages." The general shook a bundle of bandages in April's direction. He reached his hand back into the cabinet and pulled out a dark blue bottle with a red skull and crossbones on the label. It was marked IODINE. "This ought to do for you, Miss."

April grabbed the bandages and the iodine. "Yes, thank you. This will do nicely. I don't want to go back up empty-handed."

She spotted Perlman's cat slinking from under the stairs. Its eyes caught the faint sunlight and appeared to glow in the dark. "Shoo." She shook her dress and stamped her feet. "Get back up the stairs."

The orange tabby cocked his head at her and instinctively walked toward the stairs and bounded up them. He stopped halfway to the top and looked back in April's direction.

She walked to the stairs and put her hand on the rail. "You must do me a favor if I'm going to try to help you, General." She paused for a moment. "No, two favors."

"Of course, Miss. What would you like me to do?"

"If you do get back to your army, find my brother. His name is Gerald Wolff. He's a captain in the Second Pennsylvania Cavalry. Tell him I'm here and that I'm all right."

"Of course. I'd be happy to do that."

"But there's a second thing, and this is most important."

"What is it?"

"I've seen enough death and dying for a lifetime in this place. If those men up there should find you, you must promise me that you will surrender. I won't have you getting killed, and I won't have you taking the life of one of those men up there. Most of them are boys, and besides that, they're in my care. I'm doing my Christian duty, and I would expect you to do yours. I won't have any one of them dying because I concealed your presence down here."

She could tell the idea was a hard one for him to take. She knew enough about military men by now to know that most of them weren't the least bit interested in what it took to show Christian kindness when it got in the way of their duty.

"I don't know if I can promise you that."

She stepped back in his direction. "You must." She paused. "Or else I will go upstairs and report that I found you down here."

"You wouldn't do that. You're a woman of the Union."

"Don't underestimate me, General. I am my own woman, and I will do whatever I please. Right now what I please to do is to spare lives. Don't press me on this, General Schimmelfennig. I mean what I say."

He glared at her, searching her eyes. "I do believe you would."

"I always do what I say I'm going to do."

He bowed his head and nodded. "All right. You have my word. Just keep them away from here."

"Do I have your word as a gentleman and a Christian?"

He bit his lip. "Yes, madam, you do."

"Fine." She started up the stairs, once again making the awful squeak when her foot hit the stair in the middle. When she got to the top of the stairs, she pushed the open door wider and stepped into the sunlight and smoke of the living room. A few of the soldiers were standing at the windows, guns at the ready. Others were busy with making the wounded more comfortable. She watched the men as they gently lifted the wounded and moved them to a better position. There was a chorus of groans. "I have some bandages and iodine." She held them up. "Would anyone like to help me?"

A young man stepped over to her and took the bandages. "Thank you, ma'am. I'll help you."

The young soldier was slight of build with narrow, frail shoulders. He was not even close to the age for shaving, as it was late in the day and there wasn't the barest trace of a whisker on his smooth narrow cheeks or pointed chin. Two wispy locks of brown hair fell down from his cap on either side of his face, as if to give the appearance of sideburns. The boy's drooping brown eyes were sad, with the hint of a tear in them. His cap was pulled low, almost to eye level, which gave him the comical appearance of a small child dressed up in his father's clothes. But the most arresting feature in April's mind was the boy's hands. His fingers were long and narrow, almost dainty. And his nails were clean. It struck her as odd, because the last thing she expected among soldiers was to see clean fingernails.

She handed him the bandages. "Let's see if we can change some of these dressings you men put on. Did anyone boil water?"

"Yes, ma'am. We started a fire in the stove and have a large kettle of water on it. It ought to be boilin' pretty soon now."

They started to walk away when April put her hand on the boy's arm. "How old are you?"

April watched him swallow hard. He widened his eyes.

"I'm fourteen, ma'am."

"And what is your name?"

The boy raised himself to his full height and did his best to square his shoulders. Try as he might, he couldn't yet produce any semblance of a formidable figure. "I'm Private R-R-Robert Nash from Spartanburg, South Carolina, ma'am." He seemed to stammer the words, almost embarrassed by them.

April caught sight of the young lieutenant. "Lieutenant Victor, do you mind if I have Private Nash here as my assistant?"

Victor gave her a blank stare and then broke into a smile. "No, I don't mind. You can keep him if you like."

With that he walked away. April noticed that Nash's face had developed a long frown. "He didn't really mean it that way. He just meant that I could keep you to work with the wounded."

"He meant it all right."

"Well, we need to get to work with these bandages now. I am going to need your help, and I'm thankful for it."

Both April and Nash went to work changing bandages. They moved from man to man, stopping with a sergeant who moaned in pain as April unwrapped the torn dirty cloth from his chest. They both knelt beside him. Blood had soaked the man's shirt, and he was continuing to bleed.

As April unwrapped the man's bandage, he stared blankly at her and then turned his attention to Nash. His eyes narrowed, a sneer forming on his lips. April gently felt the man's wound. Her touch brought a roar from his bearded mouth. "Sergeant, you have a bullet in your chest. It has to come out."

"Jes leave me be to die here, ma'am."

April picked up a sheet and began to tear it into strips. "I will do no such thing." She looked up at Nash. "Go get the sharpest knife you can find and boil it in the water. We have to take this bullet out."

Nash got to his feet and began his search.

"I don't want no woman working on me," the sergeant bellowed. "I won't be killed by no female."

"I'm not planning on killing you, Sergeant. I'm going to save your life."

"I ain't talkin' 'bout you, ma'am."

April looked over at Nash, who had found a sharp knife. It was evident the man was talking about him, and she wasn't going to pursue the matter any further. Young boys like Nash were doing quite a bit of the fighting for the Confederacy. They should have been in school but were on the battlefield instead. No doubt grizzled veterans like the sergeant resented having to fight with children. She didn't blame him.

pril and Nash went to work on the sergeant, and April removed a bullet that had been lodged in the man's ribs. There was no way to ease the pain, and his screams filled the entire house, rattling off the walls and sending chills up the spines of the men standing at the windows. When they finished, they applied the iodine and bandages and watched him fall asleep. They then spent the better part of the next two hours changing the hastily prepared dressings that had been administered to the wounded men on the floor. Nash worked quickly with his hands, and April admired the way he seemed to take to the task.

When they finally got to their feet, April wiped her forehead with the back of her hand. "I think I'd like some fresh air. What about you?"

Nash nodded. "Yes, ma'am. I'd like that very much."

"I did see a barrel of apples in the barn when I put my mules in there. Should we get one?"

Nash looked around at the other men who were standing at the windows. "Is there enough of them to bring back for the other men?"

"Of course. I didn't look, but I'm sure there is."

Nash smiled. He walked to the door and picked up his rifle. "Okay, let's go."

Both April and Nash walked out the front door. The cannons were firing in the distance now, and numerous soldiers clad in gray were sweeping through the streets following the sound. The house was beginning to be a safe spot, and over the doorway the lieutenant had hung a red flag. April knew it was only a matter of time before the rebels would bring the freshly wounded to the house. She only hoped a doctor would be with them.

"Why are you fighting this war?" April asked.

Nash shot her a glance. "Why shouldn't I? All the men in my town were going. I couldn't just stay home, could I?"

"That doesn't answer my question. I don't care why the men from Spartanburg were going to fight. I just want to know what made Robert Nash, if that is your name, want to fight?"

Nash opened the barn door and stepped inside. "I went 'cause all you Yankees were coming down to my home, and it's my home, not yours."

April stepped closer to the boy. "But now you're here in Pennsylvania. This is my home, not yours."

Nash's face flushed. He glanced around the barn. "You said there were apples here."

April walked across the barn and stepped over to the corner behind the bale of hay she had used to feed the mules. "It's over here."

Nash followed her. He opened the barrel and bent over to take an apple.

April stepped in behind him and put her arms around his chest. "I don't want you to fall."

The boy jumped, ripping her arms away. "Don't touch me! What are you doing?"

"Your name isn't Robert Nash. You're a woman."

Nash circled around the barrel and backed up, pressing against the wall. "What right do you have to put your hands on me?"

April stepped closer. She held her hands up, apologetically. "None. I just want the truth. You have nothing to fear from me. Your secret is safe."

Nash looked at the floor, refusing to look April in the eye.

April reached out and placed her hands on Nash's arms. "I won't say anything to anyone. You've obviously gone to a lot of trouble to keep the fact that you're a woman a secret, and whatever your reason is, I respect it. I just want to know the truth. You can wear baggy clothes and fool these men here, but I'm a woman. I know these things."

Nash looked up. "All right. You're right. My name is Roberta Nash, not Robert. My daddy went off to fight along with my brothers. There ain't no men in Spartanburg over ten or under sixty. I figured I ought to go too. 'Cause if we lose this here war, there ain't gonna be nothing for me to come back home to."

It was an hour later when Nash and April returned to the house. They were carrying apples, dozens of them in a feed bag from the barn. Lieutenant Victor was assembling what was left of his men in the living room. He looked up at April. "We're going to find our outfit and join back up with the war."

"What about the wounded?" April asked.

"I'm leaving two of my men here with you and Nash. That ought to be enough to protect you till your major shows up."

CHAPTER 31

W ill and Perlman made their way back through the streets of
Gettysburg, meandering around overturned carts and broken-down wagons. Smoke rolled along the street, and
small puffs would erupt from rooms on the tops of buildings
as sharpshooters dueled with retreating federal troops. Will
and Perlman closely followed Colonel Taylor, Lee's adjutant general, and a young lieutenant from Virginia who was his assistant.

"When you reckon we ought to go back for the woman?"
Perlman asked.

Will looked down Washington Street in the direction of the
house where they had left April. It was relatively quiet, with men
dressed in butternut gray entering houses and then herding Union
prisoners out to the street. "She's probably better off where she is
for now."

"And so are we. I don't much like questioning these people as it is, and I like it even less with that woman hovering around us. We never know what she might say."

"She's pretty smart though. Tends to pick up things we might miss."

"You really think she's told us everything we need to know?" Perlman asked.

Will scratched the back of his head. "Why Sergeant, I do detect a note of suspicion in your voice. Something may come to her, but our witness is dead now. Whatever April knows is old news."

Perlman shook his head. "I've dealt with this kind before. Somebody gets mad when someone they love is murdered. They already think they have the case solved before the police arrive, and what they want to do is lead you to the one they suspect, or better yet, hate. That woman and her family have been up to their necks in fighting the South for years. She'd like nothing better than to pin the blame on one of ours. She holds us responsible anyway."

Will just looked at the man. He knew that what Perlman was saying was true. He didn't like the idea of being used in a personal vendetta, but in a way that was what the war was all about.

They rounded the corner and rode past a small creek, then continued on to a group of buildings with a sign out front, PENNSYLVANIA COLLEGE. One of the larger buildings had a bell tower from which flew the Confederate battle flag. Taylor and the young lieutenant got down from their horses, followed by Will and Perlman. They looked up at the tower.

"General Ewell up there?" Will asked.

Taylor nodded. "I do believe so."

"If he is, somebody had to carry him," the lieutenant added. "The man only has one leg."

They made their way up the stairs and into the building, then began to climb a circular set of iron stairs that led to the observation tower. On the top landing they pushed open the door and stepped inside. There on a chair they could see General Ewell, the man they called Old Baldy. The stump of his leg was hanging off the chair, and the afternoon sun reflected off his bare head. An aide was pointing out the Union positions on the hills just north of town. General Trimble and a number of other high-ranking officers stood to Ewell's right. General Early stood to his left, along with the man Will had already seen once too often, young Lieutenant Reynolds.

Perlman nudged Will's arm and motioned toward Reynolds. The man held a curved pipe in his mouth that looked exactly like the one they had bought for Tillie in Chambersburg.

Will clenched his teeth and fell silent.

Taylor walked up to Ewell and saluted. "Sir, I have orders from General Lee."

Ewell turned to face the man. "Go ahead, Colonel."

Will watched both Early and Reynolds as they spotted him standing near the stairs. Early's heavy eyebrows dropped, and his lower lip edged out. It was obvious that he was angry that Will was continuing to dog him, even into the battle. Will could see the anger building in him. The man was haughty by nature, which was typical for officers of his rank. But there was a smugness to him, an air of omniscience. Lieutenant Reynolds had a look of surprise. He jerked the pipe from his mouth and stuffed it, still smoking, into his coat pocket. It gave Will a slight sense of satisfaction to be there. If he could in any way make these men uncomfortable, he was satisfied.

Taylor leaned over the edge of their balcony and pointed in the direction of the hill with the cemetery. "General Lee wants you to take that hill if at all practicable. The federals are digging in there, with reinforcements coming in all the time."

"I can see that, Colonel. Can Pender offer any support?"

Taylor shook his head. "I'm afraid not, sir. Not at this time. The most the general can promise you is long-range artillery support.

But it is very important that you take that hill, along with Culp's Hill to the east of it. That would put us into position to roll back the Union lines."

"But Lee's orders to me were to avoid a general engagement until the arrival of the other divisions of the army. Are Longstreet's men here yet?"

"No, sir, not until tonight or early tomorrow, I'm afraid."

Ewell looked out over the town. "If at all practicable, you say?"

"Those were the general's words, sir. General Lee is not in a position to judge for himself either the condition of the troops or the difficulties they might face when approaching that hill from the north. I was told specifically, however, that you are to carry that hill occupied by the enemy, if you found it practicable."

General Trimble leaned over. "My men have heard chopping, General. Those people are preparing their defense. Allow me to attack, sir. Give me the division."

Ewell ignored the man and instead looked back up at Taylor. It was almost as if he was uncomfortable speaking with his commanders in the presence of Lee's adjutant. "Is that all, Colonel?"

Ewell's attitude made Taylor stiffen. He threw his shoulders back. "Yes, sir."

"Then I suggest you return to General Lee. Tell him we are making our plans directly."

Taylor saluted and turned to go, the lieutenant from Virginia at his heels. Will was sorry to see him leave. Having Lee's eyes and ears in the room was a comforting thing, and with him gone, there was no telling what might happen.

Ewell looked back at the men surrounding him. "Well, gentlemen, what do you suggest?" Will could see a look of despair suddenly come over his face. Lee had given him too much latitude. Jackson would have given him direct and specific orders if he were still alive. There would have been none of this "if at all practicable" with Stonewall. Ewell's eyes looked hollow and fearful, almost as if he were more afraid of making a mistake than he was of doing nothing. To do nothing would mean avoiding risk, and Ewell's eyes and the tremble in his voice showed that he was most afraid of taking a risk.

Trimble blustered and threw up his hands. "Suggest?" He practically shouted the question. "We attack, sir. Give me two brigades and I will take that hill. The enemy has fallen back. He is demoralized." He slammed his fist into his hand. "We must act quickly if we are to get there before they get that place secured. If we wait until tomorrow, my men will die en masse."

Early cleared his throat, evidently with the idea that he should be recognized. When he wasn't, he blinked his eyes and began to speak. "General, my men are tired. We have marched on Harrisburg and would have taken the place if we hadn't been ordered here. Jimmy Longstreet has fresh men. Let him do the heavy work. We've taken the town. The enemy may be strung out along the road all the way to Washington for all we know. We haven't heard a word from Stuart to the contrary. With our own army trickling in from Chambersburg, we should wait until we are assembled before we start an engagement."

Ewell took a set of written orders from his pocket. "That is what General Lee ordered me to do when we came here."

"Precisely, sir."

"All right. I've seen enough. Let's go back to the headquarters and discuss the matter further. Perhaps Lee will send us more definitive orders."

Two of the young soldiers picked Ewell up and draped his arms over their shoulders. They carried him to the door. The other officers from his staff followed, while Early and Lieutenant Reynolds stopped at the door where Will and Perlman were standing. Early looked Will in the eye and put his hands on his hips. "I thought I told you I didn't want to see you again about this matter, Major. You have no orders."

Will smiled. "That is where you are wrong, General." He pulled out the set of orders from his pocket. "I have my orders directly from General Lee."

"Let me see that."

Will handed over the set of written orders and Early practically tore them from his hand.

He read them over, his eyes falling on Lee's signature. Folding them up, he handed them back to Will.

"Is that clear enough for you, General?"

"It's clear to me that you're wiggling your way out of fighting in this war by pursuing your Yankee sympathizer's wild-goose chase."

"And it's equally clear to me, General, that you have some interest in this matter beyond what is clearly visible."

"What are you suggesting, Major?"

"You were near the man's farm when he was murdered. You had his book of Psalms, the one he carried with him at all times. Your friend is his neighbor. Perhaps you had an interest in Mr. Wolff's death."

"And perhaps your interest is in his daughter, Major. Haven't you had enough of the women of Charleston, or do you just enjoy plying women with your charms?"

"He doesn't even have a witness," Reynolds added, a cool, collected air of bragging in his voice. Will ignored it.

"Just answer my questions, General. We have ways of verifying your answers."

Early crossed his arms and began wiggling his chin with anger, shaking the part of the brown and gray beard that stood out from his bottom lip. "Very well. Ask me your questions."

"You didn't answer me when I asked you about the book of Psalms you had in York. You know"—Will paused, staring deeply in Early's brown eyes—"right before you threatened me with a firing squad." He smiled. It gave him some sense of satisfaction to bring the man's words back to him, and he could tell it had an effect on Early. The words were like the ghosts that inhabit a man's house long after he is gone. They rattle the proverbial chains and refuse to rest. "Did you get the book from General Jenkins or from your friend Slocum?" He paused to allow the words to sink in. "Or perhaps you picked it up from Wolff's body."

Early shook his head. "That's poppycock and you know it. I've never met the man and wouldn't have a reason to kill him, unless he was in a Yankee uniform. I got it from one of Slocum's kids. How he came into possession of the thing, I couldn't tell you. Perhaps he just found it."

"Then you did talk to the man that day?"

"Yes, we had lemonade and talked about the battle, the war, his farm, and how he wanted to expand it. We may have talked about his sons."

"What about General Jenkins? What's his interest in this thing?"

Early dropped his gaze to the floor. "I'm afraid that is a personal matter, Major."

"General, murder is a very personal thing. It isn't like war, the killing of strangers."

"He mentioned that he knew Mrs. Wolff. But he told me he had nothing to do with the murder of her husband. Beyond that, I can't recall. Now, is that all you have? One of us ought to get to fighting this war."

Will nodded. "It's all I have for now. I may come back to you for more questions." He glanced at Reynolds. "We would like to have a word with your aide, however."

"He won't tell you any more than you've heard from me."

"You'll just have to let us be the judge of that, General. We're finished with you now."

Early gave out a grunt and glanced at Reynolds. He then turned and headed down the stairs, leaving Reynolds alone on the observation platform with Will and Perlman.

Reynolds stood erect. "I can tell you even less than the general."

"I doubt that," Perlman said. He stepped forward and looked at Will. "You mind if I ask the lieutenant a few questions?"

"Not at all, Sergeant."

"I see you've taken to smoking a pipe," he remarked, sniffing in the pungent odor lingering in the air.

Will could see the question made Reynolds nervous. He no doubt had never expected to see the two of them ever again, and certainly not with the smell of a pipe around him. "What of it? What business do you people have with me?"

He asked the question with a flare of anger in his voice, a reaction Will had noticed among men who were guilty. Something about the pain of a man's conscience wouldn't allow a guilty man to go quietly.

"Let me see that pipe you put in your pocket," Perlman said.

Reynolds shook his head. "Absolutely not! Why should I?"

"Then perhaps you'd like to accompany us to see General Lee," Will said. "You can explain to him why you are refusing his orders."

Reynolds slowly took the pipe out of his pocket and handed it to Perlman. It was still warm to the touch.

Perlman passed it over to Will. "Would you care to tell us how you came by this thing, Lieutenant?"

"I don't know where I got it. I may have come by it on the battlefield."

Perlman took the pipe back from Will. He bounced it in his hand. "You may have come by it in Messersmith's Woods, you mean."

"I did not."

Perlman smiled. "I see. You don't know where you got it, but you're sure it wasn't there."

"What has that got to do with anything?"

"Well, you seemed so sure that we didn't have a witness." Perlman held the pipe up in front of Reynold's face. "It just happens that our witness was murdered in Messersmith's Woods. She had this pipe on her. The Major here bought it for her himself in Chambersburg."

Reynolds clenched his teeth. "I'm not saying anything more to you men. You can just charge me or leave me alone."

Will stepped over to the balcony. He looked over the edge of the rail. "Quite a view here, Sergeant. Perhaps the lieutenant would like to see it better."

Reynolds backed up. "I would not. You two just go on your way and leave me alone."

Will and Perlman looked at one another, and Will nodded. They rushed at the man, grabbing both of his arms and pulling him toward the rail.

He began to shout. "Leave me alone. Just drop me, you hear."

"Let's do that, Sergeant," Will said. "Let's drop him."

"Lead on, Major, and I'll obey."

Picking him up, they grabbed both his legs and held him over the railing. They hung on as he yelled and screamed.

"Be a shame for a young man like this to commit suicide, wouldn't it?" Perlman asked, shouting the words. He looked down at the young lieutenant. "You'd better stop your struggling, Lieutenant, before you do fall. Quiet down, too, before you attract attention."

"What do you want from me?" the man screeched.

"The truth," Will bellowed.

"I'll tell you. I'll tell you anything. Just let me up from here."

Perlman looked at Will and smiled. "Major, I do believe the young man here is ready to talk."

"Is that right?" Will smiled. He looked down at the dangling officer. "Are you ready to talk, Lieutenant?"

"Yes, anything."

"Did you kill that black woman at Messersmith's Woods?" Perlman asked.

"Yes!" the man yelled. "I did."

"Were you ordered to do that?" Will asked.

"No, General Early didn't tell me to do any such thing. He just gave me a letter for General Lee. I did that on my own. I thought I could stop this thing you were doing."

Will looked at Perlman. "Do you think he's telling us the truth?"

"I'm not sure we'd have any reason to doubt him at this point."

Carefully they lifted the man back onto the platform. They then set him down on the chair General Ewell had been using. "We will need a written statement from you, Lieutenant," Will said. He took out a small piece of paper and a pencil and handed them to the man. "You just write out exactly what you did that night and why. Be specific."

Reynolds took the next several minutes and wrote his statement. He signed it and handed it over to Will. "Is that all? Can I go now?"

"Just a few other matters," Will said. "That woman you killed was blind. You might have thought you were protecting your brave Old Jube, but all you were doing was murdering an old blind woman."

Will folded the paper the man had signed and drummed the back of his hand with it. "But I will bring you up on charges after this is over. You can count on that. You will face a court-martial." Will stuck the paper in his pocket. "If I were you, Lieutenant, I'd find a way to fight for some honor here on this battlefield. Your good name will no longer serve you. You have dishonored this army and all that we stand for."

CHAPTER 32

The house seemed deserted and yet filled at the same time, but it was filled with thoughts and sounds that sent tingles up and down April's spine. The men on the floor were restless and in pain. They moaned in chorus, some of their voices rising like opera sopranos, while others kept up a low, malcontent hum.

She was also worried. The young lieutenant from South Carolina had left without any fanfare, but with the noise of his men moving around the house now silent, she wondered if the Union general she had met in the basement wouldn't just decide to throw caution to the wind, along with his promise to her, and come out of the darkness shooting.

And then there was the matter of Roberta. This was a woman who did her duty no matter what the cost, and now she was stationed in the barn where April had planned the general's escape.

April would have to deal with it. She couldn't let the young woman see the general, and she couldn't let the general see her. Both of them appeared to be conscientious and brave, and neither would avoid a confrontation. She would have to find a way to get rid of Roberta, if only for a short time. But how?

She watched as Ulysses carried more water into the house. He was strong and determined to find his freedom, and now she had placed him directly in the path of the war. Will had told her that he had no interest in sending the man back into slavery, but that might not stop any other officer from doing just that. Without Will, she would be helpless to stop it. Just how long she could pretend to be his owner and Will's fiancée was anybody's guess. Even though her story wasn't technically a lie—Will had seen to that— it was still hard for her to tell it.

Something bothered her about Ulysses. She had worked at dismissing it from her mind. He had wanted to stay on their farm, and her father had refused. There was also the matter of his name, Ulysses Sampson. Her father had scrawled the letters **US** on the ground. But she refused to think about that just now.

She got up from her knees where she had been changing the dressings on a severely wounded man and walked into the kitchen. Ulysses had his back to her. He had just placed another large pot of water on the stove to boil and was now sharpening a long knife. The man raked the knife back and forth over a smooth stone, bearing down on it as he worked at the edge.

"What are you doing, Ulysses?"

The sound of her voice caused him to clutch the knife to his chest. Slowly, he turned around. "I's jes sharpenin' dis here knife, Miss April. Dat's all."

"What for?"

"You needed one a bit ago, and I jes wanted to make sure dere was one ready fer you, iffen you needed one."

April shook her head. "I hope it won't come to that. Maybe they'll send us a doctor."

Ulysses bobbed his head. "Yes, ma'am."

April stepped closer to him. She lowered her voice. "What if I could get you out of here Ulysses, send you behind the Union lines? You'd be safe there."

His eyes widened. "You think you could do dat?"

April nodded. "I might be able to. Perhaps tonight."

Ulysses put down the knife. "Ma'am, dat would be a wonderful thing. I sure would like to get myself out of dis here place."

April looked back toward the living room. "I need to go out to the barn for a bit to see to the man out there. Do you think you could change the dressings on the rest of those men in there?" She paused and bit her lower lip. "I know it might be hard. Those are the men trying to keep you in slavery."

Once again Ulysses bobbed his head, a continual thoughtless gesture where Ulysses was concerned. It was as if he wasn't paying any attention to the words, only responding to who had said them. "I knows dat. But dem folks in dere is hurt bad. I'll see what I can do fer dem."

April lightly patted his bare arm. "That's good, Ulysses. They may be the enemy, but they are just men, the same as you are. God made them just as He made you and me." She handed over the bottle of iodine. "You take good care of them, and I'll be back in a little while."

She turned to walk away, but Ulysses stopped her. "Miss April, you mean what you say 'bout gettin' me outta here?"

"Yes, I mean every word of it. Tonight, Ulysses, tonight."

April went out the back door and headed for the barn. The house was fortunately on the outskirts of Gettysburg, and while it had once been in the midst of the battle, it was now no more than a peaceful observer in the midst of distant cannon fire. Will had chosen it well. She had no desire to be on the roads while the battle was going on.

She swung the barn door open and stepped inside. "Roberta," she called out in a hushed voice. "Are you here, Roberta?"

"I'm up here," the girl's voice called out from up above. "In the hayloft."

April watched as the young woman stood up, slung her rifle over her shoulder, stepped to the ladder, and began to climb down.

"I just figured I could see better from up there, but I ain't seen much of late."

Roberta stepped to the floor and walked over to April. She seemed more relaxed. There was even a smile on her face. "I ain't seen me much to worry about for some time now. I figure the battle's a ways off by now."

"I hope you're right." April looked for the bales of hay and sat down on one. "Come sit by me for a while. I'm interested in knowing more about you."

"There ain't nothing much to tell." Roberta took a seat on a bale in front of April.

April scooped up some dirt from the floor and, reaching over, rubbed it gently on Roberta's face.

"What you doing that for?"

"You look too pretty for a boy, and you have no whiskers." April dug at the dirt with her toe and then picked up another small piece of the black sod. She rubbed it across Roberta's chin. "I just figure if you're going to do this thing, you might as well look the part."

"What do you care for? You're a Yankee."

"I'm a woman, just like you."

Roberta bowed her head and shook it slowly. "I hate being a woman. It's useless."

April reached over and put her hand on Roberta's shoulder. "You shouldn't say that. Womanhood is by far the most noble thing you could ever aspire to. You shape the morality of a nation and bring love into the world. This war is the creation of men and all the hatred that goes with it."

Roberta looked up at April. There was a glistening in her eyes. "My folks named me Roberta cause what they hankered for was a Robert. I figured I ought to be what they wanted, so I joined up with this here army."

April reached out and touched the black smear she had put on Roberta's face. "You know, I never had a sister and I always wanted one. Some other time, some other place, I would have loved for that to be you. You are pretty. You don't belong as a boy in the army. You need to be surrounded by love, not hate."

Roberta scooted closer to the edge of the bale. "Sides, from what I heard, you is here cause of hatred too. I heard some of the men talking. I guess that sergeant what brung you here was explaining it to the lieutenant. He said your daddy was killed and they was trying to find out by who. Said it might be one of our officers who done it. Said that was why you was with them. Ain't you got hatred for the man who done that?"

"I don't know. Perhaps I do. I like to think of it as justice."

"See! I hear that all the time. Us folks is up here cause your people done come down into our land, trying to make us live by your ways. Your men in their blue coats come down to us and burn our homes and steal our cows and horses. Ain't we got no right to hate them what done that?"

"This war is about slavery, about the freeing of men and women held against their will."

"Pshaw! I ain't never owned no slaves. Don't know many people who do, neither. The ones I do know treat them folks better than most people treat the white folks working for them. They got shoes and better clothes than I got. You want to turn 'em loose to come up here and starve for puny pay. What kind of freedom is that?"

April shook her head. "I don't think I'll ever be able to understand you people."

"That's right. You won't. But that don't stop you from telling us what to do." Roberta then waved her hand in front of April. "*You.*" She accentuated the word, then motioned with her hand over her own chest. "*Me.*"

She put her hands on her knees and leaned forward. "If you Yankees could just get that straight. You is you and us is us. We ain't gonna be you and you ain't gonna be us."

April got to her feet. "All right. You made your point." She started toward the door, then turned around. "One favor I'd like to ask you."

"What's that?"

"Those men of yours in there, some of them need a doctor. I'd like you to go into town tonight and see if you can find a doctor. Can you do that?"

"The lieutenant told me to stay put right here."

"I know, but this is important. Some of those men might die without medical help. You're the only one I can send. It's not for me; it's for them."

"All right. I suppose I can."

"Good, then I'll come and get you when I'm ready for you to go. I really enjoyed talking to you, Roberta, even if we disagree. I think you're going to make a fine, strong woman." She smiled. "You're already a good soldier."

CHAPTER 33

Will and Perlman rode through the streets of Gettysburg listening to the sound of the distant guns. It was small comfort to know the fighting was on the other side of town. War always had a way of catching up. The two men were riding to the edge of town, close to the college. They had been told that Jenkins was making camp there with his men.

They watched a mangy dog dart past them, its black coat covered in dust. It never even gave them a second look, not even so much as a bark or a whimper. The thing had taking cover in its mind, getting itself out of harm's way and fast. It ran across the street and into an alley. "I know how he feels," Perlman said. "Sometimes glory just don't matter no more."

"It matters to the people who give the orders," Will said. He studied Perlman. The man was a lot like his mule, hardheaded and plodding. When he got an idea in his head, it was difficult to shake it. "Do you think Reynolds told us the whole truth?"

Perlman laughed. "I think that man would have told us anything and everything there was to tell. He was looking at Gettysburg upside down. That would have a tendency to clear any man's head."

He paused for a moment, looking back at Will. "You serious back there? You really mean to have him court-martialed?"

"You bet I do. I don't care if Tillie was old or a slave, she was a human being." Will took a deep breath. "She was smart, funny, and a good friend to people who knew her. She deserved better than that. If a man doesn't respect human life, he has no business in the service of his country."

Perlman looked at the street. It was littered with the scraps of war. There were bodies that had not been carried away and a few wounded who were still lying on the sidewalk. "I don't see much respect for human life here."

The fields on the north edge of town were clogged with what supplies had followed the army on its way from Harrisburg. Tents had formed a city in row upon row of flapping canvas. Horses and riders were coming and going with great regularity. This was the headquarters of the Confederate cavalry. It put them in a perfect spot to intercept any Union attempt at outflanking the Rebel forces in town, while allowing them to scout out the Union rear. Will knew that this was where they would be able to find Albert Jenkins.

He trotted his horse up to a picket line and quickly dismounted. Perlman slid off his mule and tied the reins. They caught a whiff of some beef being slowly turned on spits over crackling open flames. In Will's time with the Army of Northern Virginia, he had always known the cavalry to eat better.

"Looks like we're here for supper," Perlman said. "You don't suppose they're havin' pork fat and collards do you?"

Will smiled. "I don't suppose they are. Smells to me like they've killed the fatted calf."

"Let's hope so."

They walked through the camp, making inquiries about where they might find General Jenkins. The men they stopped pointed to a set of large tents on the west side of the camp, and Will could see the battle flag flying from a staff nearby. They quickly made their way over to the spot.

Will noticed one officer who seemed to be giving out orders. He was a tall man with long black hair. His swooping mustache gave him dash and made him look like a cavalry officer. The collar around his neck was high and rigid, gold in color. It showed his rank of colonel. It also set off the large gold cuffs on the sleeves of his blouse. His brass buttons were polished and had a shine to them, and the gold stripe that came down the length of his trousers only made him look taller than he actually was.

Will stepped up to the man. "Afternoon, Colonel. I'm Major Will Chevalier of the provost marshal's office, and this is Sergeant Perlman. We're here to see General Jenkins."

The man looked Will in the eye with a hard stare. There was no life to his eyes, just two small brown stones swimming in small pools of white milky fluid. "What about?"

"I am afraid that is the business of the provost's office, Colonel. It's between us and General Jenkins."

"Listen, we've very busy here. General Jenkins has gone out on a forced reconnaissance. I don't know when he'll be back. I am Colonel Francis Updike, the general's aide. I know all of the general's business. Anything you have to say to him, you can say to me."

"I'm afraid that won't be possible, Colonel Updike."

"We might have a few questions for the colonel," Perlman added. He moved closer to Will's elbow.

Updike turned his attention to Perlman. He raised his chin and stiffened his back. There was a sudden snootiness at being questioned by an enlisted man, but Will could see it didn't bother Perlman one iota. He seemed to take delight in it.

Perlman took out a piece of paper and a pencil. He took off his cap to write on, showing his balding head. "When your outfit came north past Greencastle, did the general make any personal stops along the way?"

Updike clasped his hands behind his back. "General Jenkins has no personal life when he's in command and at the head of this column."

Perlman wrote down the comment and smiled. He looked up at Updike. "That's funny, 'cause we did see him at a funeral, a funeral for a Northern civilian. Now what do you make of that?"

"It may have been a friend of the general's family."

Perlman's grin grew wider. "Well, we did talk to the family, and none of them ever remember the general meeting the man who was being buried. Now why do you reckon he would feel the need to be at the funeral?"

"It would seem the colonel here doesn't know everything about General Jenkins," Will interjected.

Updike folded his arms and looked down the bridge of his nose. "I don't see where you have the authority to ask anybody anything. I'd like to see you men leave our camp."

"Oh, we have the authority, Colonel." Will reached into his pocket and pulled out the orders handwritten by Lee. He handed them over to Updike. "If you refuse to cooperate or hinder us in any way, you'll have to explain yourself to General Lee."

Updike grunted at the idea. He opened the orders and began to read. As Will traced his gaze down the page, he could see a noticeable change in the man's face. What had been ridicule and haughtiness quickly turned into fear. He lowered the page. "Why didn't you tell me you had orders from General Lee himself?"

"We didn't think that would be necessary, Colonel," Will said. "Now why don't you just tell us why General Jenkins would go to that funeral?"

Updike softened his stance and began to rock back and forth nervously on the balls of his feet. "The gentleman in question was the husband of a woman that the general knew quite well. He wanted to pay his respects. That's all."

"And how did he know there was even going to be a funeral?" Perlman asked. "I wouldn't exactly say these people were neighbors of his."

"General Jenkins knew they lived in the area. I think he asked questions along the way to people who might know the family, trying his best to keep in contact with them. I suppose that is where he found out about the funeral."

"The general was close to the wife?" Perlman asked. "How close?"

Updike bit his lower lip. "At one time they were engaged to be married."

"And he still has feelings for the woman?" Perlman asked.

Updike's eyebrows suddenly curved downward. It was as if Perlman had hit a nerve. "I really couldn't say about that."

"You don't suppose your general spoke to the woman, do you?" Perlman asked. "Perhaps he met with her and you didn't know."

"I would have known."

"Is there anything else you would like to tell us, Colonel?" Will asked. "If this matter does come up before a military court, your cooperation will be noted. Of course, if we should find out that you are withholding any information from us, that wouldn't look too good. It might reflect on your record."

Updike looked around and then leaned forward. "This won't get back to General Jenkins, will it?"

"Of course not," Will said. "What you say will remain confidential."

"The general took a number of rides alone when we were in the area you're speaking of. I know he was having a difficult time being so close to the woman he loves and not being able to see her."

"And did he see her?" Perlman asked the question again.

"Not to my knowledge."

J enkins's cavalry brigade had brought almost forty head of beef with them into camp. Some were milk cows that were about to be put to use in a way they might never expect, but others were steers raised for beef. Some of the men were born cowboys. Others were pretty fair butchers. Either way, it was plain to see how a unit of troopers mounted on horseback fed pretty well while in the field, especially in enemy territory. The Union army had lived off of the fat of Virginia and the Mississippi river valley for two years now, and so Will and Perlman didn't have the first pang of conscience when they cut into a slice of Yankee beef.

It was almost dark when they saw Jenkins ride into camp at the head of a column. The man was wiry and his dark beard almost covered his shirt. Updike was there to point out where Will and Perlman were taking their supper, and Will noticed him glance at the two of them while his aide explained who they were and why they were in camp. Jenkins stood straight and smoothed out his blouse, then turned and walked directly toward them.

Both Will and Perlman put down their plates when Jenkins walked up. They stood to attention.

"You men be at ease. I know who you are and why you're here. If you'll walk with me for a minute, I'll tell you everything I know. I want to get this over with as soon as possible, so there'll be no need to grill me for answers. I'm going to tell you everything I can tell you."

They began a slow walk around the camp, with Jenkins doing all the talking. "I was engaged to Christine Wolff at one time. She came up here and married Jonas Wolff." He stopped and looked at them. "It didn't change the way I felt about her, not for a moment."

He continued with his walk. "I wanted to see her, so I sent her a note asking if I could meet her. When I rode to their farm I found Jonas. We had words, but I didn't kill him. I did meet Christine later, but I said nothing about what happened."

"Did he have your note with him?" Will asked.

Jenkins nodded. "I'm sad to say that he did."

"Must have prompted a few words," Perlman smirked.

"More than a few words." He looked Will in the eye. "But I didn't kill the man."

"And just how was the note to be delivered?" Perlman asked. "I wouldn't think you'd use the U.S. Mail."

Jenkins balled his fists and twisted his neck, as if he were trying to relieve himself of some cramp. "General Early took it from me."

"Old Jube is your postman?" Perlman laughed.

Jenkins glared at him. "I would expect you to be more respectful than that, Sergeant, when referring to your superior."

"The sergeant is right," Will said. "That hardly seems like an ordinary way for mail delivery."

Jenkins gritted his teeth. "The general has a friend who was Wolff's neighbor. I asked him to convey my note to that man and make delivery."

"And did you find Wolff's book of Psalms?" Will asked.

"No. I didn't see any book. When I heard about the murder, I thought for sure that I would be a suspect. I had every reason to want the man dead. I love Christine. But I would never kill her husband. Do you understand that? I know it looks bad. If I have to face a court-martial, I will. But I will tell the same story because it's the only one I have. It's the truth."

A short time later, Will and Perlman rode out of camp. "You believe him?" Perlman asked.

"I only believed part of what he said. He didn't act guilty, but he did seem to be covering something up."

At the edge of town they ran into a familiar face. Colonel Eugene Sinclair was riding with several of his staff. When he recognized Will, he waved.

"What do you suppose he wants?" Perlman asked.

"Let's find out," Will said.

They rode up to the man, who was looking quite chipper considering they were in the midst of a battle. His mustache was freshly waxed, and he looked recently shaved. "Chevalier, I've been looking for you."

"Wonderful to see you, Colonel."

"How are you progressing on your assignment?" The man had a smile on his face, almost as if he already knew the answer.

"We're close to being finished, Colonel."

"Fine, fine. You'll be happy to know that I'm fulfilling my part of our bargain. I have a line command for you."

"And what would that be, Colonel?"

"General Pickett arrives tomorrow. You are to command a regiment of his troops. It would seem you have some very high recommendations, and if you do well, I'd expect you to make colonel in a matter of weeks or days."

"And who might that be, Colonel? Who would recommend me?"

Sinclair smiled. "Why, none other than General Bobby Lee himself, along with General Jubal Early."

CHAPTER 34

pril walked toward the barn. She could see patches of stars winking between the clouds. The sky was threatening rain, but so far it had produced only a sultry feel to the air. The occasional breath of wind was almost greasy to the touch. She had waited some time for the night to settle in and for the men Lieutenant Victor had left to feel more relaxed. One of them was already yawning, and Ulysses had shot her a number of glances that showed his restlessness. She could only hope that the general in the cellar would be patient. There was only one more matter for her to attend to. She had to send Roberta on a wild-goose chase in search of a doctor.

She eased the large door open and stepped inside. Roberta had lit a lantern, which hung on a nail under the hayloft. A shimmering yellow glow rippled across the hay on the floor and produced soft shadows on the rough boards that made up the walls. Sickles and rakes hung on the coarse wood, along with what was left of the leather harnesses that were used for the plow horses. The owners had obviously taken the animals with them, and April couldn't blame them for exercising caution. A man's plow horse made the difference in his ability to bring in a crop. With what everyone had heard about the Confederate army's need for horses, it had probably been a wise decision.

Her two mules hung their heads over the rails of their stalls, twitching their ears back and forth. Guns boomed in the distance. With each clap of artillery, the mules signaled their displeasure with their ears.

"Roberta! Are you here?" Her voice echoed in the barn.

She heard movement behind one of the bales of hay, and Roberta rolled out from behind it, her rifle in her hands. "I'm here. I was jes sleepin'."

The girl slowly got to her feet and propped the rifle against the hay. She grabbed hold of her gray tunic and began to shake the hay from it. "I weren't sleepin' too long. I coulda woke up fast."

"I'm sure you could have." April smiled. "My mules were perfectly safe." She stepped closer to the girl. "I came as I said. I need for you to go and find us a doctor."

"Aw." Roberta continued to knock the hay off her tattered gray trousers. "Can't that wait till in the morning?"

April shook her head. "No, I'm afraid it can't. Some of those men have serious injuries. If we wait until the battle begins in the morning, I'm afraid that the doctors might have their hands full." She knew that what she had told Roberta wasn't exactly a lie. A couple of the men inside did have serious wounds. But it made her feel bad that she might be shading the truth just a little, even if it was for the girl's own good. She didn't want Roberta to be anywhere close to the barn when she brought the general and Ulysses out to take the mules.

"All right, all right. I'll go. I might even find out what's happened to our regiment. Me and the boys in there will be wanting to join up with them pretty quick like."

"You really want to fight this war, don't you?"

Roberta nodded her head. "You bet I do. I want to give them Yankees a taste of their own medicine."

April stepped to the door. "You will be leaving right away, won't you?"

Roberta waved her hand at her. "Of course I will. I said so, didn't I?"

April turned and walked back to the house. There was still an odd feeling in the pit of her stomach. Getting to know these people she considered to be her enemies had challenged much of what she believed. The people were real and had dreams and shining ideals, and previously she had thought them to be only greedy slave holders who couldn't feel the pang of conscience. Now she felt like a traitor no matter what she did. She couldn't leave the general in the cellar to be discovered and captured, but she couldn't escape the feeling that she was betraying a trust. Will had brought her here to help her, and now she was deceiving him. Everything these people thought about Yankees she was proving to be correct. It galled her and sickened her slightly.

She opened the front door and spotted a young Carolina private right away. The man was standing by a broken window, looking longingly at the streets of Gettysburg in the distance. "Aren't you tired?" she asked. "Shouldn't you be getting some sleep?"

The soldier looked at the men on the floor. Some were moaning, while others maintained a stoic, worrisome silence, pain permanently etched on their faces. The private shivered. Somehow the thought of being in the same area as the wounded and dying had startled him with the notion of his own mortality. Living as he had on a battlefield meant living with death, but the dead were soon carried off and the wounded went to the rear to receive attention. He was seeing the results of war up close, smelling it and listening to it whimper. He swallowed. "I don't know if I could sleep."

April spotted Ulysses curled up in a ball just inside the dining room. He seemed to be sleeping. She wound her way past the wounded men and took the soldier's arm. "Let me fix you a place in the kitchen. It's better there, and you can sleep some. I'll wake you when I need to sleep."

He followed her like a sick puppy. It was obvious the man was exhausted and just as obvious that if he were allowed to be some-place else, anyplace else, that he wouldn't be awake for very long.

April took a blanket off the shelf in the hall closet and led the man down the hallway to the kitchen. She spread it out on the floor. "Where is the other man the lieutenant left here?"

"He's upstairs keeping an eye out."

April took the man's rifle and leaned it against the wall. "That's good. You just get a little sleep. You'll need it tomorrow. I'll take care of the men out there and come back for you."

The young man lay down on the blanket and smiled up at her. "Thank you, ma'am. I sure do appreciate it and all you're doing for us."

April backed out the door. "Just get some sleep. It'll make you feel better."

April walked back into the living room. She bent over and spoke softly to a soldier who was watching her. She checked his bandage and patted his head gently. Then she began to pace back and forth, stopping occasionally to speak to a soldier or check a bandage. She was also trying as best she could to give the man in the kitchen a chance to drift off to sleep. She knew it wouldn't take very long. She also wanted to make certain that Roberta had enough time to leave the barn and begin her search for a doctor.

Occasionally April glanced out the window, looking for the girl as she passed. She saw nothing but figured Roberta had left shortly after she'd spoken to her. By now she was probably long gone. The house echoed quietly with sounds of pain-filled sleep—snores punctuated by restless sighs and nightmare-borne twitches.

April walked softly past the men to where Ulysses was sleeping. She stooped over and shook him. "Ulysses, are you ready to go?"

The man's eyes popped open. They were like beacons in the dark room. "Go? Is it time?"

"Yes, I just have to get one more man. You two will go together. Wait for me by the door."

As he scrambled to get to his feet, April made her way to the table where she had laid the candle and matches. She sighted Perlman's cat in a corner, hunched over in a pouncing position. No doubt the thing had spotted some movement, maybe even a mouse. She only hoped he would refrain from any kill he had in mind until after she had safely taken Ulysses and the general out of the house. The last thing she needed now was noise.

She struck a match and lit the candle, then made her way to the hall that led to the stairs. Opening the door softly, she started down the well-worn stairs. She stepped lightly and then saw the particular stair that had given out the loud squeak. She had made a mental note of the thing. She lifted her foot and stepped over it. When she got to the cellar, she lifted the candle high. "General Schimmelfennig, it's me. I'm back."

The man stepped out of the gloom and into the soft light. He had his revolver in his hand. "I was worried."

"There's no need for worry, General. I told you it would be after dark. There are only two men in the house, one upstairs and the other sleeping in the kitchen. I'm taking you and a runaway slave I know out to the barn through the front door. I have two mules there, and I saw some leather tack and harness you can use. I sent the guard stationed there out to look for a doctor."

Schimmelfennig smiled, his teeth forming a bright crease in the candlelight. "You are a diligent woman. Quite rigorous. I like that."

April pointed to the gun. "You won't need that. I've taken care of everything."

He looked down at the revolver and bounced it in his hand. "I feel more comfortable with it this way. I won't use it. It makes me feel better."

"It makes me uncomfortable. I already told you that. Please put it away."

He widened his smile and stuffed the long revolver back into his leather holster. "There you are, good lady. Lead on."

April started up the stairs, holding the candle out in front of her. She climbed several of them, pausing in front of the noisy one. "Step over this one," she spoke in a low voice. "It makes a noise."

She continued up the stairs, but froze in her tracks when she heard the loud squeak. Her back stiffened. The man hadn't listened to her. She was angry and frightened at the same time. She didn't want to rouse the soldier in the kitchen. Without looking back, she continued up the stairs and turned the knob on the door leading into the hall. She quickly made her way out into the living room. Ulysses was waiting at the door. She whispered in a low voice. "This is General Schimmelfennig. He will be going with you tonight."

Ulysses seemed startled. He opened his eyes wide and ran his hand over his cheek. "Is you sure?" He shook his head. "I don't wants to be gettin' shot at."

"Just go with him. He'll take you to safety."

They went through the front door and out into the yard, then hurried toward the barn. April pushed the door open, and they stepped inside. "The mules are in the stalls over there, and there is tack on the walls. You'll have to make do as best you can and ride bareback. I didn't see any saddles."

Schimmelfennig and Ulysses led the mules out into the barn and began to fish through the various items of tack they could find on the walls. Soon they found a couple of halter ropes and bridles and began to clamp them into the mule's mouths.

"Young lady, I won't forget you," Schimmelfennig said. "You've saved me from spending time in Libby Prison, at the very least."

"Now hold on there a minute, you Yankee!" The voice came from the corner of the barn, behind a bale of hay. It startled the three of them. April's heart stopped as Roberta stepped out from behind the hay. Her rifle was lowered and pointed directly at the general.

April stepped toward the girl. "What are you doing here? You were supposed to be looking for a doctor."

Roberta smiled. "I see now why you wanted me to do that." She waggled the rifle at Schimmelfennig. "Just so's you could get your friends outta here. You Yankees are a deceitful bunch, aren't you? A body can't never trust you no way, I reckon."

Schimmelfennig held the halter rope in his hands. He stepped closer to Roberta and her rifle. "Listen to me, soldier. We're on our way out of here. We mean you no harm."

"Like the dickens, you don't. I let you go and tomorrow you'll be a killing me and my kind." She shook her head. "What do you take me for, some rawboned recruit?"

Schimmelfennig stepped closer. "Not at all. You're obviously a young man with spirit and integrity." He stepped closer. "You know the right thing to do, and I know you'll think better of this thing and just let us go."

"Like fat I will." She prodded the rifle in his direction. "You just stay right where you are, elsewise I'm a gonna be killin' myself a Yankee."

Schimmelfennig turned and feinted back in April's direction, then suddenly whipped the halter he was carrying in the direction of the barrel of Roberta's rifle. It exploded as he jerked it from her hand.

With one smooth motion, he drew his revolver and fired. The shot caught the girl squarely in the chest, knocking her flat onto the floor.

April screamed and ran for Roberta. She dropped beside her and began to unbutton the girl's gray tunic as blood formed a spreading cloud in the gray fabric. She could see that Roberta was still breathing. The girl's eyes opened, and a soft pillow of blood formed through her lips.

Schimmelfennig and Ulysses mounted their mules, and April got to her feet. She ran over to the man, her teeth grinding with passion. "You promised me."

"I'm sorry, young lady. I did what I had to do."

"There was no need for that. That rifle has only one shot."

"And it was intended for me. I did what I had to do. If you take a careful look, you'll see that soldier is wearing gray. By this time tomorrow I want everyone who is wearing that uniform to be exactly like that soldier is now."

He kicked his mule and headed out the door. Ulysses gawked at April, his mouth open. Then, without a word, he followed the general out into the night.

April walked back to where Roberta lay. She stooped to the ground and finished unbuttoning the young woman's tunic. The wound continued to pump blood, and April put both of her hands on the seeping geyser and pressed with all her might. "I'm going to help you," she said.

Roberta's eyes popped open once again. "You can't help me none now. I'm a goner. Why did you do that for? Why did you help that man?"

April shook her head and continued to press on Roberta's chest. "It's this horrible war."

"But I thought you and me was friends." She coughed and continued to spit up blood.

April began to cry. "We are. We are friends."

"Then you do me one last favor as a friend." Roberta croaked out the words.

April nodded. "Anything."

"You button up this here shirt of mine. When I die, I want to die as a man. I don't want them boys in there to think they been fightin' with a woman."

CHAPTER 35

The night sky showed the barest trace of a silver blue in the east when Will's eyes opened. It was before dawn, but he could see the shadow of General Lee in his tent. The man was sitting on his cot with the lantern still lit. He was putting his boots on, getting ready for the day.

Will and Perlman had laid down their bedrolls fairly close to Lee's headquarters tent and had slept in a field along the Chambersburg Pike. They had gotten into camp after Lee retired for the night and several of the general's staff told Will how Lee had paced back and forth during the evening, waiting for the sound of Ewell's attack, an attack that never came.

Will reached over to shake Perlman.

"I'm awake," Perlman growled. "Just laying here and looking up at the darkness. A man likes to see everything before he goes."

Will rolled out of his bedroll and picked up his boots. "You aren't going anywhere." He began to stomp his feet down into the boots, one at a time.

Perlman rolled over. "If you're going into a line command today, I sure as blazes ain't gonna hold no woman's hand while you run off to be a hero."

"I'm following orders, and so are you."

Perlman struggled with his boots. "And just what are my orders?"

Will picked up his holster belt and strapped it on. Like most of the men in the provost marshal's office, both Will and Perlman carried two revolvers, which showed the men around them that they were line closers, soldiers who shot men who ran. "You're a policeman, Sergeant. You're on a murder case. We may have solved Tillie's murder, but that doesn't take care of what brought us into this thing in the first place."

"It seems pointless to me. Jenkins is the only man with a motive, seems to me. He had the opportunity too. What more do we want?"

"I'm still not settled on the matter of Wolff's book of Psalms. I know his note to Christine was in it, but why would Jenkins take it? He's not quite the type to walk away from a murder with a souvenir."

"Early said he got it from one of the Slocum boys."

"Again, I ask myself the question—why?" Will shook his head. "There must be something we're missing, something that's right in front of us. Just because we're policemen doesn't mean we can't be just as guilty as April is of coming to a conclusion and charging off to prove it."

Will had a feeling deep in his bones that the matter was a simple thing of seeing everything they needed to see. They had Jenkins's note on them, and April still had the book. Something had to be there, something they hadn't seen.

Perlman lifted his suspenders and placed them over his shoulders. "Been my experience that when you run into a closed door, you go in through the window. We're just standing here staring at the door. Maybe we just need to get our minds on something else, like fighting this here war."

Will looked off at the horses in the field. Perlman's mule had stayed right where they had left him. The thing had a mind like an anchor. Will was glad he'd hobbled his horse, but even with his hobbles on, the big gray had bounded away to the far side of the field. The guns made them feel vulnerable in an open field. "Why don't you saddle our mounts? I'll round up some coffee for us. I need to see the general when he comes out of his tent."

"You going to find out about your new assignment?"

Will nodded.

"You should ask him who got you the job. Was it Sinclair, as promised, or was it Early?"

"I know. It seems strange. For a man who hates the sight of me, Early's going to a lot of trouble to get me in the field."

"Maybe he's just hoping a Yankee bullet might take you off this case, something he hasn't been able to do."

"That would do it all right."

"And are you going to accept this new assignment?"

Will watched Lee's shadow in the tent. The man was fastening the buttons on his coat. He stood tall even though he had the weight of the world on his shoulders. Will shook his head. "I don't know yet. I tried like the dickens to get the general to approve these orders I'm carrying; then I asked him to get me out of them. I'm going to look like a fool now if I go back to him and reverse myself once again. The man will think I'm daft."

Perlman chucked. "Hardly what he's looking for in a commander, I should think."

"And I've been looking for this assignment ever since I joined up. I'd have to be a fool to say no."

"And plunge off with some Yankee woman on a personal vendetta that ain't going nowhere."

Will nodded. "That too."

Will was back in a matter of minutes. He took a cup of what passed for coffee out to Perlman, who was saddling his mule.

Perlman sipped the black mixture of chicory and motioned toward the fire. "You go see to General Lee. He's over at the fire. I'll bring the animals when I'm done."

Will took the short walk to where Lee was warming his hands. "Morning, General. I hope you got some sleep."

Lee nodded. "I spent some time reading my Bible, Major. A general should do that before he sends men off to die. But I did get a little."

Will watched as Lee surveyed the heavily fortified Union lines in the distance. It was almost as if he could read the sadness in the man's heart. A scattered shower was starting to fall. The first drops landed on the brim of his hat with a thud. "Hope it doesn't rain today."

Lee held his hand up and looked to the west. "I expect it will be hot when this thing blows by us. It's July, you know." He looked at Will. "Are ready to take a ride with me this morning, Major?"

"Yes, sir. I am. My sergeant is saddling our mounts right now."

Lee looked back in the direction of the field. "He rides a mule, doesn't he?"

"Yes, sir. He does."

"A steady animal."

"In many ways he's just like the sergeant. The man's a plodder. He gets a notion of what he's supposed to do and he just puts his head down and goes after it."

Lee looked off in the direction of Gettysburg, no doubt thinking about Ewell and his headquarters in the town. "I wish more of my commanders were like that. We'd have a shorter war if they were. I'm afraid there's just too much timidity among our generals, Major. They seem to be so afraid of defeat that they can't reach out for victory."

"General, I saw Colonel Sinclair yesterday."

"Fine man."

"Yes, sir. He told me you were assigning me to command a regiment under General Pickett."

Lee looked at him, rubbing his hands and holding them out to the fire. "You seemed a good choice to me, Major. I like to see a man prove his potential."

"I was just wondering, General, if General Early talked up this potential of mine to you."

Lee stroked his beard. "As a matter of fact, he did. Why? What are you thinking?"

Will bowed his head. He didn't want to bring any trouble Early's way if there was no merit to the claim, but he did want to alert Lee to a possible conflict. "He does seem to be in the middle of this investigation of ours. It's like he has something to hide."

"Is the man a suspect in your inquiry?"

"One of several. I think that he's protecting someone else. I can't quite put my finger on it."

"Do you want this command, Major? It will certainly mean a promotion for you."

"Very much, sir. I've wanted nothing but a line command ever since I joined this army. But I don't want to leave things undone."

"I respect that, Major. We do need your services in the field. I'm beginning to feel that we may require all our men of character before we are finished here. And you do strike me as a someone who can meet the challenge. You'll serve General Pickett well. I will say this to you: I will leave you and the sergeant over there on this case until you have solved it to your satisfaction. But I do want you to take the command of that regiment with Pickett. That comes first. You can do the other as you have time. Do you think you can do that? Can you do both jobs?"

"I will do my best, sir."

"That's fine. That's all that I can ask."

Ewell's headquarters was in a home on the north end of Gettysburg. Will and Perlman rode with Lee and Taylor. They dismounted and went into the house. The lamps were lit, even though the sun was coming up. Ewell sat on a chair in the corner of the dining room, massaging the stump of his leg, which was joined to the wooden peg that kept him from falling over.

Early and Rhodes along with several other generals were there, and Early caught Will's look right away. He flashed him a forced smile.

"You gentlemen seat yourselves," Lee said. He looked at Ewell, who had disappointed him by not attacking the Union position the day before. "Can't you attack on this front with your corps?"

Ewell fell silent, along with Rhodes. Early was not nearly so bashful. He spoke up. "Sir, the federals have spent the entire night preparing for just such a move. I believe it would be terribly unwise. However, those Round Tops to the south seem to be almost entirely deserted by federal forces. It's a splendid opportunity. If our right could take them, they could command the entire Union line. We might very well outflank them and then come into the Yankee rear."

Ewell and Rhodes silently nodded their agreement.

"Then perhaps I should draw you men around to our right, as the line will be very long and thin if you remain here. The enemy may break through."

Again Early spoke up. "If you do that, General, then those people can turn around and face any blow to their rear. You need not worry about our position here. We are quite strong. But if we were to move, I fear what that would mean to the morale of the troops. We just took this ground yesterday."

Will nudged Perlman and pulled him back into the hall. "I think we should go back for April."

"Why? Why have that woman with us now?"

"You heard General Lee. If he decides to pull these men out, the federals can walk back in. That might cut us off from her for good."

"Would that be a bad thing?" Perlman snapped.

CHAPTER 36

I t was midmorning when April saw Will and Perlman riding
down the street. They had another man with them, a man
dressed in gray and a dirty white smock. A soft, sultry drizzle
was falling on two fresh graves. One was that of a soldier who
had died during the night, the soldier whose hand April had
held and watched as he fell asleep. The other grave was Roberta's.
A heavy sadness hung in the air, and in April's heart.

April nodded at the two soldiers who had dug the graves, and
she watched as they went back into the house. Then she stepped
out to the street.

Will got down off his horse and tied the animal to the fence
rail. He walked toward her, the stranger at his side. Touching his
hat, Will stepped aside. "April, this is Dr. Yancy from Tennessee.
He's here to take over for you."

April nodded. "Good to see you, doctor. We've been waiting for you." Yancy was an older man with stringy gray hair that fell down from the sides of his beaten gray cap. The polish had long been off his boots. The gray tunic under his dirty smock was open, and his white shirt was unbuttoned. Gray hairs peeked out from his chest. His square jaw was dotted by what appeared to be a four- or five-day-old beard, and his blue eyes looked blurry. "The wounded men are in the house. I've done the best I could."

"I'm sure you have, ma'am. The army does appreciate your service."

April fell silent as the man turned and walked into the house.

Will stepped back over to his horse and pulled out a mass of blue material from a bag he had tied around his saddle horn. He walked back toward her with a blue dress draped over his arm and a smile on his face. He held the garment out for her. "I brought this for you. It looked to be your size."

She took it and held it up. It was a light blue gingham dress with white lace around the cuffs and bodice. It did appear to be her size. "Did you pay for it?"

"Of course I did. You don't think I'd steal it, do you?"

April frowned. "Some men would."

"Well, I wouldn't. I'm no thief. Of course, I did have to wake the shopkeeper up. He squawked like a wet hen. I just thought you'd be tired of that black thing you've been wearing."

"You mean you're tired of it." April glanced back at the two graves. "It does seem to fit what I've been doing here, however." She draped the dress over her arm. "I am glad you brought the doctor. We could have used him last night."

Will looked over at the fresh graves. "Yes, I can see that. I brought you something else too." He reached into his pocket and pulled out a small pink bottle, handing it to her. It was marked DELIA'S ROSE SCENTED SHAMPOO. Going back into his pocket, he produced a small piece of pink ornamental soap, shaped in the figure of a rosebud. He took her other hand and pressed the soap into it. "I couldn't find you a bouquet of roses, but I thought these might do for you. I figure with all that water you've been boiling, you might be able to spare yourself some for a bath."

Tears welled up in April's eyes. Will had thought of feminine things for her, but at that moment her mind was filled with thoughts of Roberta. The girl had been very pretty but so uncomfortable with the way God made her. All April could think of was Roberta as the little sister she never had. She would have given anything to have known her without the war, to have been able to clean her up with this shampoo and soap and dress her in pretty things. She began to cry.

"What's wrong?" Will put his hand on her shoulder. "Did I do something wrong?"

Perlman had stepped up next to Will. He grunted slightly. "Women. You do something nice for them, and they bawl." He shook his head. "I'll never understand them."

"You didn't do anything wrong." April turned and ran into the house. She had to find a place away from people, a place where she could cry. She knew she must have looked silly to both Will and Perlman—especially Perlman—but right then she just didn't care.

She ran upstairs to the large bedroom with the extra-size feather bed and fell down into the middle of the thing. If she could cry into the mattress, then no one would hear. That would suit her fine. It was something that had to come out, all the pain, all the guilt.

It took her some time to stop crying. She felt drained. Trying to know what one's duty should be had become a crushing weight for her. It paralyzed her. She rolled over on the bed, first staring at the ceiling and then looking at the dress on the floor. It would take her putting one foot in front of the other to do it.

She sat on the edge of the bed, and thoughts about the war flooded her head. She had always prided herself in knowing right from wrong, but that had been far too easy. All this time she thought she was grown-up and had grown-up responsibilities, but she had never had to be responsible where somebody's life was involved. In many ways the children fighting for the Confederacy were more grown-up than she was. They were putting their lives and the lives of others on the line for what they believed. The most she had ever had to risk was the minor embarrassment of being wrong or the shame of having her views questioned. Teaching children to read and write, instructing them to add and play nicely in the schoolyard were one thing, but ordering people to die or allowing your own mistakes to kill them were quite another. She felt loyalty to the Union and she hated slavery. She had believed it her duty to help Schimmelfennig escape. To do that meant scheming, conniving, and pretending to help people while at the same time hiding a deadly enemy from them. She had been wrong. All of her moralizing and blind loyalty had cost the life of someone she cared about. She would never be able to forgive herself.

It was over an hour later when April stepped out of the room. She had carried the tub and the hot water up the stairs and taken the time to soak. She thought for certain the bath and washing her hair would make a difference in lifting her spirits, and it did to some degree, but tears had still formed in her eyes when she sat at the dresser and brushed her hair. She simply couldn't get the image of Roberta out of her head. The brutality of the thing and the hostility that caused it sent a quiver through her.

She stood at the top of the landing and ran her fingers down the buttons of the blue dress. They were bone and white. Will had chosen it well. It showed off her figure and made her feel alive. She could hear the steady moans of the men downstairs, and it snapped her back to where she was and who she was. These were men dying for their cause, and her belief in what she stood for had been shaken. It wasn't as simple as what she'd thought. Perhaps it never had been.

She walked down the stairs, noticing her shoes. What had been polished shoes with shiny buckles had now become battered and scuffed like old saddles. She knew that regardless of her new dress and freshly washed and brushed hair, the shoes on her feet would remain old and beaten, a victim of all she had been through. Everything else one can turn and turn about, make old look like new, but there's no coaxing shoes to look better than they are. The thought flashed through her mind that her soul was much like her shoes. It had grown worn and scuffed, scarred and blemished with death and dying. Her soul would never be new again, never feel innocent.

Will stepped over to the bottom of the stairs. He looked handsome and freshly shaved, almost as if he were waiting to take her to some glittering ball in Charleston. He gave her a subtle smile, and his eyes twinkled. "You look grand, my lady. Are you feeling better?"

April nodded. "Somewhat."

He held out his hand and guided her from the last step. "One of the men told me about last night. I'm sorry. I'm sorry about Ulysses running away and taking the mules, and I'm sorry about the young private you worked with. I didn't hear much in the way of details, just that you'd been there and that Ulysses had killed the man. That must be hard for you."

April blinked back fresh tears. "Yes, it is hard."

"Perlman and I were talking about it. Maybe Ulysses did us a favor. He might have solved this thing for us. Your father's writing on the ground, the US. Maybe he was trying to identify Ulysses. I didn't think the man capable of such a thing, but if he could kill that soldier, he just might have stabbed your father in a fit of anger."

"He didn't do it."

"How do you know?"

"Because I was there."

Will looked puzzled. "I don't understand."

April knew she would have to tell him just exactly what had happened. She would have had to tell him, even if he wasn't jumping to the conclusion of blaming Ulysses for her father's murder. Living a lie was just something she wasn't capable of, and she knew it.

She dropped his hand, walked through the hallway, and stepped out onto the front porch. Will followed her. The man had been sweet to her. The ironic thing was that she had first thought he would never be worthy of her; now she had come to the conclusion that she could never live up to the standards set by Will Chevalier. He had been honest with her, and she had lied to him. He had risked everything, including his future and the disdain of his own comrades, for her, and she hadn't been willing to put aside her own prejudices for him, not even for a moment.

"Explain what you mean by that. You weren't there when your father was killed, were you?"

"No, but I was there last night, and Ulysses had nothing to do with it. It was all my idea."

April turned her head away. She could almost see Will's eyes without looking at him. She stepped to the edge of the porch, staring off at the two fresh graves. "The man who did that last night was a Union general. I allowed him to hide in the cellar and helped him escape. He took the mules and Ulysses with him. The general was the one who shot the soldier buried there, but it might as well have been me who pulled the trigger."

She waited for Will to speak, but he said nothing. Instead he merely walked away, down the steps and toward the barn. She watched as he walked away, and she began to cry. She had been nothing but trouble to the man. A great pain settled in her throat and worked its way down to her heart. For the first time she realized that she really wanted to see Will Chevalier again. She didn't want him simply to ride away and leave her to be rescued by the Union army.

She walked back into the house and spotted Dr. Yancy as he worked with the wounded. Soon she was helping the doctor work, stooping over the wounded and washing their faces and wounds. She didn't know how much time passed. The work with the men on the floor helped to put things out of her mind.

Then she heard the front door open. Will was standing there. "Perlman and I got you a horse." He was expressionless in the way he said it, no emotion, only words. "We'd better get going."

CHAPTER 37

The three of them rode slowly through the streets of Gettysburg. April had never seen the town. Many of the shops still
had goods in the windows. Bundles of bright cloth and boxes
with colored labels were in the windows. Hats and dresses
stood to attention. A small wooden pig painted pink was
hanging over the door to the general store, along with a barrel of
apples, the price marked with bold black letters on the side, 1¢. It
was quiet except for the occasional sound of a distant cannon. A
number of shops and businesses were open, and they rode past a
blacksmith shop where the smithy was pounding away on a piece of
hot iron. He stopped momentarily as they rode by, his hammer
raised above his head. Then he seemed to sneer and bring the hammer down with authority, the sound of the heavy metal ringing in
the street.

"He don't seem too happy," Perlman said.

April was riding beside Perlman; Will was up ahead. Will hadn't said a word. He rode quietly without looking either to the right or left.

"What about your cat?" she asked.

Perlman shook his head. "Nobody owns cats. He'll come if he wants to. Can't nobody talk an alley cat into doing anything. You give him his head and he makes up his own mind."

April watched Will, his eyes straight ahead. "I can understand that," she said. "People have to decide for themselves."

Perlman looked in her direction. His plump red nose sniffed at the scent of rain in the air. "Nice dress, missy. I'm glad it fits."

Perlman seemed pleasant enough. April wondered if Will had told him what had happened back at the house. It caused her to avoid his eyes as he spoke. "Thank you."

"The color seems to suit you."

April nodded.

"I always say it's a woman's job to look pretty. It's what she does best."

The notion that the man would think such a thing would normally have caused her to erupt with some snide remark designed to put him in his place. Normally, but not today. If he wanted to think that a woman was incapable of doing anything but preen in front of a mirror, she was perfectly willing to let him do it. She just didn't feel like fighting.

As they rode on, the orange tabby trotted out into the middle of the street. He stopped and looked past Will, staring up at Perlman. The old man drew rein. He turned and smiled at April. "See, you give a feller half a chance, and he always knows what's good for him."

He leaned over the side of his mule and lowered his hand. The cat bounded into it. Curling it in his arm, Perlman looked at April. "Some people are a lot like cats." Perlman shot a glance in Will's direction. "They need their own territory. The more room you give them, the better able they are to make up their own mind about where they really belong. You give 'em up and they come back."

April forced a smile. She knew good and well the man was talking about Will, not the cat.

They came to the unfinished railroad tracks and started west. The horses and Perlman's mule stepped over the ties, picking their way along the tracks. April saw the birds first, in the distance, large black birds swerving and gliding in the air. Their wings were straight and they were carving long lazy circles in the sky. In all her years in Pennsylvania, she had never seen a vulture. But they were here now, and most likely it would be some time before they left. She then began to smell the putrefying stench of the dead.

Twisted heaps of bodies lay alongside the track, blue and gray uniforms spotted heavily with glistening black as flies swarmed the fatal wounds of war. Several men with handkerchiefs over their faces were passing along the line of corpses. They were counting the men and writing down names. The sight sickened her, but it made her problem seem insignificant. In God's grand scheme of things, the murder of her own father paled by comparison.

"I'm sorry we had to take you this way," Perlman said. "There just ain't no other way to get to where we're going. Sides, there's bodies all over the place. Ain't no place we could go where we wouldn't run into them. This here might be the best as far as we know. You'll get used to it."

"I hope I never get used to it."

It took them more than an hour to wind their way behind Seminary Ridge. The Confederate army seemed to be waiting for something. All along the way as they rode she saw men relaxing, cleaning their rifles, and checking their ammunition. They appeared to be hardened troops, not the least bit concerned about what was to follow. Some were laughing, and others simply crossed their legs in the grass and went to sleep. It amazed April that they seemed so unconcerned, given what she had just seen. It also made her wonder about the constitution of such men. What did it take to turn normal people into jaded, devil-may-care soldiers? She would never understand it.

Will drew rein near a stone house across from what she knew was Chambersburg Pike. The single-story house looked simple, with window shutters painted green. The Confederate battle flag flew from a staff positioned outside the door.

Perlman got off his mule. "This is Lee's headquarters."

"What are we waiting for?" April asked.

Perlman helped her off her horse. "I spect the major here's waiting to see his new commander."

"His new commander?"

Perlman wiped his beard and squinted at her. "That's right. Major Chevalier's got himself a line command. Might mean a promotion for him. He's going to command a regiment with Pickett's division. They don't get in till tonight though. They're marching up from Chambersburg."

She watched Will jog up the steps of the house, his broad shoulders thrown back and his chin held high. He was going into battle. The memory of the wasted bodies she had just seen hit her. This could be the last day she would ever see Will Chevalier. An odd mixture of pride and panic caused the skin on her arms to tingle and her throat to tighten. She absently bit at her lower lip.

Perlman saw the look on her face. "Don't worry none about your predicament. Will's done stuck the thing with me while he gets himself situated with that new unit of his. Troops got to get to know the man leading them into battle, ya know."

"I can imagine."

Perlman began to fidget with the buttons on his jacket. "We'll get your situation solved one way or the other. You have to remember, I'm the policeman here. The major's just a soldier boy at heart. He's doing what he needs to do, what he's wanted to do since this here war started." He waved his hand as if to ward off a diving insect. "I'll have to let him tell you though. It ain't really my place."

April looked back at the closed door of the house. "I'm not sure he's going to talk to me."

"He'll talk to you. He has to. Just remember what I told you. Some men need their own territory. The more room you give them, the better able they are to make up their own mind about where they really belong. You give 'em up and they come back."

A short time later they saw a wagon rolling down the road. The two mules pulling it were straining at their harnesses, and the young man driving them whirled a whip over their heads, popping it with repeated jerks of his arm.

April was seated on a small bench outside the house watching Perlman brush down his mule and the horses. When she saw the wagon, she jumped to her feet and started walking down the road. Perlman dropped his brush and followed her. "Ain't that the feller we saw in Messersmith's Woods?"

"Yes," April nodded. "That's Tommy Slocum, our neighbor."

April waited for Slocum to pull the wagon up alongside her. He had on a new shirt, bright green-and-red check, tucked down into his black pants. He pulled back on the reins and slammed the brake home with his foot. A broad grin spread across his face. "April, I sure didn't know I'd be seeing you here."

"I didn't exactly expect to find you here either. Why are you here?"

Slocum looked back into the wagon. "I got me some more food things to sell. Figured these here boys would be plenty hungry, and Daddy said he didn't want this stuff to go to waste."

"I take it he liked that silverware you brought him."

Slocum grinned. "He sure did. Liked it a lot." He shook his head. "Can't take none of their paper money, though." He held up his beaten hat to the sun. The heat of the day was already spreading. The soft showers of the morning were long gone, leaving only the hot July sun. "I brought me some corn squeezings too. Them boys seem to like that a whole lot."

Tommy got down off the wagon and went to the back, where Perlman had already begun to sift through the things he was carrying. April followed him. They spent a short time going over the jars of preserves, the corn, the jugs of liquor, the loaves of bread, and the hams. Tommy took his time pointing out each item. He looked at her, a sad expression forming on his face. "I didn't get to tell you how powerful sorry I was about your daddy."

"Thank you, Tommy. He liked you."

Tommy bowed his head. "I just should have give you that Bible."

"What Bible?"

Tommy bit his lip nervously. "Nothing. Never mind about that." He reached over the back of the wagon and threw the flap of the tarpaulin over the top of the food. It was as if he hoped that by turning his back on April, he could turn away from her question.

She was not to be stopped, however. She reached over and put her hand on his shoulder, turning him around. "You didn't answer my question, Tommy. What Bible are you talking about?"

"Answer the woman, son," Perlman added.

The guns were sounding in the east, and Tommy glanced over his shoulder at the explosions in the distance. "Boy, I tell you, them things sure make a powerful noise. They make me kinda scared. You reckon they'll come this-a-way?"

"I'm certain we'd have some warning before something like that happened," April said. "Now go ahead. Tell me. What Bible?"

Tommy dropped his gaze to the ground, pawing it with the toe of his boot. "My daddy said I shouldn't say anything about this to you. Said it would only bring you more pain."

"I don't care what your father said. I want to hear."

He glanced up at her. "It was that Bible your daddy carried. I should have give it to you."

"How did you come to have that thing?"

"Well, I come onto your place the day your daddy was killed. I wanted to see him 'cause I was talking to him about you."

"About me? What about me?"

Tommy stopped and turned to face her. He then began to rock his head back and forth. It was a gesture of shy embarrassment. "About you and me."

"What about you and me?"

He smiled and then wiped his mouth. He still found it hard to look her in the eye. "Well, we growed up together, sort of. We was always kinda friends, and I thought maybe you even liked me." He lifted his head slightly and shot her a quick glance. "I just figured that if I was to ask him fer your hand, that he'd tell you and you might say yes." He looked up at her. "I could take care of you. I'm a hard worker, you know."

"I'm sure you could. But go on. You came to the farm to tell him that?"

"No. I told him that a week before. I was just coming back to see if he had an answer for me."

"Well, he said nothing to me. But tell me about his book of Psalms."

Suddenly his face became twisted. He shot out his lip. "I knew I should have told you this at the funeral. I couldn't, though, 'cause my daddy was there watching me. He'd already told me not to say anything. Then that night at the woods—I should have told you then, but he was with you." He eyed Perlman.

"Tell me what?"

Tommy began to wring his hands. "Well, when I got to the barn, your daddy was bleeding and on the ground. He was kind of coughing up blood. I didn't know what to do. He sort of signaled me over to where he lay." Tommy looked up at April, directly in the eye. "And I went. I went right over. I figured there might be something I could do. Please don't hold this against me, April. I didn't know no better. I ain't been around much folks what is sick and dying."

April put her hand on his shoulder. "It's all right. Just tell me. What happened. Did he say anything?"

Tommy shook his head. "He never said much. He just handed me that Bible." He stooped his shoulders slightly and lowered his head. It was almost as if he was still trying to keep a secret even though no one was close. One would have thought his father was still hovering around him. "He said, 'Give it.' That's all, kind of."

"That's all he said, 'Give it'?"

"That's all. You figure it was somebody special he wanted me to give it to?"

April breathed a deep sigh. "Oh, Tommy. Give it to me or give it to Christine."

"No, he said no to that, 'cause I asked him. I said should I give it to Christine and he said no. Then he just sort of dropped his head to the ground and died. I didn't know who he wanted me to give it to." Tommy shook his head. "I figured maybe he wanted me to just give it to somebody to use. Your daddy was a good Christian, you know. If I knew I was dying and I had me a Bible, I'd want to give it to somebody to use."

"Oh, Tommy, you're impossible." She started to walk off.

"Did I do something wrong?"

She stopped and whirled around. "You were the last one to see my father alive, and you never said anything. I just don't understand you."

He lifted his hands and then dropped them to his side. "I just didn't know what to do."

She stepped closer to him. "Who did you give it to?"

He shook his head. "I know I was wrong, but I was worried too. I thought maybe somebody might think wrong of me. I rode off to my place and met a soldier on the road, kind of an important one too." He bit his lip. "So I gave it to him."

He began to shake his head nervously back and forth. "I just didn't know what else I could do. It didn't belong to me, and your daddy said to give it, so I gave it. Then I rode back to my place and found my daddy. I told him everything, and he said I did right. Now you say I did wrong. I'm just a mistake that's all. My daddy's always said I was a mistake."

"You're not a mistake, Tommy. You just made a mistake."

CHAPTER 38

Will waited for some time in the living room of the house before Taylor spotted him. The man was in the dining room surrounded by other officers. They hovered around a map spread out over the table. The colonel flashed him a smile and stepped through the opening of the door. Will recognized the man with him right away. It was the spy he had met at Messersmith's Woods. The man had finally worked his way into Lee's headquarters.

"Good to see you, Major. General Lee isn't here right now. We're all waiting for him." He glanced back at the man dressed in his tramp attire. "This is one of our scouts."

"We've met."

"Is that so?"

"At Messersmith's Woods."

Batist grinned. He leaned forward and gave a slight bow. "An honor to see you once again, Major."

"I take it you're here about your new assignment," Taylor said. "I don't have much more I can tell you. We are expecting General Pickett any minute. His troops arrive tonight. Our last communiqué to the man mentioned you to him, so he's prepared. I understand the man has a fine bunch of troops in his division. There is a regiment from Virginia in Armistead's brigade that you are to command. I trust that will suit you, Major?"

Will put his hat back on and smoothed the brim. "Fine. I'll just wait outside then."

"Congratulations, Major, or should I say Colonel?"

The thought of command was something Will had longed for since the war began. It was what he'd been trained to do. The very idea sent a sparkle up his backbone. But he remained calm on the outside. "We'll deal with that when it happens. I'll wait outside."

"I'll go with you, Major," Batist said.

The two of them stepped outside the small house. Will spotted April and Perlman huddled around a man and his wagon.

"Civilian salesman," Batist said. He grinned. "There seems to be no end to Yankee shopkeepers. Let's go see what the man is selling."

Perlman watched as Will walked toward them. He walked over to meet the two men, but Batist continued on toward the wagon.

"We got something here you might be interested in," Perlman said.

"I have enough to eat and don't want anything to drink," Will shot back.

"Oh, it's not what the man is carrying." Perlman jerked his thumb, pointing back to the man. "That there's one of the Wolff neighbors. We might have us an eyewitness. He says he saw the old man right before he died. He's the one who got Wolff's book of Psalms."

Will stepped off toward the wagon, with Perlman following him. Batist was plowing through the supplies in the back of the wagon. He soon found a jug of the liquor and held it up. "How much, kind sir?"

"A dollar a swallow," Tommy said.

"Blazes boy! A dollar a swallow! That's highway robbery."

"That's the price. I don't set it. My daddy does. I just sell it."

Perlman tugged on the boy's sleeve, drawing his attention. "I'd like you to tell your story to the major here. He'd be most interested."

Suddenly Batist put down the jug. He stepped over in front of the boy. "Hey, I know you, don't I?"

Tommy looked nervous. He shook his head. "No, sir. I don't know you."

Batist smiled, then broke into a grin. "Sure I do. You were out hunting with that Sharps rifle of yours. Whole lot of gun for such a slight fellow, I'd say. You were mostly scaring the game away when I saw you."

April had been patiently waiting and watching the men. Tommy was slow, and her sudden impatience showed that she'd grown tired of waiting for Will and was now even more restless while she waited for Tommy to tell him the story. She stepped over to Will and grabbed his arm, pulling him away. "Here, come over with me for a minute. Let them to their business. I can tell you what he knows, and you might find it intriguing. It just might clear at least one of your generals."

April took Will's sleeve and led him away a short distance. She didn't want her suspicions overheard. She had just begun to relate the story when they both heard the crack of the whip and the rattle of the wagon. They looked up to watch Tommy Slocum drive the team of mules back down the road in the direction of Chambersburg.

Will freed himself from April's grip and trotted over to where Perlman was standing with Batist. "That was sudden," he said.

"Very fast," Batist agreed. "I didn't even have time for a swallow."

"Mighty queer too," Perlman offered. "The man's business is here, and he seems to be going the wrong way."

Will looked over at Batist, studying him. "Tell me. Just where did you see him? Tell me about his rifle too."

Batist spent the next few minutes relating the story of his meeting with Tommy Slocum on the ridge east of Greencastle. Both Will and Perlman showed a great deal of interest in the location and also the caliber and make of the boy's rifle. April took her place behind Perlman and listened.

"Are you thinking what I'm thinking?" Perlman asked.

Will nodded. He looked at the dust being created by the wagon on the road. It was obvious that Tommy Slocum wasn't wasting any time in getting out of the area. "That just might be our sniper."

"You want me to go get him?" Perlman asked.

"No," Will said. "We'll know where to find him."

Batist and Will spent the next few minutes listening to April and Perlman tell them what Tommy had explained about the way Jonas Wolff died. They could only wonder at the boy's leaving all of a sudden like he did and trying to avoid having his movements questioned.

Later that night Will decided to take a last walk through the troops he was to command. He had been waiting for them when they arrived at camp. After the barest of introductions, he had taken the time to tell them just what he expected from them and what they might expect from him. He had spent a great deal of time instructing them on the value of depending on each other. If one man failed to do his job, if even one ran, the rest would suffer and die for it.

The men in the regiment appeared to be a hardy crew. They had their share of smooth-cheeked boys, but there were a few gnarled, sparse-toothed veterans sprinkled in among them to hold them in line. Most of the men had shoes, no doubt due to the time they had spent in Chambersburg. They also appeared fed and well rested. They would make good fighters. Will could feel it in his bones.

He walked back over to where he and Perlman had bedded down for the night. They had found a tent for April. The privacy would make her feel more like a woman. Perlman was stirring a pot of makeshift coffee over the fire, crouched in such a way that it even looked uncomfortable. April was standing behind him in the shadows.

Will stared at the dark valley below, at the blazing fires of the Union camp beyond. The hillside seemed to be dotted with thousands of stars on the ground. It was hard to think about, but he knew that around those fires were the men who would try to kill him tomorrow—and he would try to kill them. They were men with mothers and dreams. They were men who had been following a different dream, and now they had stopped. They had stopped and they were waiting, waiting for him.

He heard the clatter of hooves and the rattle of swords before he ever saw the men in the darkness. Suddenly, a group of riders burst into the dim light. Pickett was unmistakable. His boots, which had a high gloss on them that glimmered even in the firelight, came up to his thighs. His gold spurs dangled and rattled.

Pickett skidded his horse to a stop not more than a few feet from their fire, a broad grin on his face. The man was positively jovial in appearance, with a bright gold sash wrapped around his waist. There was a laugh in his shining eyes and round face even though he didn't emit a sound. His long hair dangled past his shoulders, and his cap was cocked like a schoolboy's at play. Major General George Pickett was a man people loved to be around. His mood was infectious.

He jumped off his horse and walked quickly up to Will, his hand extended. "Major Chevalier, I have heard so many good things about you."

Will saluted the man and then shook his hand. Perlman got to his feet and saluted.

Pickett grinned. "I take it this is your man here."

"Sergeant Perlman of the provost marshal's office," Will said. He motioned in the direction of April. "And this is Miss April Wolff."

Pickett took off his cap and bowed, sweeping the hat down and to his side as April stepped out of the shadows. "I am enchanted, Miss Wolff. I had no idea our camp would be graced by such loveliness." He rapped his riding crop on the side of his leg.

"The sergeant is taking her home tomorrow," Will said.

Pickett brushed aside his swooping mustache and ran his hand down his curly chin-beard. The ringlets of his hair had been soaked with perfume, giving him the aroma of a ladies department store counter. "I do hope you'll be able to see the glory of our charge tomorrow before you go. It will be a sight you're never likely to forget."

Will watched a frown form on April's face. He couldn't tell if it was due to Pickett's unabashed bravado or because she'd just learned that she'd be going home.

"We are to be the vanguard for the attack tomorrow, Major." He emphasized the word *vanguard* and stuck his finger in the air. "General Armistead and your men will be in support of Kemper's brigade. He'll take you over that Yankee wall and into their rear. It will be a glorious day."

He turned and walked back to his horse. Will followed. "I have something for you, Major." Reaching into his saddlebags, he pulled out a book. He kept the cover pressed to his chest and smiled. "It's my special gift to you, welcoming you to my command." He held it out. "Victor Hugo's *Les Misérables*. It's a fine book, and Lee's entire staff is positively devouring it. Around here it's become known as *Lee's Misérables*."

Will reached out and took the book.

"Now you must promise to keep it with you always." He waggled his finger. "I shall have questions for you on it, you know. If you are to become a senior officer on my staff, then you will have plenty of questions."

Will unbuttoned his tunic and stuck the book next to his chest. He glanced back at April. "Sir, you know my business with the provost marshal's office hasn't quite concluded, don't you?"

Pickett waved his hand and mounted his jet black horse. "So I am given to understand. No matter, Major. You lead your men into the attack tomorrow and then tend to the conclusion of your affairs with the line closers. Your command will be waiting for you when you return." He bent down and flashed Will a broad smile. "And so will I." With that, he reeled his horse around, slapped his spurs at the animal's sides, and galloped off into the darkness with the men he had ridden in with.

Will turned and walked back to the fire, the book in his hands. Perlman poured him a cup of the black substance. "The man's full of the dickens, isn't he?"

Will took the cup and looked off into the darkness where Pickett had ridden. "I'd say he's not a shy man."

Perlman laughed. "No, no indeed. You'll have to walk way around his tender feelings if disaster ever strikes him."

Will continued to look into the darkness. "If disaster ever does strike him, no doubt I won't be walking anywhere. I'll be dead."

Will turned to the fire, and April stepped closer. "Just when were you going to tell me about your plans?"

Will said nothing. He sipped his coffee and studied her over the lip of the hot tin cup.

"Were you planning to say anything to me at all?"

"Yes."

"I believe that makes the tenth word you've said to me all day."

Perlman got to his feet and smiled. "Whoa now. I'm just going to take the cat for a walk. I can see you two have a lot to talk about."

They watched him walk away, with Elmer scurrying along behind him. Will knew he'd been silent with April all day. He hadn't felt like making small talk. He knew the matter of the death of the soldier, coupled with her helping the general escape, had been eating away at her, and he thought that was a good thing. If it was one thing the woman needed, it was thought, not talk. "Perlman can take care of you until I get free here. He's good. We've done most of what can be done with this army. I really think the source of your problem is much closer to home."

"Do you mean Tommy Slocum?"

"Maybe."

"And you plan to follow me and Perlman to my home?"

"That I do."

April shook her head and walked around to the far side of the fire. She stared at him over the flames. "Do you really think that man who rode out of here is going to allow you to live?"

"It's not his choice, it's mine." He looked out across the valley at the fires blazing on Cemetery Ridge, the place he would be attacking the next day. "And those Yankees over there," he added.

"And what about me? Don't I get a choice?"

"No." The word sounded harsh even though he didn't mean it that way. April Wolff had been used to having her own way in life. She had been her father's pet. But she didn't have a choice. She hadn't chosen the woman her father had married. She hadn't chosen the manner of her father's death. She couldn't choose this.

April folded her hands and placed them under her chin. It was almost like the gesture of a small child at prayer. "I know I was wrong for what I did back at that house last night. What I did got someone killed that I cared for very much. Now I feel that you're punishing me. I believe you took this assignment because of what I did. I betrayed your trust." Tears formed in her eyes. "And if you get killed tomorrow, that will be my fault too."

"Don't flatter yourself. I'm doing what I'm doing because I believe in the cause for which this army is fighting. It has nothing to do with you. As for what you did last night, I don't blame you. In your circumstances I would have done the same thing. You did what you believed in, and I'm doing what I believe in. It's just that simple. We just happen to be on opposite sides. That's all. That's all there ever was."

April stepped around the fire. She gently slipped her hand into his and looked up into his eyes. "Is that really all there is? I believe in you, and I thought you believed in me. Isn't there anything more between us than that?"

"Do you mean love?"

"Yes, love. I know it's strange. We're so different and on different sides. Perhaps you have felt love for many women, but I've
never felt it for any man, not until now."

"You know me and you know where I've come from. I've told
you about my family, the only love I've ever seen. To tell you that I
love you would not mean the same as the love you seem to know
and need."

"Will Chevalier, that is a risk I'm willing to take. You may go
off to face your fears and hopes tomorrow, but I'm facing mine right
now." She took a deep swallow. "No matter what it is you feel for
me, Will, I love you."

CHAPTER 39

It was just after dawn when Will stirred the coals in the fire and blew them back to life. He took out his knife and shaved a small pile of wood, then carefully laid the wood onto the hissing and glowing embers. In minutes he created a healthy fire and set the coffeepot on it with its mixture of chicory that bore a faint resemblance to coffee. At least it was hot and black. He stepped out toward the ridge to look over the Union positions across the valley. They didn't appear to have been strengthened during the night, but what was there was formidable. *And then there's that open ground*, he thought, his blue eyes studying the eerily quiet mile between their lines and the Union wall on the ridge.

He noticed Armistead striding toward him. The general was the commander of his brigade, and Will had already decided when he'd met him the day before that he liked the man. He was soft-spoken and unpretentious. Will saluted.

"At ease, Major." Armistead drew close to him and stood looking out across the valley. "That's Hancock over there. He won't run. He won't budge."

"You know him?"

Armistead dropped his gaze to the ground. "Yes, he's the best friend I have in all the world. I'd die for him in a moment, and today I will have to destroy him or else he will destroy me. He was the best man at my wedding. We both swore never to take up arms against the other, and now here we are."

"I'm sorry, General."

"So am I."

Armistead looked back at the valley. "You know this is an attack Old Pete never wanted to make."

Will knew Armistead was making reference to General James Longstreet, the man Lee called his war-horse.

"Old Pete wants us to slip around the Yankees and make them attack us on ground of our choosing." He sighed. "But Lee wants a fight here. I think he's tired of this war and wants it settled today."

April stepped out of her tent. Will spotted her and signaled her over. "General Armistead, allow me to introduce Miss Wolff."

Armistead's black hat was pulled down to shield his eyes from the sun. He swung around and took off his hat, exposing his balding head. "Pleased to meet you, Miss Wolff." He motioned in the direction of the camp to the north of them. "I have a sparse breakfast in my camp." He smiled. "I was hoping the major here would join us, and I would be very pleased to have you take some with me and my officers as well."

"That's very kind of you, General."

Will could tell that she instantly liked him. Armistead was a sad thoughtful man, with deep dark eyes. When he spoke, there were actual thoughts connected to his words. He looked right at people when he talked to them.

"No, madam, the kindness would be yours if you accepted my invitation. Just your presence would remind my officers of what we are fighting for."

April glanced at Will. "Has the major explained to you that I'm from Pennsylvania?"

Armistead nodded and smiled. "Yes, last night. And he told us that you're opposed to slavery. I share much of your sentiment. But your beauty would remind my men of home. I was just about to explain to Major Chevalier that my men are all from Virginia, sons of the Old Dominion." He chuckled. "We won't hold his birth in South Carolina with any great contempt, however, nor yours from Pennsylvania."

"I was born in Virginia, General."

Armistead smiled. "You see, a reason for your loveliness." He bowed his head slightly, then looked directly at her. "I am afraid that many of my men will never see the sun set tonight, and I wouldn't want to deprive them of what beauty might be available to them this morning."

"That's most kind of you, General. I'd be pleased to join you."

Both April and Will had breakfast with Armistead and his staff. A number of the platoon and regimental commanders were present, and Will and April watched them as they joked and laughed.

Armistead walked up to them, grinning. "Major, did General Pickett present you with a copy of Hugo's *Les Misérables?*"

Will tapped his chest, making a hard rapping sound. "Yes, he did, General. He told me there would be questions."

Armistead grinned. He looked back at the other officers and shouted. "Chevalier has one, boys. You better watch out." Turning back to Will, his smile widened. "It's become somewhat of a joke around here. You must be selected for higher command, Major. That book has become a symbol of a man's knighting into the ranks of the stars. Be careful of it, and do your homework. General Pickett is a romantic, and he expects his officers to be romantic, idealistic, and fearless."

"He's all of that," April added.

Armistead chuckled slightly. "Madam, I would expect nothing less of the major with you as his inspiration. My hope, however, is that he's inspired by you and not by some wandering French thief."

It was over an hour later when they began to hear the cheers of the troops up and down the line. Men stepped forward, their hats raised. They were cheering and screaming like banshees. Will and April watched as the sight of Lee mounted on Traveler appeared to galvanize the entire army. The man was smiling, raising his hat in salute to the troops and waving to them as he passed.

"They love him, don't they?" April asked.

"They would march into hell for the man. That's exactly what they're going to do today—and I'll be with them," answered Will.

"I'm frightened for you."

"You should be. I'm frightened for me."

Lee passed where Will and April were standing. He lifted his hat, a broad smile on his face. "We go with God today, Major," he shouted. "He teaches our hands to war and our fingers to fight."

April slipped her hand into Will's as Lee rode by. "And you want me to just leave you here today and go home."

"You must. Tomorrow the roads will be clogged with wounded and dying men. It will be a sight I don't want you to see. You've seen too much already." He looked at her. It was hard to mistake the look of love and admiration in her eyes. "No matter how strong you think you are, you still have a soul of innocence. I'll do anything to protect that. I lost mine years ago, and I won't have you losing yours."

"You sound like you think you're going to lose this battle."

Will took her arm and led her forward to the crest of the ridge. "You see that open space out there? This afternoon that portion of our sweet planet will become hell. Your army will open up with long-range cannon fire and then switch to double canister when we reach that fence you see out there. The small rounds of metal will tear huge gaps in our line and may even take out my whole regiment in one bite. Then the Yankees will open up with their rifles from behind that wall. What's left of my men will be chopped to pieces before we've even fired a shot. If any of us do reach the wall, there won't be enough left to make a difference. The Yankees will crash into us with reinforcements in great numbers. That will be the end of this day, this battle, this war, and the Confederacy. Tomorrow will be the funeral of private joy I spoke to you about. They'll make speeches here, but under all those words will be their hatred and their absolute glee at what they've done."

"Then why are you doing this?"

"Duty." Will paused to let the word sink in. It was a word that was foreign to many people's thinking. "Duty and honor. General Lee is tired of this war. He wants to end it here and now, and unfortunately, he thinks we're invincible. We've had so many victories, but those were in Virginia. We knew the terrain and we had the good ground. He has a few officers who still lust for glory, men like George Pickett. It's their birthright, and they've been denied it so far. This is their grand opportunity, a place for a stroke of genius mixed with our blood."

Just then they heard the shouts of General Pickett. The man sat astride his sleek black horse like a jaunty jockey off to the races. He rode up and down the line of men, shouting out orders. He was almost desperate looking, with wild eyes that set off the double row of fire-gilded buttons on his breast. He waved his riding crop, shouting out orders to the officers. Then he rode on.

Will turned to April. "I should join my men now. Perlman will see you home."

She reached out to him, but Will stepped away. He was determined not to look back at her. He joined the front of his regiment and turned to shout. "Forward march." Setting the regiment in motion was not a quiet thing. Shouts and grunts and the creaking of rifles, packs, and weary bodies echoed as dust swirled in the morning sunshine.

As Will turned to look over his shoulder at the mass of men at his back, he caught sight of April on the ridge, framed by the trees. Her arms were crossed protectively, and emptily, around her waist.

She was watching him. He touched the brim of his hat and turned away, shoving down his mixed-up feelings. He didn't have time to sort out why the mere sight of her made his stomach flutter, nor figure out why even her belligerent ways made him want to chuckle. He had to think of these men first. Will didn't see Perlman gently tug her away as he marched out of sight.

The march was a shady one through woods that screened the troops from the Union artillery. It was an easy walk, with the men now almost silent. The noise of their rifles and canteens banging against their bodies were but soft thuds.

When they arrived at the place they were to assemble, Will began to move through the ranks. He motioned with his hands. "Take a seat, men, and relax a mite. We'll be at it soon enough." He watched as the men began to first squat, then sit and lie down.

He looked up to see General Lee riding down the line of men. They had all been given instruction not to shout, but it didn't prevent them from jumping to their feet and taking their hats off in silent salute. Lee nodded, smiling, as he passed.

It was some time later before General Armistead stepped over to the men and motioned for them to move forward. Will walked to the front of the long line and watched the men struggle to their feet. The men were wearing their best gray uniforms. The clean, crisp gray wool of some made it obvious that they had just received packages from home with uniforms that wives and mothers had stayed late into the night to proudly sew.

The white belts were the most striking feature of the regimental uniform. A pair of white leather straps crisscrossed a man's body and joined in the middle at the man's chest with a brass regimental insignia. Will knew the soldiers liked the striking effect of the X on the gray. "All right, you men," Will shouted. "Take off that white leather, right now."

The men, puzzled, began exchanging glances. Slowly, they removed their white leather Xs, dropping them to the ground.

He then moved from man to man, checking their rifles and making sure they had enough ammunition to return fire. He stopped in front of a young private with a babylike face and fuzz covering his cheeks. The young man was fumbling in his cartridge box, a worried expression on his face. "What seems to be the problem, soldier?" Will asked.

The man glanced up at Will and gulped. His Adam's apple bobbed up in his thin throat and the dimple in his chin quivered nervously. "I lost my patches, sir. I had me some nice ones too."

"What's your name private?"

"Robertson, sir, James Robertson of Lexington."

Will studied the young man's blue eyes. He fought his emotion. He really didn't want to know these men. He almost felt fortunate that until yesterday he'd been a total stranger to them. To watch a man die that you knew was to watch a little bit of yourself die with him. "Robertson, coming from a place with the Virginia Military Institute, I'm surprised at you. You lose your patches, you might as well lose your rifle."

"Yes, sir. I know, sir."

Robertson had the face of a starving kitten and eyes with a prayer for mercy written in them. Will reached into his pocket and pulled out a silk handkerchief. He then drew out his knife and cut the thing in two. Quickly, he began to make the two large pieces into smaller pieces.

"That's your handkerchief, sir."

"And a nice one too—silk. You ought to be able to get another fifty yards by using silk." Patches were used to position the ball in place before ramming it down the barrel. They created a tight seal around the charge. Most men used pieces of cotton fabric to seal their shot. Silk was always tighter and smoother and made for more accurate shooting, but it was hard to come by.

"Sir, if you don't mind me asking, why'd you order us to take our leather off?"

Will glanced up at the boy. "With all that smoke we're going to have in the field, our gray uniforms will be hard to pick out. Those Xs across the chest make fine targets. We don't want to give them any better aim than they already have." Will handed the small pieces of silk over to the boy. "Just shoot straight, son."

"Thank you, sir. I will."

Moving back to the center of the line, Will shouted, "Fix bayonets."

The men reached for the cold steel at their sides and, one by one, began to slide the shining metal spikes into place. Their eyes were focused on the trees up ahead, the last line of concealment they had from the massed Union cannons. Soon they would be visible and nothing would stand between them and the enemy.

The sound of thundering hooves brought every head up. It was Pickett, and he was waving his sword. He skidded his horse to a stop and then turned it around to face the men. "Men of the Old Dominion," he shouted. "Today you are fighting for your sweethearts, your wives, your families, and your homes." He waved his sword in the air. "For Old Virginia!"

Will watched as General Pickett moved his brigade out, but he kept his eyes trained on Armistead. The man turned slowly to face the brigade. He drew his sword. "Gentlemen, follow me over the wall."

All up and down the line, officers barked out the order to march. When it came Will's turn, he swung around and shouted, "Forward march." All at once the line of men in his regiment lurched forward. It was like a line of gray dominoes wobbling on a table someone had bumped into. They seemed to shudder forward. Up ahead were their own cannons, rumbling and belching out fire and great plumes of smoke that rained down on the Union lines.

Minutes later Will's regiment cleared the trees. They could see the rebel cannons as they fired round after round, bucking like sleek elephants of steel, spitting out plumes of smoke. The cannons fired in sequence from right to left. As the mass of men slowly passed them, the cannons fell silent. Rebel gunners turned and cheered, waving their hats in the air.

As Will moved in front of his men onto the field, he could see the Union guns erupt on the far ridge. A hail of steel torpedoes arched up into the sky and then rained down on the mass of men moving into the valley. It seemed to go on forever, men suspended in a slow walk, the high, hard-blue sky murky with stormy fumes of gunpowder. The sun turned bright red as the smoke and fire shadowed the field like a funeral pall.

Armistead gave the order for the brigade to assume a prone position, and all along the line men flopped down on their bellies like gutted fish being laid out in a sunny marketplace, listening as projectiles whooshed overhead. In brave disregard for his own safety, Armistead walked among the prone men. Will watched as one man rose in protest. The general simply waved him back into position. "Never you mind me. We want men with guns in their hands."

In short order they were back on their feet, dressing their lines to impress upon the Union troops on the ridge that it was useless to resist so formidable a foe. They stepped forward in formation as if drawn by some irresistible force that appeared to be willing to throw them off a cliff en masse. The murmur of trouser legs and jingle of equipment mixed with the rustle of thousands of feet in the stubble of the field. Dust and chaff were stirred up in front of them like churning waves washing the prow of a vessel on the high seas.

Union batteries recovered and began to rain down upon the men, tearing them like rag dolls being thrown on an ash heap. The lines closed, moving swiftly past moaning men. Flags pitched forward in the still air, only to be picked up again by new color bearers.

"Double quick march," Armistead shouted. The mass of men surged forward. They came to a line of rail fence, and the men began to climb. Some fell backward, others clung to the fence as shot poured into them. Will stepped up to the rail barricade and began to help the men climb over.

He spotted Robertson and waved for him to come quickly. The boy ran and planted his foot on Will's hand. He boosted himself up, then suddenly fell back into Will's arms. Will could see the blood spreading over the boy's tunic, a cloud of red over a mass of gray. Robertson's eyes stared right at him. A small frown formed on the young soldier's lips, followed by a smile. Will bent to lay him back on the ground.

Will got to his feet and climbed the fence with the men who had formed the new wave. Not ten yards down, a mass of the rail fence was blown away by Union canister. Dozens of men flew in all directions. The army had ceased to be men you could name. It was now an animal sniffing for a place to die.

Will spotted Armistead up ahead. The man had his black hat on the tip of his sword. He was waving the troops on and they came, rebel yells puncturing the air, a mixture of screams and ghostly wails.

Will saw a gunner touch the fuse to a Union cannon up ahead. The cannon bucked, hurling smoke, fury, and fragments of steel in his direction. The blast spun him around, and he hit the ground on his face. Pain stepped up and down his spine, and he felt the warmth of his own blood. He closed his eyes. Everything went silent and black.

The
RETREAT

CHAPTER 40

April stood at her father's grave. The creek flowed peacefully by the waving grass, gently lapping and gurgling past the exposed roots of the old oak tree. April lifted her hand over her eyes, blinking at the noon sky through the branches. Thoughts flooded her mind, her father's hopes and dreams. He had left Virginia to make a new life, a life without slavery. His dream had always been a country without the scourge of keeping people in bondage, and now, if what Will had told her was true, there would be one. Her father would never see it, but he would have been pleased all the same. While the results of the war might prove pleasing to her as well, she could never recover from the sight of the price that had been paid for it.

She watched as Perlman walked from the barn and started in her direction. There was a sadness in the man's eyes, and his walk was slow and deliberate. All the way home yesterday April had known that the last thing Perlman wanted to do was leave the battle. She knew his feelings about continuing this investigation with a battle underway, and she could see the mixture of worry and disgust written across his face. He had a deep, brooding scowl that even his gray beard couldn't conceal. He was doing his duty, but he didn't like it. His tunic was unbuttoned in the heat of the sun, and he removed his cap, wiping his forehead.

"I got the horses put away." He shook his head and glanced back toward the house. "And I spoke with your stepmother."

"You told her about Tillie?"

"No, I didn't. I figured I'd leave that to you."

April nodded. "That's all right. You've had enough unpleasantness. I suppose that does belong to me."

"That's what I thought. That's none of my business. What's between you and that stepmother of yours belongs to you."

April squatted down and pulled the ladle out of the bucket of water she had brought. It had holes in it, and she softly sprinkled water over the top of her father's grave. Even though it was in the shade, the water would help to keep it cool. She glanced up at Perlman. "You know, you remind me of my father."

April's words caught him off guard. The scowl disappeared, and his eyes got bigger. "How's that?"

April looked back at the grave. She dipped the ladle into the bucket once again and laid down a pattern of cool water over the mound. "He was a man who did his duty even when he hated it, a family man."

"I ain't got no family."

"But you're still a family man." She continued to make a pattern over the grave with the fresh water. "I know you. You become a part of every man's family that you come in contact with. People respect and admire you." She looked up at him and got to her feet. "I respect you. I know this is hard for you, and I know you don't even believe in what you're doing here. You're doing it because you've been told to and because it's your duty. That's just the kind of thing my father would have done. I just hope you come to for-give yourself."

"Why would you say that?"

April shook her head and looked at the ground. It was still hard for her to forgive herself for what she'd done in Gettysburg. The face of Roberta still haunted her, and she felt responsible. She might have that young girl's face in her mind forever. "Knowing what is a person's duty is so confusing at times. Do you do the thing you've always thought was right, or do you do what you feel like doing? I get confused."

"Look, Miss April, the major told me what you did back at that house. He wasn't angry either when he said it. It was almost as if he figured something like that, coming from you."

The thought jarred her. She stared at him. "Do you mean he doesn't trust me?"

Perlman pulled at his beard. "Not when it comes to politics, I suppose. You're a Yankee. You think like them people."

"But I have come to understand more of your side and why you're fighting this war. It's much bigger than what I was led to believe. I just saw one thing, and now I see so much more." She bit her lip. "It's hard though."

Perlman stopped her, his hand on her shoulder. "I'm a mite worried 'bout you, missy." He glanced at the house. "And this here farm of yours."

"Why is that?"

"Everybody has enemies, and I spect you got some neighbors somewheres round here that would just as soon see you gone and burnt out. You been spending lots of time with us rebs. We was even at your daddy's funeral, which may have been a big mistake."

"What are you saying?"

Perlman looked her right in the eye. "They might just spread it around that you folks is Copperheads. That army of yours gets here, they could burn you down just the same as they do us."

"That would never happen. We've been sheltering slaves."

Perlman shook his head. "You ain't got none round here now. I'm just sayin' that we better be careful. You never know 'bout folks you been breaking bread with. They stick their feet under your table, but lots of times there's envy in their hearts."

She began a slow walk back toward the house. "People are complicated, aren't they? You think you know them, and then you find out that you don't know them at all. Perhaps you never did."

"How well do you know this stepmother of yours?"

"Christine? I suppose I don't know her very well. My father didn't know her that well when he married her. She was the daughter of an old friend. I'm not sure he'd seen her in years before he arranged their wedding by mail."

"You folks is mighty strange, if you ask me. Where I come from they talk about love, not arrangements."

"I think the feeling was that real love is something that people grow into. You learn to trust someone with time."

"I don't see you heading off to marry some man you've never met. You fight the menfolk you have met."

April looked off toward the house. "Christine and I are very different. I think she was more motivated by a need for security and adventure. She talks about travel a lot."

Perlman smiled. "From what you tell me about your daddy, he don't seem the type to drop things around here and plow off looking for sights to see."

"No, you're right. I haven't been home all that much since they were married, but Tillie did tell me about some of their discussions. From what I hear, there wasn't a lot they agreed on. I think my father thought the baby would change that."

"And did it?"

"I think it made her more anxious. Some women are like that. They see their lives as being over, all of their girlish dreams dashed. Some women believe their dreams will be satisfied by a man"—a slight smile crossed her face—"only to find them ended by one. I've always made certain that my dreams were something I could accomplish on my own."

"And what if your dreams were wrapped up in one man, and then you just left him to marry someone else, someone you thought could make you more comfortable." Perlman gestured with his hand. He seemed more at ease when he was talking with his hands. "And then as time passed, you thought about the man you left more than the man you married. Don't you think the disappointment would grate on you?"

"You can't be talking about Christine."

"I'm not saying I am and I'm not saying I ain't. I'm just supposing for a spell. Now let me ask you this. Was your daddy the type of man to go prying into other people's letters?"

April shook her head. "No, he'd never think of doing such a thing."

"Then how'd he come upon that note from Jenkins?"

"I'm not sure."

"You think she left it out for him to find?"

"Why should she do that? I would have destroyed such a thing."

"Maybe you would have, but Christine didn't. Fact is, she let it be found. Let me ask you something else. Was your daddy the type of man to get himself all excited and angry?"

April bowed her head. "He was a thoughtful man. He was never one to erupt at the drop of a hat." She looked up at him. "But I would have to say that when aroused he could lose control of himself."

"And wouldn't you have to say that a note from your stepmother's old fiancée, a note suggesting a rendezvous, might be enough to arouse him?" Perlman smiled. "It'd get me plenty worked up. I'll say that."

"Yes, it might."

"And what about this neighbor of yours, this Slocum feller. He and your daddy ever have any quarrels?"

"The two of them have been friends for a long time. You know how those things are. A man begins to think that friendship allows you to take liberties. There were times my father became absolutely infuriated at the way John would just assume things."

"Like selling his farm."

"I suppose. We never discussed that. I don't think my father thought the farm was my business."

"What then?"

April stared at the ground. It was an uncomfortable thing to talk about. "Slocum always thought our families should find a way to join, you know, to keep both farms in the family."

"That's interesting. This Slocum don't have no girls does he?"

"No, just boys. Why do you ask?"

"Well, that sort of leaves your brother out of the picture when it comes to joining up the families, don't it?"

"My brother, Gerald, is in the war. I'm not sure either my father or Slocum ever thought he'd come back. They were opposed to war and I think they sort of blanked him out of their minds when it came to planning."

"Then that just leaves you, don't it? You marrying up with the Slocum boy."

"I don't want to think about that."

"Oh yes, I remember. You want your dreams to be something done on your own, without a man." Perlman smiled. "You still feel that way?"

"If you mean Will, I'm anxious about him. I'll feel better when I see him ride up."

"And you really think that's going to happen?"

"Why shouldn't it? He promised me."

Perlman stopped in his tracks. "Dear lady, every man on that field we left made promises, promises he'll never be able to keep. A man makes a pledge to ease a woman's mind, but it's one that other folks don't intend for him to keep."

They walked into the house and could hear the sound of Christine's voice in the kitchen. The woman was singing. They stepped into the dining room and made their way to the kitchen. Christine had her hands on a rolling pin, smoothing out a sheet of dough. She looked up at them and wiped her forehead with the back of her hand, leaving a white streak of fine flour. She smiled.

"There you are. I was making a pie for Mr. Slocum. He likes apple pie."

April walked over to the table and sat down. "He's coming here?"

Christine turned back to her piecrust, rapping the pin on it and rolling it. "Yes, he is. I invited him for supper tomorrow night."

"And I take it he still wants to buy the farm?"

"More than ever. I saw him a couple of days ago, and he wanted to discuss terms."

"Both of you seem a little anxious, I'd say," April added.

Christine turned to face her, her hands on her hips. "Why shouldn't we be? This war will never end." She glanced at Perlman. "With those rebels coming up here, who knows when this thing will end. We could be burned out for all you know."

"I seriously doubt that. Wouldn't you agree, Sergeant?"

Perlman was thumbing through a stack of papers on the sideboard, lost in thought. "You planning on taking a trip?"

"Oh, those old things." Christine waved her flour-caked hand at him. "I've had those for a long time. John Slocum gave them to me."

Perlman held up the brochure for April to see. "Advertisements for a boat trip to England," he said.

Christine turned back to her work, lifting the crust and laying it gently in a pie tin. "I showed those to Jonas when he was alive. He just grunted; said the thought never appealed to him. A girl should travel though, shouldn't she?" She glanced back at April. "You've always wanted to travel, see the sights, haven't you, April?"

"We've never had the money for such thoughts."

Christine turned and smiled. "Well, now we do. We can't stay here. We have no idea if Gerald is even coming back from this war, and it's too much for me to handle. All the men who could even be hired to work the place are already off fighting the war."

"And Slocum is interested in buying the farm?" April asked.

Christine picked up a knife. She circled the edge of the pan with it, cutting off strips of dough. "He's very excited. He said he's always wanted it, but Jonas would never sell. Said one big farm was more valuable than two small ones. He seemed most anxious about it, and he has cash."

"You haven't asked us about Tillie," April said.

Christine turned to face them. "Yes, where is she? The baby will be needing her."

"She's dead, Christine. I suppose you'll have to take care of the baby yourself."

Christine put down the knife and picked up a cloth, wiping her hands. "Dead? That's awful."

"She was murdered."

The thought seemed to jar Christine. She walked over to a chair and sat down. "Murdered? Who would want to kill Tillie?"

"It was a Southern officer who thought she might implicate someone."

Christine took a deep breath. "I knew it. It was one of those people who killed Jonas. Did you find out who it was?"

"I'm afraid not, Mrs. Wolff," Perlman said. "It would seem the man was protecting someone by mistake. Near as we can tell, the murderer is someone closer to here."

"That's impossible. Jonas was well liked. No one around here would do such a thing."

"What about someone who wanted your husband's farm?"

Christine shot to her feet, glaring at Perlman with eyes suddenly turning to hard blue steel. "I find your suggestion impossible. Mr. Slocum goes to our church. He's a fine Christian gentleman."

"Madam, we just left a place where Christians were murdering Christians by the thousands. Anything is possible."

CHAPTER 41

erlman saddled his mule late in the afternoon. The heat of the day was beginning to fade with the last of the western sun filtering softly through the cracks in the barn door. He could see the dust in the air, trails of powdery dirt and hay sailing through the shafts of yellow light. There was a peacefulness about the place that almost made him forget the war, a quietness of the spirit. It wasn't like going home, it was almost like going back in time, to a place where people smiled at each other on the street. He'd been a policeman in Atlanta before the war. He'd walked the streets, smiling and chatting. Now he wasn't even sure if there would be a street to walk down when the war was finished.

The orange tabby curled around through the slightly open door, cocking his head and studying Perlman as he cinched his saddle. The cat stepped lightly into the barn, drawing a smile from the sergeant. "If you're here for more cream from bossy over there, you're too early. You better get to mousing, old son. Man's got to work before he can eat."

The big cat stepped over to where Perlman was tightening his cinch. It swept its body through Perlman's legs, curling its tail around his pants leg like a furry snake. It let out a loud meow, followed by a rumbling purr.

"Ain't no amount of sweetness going to fetch one drop of milk before it's time, Elmer. Menfolks got to learn that. You can coax all you want, but if it ain't there, you ain't getting any." It did him some good to talk to the cat, mostly because the thing didn't talk back. He had no fear of being contradicted. He could be listened to by something that had eyes. Most of the time that was what men needed the most, just to be listened to. To have someone blink and purr in admiration as you spoke was a luxury that few men had.

The door creaked open farther, and April stepped inside the barn. She was wearing a pretty yellow dress with white lace outlining the top of her bodice. There was a bright yellow ribbon in her dark hair.

"That's mighty pretty, Miss April. You look like you're dressing up for a party."

April looked down at her dress. "I suppose I am. I was just hoping . . ."

"Hoping the major would keep his word and show up?"

April nodded. Perlman could see a look of shy embarrassment in her eyes. She batted her lashes and looked down at the barn floor. He continued to check his saddle. "I wouldn't stay on pins and needles over that if I was you."

"So you don't think he made it?"

"Ma'am, I don't rightly see how many of them men will ever come back, to say nothing of Major Chevalier. Bravery is an issue with him, you know."

"Yes, I know. He's got to prove how much of a soldier he is."

"And I don't reckon he's about to stop either, at least not on his own." Perlman turned to check the rifle in his saddle boot. "When that man gets all excited about something, there ain't much in this world that's going to stop him."

He turned back to look at her. "Ma'am, if I was you, I'd just try and put the major plumb out of your head. Best to face what's ahead of you, not what's behind." He knew the truth of what he was saying, but somehow it didn't seem very comforting. What lay ahead of him was burned empty houses and full graves. What was behind him seemed much more inviting.

"And I suppose you're leaving now too."

Perlman wiped his beard, spreading his gray whiskers with the back of his hand. He had a plug of fresh tobacco in his mouth, and he chomped down on it with his back teeth. "Ain't likely. I got my orders here, and I aim to see them through." He spat on the ground. "If it kills me."

"Then where are you going?"

"I figured to take me a little ride over to that neighbor of yours."

"John Slocum?"

Perlman shook his head. "Naw, least not today. I'd like to have me a little talk with that boy of his. He's our only eyewitness, and he's a witness that tried to shoot us, if I got him figured right. That don't make much sense to me, and I spect he's going to have some 'splainin' to do."

"So you're staying?"

"Just till we get this here matter settled. Near as I can figure, one of them armies, maybe both, ought to come by late tomorrow. That don't leave us much time, and I don't figure it'll take all that much. All I'm going to need are directions from you."

"Did you mean what you said about our neighbors?"

"About them being suspects?"

"No, about them throwing suspicion on us and making us rebel sympathizers?"

"Ma'am, you say you is tight with your neighbors, but I don't think they take too kindly on us for coming up here and bringing this war your way." He spat a gush of brown tobacco juice onto the barn floor, which landed with a splat. He wiped his mouth with the back of his hand. "You got to admit you been mighty sociable with men wearing this here uniform I got on."

"But we were looking for my father's murderer."

"That won't make no difference to them, I reckon. None at all."

"I hope you're wrong."

"I do too."

I t was close to suppertime when Perlman rode up to the trees surrounding the Slocum farm. Row upon row of tall sycamores stood like sentinels along the drive that led up to the house. Like the Wolff place, it looked prosperous. The house was three stories and painted a bright, candy-apple red with white shutters and gingerbread trim under the windows. There was a large barn and a set of pens for the hogs. The sound and aroma of the dirty animals carried all the way to where the sergeant sat on his mule. He'd never been much of a farmer. To him, the hogs just smelled like bacon. Of course, a man would have to use his imagination for that. But it was better thinking about what they produced than what they smelled like.

He got off his mule and began to walk the animal along the line of trees, keeping his distance from the windows. Being shot for a prowler was something he didn't have in mind. When he got to a safe enough place, he sat down beside a tree and waited. It gave him some time to think the matter over. This Slocum boy was no doubt their only eyewitness and most likely was the one who had tried to ambush them along the road. It didn't figure, but only the boy himself knew the answers, and Perlman was determined to find out.

Shortly after dark he saw the back door open. A young man went down the back stairs and into the barn. Several minutes later the young man emerged from the barn with two full buckets in his hands.

Perlman left his spot by the trees and skirted around toward the area of the hog pens. He could hear the squeals, which meant it was feeding time, just the chore Tommy Slocum would be performing. He could hear the boy singing out to them. "Piggy, piggy, piggy! Here piggy, piggy."

Perlman made his way around the barn, glancing up at the back window in the kitchen. A light was there, but no one was at the window. The hog pens were situated some fifty yards from the barn in an area mostly downwind from the house. He could only imagine what it must have been like for the wind to occasionally blow in the other direction. People would have to have a strong stomach. Dinner in the home would mean closed windows, even on a hot summer night.

He spotted Slocum leaning over the fence, pouring out the contents of his last bucket into the feeding trough. The hogs were gathering, a milling black-brown-and-red-spotted mass, snorting and squealing at the fence. Slocum bent over the fence, shaking out the bucket.

Stepping up behind Slocum, Perlman drew out his revolver. "I see you're taking good care of some gentile's dinner," he said.

Tommy dropped the bucket into the mass of hogs and whirled around. He hung on the fence, his eyes widening at the sight of Perlman and his revolver. "What are you doing here?"

Perlman wagged his revolver at him. "That pretty much depends on you. You just climb down off that fence before you fall in. I'd hate to see just what those hogs of yours would do to you. There wouldn't be enough left to bury."

Tommy dropped to the ground and brushed off his hands on his pants. "What do you want with me?"

"I want to ask you a few questions, and if I don't get the answers I'm looking for, I'll feed you to those hogs myself."

"I done told you ever'thin' I knows." His eyes looked wild, glancing around to where he could see the farmhouse in the distance. "I done told April what I seen. I ain't got much more to tell."

"You let me be the judge of that. Let's start by talking about what you didn't tell, say, why you took those shots at us from that ridge overlooking the road. And don't try to deny it, because you were seen with that Sharps."

"I was just out hunting, that's all."

"You might have been out hunting, but you were hunting us." Perlman stepped closer to him. "Was a durn fool thing to do too. You might have shot April by mistake."

Tommy shook his head violently and held up both hands. "I wouldn't do that. Ain't no way I'd do that. I'm too good a shot for that."

"Not hardly. If you were, we'd both be dead. April came close to being shot. You were just aiming at anything moving, anything that happened to cross your sights."

Tommy twisted his face in pain. "I didn't mean to do that. Please don't tell her nothing."

"You just tell me why and, if I'm satisfied with your answers, then I won't say anything about it to April."

Tommy once again glanced at the house. It wasn't a look of hope that he would be rescued. It was more a look of fear. Perlman could see it in his eyes.

"Look, son, you have nothing to fear from the truth. Did you kill Jonas Wolff?"

Once again Tommy began to shake his head violently. "Oh no. I didn't do no such thing. I wanted to marry up with April. I'd asked him for her hand. I just wanted to come and talk to him some more about it. That's all. Honest, mister. Why would I up and kill the father of the girl I wanted to marry up with?"

"Then why did you take those shots at us?"

He hung his head and began to paw the ground with the toe of his boot. Then he looked up. "When we seen you ride off that day, my daddy said you fellers was the ones who had started this here war. Said if it hadn't been for you, then we wouldn't be sending men off to die. I ain't never seen me no Johnny Rebs before. I jes figured I'd be doing me a good turn to up and kill you boys."

"Poppycock! Then why don't you go and join the Union army? Then you can fight us full time and not just for a hobby."

Tommy shook his head. "Naw, I can't do that. We don't believe in war in my family. Daddy says it's the devil's business."

Perlman chuckled. "You beat all, boy. You don't believe in war, but murdering people from ambush is all right by you."

"I can't rightly splain how I was thinking about it, but I know at the time it seemed clear in my head."

"I can't say as I believe you, boy. You go out of your way to kill total strangers, but you don't believe in war. Next thing we know about you, you've got a wagonload of goods you're selling to our army, men you hold responsible for this war. That doesn't quite figure."

Tommy suddenly slammed both hands into his temples, pressing them to the sides of his head. He looked confused. He gave the appearance of a frustrated five-year-old who had been asked to recite a spelling word he couldn't quite remember. "I just do what my daddy tells me to do. That's all I ever do."

Perlman scratched his beard. "And in your mind, no doubt, he was telling you to kill us. Well, it's plain to see you're not the mastermind of this operation."

Perlman's words ripped right through Tommy. He dropped his hands, balling them into fists. Letting out a roar, he lowered his head and charged like a bull, screaming and bellowing as he came.

The sudden fury of the boy caught Perlman off guard. He had a gun on him, but obviously that didn't mean anything when anger took control of Tommy Slocum. Perlman stuffed the revolver into his trousers and stepped aside as Tommy got close. He grabbed the young man by the shirt and continued his run, finally flinging him at a post at the corner of the hog pen.

The sound of the collision was a dull thud. The fence rocked back and forth. Turning the boy over, Perlman climbed on top of his chest. He pulled out his revolver, cocked it, and then pointed it directly between the boy's eyes. "You got yourself a temper, son. Makes me kinda wonder. If you was to get yourself a no from April's daddy, and if he did spell out his reasons in a way that you didn't like, you could have stabbed the man. You're as liable to lose control as a swarm of mad honeybees."

"No." Tommy's eyes were wild, staring at Perlman's Colt.

"Maybe you figured that your father killed Wolff. Maybe you thought you were protecting him."

Tommy held up both hands and shook them, as if warding off a swarm of hungry mosquitoes. "I never said that. I never said that at all."

"But your father wasn't home when you rode off to speak to Wolff, was he?"

"Yes, he was here."

"You're a lousy liar, boy. Pick something you're better at."

"It don't make no difference where he was. He was busy."

"And he did want to buy the Wolff farm, didn't he?"

"What if he did?"

"And Wolff didn't want to sell."

Tommy shook his head from side to side on the ground. "That don't make no difference. My daddy and Mr. Wolff was friends. He wouldn't do such a thing."

"You had to figure you were protecting someone important to you to go off and try and kill a couple of strangers, unless you were trying to cover your own sorry hide. Not many men would do a thing like that without some very good reason. Did you ever ask your daddy if he killed the man?"

Tommy put both hands to his face, covering his eyes. Then he slid them down slowly. "I could never ask a thing like that."

"But you figured he might have, didn't you?"

Tommy began to cry. "I didn't know. I just didn't know."

"Boy, I feel sorry for you. There's a world of things that you don't know. Now you listen to me. Tomorrow night your father's coming to dinner. You make sure you're with him. Don't make me come and get you."

Perlman got up from on top of the boy and walked over to the gate. He then lifted the latch and swung it open. A number of the hogs bolted out, squealing with delight on their way toward the open field. "There you are, boy. That ought to keep you busy here. We'll see you at dinner tomorrow."

CHAPTER 42

The following day passed slowly for April. She had put on a blue dress trimmed in white lace around the neckline. She was fast going through her Sunday wardrobe, but that didn't matter to her. She wanted to look her best. Normally she would have worn a simple everyday dress, and she could see from the way that Perlman looked at her when she stepped out onto the porch that there was no fooling the man. Hope died hard inside of her. Her ability to keep on going and never give up hope was what had prompted her to begin this search for justice.

Perlman was sitting in the rocking chair that Tillie had used. He was rocking back and forth and cleaning his guns. There was something appropriate about it. It had been Tillie's throne, the seat of wisdom for the house. Now, with her gone, Jacob Perlman had assumed the role of lawgiver and sage. The title seemed to reflect his personality. It suited him well. He had told her about his ride to the Slocum farm, but he hadn't told her much. The man was rather reluctant when it came to the investigation. He was the type of man who had to work through everything before he made his final judgment. He didn't think as he talked. He thought first, then talked. Perlman glanced up, then looked back at the pistol on his lap and continued his rocking. "It shouldn't be long now, one way or the other."

April stepped out farther on the porch and placed her hands on the rail. She took a long look down the road that led to their house. The minutes of this day seemed to be crawling by like hours. This might be the day that would make her life either empty or full. There was a pain in her empty stomach from the worry. "You seem so calm about this."

"A body's got to be calm about what he can't change. When a man puts on the uniform, he comes to peace with death, his and that of the men around him. You can't look back. As long as you got breath inside your chest, you got to look ahead. I figure to wind this thing up tonight and be on my way. I'll find out where the army's gone and join up with them there."

"Then you do think it's someone around here?"

Perlman nodded. "That I do. I'm not your civil authority, though, so I'm going to have to leave the matter with you when I'm gone." He grinned. "They ought to dig themselves out of the woodwork they crawled into in a couple of days or so. You can go on down to Greencastle and tell them what we found out."

"And you think it's going to be someone who comes to dinner tonight?"

"Yes, ma'am. That's right."

April shook her head. "That hardly seems possible."

"When you throw out the possible, you're left with believing the impossible. I'm afraid that's what we have here, the impossible."

April looked down the road. "Then that's what I should believe too, the impossible."

Perlman put down his revolver and picked up April's father's book of Psalms. He opened it and began thumbing through the pages. "You know our faith is made up of the believable, but the impossible I'm never sure about."

"Our faith? But you're Jewish."

"We have the same God, don't we? You just carry it farther than we think we can just now. Your Messiah's already come and been killed. Ours is coming back in front of an army that can never suffer defeat."

April turned to face him. She knew Jacob Perlman was a Jew, perhaps even a devout one. He knew who he was and where he'd come from. Not many men knew that, and she respected it. "It's the same man, Jacob. He rose from the dead, and He's coming back. You just have to believe that He's the one who died for our sins. He's the sacrifice that you've been celebrating all these years."

"Maybe my impossible only goes so far, not nearly as far as yours, it seems."

She turned back to face the road. "I like my impossible better. It made me trust you, and it makes me wait for Will Chevalier. He's going to come. I just know it."

April stepped inside the house to begin her housework. She took a mitt made out of lamb's wool and began to dust the dark cherry furniture, the type her mother had always wanted. Unfortunately, her father had gone to Harrisburg and bought it just before Christine arrived. He had wanted to impress the woman and had spared no expense in doing just that.

It grated on her that Christine got to live with things that her mother had wanted but never had. The thought of her stepmother selling the farm now infuriated her. Her brother might survive the war. By all rights the place should be his. To have Christine sell it after only being married to her father for three years seemed too much to bear. April almost hoped that Perlman had found John Slocum to be the murderer. If he was arrested, then he couldn't buy the farm. She knew such thinking wasn't Christian. It was selfish. She wanted justice, not just to preserve her father's farm.

She took the rugs out and hung them over a line to beat them. She would stay busy, somehow, to take her mind off the identity of her father's killer and the hoped-for sight of Will Chevalier. The more she thought about Will and the more she thought about the farm, the harder she beat the rugs.

The house was bright now, almost cheerful. She took the time to dust the paintings, which had been hung with care. The maple floor shone with polish, and she made certain all the globes in the lamps were clean. They sparkled, the light from the heat of the day causing them to gleam. She could see that Christine was also working, baking bread and cooking the roast they would have tonight. It was obvious to April that Christine wanted to make a favorable impression on Slocum.

April got a bucket of water mixed with vinegar and began to wash the windows. Those in the front of the house would get a special wash, but not because they were sure to be seen and would make the best impression. April wasn't kidding herself any longer. She took longer to clean them because she could watch the road as she did. It didn't matter that she was doing such dirty work in a nice dress. If Will came back, she wanted him to see her in it. If he didn't, she wasn't sure if she would ever want to look attractive again.

It was close to midafternoon when she finished cleaning the front windows. She squinted out and thought she saw a lone figure on foot some distance away. She continued rubbing the window, staring at the figure in the distance. Will would be riding his big gray horse. No doubt the man at the end of the road had lost his way. Perhaps he was even a straggler who had refused to fight. April hoped Perlman wouldn't make a scene. They had enough on their hands without him trying to apprehend a deserter.

The man continued his struggling march down their road, and April dropped her cloth in the bucket and stepped out on the porch. She walked over to the railing and clasped the smooth wood. She could see the man more clearly now. He walked with a limp but appeared to be about the same height as Will. He had no hat and wore a bandage around his head, but April could see that the dark tuft of hair sticking out above the bandage was the same color as Will's. It was then that her heart began to pound. She breathed a prayer.

Moving to the steps, she started down them one at a time. Perlman had long since gone to the barn, and she was almost grateful for that. The man would be laughing at her now if he was still there. She did feel a little foolish.

The man in the distance picked up his pace. It was a determined walk, and April quickly stepped off the last of the stairs. She began to walk up the road in his direction. As he caught sight of her, he stopped. She walked faster, then lifted her skirts and began to run. It was Will. She knew it. The way he carried himself in spite of the hobble was enough for her.

She threw open her arms and charged toward the weary man. She wouldn't wait for him. She flung herself into his outstretched arms. He spun her around without thinking. He winced, but held her tight against him. "I knew you'd come," she gasped. She could smell sulfur mixed with sweat. "You promised me, and you always keep your word."

He pushed her back and brushed away her hair. "You're the most beautiful sight I've ever seen," he said.

She couldn't help but cling to him. She brushed away the small lock of hair hanging down below the bandage and ran her fingers over his face. "I knew I would see you. Perlman kept telling me to give up hope and just go on with my life, but I couldn't. I could never do that. Not now."

April gingerly touched his arm. "You're wounded."

Will nodded. "Yes, but I'll heal. I can't stay long. I have to rejoin my troops, or what's left of them."

"What happened there? Can you tell me?"

They began a slow walk toward the house. "We got whipped. It's just that simple. I couldn't begin to tell you about the wagon train I left to come here."

"Tell me. Please tell me."

Will stopped and looked at her. "I'm glad you didn't see it. We're carrying back the wounded we felt might make it, mile after mile of wagons filled with screaming men. I listened to men beg to be put out of the wagons and left to die, begging and pleading, mind you."

April slowly shook her head.

"I was told that it would take a man seven hours riding at full gallop to go from the wagons in back to the ones in the front of that train. I've been listening to nothing but men screaming in pain all night long."

April listened, soaking up his words. She knew Will needed to talk about what had happened, and she also knew it was something he was hesitant to do. She didn't want to say anything now that might cut him off or distract him. His uniform was torn and bloody and caked with dirt. There were large holes in the breast of his tunic, and several buttons were missing. None of that mattered to her. She drank in the sight of Will Chevalier, of Will breathing and talking.

She put his arm over her neck and wrapped hers around his waist. "I want to hear everything. I want to hear all about it. We'll get you into the house, and I'll change your dressing. You'll feel better after a hot bath."

Will smiled at her. "I just won't use that pink-colored soap I bought you."

When April settled Will into a living room chair, she slowly took off his boots. She watched the pain shoot through the man as he twisted in the chair, his eyes closing and his mouth twisting in agony. "You knew I would wait for you, didn't you?"

Will smiled. "Yes, I knew. I suspect Perlman had a tough time getting you to ride south. I halfway expected you to be on the field looking for me."

April nodded. "I would have too, if he'd have let me. But you know how determined the man is."

"And I'm glad for that."

April bowed her head and then looked up into his eyes. "I spent some time feeling ashamed of myself."

"Ashamed? Why?"

"Because of how forward I was with you that day. Those were words I've never spoken to a man, and feelings I've never had."

Will reached out and patted her head. Then he ran his fingers down her cheek. "Sometimes it takes extreme circumstances for people to figure out what they really feel. I'm glad you did. Last night in that wagon, those words and your face were all that kept me going. I felt so much hope drain out of me after that final day. I needed what little bit you gave me."

April smiled. She knew Will didn't have any problems with talking about matters of the mind, but things from the heart were a different issue. "I am glad what I said meant something to you."

He tipped his head and smiled at her. "Yes, April, I had to make it back to see if you really meant it, or were just throwing a soldier a good-bye kiss."

April looked at him sharply, but the roguish smile told her he was teasing her. Her eyes teared unexpectedly. April wanted so badly to hear from Will that he loved her. She couldn't say the words for him, though, and she couldn't produce his feelings. A tear trickled down her cheek. "I didn't know if you'd ever forgive me for what I did at that house."

Will traced the tear's path with a rough index finger, then touched her cheek. "There's nothing to forgive where I'm concerned. How can I fault a woman for doing something she believes in? That's who you are. And that's what—"

He stopped, pulling his hand away from her face.

She wanted to finish his sentence but instead fingered the holes in his tunic. "What made these?"

"Union canister shot. By all rights I should be dead."

April looked puzzled. "Then what—"

"What saved me?"

"Yes."

Will gave off a wide grin. "Victor Hugo." He reached into his tunic and pulled out the copy of Les Misérables that Pickett had given to him. He handed it to April.

April took the book and ran her hands over two large holes in it. She opened it and found where the lead balls had stopped, almost at the very end of the novel. Then she held the book to her breast and looked into his eyes. "I think this has just become my favorite novel, and I haven't even read it."

"Mine too," Will agreed.

CHAPTER 43

pril peeled apples on a stool in the kitchen and watched Christine spoon flour into what was going to be the gravy. The smell of slow-cooked beef filled the room, and mounds of potatoes waiting to be mashed sat on the side of the stove. Christine took the last of the silver serving spoons out of the cupboard and sailed out the door to the dining room.

April watched Will and Perlman try their best to stay out of the way. It was still warm, and the heat from the kitchen made sweat beads form on the back of her neck. She could only imagine how the men must feel in their uniforms. Of course, Will's uniform was the worst for wear. He had given her the thing to wash while he took a bath, and there had been enough heat in the air to allow it to dry while the sun was still up. While it did look clean, the tatters and holes made it look barely fit for wear. *I'll have to sew it for him,* she thought.

She carried the apples into the dining room. The table was laid with a lace cloth that her mother had made. April set the apples down and lightly fingered the lace, running her hand along the loops in the intricate border design. The delicate pattern had taken her mother the better part of a winter, and the sight of it brought back memories of the two of them sitting by the fire. Some of their best conversations had happened when her mother's hands were busy.

She let out a deep sigh. Today was a happy day for her, and the memories of her mother added a special warmth to it. Then, almost without warning, her mind turned to thoughts of selling the farm. She shook it off. Will's return had been an answer to prayer. She wasn't going to let thoughts of envy or malice toward Christine spoil it. Then she heard the baby cry.

April ran out of the dining room and up the stairs to the baby's room. Reaching into the crib, she picked up her baby brother, her father's child. April rocked the boy in her arms and walked back down the stairs. She went through the dining room and into the kitchen.

Christine was giving the potatoes a stir when she turned and saw April holding the child. She dropped the spoon, a frown forming across her face. "Here, give him to me. He's my baby," she said harshly.

"I was only trying to help," April said. "He was crying upstairs."

Christine took the baby in her arms and walked out to the living room. Perlman smiled at April. "Women get kinda touchy about their children, I guess. Want what belongs to them."

April bit her lower lip. "Some want what belongs to others too." April felt bad about the biting remark when she said it. Even though this was her home and she had grown up in it, Christine had every right to provide for herself and the baby. She let out a sigh.

"So the Slocum family will be at dinner?" Will asked.

"Just John and his son Tommy," April said. "John's wife died a few years ago, and his other sons are all married and moved away. I guess his farm is too small to support three families."

"Could be that's why he wants your place," Perlman said. "A man likes to have his whole clan close by if he can have it that way."

"You're probably right," April said. It still didn't change the way she felt about the man. She saw him as an opportunistic vulture who couldn't even wait until her father's body was cold in the ground. She looked at the roast. No matter how wonderful the dinner was, she had already lost her appetite.

A short time later John and Tommy Slocum arrived. They were both escorted by Christine into the living room, where April joined them along with Will and Perlman. Christine then left for the kitchen. John Slocum wore a black suit and boiled white shirt. It was his Sunday best. His boots were shined and his beard trimmed. His dark eyes appeared to glow in the lamplight. His stocky build seemed squashed in the chair, like a mountain of lard in black pants. Small talk was difficult for John, especially with men with whom he had little in common. April watched as he made deliberate attempts not to make eye contact with either Will or Perlman. Tommy, his hair parted at the middle and slicked down with shiny grease, was quiet. He shifted his feet nervously under his chair.

Later, when they had finished dinner, Slocum pushed himself back from the table and patted his beard with a napkin. He glanced at Christine. "That was a most delicious meal, Christine." He cleared his throat. "But now we have some business to conclude."

"Would you like some coffee?" Christine asked.

Slocum again cleared his throat. It was a rumble from deep down. "Certainly, if you have some." He swatted lightly at the bottom of his beard as if to knock stray crumbs to the table.

Perlman got to his feet. "Why don't you let me build up the fire in the stove?" April could see that the man was bored by their conversation and would have paid any price for escape. "Then you can come in and put the pot on."

Christine had a panicked look on her face. She shot to her feet. "No, that won't be necessary. I'll do it."

"Nonsense," Perlman said. "That's not woman's work. You stay here and entertain."

Christine started to move to the door ahead of Perlman, but April took her arm. "He's right. These are your guests." She got up and dropped her napkin on her plate. "I'll put the coffee on, and he can start the fire again. It's cool enough now."

She followed Perlman into the kitchen, closing the door behind them. "I did so want to get out of there," she said. "I don't think I could stand the thought of sitting there and watching her sell off my father's farm."

"I can understand that." He grinned. "But I think the major may have a few questions for them before that happens. We talked this afternoon. I wouldn't want you to miss that." Perlman pulled several pieces of kindling from a bucket beside the stove and opened the iron gate. He stirred the coals.

April took the cobalt blue coffeepot down from the shelf. She set it on the counter and reached for the heavy jar that contained what remained of the coffee. Holding it up, she shook it. "I think we still have some left. Lucky us."

Perlman was down on his knees, digging in the stove. April heard him mumbling to himself. Suddenly, he sat back. "It might be very lucky for us." Turning around, he held up a charred end of a pitchfork. "Do you know what I have in my hand here?" he asked.

April took a step in his direction, the pot in her hand. "It looks like our old pitchfork. One of the tongs was broken off. Why would that thing be in the stove?"

Perlman grinned. "That's a good question. But more than that." He paused, allowing April to get closer, then he stood up. He held it out to her. The prongs were still intact, three prongs of an iron pitchfork. The wooden handle had been broken and was charred down to the base. There was only an inch or so left from where it joined with the prongs. "I would say that what we have here is the murder weapon."

April dropped the pot to the floor.

Perlman picked up a set of dishtowels and gently wrapped the pitchfork in them. "You'd better get that coffee ready so we can go back for dessert." He smiled. "I have a feeling it will be mighty sweet."

Perlman coaxed the fire to life while April fixed the coffee. A million questions flooded her mind, but she knew from the set of Perlman's jaw that he wasn't in a talking mood at the moment. He was thinking, hard. Her hand shook as she took down a set of china cups and saucers along with a hand-painted china coffee server. "I want this to be special," she said.

"Oh, it will be special all right. I think what I have wrapped up in those towels will make this a night to remember."

April put out a bowl of sugar and filled the china creamer. Then, carefully, she poured the coffee into the server and lifted the tray.

"Allow me, little lady." Perlman opened the door and picked up the wrapped pitchfork. "Don't want you dropping anything else."

They walked into the dining room where Slocum had carefully laid out papers and a bill of sale. He glanced up at her and smiled. "I see you made it back for the important part."

April noticed the knowing smile on Will's face. He was seated with the leather-bound book of Psalms at his side. It was open. He couldn't possibly know what they had found in the stove, nor could he understand what she had on her mind. But there was a sense about the man, almost like a lion who knew that it was the time for a kill.

April set the tray down on the table. She returned Will's smile with a wide grin and responded to Slocum. "I wouldn't miss it for the world." She then handed Will a cup on a saucer. "How would you like your coffee, John?"

Slocum sat back. "I take mine with cream and sugar, if you please."

April began to pour the coffee. It wasn't often that she gave in to temptation, but she was going to do it this time. Perlman hadn't said a word about whom he suspected and Will hadn't shown his hand, but she couldn't get over the burning feeling in her stomach when she looked at Slocum. She poured the coffee first into his cup and then trailing over the cup and down into his lap. "How about hot, John? Do you like it hot?"

Slocum jumped to his feet, bellowing like a bull. He was followed by Christine, who screamed at April and took her napkin to the man, swatting at the dampness in his lap. "April! That was a terrible thing to do!" Christine bellowed. "I never thought you were capable of such a thing."

April backed away, a smile still on her lips. "You would be surprised at what I'm capable of doing, Christine. But I'm more surprised at you."

"At me? What did I do?"

Will got to his feet. "Why don't we all sit down for a minute. Just calm yourselves. I'm sure everything can be explained." He looked over at April. "Why don't you bring us a pencil and paper?"

Slocum slowly got back into his chair, glaring at April all the while. Christine moved to her seat and sat down, leaving her chair pulled away from the table. April got the pencil and paper and laid them in front of Will. She noticed that Tommy Slocum had been amused by his father's discomfort, but he was trying hard to hide it. He rubbed his mouth back and forth trying his best to stifle a smile.

"All right, Major, the floor is yours," Slocum said. "But this had better be good."

Will leaned over the paper and drew the familiar US, making the X mark underneath it. He passed the paper around the table. "This was the writing on the floor of the barn that April found near where her father died. It's something that has had the sergeant and me puzzled for a long time."

He looked over at where Tommy Slocum was seated. "It might have been that belt buckle of yours, the US."

Tommy gripped the arms of his chair. He stood up and looked down at his belt. He was wearing the brass Union buckle. He fingered it. "It weren't me." He shook his head. "I found him before he died, and he gave me that Bible of his." He pointed to the book of Psalms at Will's place. "He gave it to me and said, 'Gave it'. I thought he was talking 'bout Christine, and so I asked him, 'Do you want me to give it to Christine?' But he said no. He just said, 'Gave it.' And then he died. He died right there in the barn, but I didn't kill him."

"I thought he said, 'Give it'," Will said. "I thought that's why you gave it away."

Tommy shook his head. "You're right. He said, 'Give it.' I'm pretty sure."

"But you did try to kill us?" Will asked. "You tried to take us at ambush?" He glanced at Perlman. "The sergeant and I talked today."

"Yes." He shot a glance at his father. "But just because you was rebs and cause my daddy said you ought to die, that it would be better for everyone if you did."

Will took a long look at Slocum. "I'm sure he thought it would have."

John started to get to his feet. "You don't think I had anything to do with Jonas's death, do you?"

"Just sit down, Slocum," Will said. "We'll get to you." He reached over and took the paper, then slid it in front of Christine. "Do you think those letters could be the word *us*, Mrs. Wolff? Perhaps your husband was implying that you and he were over with?" He looked at Christine. "Your husband might have left the X mark under the word *us* to show that you and he were finished."

Christine shook her head. "You're mad." She reached down to the cradle by her feet and picked up the baby, holding him in her arms. Looking back at Will, she let out a soft, "Surely you can't be serious."

"I could be very serious, Mrs. Wolff." He reached over and slid the book of Psalms in front of him. "But it wasn't all he left." He reached into the book and took out the note from Jenkins. He held it up. "This is what you must have been looking for that night you came into the barn, a note from your former fiancé, a note suggesting a meeting."

Christine continued to rock the baby, shaking her head.

"You left it out for him to find, knowing it would make him jealous. You wanted him to sell his farm and take you someplace, someplace with no war and no slavery. Some women will use a man's feelings to get him to do what she wants him to do. I suspect you're a woman like that."

"Is that all you have, Major?" Slocum asked.

"No, it isn't," Perlman said. He stepped forward and dropped the wrapped pitchfork on the table. "I found the murder weapon in the stove."

As Perlman unwrapped the tongs on the pitchfork, all eyes went to Christine. She continued to rock the baby, then began to cry. "I didn't kill him. I didn't."

"Then who did?" Will asked.

"I left the note for him to see and, yes, I did meet with Alfred. I thought that when Jonas found the two of us together he would want to take me away. But when he came out and saw us, he flew into a rage. I couldn't talk to him." She began to cry. "Alfred rode off and left me there, and I went up to my room to cry."

Perlman picked up the burned pitchfork. "Then what about this?"

Christine nodded and began to dab her eyes with her napkin. "Yes, I found it when I came back to the barn." She blurted out the words. "I was going to try to say I was sorry. But I just found him there. I took the pitchfork and chopped it up and burned it." The tears began to fall. She buried her face in her napkin. "I thought . . ."

"That Jenkins had come back to finish the job?" Will asked.

She said nothing, just nodded her head in her napkin.

Suddenly, they heard the sound of horses in the front of the house. April jumped up from her seat and went to the front window. She could see men and horses and heard the sound of metal—

swords, spurs, and rifles. She moved to the front door and opened it. There was a large group of Union cavalry. A tall officer got down from his horse. He took off his hat, showing a flowing mane of brown hair. The smile on his face brought instant recognition. It was her brother, Gerald. He had come home.

CHAPTER 44

erald and several officers walked up to the steps. Gerald had filled out some in the last two years. All that April had to remember him by were old photographs, some of him as a little boy standing with the family, looking somber, serious, and so young. Now he stood before her in person, tall and handsome, with a brown mustache. She knew at once that in spite of her father's opposition to the war, he would have been proud just to look at Gerald now. He threw his arms open and lifted April off the steps. "There she is, the most beautiful woman in Pennsylvania, and my sister." He kissed her cheek. "It's so good to see you, Sis. You have no idea of how much I've waited for this day." He smiled. "Of course, I thought it would be after we had won this war."

April swallowed hard. Ordinarily, nothing could have pleased her more than the sight of Gerald, but not tonight, not just now. It was the worst of all possible times, but how could she tell him?

Gerald put her down. He beamed a bright smile at her. "You don't know how much I've wanted to see this place too." He looked up at the house. "It's just the same as I remember it. Nothing has changed. Of course, I have."

"Yes, you have," April agreed.

"And, Sis, you have no idea what we've been through. We've just come from a terrible battle in Gettysburg." He shook his head. "Just terrible."

April knew that the general she had rescued evidently had not gotten any word to him about her being at Gettysburg. She had seen enough of the battle to describe it better to him than he ever could to her. She'd even met with General Lee. She knew the South's courage and what they were fighting for. But it was something she couldn't tell him, not yet.

He went on. "But all I've been able to think about was getting home. I was planning to have my men camp here for the night and thought maybe I could get my bed back." He smiled. "And maybe some of your good food."

April gulped and took Gerald's hand. "I'm afraid that won't be possible."

He looked surprised, as if someone had just told a small child that Christmas had been canceled. "Why not?" He glanced back at the more than forty men who had ridden in with him. Many were just getting out of their saddles. "My men have been looking forward to it. I've been telling them so much about the place."

He looked up at the open door. "Where's Pa?"

"That's part of what I need to talk to you about." She scanned the formidable group of men over Gerald's shoulder. They looked battle hardened and weary. Some were unshaven, but most looked robust and burly. Their uniforms were in good shape, with the brass shined, and they all had good boots, something she had seen so seldom on the men her brother was fighting. She was sure they would like nothing better than a good night's rest and two rebel prisoners, one an officer. "But I need to talk to you inside," she said, "and alone."

"Okay, little sister. Anything you say."

He looked back at the men. "You boys stay here for a bit. I'll just go in with my sister. I won't be more than a few minutes, and then I'll find us a place to make camp." He grinned. "I might even see what's keeping our pie and coffee."

She led him up the steps and into the hallway. He could see the lights on in the dining room and could hear the sound of talking. He craned his neck to catch a glimpse of what was happening there, but April led him to the living room.

The living room was away from where the people were gathered in the dining room. April's mind raced. She had to find a way to get rid of her own brother. But after he had come so far and had been gone so long, it wasn't going to be easy.

"What's going on here, Sis? Sounds like you've got a party or something." He looked back toward the hall and the dining room beyond it. "Is Dad in there?"

"No, that's one of the things I wanted to talk to you about." Her eyes went to the floor. In the past few years she knew that Gerald had been a disappointment to his father. Their last conversation had been an argument about Gerald leaving home and joining the army. She looked up at him. "Our father has been killed."

The words took Gerald hard. He almost rocked back on his heels. His eyes grew larger and his mouth dropped open. "Killed? I can't believe it. What happened?"

April took his hand. "I'm still not certain. You can come back to see me tomorrow, or I can write you and tell you more."

"I can't do that. What are you trying to do, get rid of me?"

She looked out the living room door, toward the kitchen. She was trying to see if anyone had ventured into it. The last thing she wanted was to mix Gerald up with what was going on. "He's buried out back, next to Mother."

"When did it happen?"

"A week ago."

"Are Tillie and Christine all right?"

"Christine is fine, and so is the baby. Tillie's dead. We buried her in Cashtown."

"Cashtown? Why Cashtown?"

April patted his hand. "It's a very long story, and I'm not even sure of the ending. I'll have to write you and tell you what happened."

Gerald was shaking his head. "I can't believe this, Pa and Tillie."

"I know. It's been awful. I just have to ask you to trust me tonight. It would be better if you and your men rode on. Don't ask me why. I can't tell you right now. Just trust me, please."

He grabbed her arm. "April, are you in some sort of trouble?" He then sighed. "I've been gone such a long time, and it's unfair that all this has fallen on you."

"No." She shook her head. "You don't understand."

It was then that the worst thing she could imagine occurred. Will walked through the hall and up behind her. "Is anything wrong, April?" The sight of Gerald stopped him in his tracks.

Gerald's face grew pale. He dropped April's arm, reached for his holster, and pulled out his revolver.

Just then Slocum came into the room, followed by Perlman.

Gerald seemed surprised, especially by the sight of another man in a Confederate uniform. He blinked his eyes, then shook his revolver in Perlman's direction. "Come closer. I'm taking you two men prisoner."

"Good, boy," Slocum shouted. "You do that." The big man forced his way past April. She could almost see his chest swell as if he were gloating.

April put her hand on Gerald's arm. "Please stop! You don't understand."

"I understand all right. These men are holding you prisoner, hiding out. Well, we'll put a stop to that. How many of them are here, and where are they?"

April looked back at where Perlman was standing. She knew he was armed, but Will had placed his sidearm on the kitchen table earlier that night. He almost seemed undressed without it. "There are only these two men, but you don't understand."

"I understand all right. Mr. Slocum, open that door and call my men."

April grabbed Slocum's arm. "Don't take another step." She turned back to Gerald. "Please, you've got to let me explain. I don't want your men in here, and I don't want these men taken prisoner. You've got to ride away and forget that you've ever seen this."

In the confusion, Perlman drew his revolver. The sound of the gun as he cocked it, brought every head around. "We seem to have a standoff here." He held the pistol out, pointing it directly at the young captain. "Now perhaps you can take the time to listen to this sister of yours. She's got good sense and deserves to be heard."

Gerald looked at April. She could see the confusion in his eyes. She had been the only one in the family who had supported his decision to join the army. She had given him her blessing when their father wouldn't. "I can explain," she said, "if you'll only give me time."

"What am I to think when one of your guests has a gun on me?" He looked at Perlman. "And you must know, if you were to pull that trigger, my men out there would be in here quick as a cat."

"But then you'd be dead, Captain Wolff, and your sister would have more grief, all because you wouldn't give her your attention."

Gerald stared April in the eye. She could see his mind turning over the situation, and she knew the next word spoken by her would seem more of a plea that an appeal to his wisdom. She prayed silently.

"All right," Gerald said, "I'll give you five minutes." He motioned with his pistol in the direction of the door. "But those men of mine have had a hard ride. They're already edgy. I can't promise that I can hold them any longer than that." He looked at April. "I just can't believe you'd be involved in anything like this. I know you. You hate the rebs, and here you are hiding them."

Will edged his way forward. He held his coat open with his good arm to show that he was unarmed. "Captain, if you'll give your sister and me that much time, I'm certain we can explain this. As you can see, I am unarmed. You have my word as an officer and a gentleman that our presence here is all for you and your sister's good. If we can't explain it to your satisfaction, then you can take me and the sergeant here as your prisoners."

April was shocked at his statement. She knew that the last thing Will wanted was to be put up in a Union prisoner-of-war camp for the duration of the war. She swallowed hard. "Please Gerald," she said, "trust me."

"All right," he said, "You have five minutes."

Perlman stepped forward, his gun still drawn. He took Slocum by the arm. "You folks talk. I'll take your neighbor here into the dining room for more coffee."

April motioned toward the sofa. "Please have a seat and put your gun away. I know he means what he says."

The captain stuck his revolver back in his holster and took his seat. April and Will followed and took chairs beside him.

Will looked at the man. "I'm Major Will Chevalier of the provost marshal's office of the Army of Northern Virginia. I volunteered to help your sister solve your father's murder." He glanced at her. "Initially we thought our prime suspect was a member of our own general staff, but now our investigation has led us back here. That is not to say that we don't share some responsibility for what happened. We do. But it will be left up to me to bring any charges involved."

"I don't understand," Gerald said. "You're here conducting an investigation against your own army?"

"Yes," April said. "But there's more." She looked at Will. "Much more."

"How much more could there be?" he asked.

April scooted close to Will and laid her hand on his. "This is the man I love, Gerald."

Gerald's face turned pale.

It was then that Perlman stepped back into the room. "Scuse me for interrupting. I just thought you should know. Christine's gone, and she took the baby."

CHAPTER 45

A fter Will and Perlman discussed what they had found out about the murder, Gerald left the house. It was a short time later when Will and April joined him beside their father's grave. The moon, which looked like a large cantaloupe cut in half, had risen and was riding low over the hills.

"I thought I would find you here," April said. He looked so handsome in his blue uniform, she was certain her mother would have beamed with pride. Even their father would have had a secret admiration for him. Her father had never made it a point to say when he'd been wrong, but she was sure he would have come close now.

Gerald had his hands folded. He was staring at the mound. "Do you think he could have ever forgiven me?"

"Father?"

Gerald nodded his head.

She slipped her arm around him. The army hadn't changed his soft heart, and she was glad about that. From what she had seen of the horrors of war, there wasn't much about a man that it couldn't change. "There's nothing to forgive. You did what you believed in, no matter what the cost." She looked down at her father's grave. "He did the same thing when we were children. Don't you remember? You were small and didn't want to leave your friends in Virginia. Mother told me you cried. That must have been hard on him, but he came here anyway, for what he believed."

"Yes, I remember."

"People can only follow their conscience. He followed his, and you're following yours. The Lord would be pleased with both of you."

Gerald looked at her, then glanced at Will. "What about you? Are you following your conscience?"

April reached out and took Will's hand. Gerald was still her older brother. He'd always protected her, and it didn't look like he had any plans to change that. "If you mean Will, it's something I never planned on."

"What did he say to you?" Gerald cocked his head, studying Will. April could see that her brother recognized that Will was a handsome man. He'd already seen how well spoken he was. It would have been natural to assume that such a man could have and probably had swept many women off their feet.

April smiled, then chuckled. "He hasn't said anything." She glanced at Will. "I even feel like a fool. He hasn't even told me how he feels about me. For all I know, I'll never see him again."

She leaned toward Gerald. "My feelings are almost preposterous for me. I've never given any man a second look in my whole life, and Will's a man I started out never wanting to look at the first time."

She glanced at Will. "But that changed, and it changed because of his character. He's honest and kind and given to duty. I know very little about his background and understand even less. I just know how I feel. I love the man." She squeezed Will's hand. "Nothing can ever change that, especially not politics."

"You didn't used to call it politics," Gerald said.

April nodded. "I know. But I've learned so much; I've learned about people. It's not as simple as we thought it was. These people you're fighting aren't devils, no matter what you think about them. There's so much hatred in this war. It's got to end, and for me, it's ended right here."

Gerald stepped around April and faced Will. "Look, Major, I don't know anything about you, just that you wear that uniform. But my sister's always been a good judge of character. If she says she loves you, that's good enough for me."

He shot April a look. "Although I can't for the life of me figure it out."

"Nor can I," Will agreed.

"Well, no matter. I just want you to promise me that you won't break her heart."

Will studied the tops of his boot for a moment. "I don't know what I can promise you. To be honest with you, I've never had much of a teacher when it came to love. Frankly, I've never believed in it, beyond poetry and empty platitudes." He looked April in the eye. "I will say this: What little I know about love, I've learned from your sister."

Gerald stuck his finger in the air and shook it. "Good. Then don't you miss one day of school, 'cause she's a good teacher."

They began to walk back toward the house. There was a slight breeze from the south. It carried a faint odor of acrid gunpowder. There seemed to be nowhere that one could escape the war. "Did you find Christine?" Gerald asked.

"No," Will said. "Either she's hiding or she ran."

Gerald shook his head. "This is just so hard for me to believe. Do you think she did it?"

"It doesn't look good for her," Will said. "For some people, even thinking about a deed like that makes them feel guilty. Just the burden and the sense of responsibility for the thing might have caused her to burn that pitchfork. It might have made her run too. She just didn't want to look either of you in the eye."

"What about Tillie's death? Was that ever solved?"

"Yes," Will said. "It was an overzealous lieutenant who thought he was protecting his general." Will looked off at the moon. "I found out he was killed at Culp's Hill in Gettysburg. It solves part of my problem to have God give out justice."

"I sent my men down the road to find a camp, but if I were you and your sergeant, I wouldn't spend the night here. My whole army's coming down the road, and they don't have sisters that love you."

April took Will's hand and chuckled. "We can't be so sure about that." April was actually enjoying the idea of being in love with someone so far from what others would have chosen for her. There was a freedom to it, a semirebellion, an expression that seemed to shout, *This is my choice, not yours.* The feeling was liberating, and she didn't want to lose it.

"What happened to Slocum and his son?" Gerald asked.

"The sergeant was supposed to send him home, after your troops left." Will smiled. "He seemed anxious to play the part of the good citizen."

"I'll just bet he was," April shot back.

They watched Gerald mount his horse. He turned and leaned down to give April a kiss. "If I can, I'll be back. We're chasing the rebel army now, so I don't know when that will be." He looked up at Will. "If we can catch them this side of the Potomac, maybe we can bring this war to a close."

As they watched him ride away, Will turned to April. "We'd better join Perlman in his search. The quicker we can find Christine, the quicker we can leave."

They walked up the steps to the hall. The trap doors that had hidden the escaped slaves were on the floor, with nothing but the empty hole in the staircase wall to show for it. Will picked up a lamp and shoved it into the opening. He then called out. "Sergeant, are you in here?"

A voice came out of the darkness, followed by a flickering lamp. "You durn tootin' I am."

Will watched as Perlman, squatting, walked his way under the sloping ceiling. He held up his lamp to make sure he'd seen all of the ceiling beams. Hobbling his way toward where Will was holding out the lamp, he seemed out of breath. "This stooping is too hard on an old man's back, but there's nobody here."

He handed his lamp to April and climbed out of the hole and into the hallway. "I've checked the entire cellar, and there's no sign of the woman down here. I spect we'd better go to looking upstairs in the bedroom area. Likely as not, she's hunkered down up there crying."

The three of them made their way upstairs. The long hallway had been hung with a lavender-flower-print wallpaper. There were several sideboards designed to hold sheets and towels, and one of them had a mirror. Two of them held vases of dried flowers. Brass lamps hanging on the walls gave off a soft glow over the wheat-colored carpet. The mirror caught the light from one of the lamps, brightly illuminating the very middle of the hall. "I'll start down at that end," Perlman said, pointing in the direction of the bright light, "and we'll work our way toward the middle."

Will and April walked away from the lighted middle of the hallway and toward the bedroom that was in the front of the house, Christine and her father's room. They opened the door, and April reached for a match in her apron pocket. She struck it on the top of the bureau and lifted the globe on the lamp that was sitting on the bureau. She touched the flame to the wick, and it sent out a soft glow over the room.

The large, four-poster bed was mahogany with a lace canopy. Her father had never liked it. It always made him feel trapped. He had said it made him feel like he was waking up in his coffin. But he had bought it for Christine anyway, at a shop in Chambersburg. The one thing he had to brag about where the bed was concerned was the fifty dollars he had haggled the shopkeeper out of. Of course he was the first to admit that it was no doubt due to the fact that no self-respecting farmer in the region would dare sleep in a thing like that. It had given him small comfort, but he never liked the bed.

The quilt over the bed was an orchid-patterned lavender and white one that her mother had made. Her mother had gotten the idea from a book on the South Seas, another place that she would never visit but wanted to be reminded of it. Now it was on the bed that her father had shared with Christine.

Will gave the place a swift examination and stepped out into the hall. April stayed behind. She opened one of her father's drawers and began to take out some of his clothes. Will and Perlman would need something to replace their uniforms. With Union troops all over the roads, she had no intention of them being caught.

A few moments later, she caught up with them in the hall.

Perlman shook his head. "I don't think she's up here. She must have lit out."

She held out the clothes. "Here, take these and change. I don't want you caught out on the road with those uniforms of yours."

Perlman held up the lapels of his Confederate tunic. "I'm getting sort of used to these things. They've been with me for quite a spell now. They catch me in that thing and they'll hang me for a spy."

"Here, take this, silly." She handed him a set of dungarees along with a red-and-black patched shirt. "Just tell them you're a farmer, and look surly. You're good at that."

She then handed Will a black suit and white shirt.

"What am I supposed to be?"

"A preacher, of course." She patted his cheek. "You would make quite a handsome preacher too."

Perlman laughed. "Well, with that bath you took today, you'll smell like a preacher." He looked at April, grinning. "At least you could have given that preacher outfit to someone who knows the Bible."

Will took the suit. "I know the Bible." He threw his shoulders back. "I wouldn't let all that education of mine from Saint Mary's Academy go to waste. And I'll have you know that my mother in Charleston has a Sunday school perfect attendance pin with my name on it in her parlor."

"Well, pardon me." Perlman grinned and bowed. "I had no idea I was in the presence of a Bible scholar. Perfect attendance? Must have been fear of the strap."

"All right you two, get dressed and I'll meet you in the barn with your horses. I want you gone before more troops get here. Just leave your uniforms in the room, and I'll hide them."

A few minutes later Perlman and Will joined her in the barn. She handed them a gunnysack. "I packed some food for you two. I hope you don't mind." She looked over at one of her bay horses. "You can have that one, Will. He's a four-year-old gelding, and he rides like the wind."

"Thank you. I was afraid I'd have to double up on the sergeant's donkey."

"You watch what you say about my animal," Perlman shot back. "He's been with me since this war started."

Perlman then started roaming the barn, looking for his cat. He found the orange tabby, picked him up, and stroked his head. "It wouldn't do to leave this old thing to the Yankees. They just might skin him for his fur."

"That old thing will survive this war, sure enough," Will said.

Perlman set the cat on the ground. "Why not? They have nine lives don't they? With what we've got to go through, he just might need all of them."

Quickly, Will saddled his horse and Perlman his mule. Perlman once again picked up the cat and swung himself into his saddle. He walked the mule around the barn and looked down at Will. "Well, I'll let you two say your good-byes. I'm looking forward to Virginia." He touched the brim of the brown hat April had given him. "Ma'am, I can't say it's been a pleasure, but it's sure 'nuff been an adventure."

April reached up to him and took his hand. "It has been a pleasure for me, Sergeant. My only disappointment is that I couldn't make you a Christian."

"Many have tried, little lady. I'll probably get into camp just in time for their next revival. I think after this, they'll be ready for it." With that, he rode out of the barn.

Will held out the book of Psalms he was still carrying and placed it in her hands. "I would have liked to have kept this. Might make good reading."

She pressed it back into his hands. "Then by all means keep it. I can't think of anyone my father would have preferred to have it more than you."

"Thank you." Will turned around and unbuckled his saddlebag. He put April's sack and the book into it. Turning back around, he began to speak. "You know—"

April stopped him and put her hand on his. "Don't say anything. It would just ruin it for me." She smiled at him. "I'd just like to use my imagination when it comes to your words right now. It's better that way. I like what's in my head."

Will smiled. "How do you know? You just might like what's in my mind."

"You know I said those things about the way I felt about you for Gerald's benefit. I thought it would keep you from a fight."

"Are you telling me you didn't mean them?"

"Of course I meant them." She rubbed his hand with her thumb. "I meant every word. I just would have rather said them to you alone, without anyone else listening."

Will looked around the barn, then back at April. "Well, we're alone now. May I tell you what I have on my mind?"

She nodded. "Yes." Then she bit her lip.

Will held her hand. "I don't really know what the words mean, April, but I do know what's in my heart. I love you."

She put her hand up to his lips. "Don't say that unless you mean it."

"I do mean it. I've never meant anything more sincerely in my life. I don't know how this war will turn out, but I can guess. When it is over and if you're still of the same mind, I will come back. I will come back and ask you if you'd do me the high honor of becoming Mrs. Will Chevalier. I want to take you to Charleston, or what's left of it."

April nodded. Her eyes were tearing. "I'll be waiting then, and my answer will be yes."

Will bent down and almost kissed her. Then he stopped himself and turned away. He gently pushed her back and got on his horse. He rode out of the barn, not looking back.

CHAPTER 46

A pril sat down at the piano in the living room and ran her fingers lightly over the keys, not actually playing it. The silence of the house was almost too sweet to part with. It was the first time she could remember being alone there since she had been sick at age fourteen and had to stay home from church. There simply had never been another opportunity to be away from the sound of voices.

She looked down at the keys and remembered her mother teaching her to play. Her mother would put her hands over April's and whisper in her ear, "Just hold your fingers lightly, darling, and let mother play through you." In a way she hoped her mother was still playing through her. She wanted to do the things her mother would have done if she'd been here, feel the same feelings, think the same thoughts. Her mother was who she thought of when she heard the word *Christian*. All that was contained in the word was found in her mother. It caused April to wonder if her mother would approve of her loving Will Chevalier.

She put her hands on the piano bench and leaned back. She then looked at the hall and the stairs. *What if Christine is still here?* she wondered. She thought that if Christine were still in the house, the sound of silence might just bring her out into the open. They had looked for her, but there were other places to hide, places that perhaps her father had built for the underground slaves in the past few years that she didn't know about.

It suddenly gave her an ominous feeling. If the woman had murdered her father, then what was to stop her from trying to kill again? With her out of the way, Christine would be free to sell the farm, and no one would have to know. April suddenly felt very alone without Will. She almost wished she had thought to hide the both of them under the stairs and have them stay. But she knew they wouldn't have done that. They were both too intent on rejoining their own army. Their army needed them now more than ever.

S he slid off the piano bench and went to the kitchen. Taking a large pot from the counter, she filled it with water and set it on the stove. She would do the dishes. The work would be good for her. It would take her mind off what had happened and perhaps enable her to do something she was growing ever more fearful of, spending the night alone in the house.

She pulled some kindling out of the pail next to the stove and opened the grate to stir the coals that Perlman had created when he made the fire for the coffee. She would need more wood. She looked at the back door and the axe that was leaning next to it. She would have to go outside and cut more.

She walked across the kitchen and picked up the axe, then opened the door and stepped out onto the back porch. The back porch was more of a small platform with a set of stairs and a railing. It led down to where a stack of wood had been placed along the side of the house. She walked down and picked up several likely pieces of wood. Placing them lengthwise up on a stump, she began to split them. It wouldn't take more than five or six pieces to have enough for the dishwater and then have some left over for breakfast.

When she started to chop the fourth piece of firewood, she heard the sound of galloping horses. A large group of Union cavalry were riding down the road toward their house. She dropped the axe and stepped out from the shadows of the house. She wondered if perhaps it was Gerald who had come back, but this looked like a larger group of men, heavily armed. Behind them, two teams of horses pulled two cannons.

Picking up the axe, she walked toward the front of the house. If they were hungry, she would try to feed as many of them as she could. If they needed water, she could supply enough of that.

She stood in front of the house as a number of the soldiers surrounded her. "I don't have much to feed you if you're hungry," she said. "But you're welcome to water your horses."

It was then that an officer appeared, brushing his horse past the rest. The men separated for him. April recognized him right away. "General Schimmelfennig! I didn't expect to see you here."

He brought his horse to a stop and leaned forward, his hand on his sword. As he looked at her, a look of astonishment came over his face. "You!"

April knew there was no way she could erase the look of indignation on her face, no matter how hard she tried. This was a man she had gone to a great deal of trouble to rescue, a man who had betrayed her confidence and killed a friend. She felt slightly sickened at the sight of him. She took a deep swallow. It had always been hard for her to hide her feelings. Turning, she motioned with her hand to the house. "This is my house. You are most welcome to whatever hospitality I can give you."

He moved his horse closer to her. "Is this the Wolff farm?"

April nodded. "Yes, how did you know that?"

"We have it on very good authority that this home is a nest of Southern sympathizers, that you are Copperheads. Now that I see it's you, I can believe it. You were helping to nurse the rebels at Gettysburg." He motioned to several of his men. "Search the house," he shouted.

April shook her head. "No, that's not true. Who told you such a thing?"

"We have our sources, very reliable sources."

April could only imagine how they must have met up with Slocum on the road. The man couldn't have the farm, so now he was doing whatever possible to make it not worth having. "General, jealous neighbors are hardly a good source. We have done nothing but support the Union cause here. My family was involved with smuggling slaves north. Surely you can't believe such a thing."

"Why should I believe that?"

"I sent one of our runaways with you. Ulysses must have said something?"

Schimmelfennig shook his head. "The man said nothing to me. He just rode on once we found our way safely to our lines. I have no way of knowing if what you said is true or false. I just heard that you were Southern sympathizers and that you had been consorting with Confederate officers."

Schimmelfennig got down from his horse. Turning back to April, he dropped his reins. "Normally I might just take your word for such a thing, but you were in Gettysburg and you were nursing the rebel wounded."

"I did more than that. I got you away to safety, didn't I?"

He nodded. "All while trying to give comfort to and heal the rebels, making quite an effort to protect the rebels, if you ask me. One would think you had a personal interest in them. What am I to think? Perhaps you do favors for any and all officers with money, no matter what uniform they're wearing."

April stepped up to him. She wanted to slap him, but she stopped herself. She still had the axe in her hand. She gripped it tightly. "That is an awful thing to say to a lady."

"Madame, you haven't demonstrated to me that you are a lady. I know what I saw and what others tell me about you."

Two of the men who had been sent to search the house came running back down the steps. "General, we found a hiding place under the stairs. The door's off the thing, and it looks like people have been there."

Schimmelfennig glared at her. "You have a hiding place for rebel spies?"

"No." April shook her head. "It's as I told you. We've been involved in smuggling slaves out of the South. We used to hide them there in case people came." She pointed to the iron lawn jockey close to where he was standing. "My father would tie a red ribbon there if it wasn't safe."

"Signals?"

"Yes, signals in case he had runaways and didn't want one of us to give them away."

Just then, two more of the men came running down the steps. "Look what we found, General." They were holding Perlman and Will's uniforms. They handed them to the man. He held them up for her. "And how do you explain these?"

April shook her head. "I can't, General. It's too long and complicated, and you probably wouldn't believe me anyway. But it's perfectly innocent. Please believe me." She grabbed hold of his arm. "I even have a brother who's a captain with the Second Pennsylvania Cavalry. He was here not more than an hour ago."

"So you say. It's been my experience that traitors are bound to make up any story when they've been caught in their lies and deception." He turned to his men and shouted. "Burn the house and barn. Burn them down at once."

April jumped in front of him, waving her hands. "Don't do this. My father built this house. He came here from Virginia to escape a slave state and work to free them. You can't do this!"

"You are from Virginia?"

"Yes, I was born there, but—"

He waved his hands at her. "That's enough. I don't need to hear any more of your lies. You even come from a rebel state." He turned to the men who were lighting the torches. "Put that place to the torch and all the buildings. I don't want to see one of them left standing."

April watched as the men ran around the house, setting fire to the buildings. She saw several men run to the barn and to the smokehouse. Streams of men soon followed them and began bringing back whatever it was they could find. Some had hams and other meats, others led out the mules and what remained of her father's horses. She watched as the flames began to climb the sides of the house.

Schimmelfennig got back on his horse. He looked down at her. "This will serve as a lesson for all those who share your sympathies, madame. I trust you will learn your lesson and they will learn theirs."

He circled his hand and waved at the troops. "Let's go men, at a gallop."

April watched the soldiers turn their horses around and begin to ride off. She made her way to the steps, watching helplessly as her childhood and family memories crackled in the flames. Slowly she began to climb the steps, walking into the entryway. Then her slow walk broke into a run. *What if Christine is still in the house?* She raced upstairs to the hall. "Christine! Christine! The house is burning. You've got to get out with the baby."

She began to run from room to room shouting, "Christine! The house is burning. Please come out now. I don't care what you've done. You've got to get out."

She watched the fire lick its way up the back of the house. She could see it through the window at the rear of the hall. The flames were rising, and the smoke began to roll up the stairs, sailing on the breeze, clouding the ceiling, and lapping around her dress.

She held her hand to her face and stumbled toward the stairs. The stairway had become a smoking funnel, with the black fumes rolling up them toward the top stories of the house. She made her way down the stairs, choking and gagging. Then her feet slipped and she tumbled down, rolling over and over through the black smoke.

When she finally hit the downstairs hallway, she was sent sprawling on the floor. Everything went black.

The next thing April knew, she was being carried down the steps of the porch. She coughed at the smoke and gulped the fresh air. She could see two figures, men who had carried her from the house, but she couldn't make them out. The tears in her eyes and the smoke refused to allow her to focus. It was the voice she recognized first. A hand was on her face. "April, April, are you all right?"

She forced her eyes open and wiped them with the back of her hand. She threw her arms around the man. "Will, oh Will," she sputtered, "you did come back."

"Of course we came back." He looked up at Perlman. "You can thank the sergeant, though. He carried you out. I can't lift anything with my arm."

April reached up and took Perlman's hand as he bent lower. "Thank you, Sergeant."

"Why'd you want to go into that burning house?" Perlman asked.

She gulped, trying to force some moisture down her throat, then coughed. "I thought maybe Christine was still in there with the baby. I had to go."

Will was on the ground next to her. He looked up at Perlman. "Go get her some water."

"I thought you were gone," she gagged.

"We were up on the ridge when we saw those soldiers riding in. We thought we should wait and see if everything was all right here."

"I'm glad you did. They thought I was a Copperhead. Someone told them that."

Will looked up. "They probably met up with Slocum."

She began to cry. "I find that so hard to believe. I've known that man all my life. He and my father were best friends."

"Yes, and Cain and Abel were brothers."

CHAPTER 47

April sat up while Perlman held the cup to her lips to drink. He had a bucket of water from the well. Will wiped her face with a cloth that he dipped in the bucket. It felt cool to the touch.

"I see they at least left you something to ride," Perlman said.

She looked up and saw one of the mules grazing on the grass in front of the house. The mule lifted its head occasionally to see the sight of the burning house, and then it once again turned its attention to feeding. The mule was a picture of contentment in the midst of chaos.

"That's better than they do down where we come from," Perlman went on. "Usually they take it all."

Cupping her hands around Will's, April took another drink. She could see the look of compassion in his eyes. He hadn't said a thing about the irony of having her own house burned down by the

Union army. She had been so sure of who she was and what she believed before she met him. She had been full of self-righteousness. She knew she couldn't fault the cause that she believed in just because of the actions of a few, but neither could she condemn those who stood on the other side. They were not devils. They were human beings with compassion and values, the same as the rest. It had been much too easy to paint them as monsters.

The house was fully in flame now, spirals of fire and sparks rising into the black sky. The sparks and cinders rose and fanned out with the wind, and the heat from the house was now scorching her face.

"We'd better move," Will said.

Perlman reached down and picked April up. He bounced her in his arms. "You are light, little missy." He began to walk into the grass. "It's been such a long time since I held me a pretty woman in my arms. Feels kinda nice."

"You find your own pretty woman, Sergeant. That one's taken." Will looked at her. "Quite taken."

Perlman looked down at her. "I suppose she is at that." He put her down when they had cleared the worst of the heat, and April took a seat on the grass. Her legs were still a bit wobbly. Will turned to Perlman. "Is everything gone?"

The sergeant nodded. "Everything." He picked up the cat that had followed them and held it in his arms. He was petting it, running his hand over the cat's fur from head to tail. "The barn went right off, and then the smokehouse. They didn't leave enough to give shelter to old Elmer here."

"My father built that house, stone by stone, board by board. He put all that he had into that place. It was his life. I just never thought I'd live to see it destroyed by people who are fighting for the cause he held so dear." Her voice seemed to trail off with emotion as she watched the fire. "Everything he had is gone, everything he built."

"Not everything." Once again Will wrung out the cloth. He stooped down and wiped April's face. "What is most important is still here—you."

She put her hand on his. "You always seem to know the right thing to say."

A smile crossed his lips. April thought that Will Chevalier's smile communicated understanding and love. "I just tell the truth," he said.

She watched the fire as it continued to burn. "Now I have no place, no home."

"April, you can come with us. I'll send you to Charleston with a letter to my mother. We have a wonderful home there, and you'll be very comfortable until the war is over. Then I'll come to you."

She patted his hand. "Thank you. I'll have to think about that. I have my teaching job and a cottage by the school. I should go back there this fall."

"Well, think about it. You have a home no matter what."

"Should we tell her about the other matter?" Perlman asked.

"What other matter?"

Will looked down at her. "I think the sergeant has solved your father's murder." He looked off at the burning house. "This only confirms it."

"Confirms what?"

Will got to his feet and walked over to the mule. "See if you can make a halter for this thing, Sergeant."

April got to her feet. "Confirms what?"

"It confirms that we have to make a ride over to the Slocum farm tonight. If what we figured out is right, he's your father's murderer. Your father left us a message."

"Two messages," Perlman added.

"Yes, that's right." Will nodded. "One of them written with his own blood."

They began their ride, Will followed by April and Perlman on their two mules. The smell of smoke was everywhere in the valley. For a while, ashes rained down on them, and then only smoke and the glow of the farm in the distance filled the air. They stamped their mounts through the cool creek, pausing to let them take a long drink.

They soon came to the small section of the valley that held the Slocum farm. John Slocum's farm had been smaller than her father's, but it had greener pasture for grazing, better water, and more trees. Her father had allowed him to have first pick between the two properties when they had come up from Virginia, and he had lived to be thankful for that decision. Where they had settled turned out to have better ground for farming and wheat. It was something her father had been proud of. He had told her, "If you let God do the choosing, He'll always choose the best for you." She had come to believe that, especially since falling in love with Will Chevalier.

Riding into the trees, they could see the Slocum farm. The lights were on, glaring out over the grass and shining on the creek. "That's it," she said.

"Yes," Perlman agreed. "I can smell the hogs. Smells like bacon."

Will pulled up on his reins. "Smells like bacon? Not by a long shot."

Perlman smiled and slid off his mule. "That's the difference between some folks, Major." He chuckled. "Some folks see things that is. Other folks see things for what they ought to be. I just smell those hogs for what they're becoming, the main course of a gentile breakfast table. While I can't eat it as a Jew, I can appreciate the aroma." He leaned back and took a deep breath, then let it out and grinned a toothy grin at Will. He pointed his finger at Will as if to drive home the point. "That's the difference that makes a leader. If you're ever going to be a general, you had ought to learn that, Major. See and smell things for what they ought to be."

Will grinned. "Sergeant, you're not only a policeman, you're a theologian and a philosopher. Some college would be mighty proud to have you teaching there once you finish your education."

Perlman hitched up his belt. The dungarees she had given him were slightly large for him. They had been passed down to her father by the widow of another man, a very large man. Her father had never worn them, so they were almost new, and looked like a tent on Perlman.

"We should go on by foot from here," Will said.

"Lead on, Major."

The three of them made their way through the trees, winding their way in and out of the sycamores. The smell of the hogs stifled whatever scent might have alerted the dogs to their presence. The wind was blowing from the east, over the ridge and past the hog pens toward the house.

They crept up to the house, and Will looked in the living room window. He looked back at them. "There's no one in there."

"They must be in the kitchen," April said. "It's around back. It has a large table they use for occasional eating when they're not having company."

"Is there a back door?" Will asked.

"Yes."

Will drew his revolver. "All right. Since you know the layout of the house, you and the sergeant go through the front door. I'll go around back."

April watched Will disappear around the corner of the house. Perlman pulled out one of his revolvers and smiled at her. "No time like the present, I'd say."

April nodded.

They walked up the steps, and April warily opened the door. The door had a slight squeak to it, and she gave it a quick push. Taking it slowly would only prolong the suspense and the noise.

She looked back at Perlman as he stepped through the door and whispered, "Leave it open."

He nodded and moved into the hall behind her.

April tiptoed down the long hall with Perlman behind her. The hall was lined with side tables, and pictures hung on the wall. The relatives in the photos were long since dead and gone, but April stopped in front of one of them. It was a photograph of the two families that had been taken when she was small. Both families seemed to be happy and content. Her father had his arm over John Slocum's shoulder. It made her shake inside.

She could hear the sound of voices from the kitchen. She turned back to Perlman and whispered. "That's Slocum and Christine. I don't hear Tommy."

"Maybe you should let me go first. I can take it from here."

April stepped aside as Perlman walked past her.

He marched into the kitchen. "Good evening, folks. Nice to see you." He looked at Christine. "Both of you."

April stepped into the kitchen behind him. She looked at Christine.

Christine's eyes studied her. April's dress was covered with ash, gritty in places and smeared with traces of smoke. "What happened to you?"

"Ask your benefactor there." April shot a glance at Slocum. "I take it you decided to talk to Union troops on your way home."

Christine looked at him, studying him. "Yes, he did."

April continued to have her eyes locked on John Slocum. "And you told them we were Southern sympathizers."

"I only told them the truth." He straightened himself in his chair and held his head up. "That you were harboring rebel spies."

"And you didn't tell them that we helped escaped slaves or that Gerald was serving as an officer in the army."

"I told them what I told them."

The back door opened, and Will walked in. His gun was drawn. He put his hand to his hat and nodded at Christine. "How are you, ma'am. We didn't have the chance to tell you good-bye." He then looked at Slocum. "And you were a bad boy. You were supposed to go right home and not stop to get social with Union troops. Did you tell Christine here what you did?"

"I don't think the man's armed," Perlman said. "I suppose we can put these away."

"Tell me what?" Christine asked.

Will lifted the flap on his leather holster and stuffed the pistol down into it. "Well, for starters he told the commander of those troops that your stepdaughter was a Copperhead and that your house was a nest of spies. Of course that's not the worst of the man's sins. There's more."

"They found the hiding places for the slaves," April said.

"I'm afraid the sale price on that farm of yours is going to go way down," Perlman said. "Those Yankees burned the house and all of the buildings." He shoved his revolver back into his holster. "Burned them down to the ground."

Christine's eyes moistened. Her voice cracked. She looked at Slocum. "Did you know they were going to do that?"

He shrugged his shoulders at her. "How could I have known that?"

It was then that he looked toward the dining room. It opened onto the kitchen from another direction. He smiled. "Come on in, boy. Show yourself."

Tommy Slocum walked into the room. He had his Sharps rifle leveled at Perlman, but then, catching sight of Will, he swung it around.

John got to his feet. "We seem to have caught us some rebel spies here, son. They have no uniforms on, and we are going to be heroes when we kill them and turn their bodies over to the army." He grinned through his black beard. "The government might even reward us. You never know."

Will looked at Christine. "Do you see who you've gotten involved with?"

April looked down at her dress, then back at Christine. "I went back into the house to find you. I couldn't let you and the baby burn. I ran all over looking for you."

"She almost died," Will added.

April looked over to where Tommy was standing. The boy was taking it all in. She knew that in spite of being a hothead and a simpleminded person, Tommy Slocum was walking the line between what it meant to be good and bad. She also knew that he loved her deeply. She had spent years avoiding that love of his, and now she was going to have to try to use it.

"Yes, I almost died Tommy," she said sweetly. "And because your father lied."

She caught Perlman's eye. She knew that he was almost reading her mind.

"Maybe we should tell Christine and Tommy here what else this man is responsible for," Perlman said.

"All right, that's enough," Slocum shouted, standing up and waving his arms. "I know what you're doing. If you think you can walk in here and accuse me of murdering Jonas Wolff, then you can go to blazes. That's a wild accusation, and you have no proof."

"We have proof," Will said, stepping forward. "We have proof that you use people to get your way. You wanted to use Christine to get her husband to sell that farm. You even gave the woman travel brochures, just to feed her thinking."

April could see the wheels turning in Christine's brain. She was piecing together all the friendly times with Slocum when she thought he was just being helpful.

"When that didn't work, you passed a note to her from her former fiancée. You thought that might make things move quicker."

"Oh no," Christine began to cry.

"You even led her to believe that it might have been Jenkins who came back and killed her husband. You thought if you could throw suspicion on her, on anyone but yourself, that you would be free and clear to take your lifelong friend's land."

Christine continued to cry, nodding her head. "He did. He did."

Slocum slammed his fist down on the table. "You have no proof."

"I think we have enough," Perlman said. "If you were in Atlanta, I think I could arrest you and get a conviction."

"You see, the sergeant and I pieced two final parts of the puzzle together after we left you tonight." Will motioned to Perlman. "Go ahead and tell them, Sergeant."

Perlman pulled out a piece of paper and a pencil. "It was that US thing and the X that were written on the barn floor. We thought it might have been the word *us*, referring to him and Christine here, but now we know better. He was trying to draw out initials. Only thing was, his finger slipped. You see JS can become US if your hand is shaky and you're bleeding."

"You probably came back and rubbed that writing out yourself," Will said.

Tommy looked at him. "Was that what you was raking in the barn, Daddy? That man's writing?"

Slocum growled. "That was of no consequence."

Perlman looked up at Slocum. "He was talking about you and him, Slocum—John Slocum. But there's more. The major can show you."

Will reached into his pocket and pulled out the book of Psalms. He opened the cover. "Jonas Wolff left us a message here." He looked over at Tommy. "He was trying to tell you, boy. He said, 'Gave it.' He didn't mean for you to give it. He was referring to who gave it to him."

He opened the page where the title of the book was printed. He held it up. "There's a spot here for the occasion of the gift of this book, and the giver is listed. You can see that it was given to Jonas on his birthday"—Will looked Slocum in the eye—"by you, Slocum. It's written right here. 'Given to Jonas Wolff on the occasion of his birthday by his best friend, John Slocum.'"

"There's a further indication of what Wolff had on his mind." He held the book closer for them to see. "He left a bloody fingerprint on your name Slocum, his own blood. He was trying to say 'gave it.' Which is why when Tommy asked him if he wanted to give it to Christine, he said no. He was trying to tell you, Tommy, who it was who killed him. The man who gave this book of Psalms to him was the man who killed him."

Slocum stepped closer to Tommy. "Don't believe him, boy."

Perlman moved closer. "Tommy, remember who it was who told you to kill us, who told you it would be better if we were dead. He didn't want you joining the army, but he did want you to kill us. And you almost shot April when you tried."

"Is that right, Tommy?" April asked. "Was it you who tried to shoot us on the road?"

"Yes." Tommy pointed the rifle in Slocum's direction. "He told me to, told me it would be better if they was dead."

"But, Tommy, you almost killed me."

April could see his lower lip quivering. He was trying hard not to break out into tears. She moved closer to him. "And tonight I almost burned to death because your father told the soldiers we were spies. I thought Christine and the baby were in danger and I tried to save them, even though I thought she might have killed my father. I still tried to save her. You can save us, Tommy."

She glanced at Slocum and then back to Tommy. "He lied to them, Tommy, and he lied to you. He wanted our farm because he wants your brothers and their wives back here to live close to him. He needs them to be close, Tommy, because he doesn't think you're good enough."

"All right," Slocum roared. "That's enough. Give me the gun, you idiot."

He reached for the rifle, grabbing the barrel. It exploded, filling the kitchen with a flash of light and flame and smoke.

Slocum was catapulted back into the table, knocking it over and spilling Christine to the floor. Perlman grabbed for the rifle, snatching it from Tommy's hands. Tommy followed Will to his father's side. He swung himself around and placed his father's head on his lap.

"Daddy, I'm sorry. I didn't mean to do it." He looked up at Will and Perlman. "I didn't mean to do it."

"We know that, son." Perlman put his hand on the boy's shoulder. "It was an accident."

EPILOGUE

I used to think I knew what heartache and despair felt like. Especially after my mother died. What a child I was, how arrogant. Only standing there beside my father's fresh grave, the ash and embers of my childhood home still crackling and snapping in the first light of dawn, I let the raw waves of sorrow flood my soul.

Worse yet, I kept waiting for Tillie to comfort me, just like she had when my mother died. I ached to hear her gentle wisdom and cackling laughter just one more time. I even missed her smelly old corncob pipe. Somehow, in spite of all the heartbreaks in her own life, she always had time for mine. Without her eyes, she saw far more of me than I ever admitted.

If it wasn't for Will by my side . . . I don't even want to think of how lonely and abandoned I'd feel. Only a short time ago, he had been a stranger—worse yet, an enemy. Now he was the only one who cared.

I looked up. The cloudless sky looked like a canvas someone had painted with an ocean spray. The only blemish was the plume of dirty brown smoke still rising from the ashes that had once been our farm.

Will slipped his arm around me. "I know this is a day that seems empty to you, and I wish there was some way I could make it up to you."

I put my arm around him. "Just you being here with me makes all the difference. I thought you were going to ride out with Perlman last night."

Will gazed at the ground. "I would never do that to you. But I have to go today. I was hoping to go with you."

"I can't do that. I do appreciate your offer, but how could I stay in your home and watch the window for what might be years to come, just waiting for word from you, hoping that I wouldn't hear that you've been killed. I'd cringe every time someone came to the door."

The thought filled my heart with dread. I knew if I could stay as far away from him and the war as possible, then I could just go on imagining him to be alive, alive and coming back for me. I'd never been given to fanciful thinking, but it seemed to be the only luxury I had left and I wasn't about to abandon it.

"I'd have nothing to do but fret all day. At least here I have my work and the children in my classroom. Their laughter will go a long way to lifting my spirits." I paused and swallowed. "Did Perlman take that cat of his?"

"Of course. Do you think he'd be without that mangy thing?" He smiled. "You know, I think he keeps that old Tom around just to attract fleas. He thinks that if he can keep the little varmints hopping on that cat, then they'll leave that beard of his alone."

I didn't want to laugh, but I had to. He wanted to take my mind off of all this and our farewell. I hated good-byes, especially during the war. Something about them seemed so final and they saddened me. Men were always saying good-bye to women only to disappear into the ground of some state far away, someplace where there was no family and no one even to lay a sprig of flowers on the grave. I had seen it over and over in the past three years.

"Then you will wait for me?" Will stepped in front of me and took my hand. He was smiling that charming knowing grin. "You are my fiancée if you recall. You even told me that you loved me."

The man made me laugh again. Just the thought of that time when he had forced me to accept his proposal of marriage, with Tillie behind me egging him on, was enough to make anyone laugh. It was a small, lighthearted chuckle, but a laugh nonetheless.

Will had a way of doing that, catching me off guard with something to smile about. He never seemed to take serious times seriously. "Yes, that was when I hated you. You seemed like the most arrogant man I'd ever met."

"Confident. Just confident. I'm not certain you've ever dealt with a man who knew who he was, what he believed, and where he was going. Yes, you even told me you loved me." He chuckled. "It was hollow, I know, and Tillie was goading you into it."

"She certainly was. I think she took delight in me being uncomfortable." I looked him in the eye. "I also somehow think she knew just how I would eventually feel about you. It was like she was steering my heart into a direction I didn't want to go, but one she knew would be best for me. She had always done that to me."

"I sure do miss her. She was confident and, as you put it, arrogant, just like me."

"Yes, but with her it was cute. With you it's maddening." I looked up at the ruins of the house in the distance. "I wonder what will become of Christine and the baby?"

"I wouldn't worry about that if I were you," Will said. "I don't think attractive widows last very long in this country. I spoke to her this morning before we left. She will sell the farm and split what money it brings three ways. Unless, of course, you all decide to rebuild."

"Gerald would never agree to selling, and neither will I. Our parents are buried here. We will just have to trust God's providence in bringing him home after the war."

"He does seem like a fine officer."

"Yes, so much like my father." I squeezed his hand. "One thing does worry me about you, Will Chevalier."

"And what is that?" He chuckled. "You have so much to choose from."

"We speak of the providence of God, and yet I'm not even certain you believe that, or in Him, for that matter."

"Just because of what I said about my parents' marriage?"

"That among other things."

"So marriage of the miserable represents the test case of Christian identity to you?"

"No, I suppose not. But it is something."

"Yes, it's insane. If you want to find something to indicate a person's credentials to the kingdom, I would hope you would pick joy and not misery."

"Duty is important."

"Yes. That I can accept. I faced duty when I led those men to their death on the battlefield. If I have to, I will face that every day for years to come. It doesn't mean that I like it; it just means that I do it. I wouldn't worry about me doing my duty if I were you, not in the army or in my marriage to you."

"What about to our Lord?"

"April, my early years were spent at church. In some ways I think it would be safe to conclude that my decisions as a boy have lain dormant for years, asleep in the middle of living." He gripped my hand. "But you changed that. You've shown me what it means to have a faith that is devotion along with beauty. I thank you for that."

"I'm glad to hear that." I put my hand to my breast. It was a good feeling to hear of Will's faith from his own lips. "It's a relief."

He reached out and took my chin in his hand. "One thing more, my dear. It's my turn for a question. When you agreed to become my wife during that farce of a proposal, Tillie told you to kiss me and you said"—he looked up at the sky, trying to get the exact words—"let's see if I can recall. 'Not now, not ever.' Yes, I think that's right. Do you remember that?"

I nodded and had to smile. "Yes. I don't think I could ever forget it."

"Were you right or were you wrong about that?"

It was another of Will's infuriating habits, putting me in a place where I had to admit that I was wrong and then giving me a chance to feel good about being mistaken. "I was wrong and you know it."

Will grinned. "Well then, I think an admission like that deserves a kiss, a nice big one." He bent down and kissed me. It was a long tender kiss, warm to my mouth. He leaned back, looking deeply into my eyes. "That, my darling, is the first of many."